Also by Jill Mansell

should I tell you?

Jill Mansell

sourcebooks
casablanca

Published by Sourcebooks Casablanca, an imprint of Sourcebooks
P.O. Box 4410, Naperville, Illinois 60567-4410
(630) 961-3900
sourcebooks.com

Originally published in 2022 in the United Kingdom by Headline Review, an imprint of Headline Publishing Group.

Library of Congress Cataloging-in-Publication Data

Names: Mansell, Jill, author.
Title: Should I tell you? / Jill Mansell.
Description: Naperville, Illinois : Sourcebooks Casablanca, [2022]
Identifiers: LCCN 2022004388 (print) | LCCN 2022004389 (ebook)
Subjects: LCGFT: Novels.
Classification: LCC PR6063.A395 S56 2022 (print) | LCC PR6063.A395
    (ebook) | DDC 823/.914--dc23/eng/20220203
LC record available at https://lccn.loc.gov/2022004388
LC ebook record available at https://lccn.loc.gov/2022004389

Printed and bound in the United States of America.
POD

For Sue Gregson "I Wanna Be Adored"
Love, as always, Mark xxx

chapter 1

CHOPPING, SLICING, AND DICING WAS LACHLAN'S FAVORITE thing. He liked it when the flashing blade of the knife became a blur; every time he did it, he tried to go faster and beat his own record.

He always wanted to do better, *be* better…and he might have succeeded if at that moment the restaurant phone hadn't sprung to life.

Lachlan grabbed it and said, "McCarthy's."

"Hi!" said a voice he didn't instantly recognize. "I left three messages on your phone and you didn't get back to me, so I thought I'd try this number instead. And here you are!"

That narrowed it down. "Hi, Nell. Sorry, rushed off my feet. What was it you wanted?"

"Well, *I* wouldn't say no to rushing you off your feet! OK, remember back in March, you took me to your friend Amber's stained-glass studio and I bought that suncatcher? Well, I accidentally broke it, so I wondered if she'd make me another one because I loved it so much."

"I'm sure she would. You can ask her yourself," said Lachlan. "The number's on her website."

"I know, but I couldn't remember the name of the studio. You know what I'm like…"

"It's Lanrock Glass."

"OK, I'll give her a call. Anyway, how are *you*? It's been ages!"

There was a reason for that. Nell had always used a lot of exclamation marks. Her enthusiasm was exhausting. She'd also worked hard to turn their brief fling into an actual relationship. "Busy," Lachlan said as he put her on speaker and got on with the food prep.

"But you don't work on Mondays. I thought maybe I could come down and see you then?"

"I'm not sure. I might have something else on."

"Lachlan, I'm not asking you to marry me. I just thought it might be fun."

He stopped chopping the potatoes. It wasn't like him to say no. And it *would* be fun…

Tinggg went his phone, and a text from Amber flashed up on the screen:

On my way.

Into the phone, he said, "Look, I'll see how the next few days go. I'll give you a call."

"Make sure you don't forget to do that." There was an edge to Nell's voice now.

"Call Amber about the window thingy. Lanrock Glass," he reminded her. "I'm sure she'll make you another."

"Oh, I'm not bothered. It was just an excuse to speak to you." With a burst of honesty, Nell added, "I only bought the first one because I thought it'd make you like me more."

He laughed. "It did make me like you more."

"But not enough to want to see me again." Her pride was wounded; she'd called him up, and he'd turned her down.

"Look, I'm sorry. I've been kind of seeing someone. I'd feel bad going behind her back."

"Fine, I get it. No worries. You have a nice time with her. Maybe I'll bump into you sometime."

"It's been good talking to you."

"I think you're just saying that, aren't you? Bye, Lachlan."

The call ended. Lachlan smiled to himself, carried on chop-chop-chopping potatoes into tiny dice, and thought how impressed Amber would have been if she could have heard him.

Maybe it meant he was becoming a better person at last.

Reaching for the next potato, he glanced up at the clock on the wall. Amber would be here soon.

Amber's mum had always maintained that anyone with a scintilla of natural instinct was capable of applying lipstick by feel alone. It was a life skill worth honing, she'd said. Even on the day she'd died in the hospice, her body might have faded away, but her lipstick had been perfect.

The brunette in front of Amber today clearly wasn't taking any such chances. Pausing at the entrance to McCarthy's restaurant, she peered into a small mirror and pouted as she touched up her own lipstick.

Rather than attempt to squeeze past, Amber hung back on the sunny sidewalk and idly admired the woman's city-smart black pencil skirt. You didn't see many of them down here in Lanrock, on the south Cornish coast.

A fresh layer of crimson duly applied, the woman smoothed her hair and unfastened one more button on her shirt before pushing open the door and disappearing inside.

Thirty minutes later, seated in a quiet corner of the restaurant with her laptop open in front of her, Amber finished the design she'd been working on for a stained-glass mirror surround and began eavesdropping on the conversation taking place three tables away between Lachlan and the lipstick woman, who was evidently a journalist.

"So you've achieved a great deal, career-wise." Lipstick woman leaned closer, her tone confidential. "How about your personal life?"

Lunchtime service was over, but Lachlan was still wearing his chef's whites. He reached for his bottle of iced water and said, "My personal life's fine, thanks. But it's not my number one priority right now. This place is."

"And that's completely understandable. But no girlfriend at all? That seems like such a shame!"

Oh, here we go. From across the restaurant, Amber cringed on the journalist's behalf because she was shifting into flirt mode now, her eyes sparkling as she studied Lachlan's face, gauging his reaction and the likelihood that he might fancy her.

"No girlfriend," said Lachlan. "But I get by."

"I'm sure you do." She was smiling, twirling the stem of her empty wineglass. On the table between them, her phone recorded a couple of seconds of deliberate silence.

"Actually"—Lachlan glanced at his watch—"I need to get back to the kitchen pretty soon."

"Really? But you don't open again until seven."

"I need to prep though. Unlike some places, we don't just take bags of fries out of the freezer and dump them in vats of oil."

"Hahahahaha." The woman ran her tongue over her upper lip, clearly excited by the mention of fry-gate. "I believe another chef wasn't too happy when you said he used frozen fries. Have you heard from his lawyers yet?"

"Of course not," said Lachlan. "It was true."

She adopted a conspiratorial tone. "I've also heard some gossip about you refusing a request from a TV company to costar in a show with a certain well-known Michelin-starred chef."

"Have you?"

"And is that true as well?"

"Might be." He took a swig of water.

"Why would you turn down an offer like that?"

"Because the certain well-known Michelin-starred chef is a dick."

Oh, he went there. Across the restaurant, Amber was tempted to give a coughing-major-type warning. But really, what would be the point? Lachlan would only ignore her; keeping his thoughts to himself had never been his forte.

The journalist gave a trill of laughter. "I can't say I'd disagree with you there! You mean Gerry Walsh, am I right?"

"You might think that. I couldn't possibly comment."

"But wouldn't you like to have your own series on TV?"

"It's not the be-all and end-all. I'd rather my customers came here to eat having heard the food's fantastic than because they've seen my face on some crappy show." Lachlan spoke with an air of finality. He checked his watch once more. "Look, I'm really sorry, but there's a ton of prep I need to be getting on with in the kitchen."

"You want to be the best," said the woman.

"Of course. And I'm on my way there."

"It's wonderful that you're so passionate about what you do."

Lachlan said, "Well, I'm glad you think so."

Keeping her head down and tapping busily away on her laptop, Amber heard the sound of chairs being pushed back and guessed what would happen next.

"Actually, I was going to head back to London this afternoon but I'm thinking now that it seems a shame to come all this way and not try your delicious food." The woman was visibly checking out Lachlan's body now that they were both standing. "I'd love to book a table for this evening…"

And then we'll share a few drinks afterward while I tell you how amazing you are, then I'll miss the last train home and end up having to spend the night with you.

Amber hid a smile, because it was so predictable. Honestly, every time.

"What a shame." Lachlan looked regretful. "If only I'd known a week ago, I could have held a table for you. But we're fully booked."

"Oh." The journalist's face fell. "And there's no way…?"

"I'm sorry. It's been fantastic to meet you, though. Next time you're in the area, you must let me know."

"I shall." She switched off the voice recorder on her phone. "Could we have a photo together?"

"Of course. Amber, will you do the honors?"

She'd guessed this would happen too. The journalist handed over her phone, and Amber took several snaps of the two of them, with Lachlan's tanned arm around the woman's shoulders. She looked pink-cheeked and excited, while Lachlan was…well, as effortlessly charismatic as ever, with that gypsy-dark glitter in his eyes, his glossy black hair, and his deceptively angelic smile.

When the photos had been taken, the woman murmured, "And who is she?"

Lachlan grinned. "Amber? She's… Let's just say we're close."

He thought it was funny. Amber waited while they finished exchanging cheek kisses and saying their goodbyes. As he opened the door to let the woman out, she belatedly called out, "Not *that* kind of close."

When the door had swung shut and it was just the two of them, she said, "You have to stop doing that, using me as an excuse. I hate it." She especially wished it didn't make her blush.

Lachlan grinned. "That's why it's fun. How are you, anyway? All right?"

"Not too bad, considering you asked me to come over here and then kept me waiting for an hour."

"I know, sorry about that. Forgot about the interview."

"She was angling for more than dinner tonight."

"I know that too. But I didn't go along with it. Aren't you proud of me?"

"Very proud. You're learning. Well done," said Amber, because last year he'd slept with a journalist who'd taken umbrage when he'd neglected to call her afterward and had subsequently got her revenge in print. It hadn't been pretty, put it that way.

"How d'you think this one went?" As if he ever took a blind bit of notice of anything she said.

"You shouldn't have called Gerry Walsh a dick."

"I didn't. I didn't utter his name."

"But we all know who you were talking about."

He spread his hands. "Because we all know he's a dick."

"It makes you sound arrogant."

"Is it arrogant to know you're a better chef than someone else? Because I *am* better than him," said Lachlan. "And I'm less of a dick."

"So modest too."

His dark eyes danced. "I prefer honest."

"Whatever you say." She hopped up onto one of the high stools by the bar. "Anyway, tell me why I'm here."

Lachlan pushed his fingers through his hair, raking it back from his tanned forehead. "It's Teddy."

"What?" If it was terrible news, he'd have said it right away. "He's OK, isn't he?"

"Oh, *he's* OK. He's having a whale of a time. Something's bothering me, though."

"What kind of something?" She couldn't begin to guess. Teddy was currently sailing off the coast of Greece, over halfway through a twenty-four-day cruise. It was three years now since May had died, and he'd finally been persuaded to take a holiday. They'd all encouraged him to go, and cruise ships were friendly places, geared up to the needs of solo travelers.

"I wouldn't enjoy it." Teddy had been adamant when Amber had first presented him with the glossy, enticing brochure. "Where's the fun in going away on my own?"

But she'd persisted, showing him online reviews and explaining that there were daily get-togethers for those traveling singly, big shared tables at dinner, organized trips ashore, quizzes and competitions and as much company as anyone could wish for, should they want it.

Then, when he had finally been persuaded, there'd always been a chance it could all go horribly wrong. Thankfully, that hadn't happened. Two days after departing on the ship from Southampton, Amber's phone had rung, and for the next twenty minutes, she'd had to abandon work in order to listen to Teddy extolling the joys of every single aspect of cruising. He was with his group of new friends, having a drink at a sunny harborside bar before they all set out together to explore the shiny delights of La Coruña.

"Remember how much you love it when it turns out you knew best after all?" he'd said happily. "Well, you were right."

"I'm always right." The relief was enormous. "You should know that by now."

"The food's incredible, everyone's so friendly, and there's nothing better in the world than sitting up on deck with a cocktail watching the sun go down over the sea."

"Oh my God, you're drinking cocktails now?" Teddy had been a pint-of-cider man his whole life.

"I know, can you believe it? They're amazing! They have umbrellas in them, and they don't even taste alcoholic. But they definitely are."

She laughed. "Which one's your favorite?"

"Well, here on the ship, it's called Fun on the Beach, although in real life, it has a naughtier name than that. I won't tell you what it is."

Amber's heart gave a squeeze of love for the kindest man she'd ever known; she might be twenty-nine years old, but Teddy still wanted to cocoon her from hearing about a cocktail called Sex on the Beach.

"And you won't believe this," he went on, "but out of all the people in our group, only a couple of us have never cruised before. The rest of them are mad for it, do it as often as they can. And now I can see why!"

"That's brilliant," she told him. "So d'you think you might book another one?"

"There's a travel agency right here on the ship," Teddy said. "I definitely will."

That phone call had taken place a fortnight ago. The group of friends he'd made on board was still going strong, and the photos he'd been sending her showed him growing steadily browner and—if it was possible—even happier as the days went by.

"Tell me," Amber prompted now.

Lachlan was busy scrolling on his phone. "Hang on, signal's dodgy…"

"Hello? This is me," she chided. "That's the excuse you give girls when they want to know why you haven't called them."

"Just be patient. OK, got it now." He raised his head, looked at her. "Remember when you were at school and had a massive crush on Lee Cope, and you were always levering him into conversations?"

"What?"

"Like, if someone said their favorite color was green, you'd say your favorite color was purple and guess what, purple was Lee's favorite too?"

"I didn't say that!" Amber was indignant. Lee had been her fantasy boyfriend in tenth grade. What was more, his favorite color had been black.

"OK, I'm just paraphrasing, but you were obsessed with him and couldn't stop talking about him. Like, *all* the time."

Belatedly, she did the math. "Hang on. You weren't even there. You'd left by then."

"I know, but I heard all about it from Raffaele. He said it was hilarious. They used to lay bets on how many times you'd casually mention his name."

Of course it had been Raffaele; the pair of them had loved to tease her.

"Fine," said Amber. "But you still haven't told me why you've got me over here now."

"Take a look at this." Lachlan passed her his phone. Talk about a massive letdown. She glanced at the photo of Teddy and his group of new friends on the cruise ship, around twenty of them gathered out on the top deck at sunset, beaming as they raised their glasses for the camera.

"I've already seen it. He sent me this one last week."

"I called him this morning while they were docked in Mykonos. We had a good chat. Obviously, he's still loving it."

"And?"

"And in the first five minutes, he casually mentioned someone three times."

"Oh!" Finally the penny dropped. Now this was more interesting. She expanded the photo. "And it's one of these women? Which one? Tell me, tell me!"

"What makes you think it's a woman?" said Lachlan.

Amber's head jerked up. "*What?*"

"Joking. Ha, your face."

She returned her attention to the happy group on the screen, checking out each of the likely candidates in turn until she came to a smiley one in a peach dress and matching pashmina. She had plump cheeks, a sweet smile, and neatly styled short brown hair.

"Got it." She tilted the screen to show Lachlan. "She even looks a bit like May. Oh, this is good news. She looks perfect!" For the last year or so, they'd been attempting to gently persuade Teddy to at least consider the idea of moving on, but he couldn't have been less interested. May had been the great love of his life, he'd explained; what would she say if she knew he was dating another woman?

And when Amber had said, "But she'd want you to be happy again," Teddy had shaken his head, dismissing the idea out of hand.

"I'm fine as I am, love. If I can't have May back, I'm not bothered about being happy again."

But now, fingers crossed, there was a chance that it could be happening anyway. The thought of love creeping up on Teddy and catching him by surprise made the backs of Amber's eyes prickle with emotion, because if anyone deserved to be happy, it was him.

She didn't cry, of course. That would give Lachlan too much of an opportunity to make fun of her.

"She does look perfect, doesn't she?" he said. "Just right for Ted. Except it's not her."

"Oh."

"I know."

"Why not? She's so obviously the best match." Amber snatched the phone back and took another look. "So…it's the one with the gigantic glasses?"

"Nope."

"The flowery cardigan?"

"Not even warm."

"Show me, then."

Lachlan pointed. Amber peered and did a double take, then gave him an accusing look, because it was surely another of his jokes.

Reading her mind, he shook his head. "This time, I'm serious. Her name's Olga."

chapter 2

OLGA. AMBER ZOOMED IN AND STUDIED HER WITH MICROSCOPIC attention to detail. Olga's hair was like a sleek blond waterfall, scooped up on the left side with a jeweled comb and falling to her waist on the right. She was tall, her height enhanced by sky-high silver stilettos. Her dress was low-cut, figure hugging, and bright purple. At a guess, she was in her early forties. She was also strikingly attractive, with a full face of makeup and a minxy, flirtatious smile.

It was a mixed age group, and while Olga might not have been the youngest, she was the only one dressed as if she were performing in the halftime concert at the Super Bowl.

Amber looked up and said, "Are you sure it's her?"

By way of reply, Lachlan indicated with his finger that she should scroll to the next photo, and there they were. Sitting together this time, in a glitzy-looking bar, the two of them perched side by side on high stools, leaning toward each other as they posed happily for the camera.

"When he mentioned her for the third time, I asked him who Olga was," said Lachlan. "And that was it, there was no stopping him. I got the whole story."

In this photo, Amber was able to see up close that Olga had almost luminous green eyes fringed with heavy false lashes, expertly contoured cheekbones, and a pillowy mouth accentuated with lip liner and magenta lipstick. Her fingernails were decorated with three blended shades of gel polish and multicolored crystals.

"We wanted him to have a great time," she said. "Maybe it's what he needs, just a harmless holiday friendship. All they're doing is sitting next to each other in a bar on the ship. It doesn't have to mean anything…you know, more than that."

"She grew up in St. Petersburg. Her parents died when she was ten, and she was sent to live with an aunt and uncle who beat her. They were alcoholics, and they didn't feed her. She ran away and lived on the streets until someone took her in…but she studied hard and worked twenty hours a day, and now she lives in Reading and works in a beauty salon." Lachlan paused. "Teddy also mentioned that she's keen to see the Norwegian fjords, so he's thinking of booking for them to go on another cruise together."

"Oh God, really?" This all seemed a bit sudden.

"I mean, maybe I'm reading too much into it. I really hope I am. But what if she has ulterior motives?" said Lachlan. "I think you should give him a call. Have a casual chat, see if he mentions her. I'm pretty sure he will. He sounded completely smitten to me. Before he hung up, he said he couldn't wait for us to meet her when they get back."

Amber exhaled. It wasn't just that Teddy was probably more than twenty years older than Olga. Appearance-wise, they weren't exactly a matching pair. "You think she's latched onto him because she's out for what she can get?"

"I hope not," said Lachlan. "But you have to admit it's a possibility. Think about it: she spoke to him, heard his life story, discovered what kind of guy he is. He'll have shown her photos of his big house, talked about when he retired and sold the company. He made a lot of money when he did that, remember. And women with those kinds of interests know what they're doing. We used to see it all the time when I was working in London. They're the experts, and men like Teddy don't stand a chance."

What he was saying made sense. Teddy had worked hard all his life and over the years had built up a hugely successful printing business employing hundreds of workers. Now retired, he might not be the outwardly flashy type, but he was without doubt a very wealthy man. The prospect of him being fleeced and having his still-fragile heart broken all over again was just too agonizing to contemplate. Amber said, "Did you tell him that?"

"Not yet. And I don't want to. But I think we have to warn him at least."

"I can't bear it. Maybe we're wrong and Olga's lovely and it's all completely innocent."

"Maybe." He paused. "Let's hope you're right."

"If I'm wrong, will it be all my fault?" She'd been the one who'd persuaded Teddy to book the cruise, after all.

"Course it will be." He gave her a playful nudge. "Hey, don't look so guilty. Have you been over to the house today?"

"Not yet. I'll do it now."

Lachlan disappeared into the kitchen, returning with a small carrier bag of bread rolls. "Here, take these with you."

"And I'll give Teddy a call later, let you know what he says."

Lachlan headed back to work, prepping for the evening service. Amber made her way along the narrow winding streets, swinging the bag of bread rolls. They were yesterday's, which meant they couldn't—heaven forbid!—be served in the restaurant, which was why they were destined to feed the birds in Teddy's garden. But there was actually nothing wrong with them; they were still completely delicious. Opening the bag, she selected an oval focaccia studded with sun-dried tomatoes and sunflower seeds. Left to her own devices, she bought cheap white sliced bread, but that was because she could never be bothered to make her own. Luckily for her—and for the birds that flocked to Teddy's garden—Lachlan could.

Even better, he was good at it. The bread he baked was out of this world. Tearing off a chunk, she turned right and took the steep shortcut up Smugglers' Steps.

Minutes later, she reached Wood Lane and paused to catch her breath outside Teddy's house. Number 19 was a large gabled Victorian property set in a wraparound garden, its west-facing front windows reflecting the afternoon sun. As always, Amber remembered the first time she'd set eyes on the place—it was like a Pavlovian response, replicating the emotions she'd felt all those years ago.

She'd been fourteen and terrified about what the future held. The previous year, her mum had left the latest in a long line of unhappy relationships and decided a move away from Milton Keynes was in order.

They'd ended up in Plymouth, in a quiet back street where the occupants kept to themselves. Which had been OK until her mum became ill and there'd been no one else around to help out and offer support.

It was cancer, the doctors eventually discovered, but hopefully slow-growing. It was horrendous news, and the surgeons wanted to operate to remove as much of the cancer as possible, which was scarier still. The social worker had explained to Amber that while her mum was away in the hospital undergoing surgery and recuperating afterward, she couldn't be left in the flat on her own, and there were no friends or family to offer to take her in. Amid the trauma of being worried sick about her mum, she found herself being driven from Plymouth to the much smaller sea-side town of Lanrock in Cornwall, almost twenty miles away.

The social worker reassured her that the Penhaligons were a wonder-ful couple who'd been fostering children of all ages for years, but that had done nothing to stop Amber feeling churned up with anxiety and as jumpy as a cornered cat. Already confused and terrified, she'd also read enough books and watched enough TV shows to know that not all foster parents were as great as they liked to make out.

And as for these Penhaligons…well, she wasn't even going to speak to them. If they tried to force her, she'd just run away, head back to Plymouth or maybe Milton Keynes, then just hide somewhere until her mum came out of the hospital.

By the time they finally drew to a halt in front of her temporary new home, she was trembling all over and ready to leap out of the car to throw up in the nearest hedge.

Then the bright red front door was pulled open, and a middle-aged couple came hurrying down the front path to greet them. Amber froze and took a step back.

"Oh, sweetheart, it's OK," cried the woman. "I know you must be worried sick. We're just going to be looking after you until your mum's back on her feet. I'm May, and this is Teddy, and we're *so* glad you're here!"

She held out her arms. And Amber, who hadn't planned on even speaking to these complete strangers, let alone making physical contact, found herself stepping forward into May's welcoming embrace and bursting into gulping, noisy, long-overdue tears.

The relief, coupled with the fact that one of the worst days of her life had within seconds taken a turn for the better, was what had imprinted the scene so indelibly in her mind. May and Teddy had swept her up, drawn her into their lives, and made her feel completely loved and secure.

Now, as she made her way across the drive to where the path led around the side of the house to the back garden, Amber glanced across at the neighboring property. One of the other enduring memories of that day fifteen years ago had happened later in the afternoon while she'd been outside exploring the garden and the old man next door had been clipping his yew hedge. He'd looked over at her for a stony second before turning away and muttering, "Oh God, not another one."

Which was when Raffaele had suddenly materialized at her side and said in a carrying voice, "Ignore him. He's going all out to be crowned misery of the year."

"You watch what you're saying, lad." The man's eyes narrowed.

"I'm just letting her know what you're like." And when the man walked off in a huff, Raffaele said, "He's a grumpy sod. Don't let him get to you."

Amber turned and managed a smile, because it was nice to have someone on your side. "Thanks. Is he always like that?"

"Pretty much." Raffaele shrugged. "Especially when people chuck slugs over the hedge into his garden."

"How often does that happen?"

"As often as we can find them."

"How long have you been here?" She took in his tight white T-shirt and slouchy jeans, flecked with grass clippings from where he'd mowed the lawn after getting back from school a couple of hours ago.

"Me? Nearly two years."

Two years. "That long? Wow." She wanted to know why, but it seemed rude to ask.

"I know." He grinned at her. "I struck lucky."

Now, Amber opened the carrier bag and examined the contents.

There were five rolls left: four for the birds and another one for her. She sat down on the wooden bench in the shade of the rowan tree and began breaking up the bread, throwing it onto the dry grass. The birds were already on high alert, excitedly gathering along the top of the fence. The trick was to let the little ones, the robins and the sparrows, have first go at the crumbs while shooing off the hooligan gulls that were already greedily circling overhead.

It was a routine that had been begun by May and Teddy twenty years ago and had continued ever since. Every day, they'd come out and sit here on their favorite bench, accompanied by one or more of the many children they'd welcomed into their happy home.

"No, stop it." Amber wagged a finger at a magpie as it dive-bombed the lawn, briefly scattering the robins and sparrows. She clapped her hands, the magpie flew off with a chunk of cranberry-studded whole wheat roll in its beak, and within seconds, the tiny birds were back. May had invented names and characters for them, making up stories about their adventures and teaching the smaller children about the importance of learning to share. These days, they no longer had names, but while Teddy had been away on his cruise, Amber had come to recognize the regulars. A pair of blue tits that had been nesting under the eaves flew down to join the others as she watched, and a sparrow hopped companionably aside to make room for them.

Did birds have friends? Did they get to know each other, keep in touch, show off their babies, and continue to meet up as the seasons moved on? Did their various offspring become friends too? Did they argue and fall out, then make up again—

Amber pulled the ringing phone from her jeans pocket.

"Where are you?" said Raffaele. "I'm at yours, and you aren't there."

"I'm feeding Teddy's birds. *Go away.*"

"Fine, no need to shout."

"Not you. I'm talking to the crows." She waved her free arm at them. "*Don't be so greedy.*"

"Stay where you are," said Raffaele. "On my way."

chapter 3

HE PULLED UP THREE MINUTES LATER. AMBER WATCHED HIM climb out of the car, taller and leaner than Lachlan, just as tanned, but with his light-brown hair cut close to his head and his light-brown eyes narrowing against the afternoon sun as he approached.

"Why are you looking at me like that?" Raffaele joined her on the bench.

"It's still so weird to think you're going to be here again full-time." She breathed in the familiar scent of him; he smelled of the sea and faintly of limes. "Last week, Lachlan came over to mine on his night off, and we ended up watching *The Blues Brothers* on Netflix. And when they tell their old friends they're getting the band back together, Lachlan said, 'Just like us.'"

Raffaele grinned. "I suppose it is. Except you have to promise not to sing."

Amber gave his ankle a kick, because making fun of her attempts at karaoke was what he and Lachlan had been doing for years, and to be fair, they had a point. But the actual getting-back-together part gave her a warm glow every time she thought about it. Over the years, the Penhaligons had fostered almost a hundred children, some for a matter of days or weeks, others for longer. Many of them had stayed in touch, and when May had died three years ago, the church had been full to bursting; so many of their former charges had wanted to pay their respects.

The strongest bond, though, had been forged between Raffaele, Lachlan, and Amber during their overlapping stays, and their friendship had endured ever since. When they'd returned to Lanrock each Christmas, May and Teddy had welcomed them with open arms, exclaiming that the Three Musketeers were home, and it had never failed to feel wonderful.

At May's funeral, the three of them had stood together and given a joint eulogy, explaining the effect she'd had on each of their lives.

Amber closed her eyes briefly; when you loved someone that much, did the grief ever really lessen, or did you just get used to walking around with the gaping hole their loss had brought to your life? She wondered if maybe it was the fear of losing people she truly cared for that had prompted her to steer clear of serious relationships herself, in case they turned out to be more trouble than they were worth. She'd had a few brief romantic interludes over the years, but nothing earth-shattering; it had always seemed safer and easier to concentrate on building her career.

Anyway, never mind that now. She'd been the first one to return to Lanrock, at the age of twenty. Then Lachlan had come back two years ago. And now Raffaele was joining them too. It was happening, as if some invisible thread had drawn them together once more.

"I bet I know what you're doing," said Raffaele.

"What am I doing?"

"Singing along to some *Blues Brothers* song in your head."

Amber laughed, because he was right as usual; in the background of her thoughts, the music to "Everybody Needs Somebody to Love" was playing, her foot had been jiggling along with it, and the words were being sung by an imaginary version of herself but with a much better voice.

"You know me so well." She changed the subject. "How's the refit coming along?"

"On course to be finished by the end of next week."

"I still can't believe you're doing it."

"Neither can I." His tone was wry. "This is what happens when you give in to emotional blackmail. It could turn out to be the biggest mistake of my life."

"Or the best move you ever made."

It had happened six weeks ago, during his last trip down from London. They'd been seated at a wooden table outside the Harbor Inn, watching the setting sun sink into the sea, when old Eric Kempner had come out of the bar with his pint of Rattler to engage Raffaele in lugubrious conversation.

"Saw you on the telly t'other night. Doing well for yourself, lad. Good job." He nodded. "Pleased for you."

"Thanks, Eric. And you were the one who gave me my first break." At the age of fifteen, Raffaele had taken a Saturday job in Eric's barbershop, initially washing hair and sweeping the floor before progressing to buzz cuts and trims for the older, less discerning customers. He added, "How are things with you?"

"Not great, lad. Still no buyer for the business. Thought it'd be snapped up, but no luck. It's been three months now."

Amber felt sorry for him. Eric was nearing seventy and had looked after his dad for the last fifteen years. Three months earlier, his father had died at the age of ninety-three, and as soon as the funeral was over, Eric had put the property on the market. Rheumatoid arthritis had made holding scissors increasingly painful. The time had come to retire and move abroad.

"The right buyer will come along." Amber's tone was consoling. OK, it wasn't the most salubrious of businesses, but someone would buy it; they always did. "Oh, don't worry," she exclaimed, because he looked so despondent. "It'll happen eventually."

His face reddening, Eric took a swallow of cider and sat down heavily on the bench facing them. "Thing is, I've gone and got myself a lady friend."

Well, this was news. "Eric, congratulations! We didn't know that!"

"No one knows. I met her online last year in a chat group for older caregivers, what with me having Dad and her looking after her aunt in Benidorm. We've been talking to each other on Skype for over a year. It kept us both going, y'know? Then her aunt died after Christmas. After Dad went, we planned for me to sell my place here and move to Benidorm, get an apartment with a view of the sea." He paused, jowls quivering, and blinked hard. "So we can be together at last, you know? Well, that was the plan. Except the days go by, and I still can't find a buyer… It gets you down after a while, know what I mean? God, sorry." Ashamed, he rubbed his eyes. "It's just, we waited so long, and now I'm starting to wonder if it's ever going to happen. Knowing my luck, I'll probably drop dead first."

Raffaele had been listening intently. "Look, let me help you." He kept his voice low. "I can lend you enough so you can go over there right away. Let the agents take care of the sale. How about that?"

Eric turned his head to one side as if he were gazing out to sea. His Adam's apple bobbed in his throat. Finally, he turned back and shook his head. "Thanks, that's good of you. But I couldn't let you do it. I've never been in debt in my life. My dad taught me that much. And he made me promise I'd never borrow money from anyone." He exhaled heavily, then glanced at Amber. "It's fine. I'll wait. Like you said, it'll happen sooner or later."

"I understand." Raffaele nodded. "But if you change your mind, the offer's there. Just say the word."

Eric nodded and rose to his feet. "You're a good lad. Don't go telling everyone about my lady friend, will you? None of my mates know about her. Don't want them taking the mickey out of me." He gestured awkwardly in the direction of the tiny back bar of the Harbor Inn, where the older locals tended to congregate. "You know what that lot are like."

"We won't say a word," Amber promised. "What's her name?"

"Thanks, love. Her name's Maureen." Unable to resist, Eric took out his phone and showed them a photo of a rosy-complexioned woman with a neat perm, bushy eyebrows, and a shy smile.

"Oh, she looks lovely," said Amber. In truth, Maureen looked like the kind of woman they might have expected Teddy to choose, homely and sweet.

Eric nodded proudly. "She is. She's like a dream come true."

Those words struck a chord. Amber remembered Raffaele saying them a few months after he and Vee had first got together. This was it, he'd told Amber, too much in love to even be embarrassed by what he was saying. Vee was the one he'd been waiting for; she was everything he'd ever wanted. And having gotten to know Vee herself, seeing the two of them together, Amber had agreed that they were a perfect match, funny and happy and the best couple you could imagine. "She's like a dream come true," Raffaele had said as they'd sat on the beach that night, watching Vee dancing under the stars.

"I love her," Amber had told him. "You're so lucky."

And Vee, overhearing them, had run over and pulled the two of them to their feet to join in with the dancing. Her eyes sparkling, she'd said, "I'm the lucky one!"

Everyone had thought they'd be together forever.

But that had been then, and this was now. Oh well. Hopefully things would work out better for Eric and Maureen.

A week after his conversation with Eric, the increasingly difficult relationship between Raffaele and Vee had broken down completely. After a massive showdown at the salon culminating in a hairbrush being hurled at his head and a set of straighteners flying out a second-floor window, it became apparent that working together was no longer an option. Everyone had warned him it could prove to be a mistake when they'd formed their business partnership, and everyone had turned out to be right. The next day, Raffaele traveled back down to Cornwall, paid a visit to the dilapidated barbershop with accommodation above it, and saw for himself why no one else was interested in taking it off Eric's hands.

But he hadn't been able to get the older man's emotional words out of his head. And this seemed as if it could be the answer. Eric might be too proud to accept a loan, but a straightforward business transaction was another matter entirely. It would help both of them out.

Raffaele offered the asking price. The last eight years in London had been hard work but exciting as he'd built his career and achieved more success than he'd ever envisaged. Now he needed to get away, regroup, and take a break from all the stress and drama. And as Amber had reminded him when he'd told her, where better to do that than back here in Lanrock, the place he'd always thought of as home, where life was easy and he had friends he knew he could trust.

Now, as they sat together in Teddy's garden watching the birds squabble over the remains of the bread rolls, Raffaele said, "I'll need to head off soon. Will you keep an eye on the work going on at the salon until I get back next week? Let me know if there are any problems?"

"Course I will." She knew he still had plenty of business commitments to sort out before he could move down here properly, and Vee wasn't making things easy for him. Amber gave his arm a consoling squeeze. He insisted he was fine about the breakup, but he and Vee had been together for over four years, and they'd been so happy together up until last year, when it had all started to go wrong. It had to hurt. "You OK?"

"I'm great." He nodded, his smile faint but reassuring. "How about you?"

"You know me. I'm always great."

"Oh, before I go, I got a text from Lachlan telling me to ask you about Olga. Who's Olga?"

"That's the million-dollar question." Taking out her phone, Amber showed him the photos Lachlan had forwarded to her and relayed the whole story—well, as much as they knew of it, which actually wasn't much at all. Lachlan had been googling Olga and checking her out on social media, but other than an Instagram account showing photos of false lashes, false nails, and iridescent eyeshadows, there was little to check out.

"Right." Raffaele nodded slowly when she'd finished. "So she looks like someone out of a Bond movie and probably has an accent like a Russian spy."

"Pretty much. What d'you think?"

"I think maybe Lachlan's finally gotten around to watching *Killing Eve*."

"I'm not saying she's going to persuade Teddy to leave everything to her in his will before chucking him off the nearest cliff," said Amber. "But do you think she could be after him for his money?"

"Maybe. Maybe not." Raffaele shrugged and stood up, ready to leave. "But there's nothing any of us can do about it right now. It could be a harmless fling that'll be over by the end of the cruise. We'll just have to wait and see what happens next."

Amber hugged him. "Well, drive carefully. And give—" She stopped abruptly, because it was no longer appropriate to add "And give Vee my love."

But of course Raffaele knew what she'd been about to say. He took out his car keys and said with a rueful half smile, "Don't worry. We'll get used to it, in time."

....

It had happened four years ago, and it most certainly hadn't been love at first sight on Vee's side. The hairdressing competition was being held in one of the hotels bordering Hyde Park, and Raffaele was the guest judge, just back from a trip to LA where he'd been working flat out during awards season, styling the hair of those who'd be walking the red carpet.

He spotted Vee early on and liked what he saw. Later, he would learn far more about her: that her father was Jamaican and her mother was Welsh, that she couldn't go a fortnight without adding to her collection of colorful earrings, and that when telling a joke, she invariably creased up with laughter before getting to the punch line. But at the time, he was more interested in her athletic physique, her close-cropped hair dyed white, and the look of intense concentration on her face as she worked on the hair of the model in front of her.

The more he looked, the more he liked what he saw. She was chatting animatedly with other people around her. Her huge dark eyes were mesmerizing, her laugh infectious. She was wearing a black T-shirt, black jeans, red stilettos, and red lipstick, and it wasn't long before she noticed Raffaele watching her. From then on, fleeting glances and tiny smiles were exchanged whenever he found himself in the marked-off vicinity of her workstation. Well, there was nothing like a bit of unspoken flirtation to brighten the day.

Until it came to the judging, when as guest judge, he had to choose his own personal winner.

Awkward.

Other categories had already been judged and awarded, but this one, arranged by the sponsor who was paying his appearance fee, was purely down to him. Now Raffaele found himself with a dilemma, because he genuinely couldn't decide between Vee's work—he'd found out her name by now—and that of a young lad from Coventry who'd achieved an entirely different but equally spectacular result.

He was torn, but in the end, it came down to sheer physical attraction. The boy was gaunt and pale, with prominent teeth and the narrow, mistrustful eyes of a cornered fox. Vee was stunning and exuded sex appeal.

What else could he do? With the eyes of the room upon him, Raffaele knew he had no choice but to make his way over to the boy's chair and present him with the winner's trophy.

As he was leaving the event an hour later, he saw Vee carting her kit bag across the road to the bus stop. Hurrying after her, he caught up just as the bus arrived.

"Hey—"

"Come to say you're sorry? Too late." No longer smiling, she waved him away and jumped onto the bus.

It was heading in the opposite direction to where Raffaele wanted to go, but what other choice did he have?

"Please go away," said Vee when he sat down next to her.

"I've spent the last hour looking for you."

"That's a coincidence. I've spent the last hour actively avoiding you."

"Look, I'm sorry."

"I should have won."

"I know you should have won."

"My work was better than his."

She was right. He nodded. "It was."

Vee turned to look at him, and he saw the hurt and disappointment in her eyes. "So you knew it and I knew it, but someone else gets to go home with the trophy."

"I saw you. I liked you. I mean, really liked you," said Raffaele. "I heard you joking with your model about being too busy to find a boyfriend, and I knew I wanted to get to know you, ask you out. Then I realized how that would look if I announced you as the winner, then people saw us together afterward. They'd say the competition was fixed from the start, and that wouldn't do either of us any good. Which is why I had to give the trophy to the other guy instead."

"You mean so you could get my number and meet me for a drink?"

Honesty had to be the best policy. "Yes."

Vee exhaled. "And did it occur to you for one moment that given the choice, I might have preferred to win the competition?"

He'd put his own feelings first. "I messed up. I'm sorry."

"Me too."

They sat in silence for the next few minutes. Raffaele pretended to be looking out the window. In the reflection of the glass, he could see Vee's long fingers tapping impatiently against the knee of her black jeans. He'd gotten it wrong, and he didn't know what to do. He appeared to have gotten himself into a lose-lose situation.

Finally, she said, "Where are you going?"

"No idea. Where are *you* going?"

"Wandsworth."

He snapped his fingers. "That's the name I couldn't remember. Wandsworth. That's where I'm headed too."

"Why?"

He pointed to her bulky canvas kit bag. "So I can carry that for you."

"You think I can't carry it myself? I box in my spare time. I bet my muscles are bigger than yours."

He was getting nowhere fast. In desperation, he said, "What's Vee short for?"

By way of reply, she turned and raised two fingers at him in a rude gesture. "It's short for this."

Which served him right but was at the same time faintly encouraging, because there was a spark in her eyes that hadn't been there before, along with the tiniest glimmer of a smile.

"Short for fuck off." Sympathetically, he nodded. "Must have been interesting, growing up."

Against her will, the smile grew. "Very good, but I'm not letting you off that easily. If you want to take me out, you have to grovel."

Sometimes, when you're unexpectedly granted an opportunity, it's necessary to just grab it. Raffaele's heart leapt as he slid off his seat onto one knee in the middle of the aisle. Clasping Vee's hand, he said, "I'm sorry, I'm an idiot, I was wrong, and I don't blame you for being mad with me. But if you'd let me take you out, you'd make me the happiest man on the planet." He paused and clutched his heart. "What else can I say? I'm sorry, I'm sorry…"

"That's the lad we saw on the telly, remember?" An older woman on the other side of the bus gave her friend a nudge. "Is this one of them hidden camera shows?"

Vee dragged him back onto the seat beside her. "Shh. Stop, you're being embarrassing."

"That's your fault," said Raffaele. "You made me do it."

The older woman across the aisle said, "So are you going to go out with him, then?"

"Haven't made up my mind yet," said Vee.

"He did say he was sorry."

"Several times," said Raffaele.

"He's a hairdresser, love. Always handy to have around."

"I suppose," said Vee.

A girl sitting in front of them turned to look at Vee. "Not that I'm speaking from bitter experience or anything, but if he's a hairdresser, you might want to make sure he isn't gay."

Five days later, after their third date, Vee Harper allowed Raffaele to prove he wasn't gay. He'd also come to realize by then just how special she was. After a decidedly dodgy start, this brand-new relationship was turning into one he didn't want to end. Vee—it was short for Alvita—worked as a senior stylist at a salon in Covent Garden and had begun making a name for herself as an Instagrammer, demonstrating her skills with both hair and makeup. Thanks to her engaging manner and witty asides, she was steadily building her online audience while becoming more and more in demand at the salon.

As the weeks passed, Raffaele was increasingly relieved he'd found her. She was a year older than him, funny, hard-working, ambitious, and perfect in every way. He'd come so close to messing up and missing out, but fate had taken pity on him and given him a second chance with this amazing girl who loved to eat carrot sticks dipped in Marmite, who could dance forever, and who burst into tears every time she saw that schmaltzy

TV ad with the gray-and-white kitten left out in the rain. ("Oh, I can't bear it. Turn it off… No, *don't* turn it off. Look at his little face. He's so sad!")

The two years that followed were golden, the very happiest of his life. There were trips to get to know Vee's mum's relatives in Cardiff as well as a holiday in Jamaica to meet her dad's side of the family. They were a proper couple, and he was in love for the first time. The salon was doing fantastically well. Vee's star was rising too. Best of all, she wasn't one of those obsessive Instagrammers who made their boyfriends take endless photos of them all over the place; when they were out and about together, she took her own snaps in twenty seconds flat, then put her phone away. They worked hard, went out often, and hardly ever argued. As relationships went, theirs couldn't have been better.

Then the owner of the salon Vee worked in decided to sell and move abroad, and Vee found herself having to look for another job. As they were discussing it over dinner in the flat one evening, Lachlan joined in. "Look, everyone knows you as a couple, they're invested in your relationship, so why not go into partnership?"

It had seemed like the perfect answer, a fail-safe decision. So they had.

And that was when it had all started to go horribly wrong.

OK, time to stop thinking about Vee. As he reached the dual carriageway, Raffaele pressed his foot down on the accelerator and turned the radio to top volume so the music could drown out the unhappy memories in his head.

chapter 4

WHILE LACHLAN WAS FINISHING PREP, PEGGY SMART'S DUSTY white four-by-four skidded to a halt outside the restaurant, and she came flying in.

"Darling! Table for five at seven thirty. Can you squeeze us in?"

It was an order rather than a request. Whatever Peggy wanted, Peggy got. This afternoon, she was wearing a voluminous orange-and-purple kaftan, flat gold sandals, and turquoise-framed sunglasses perched on top of her head. There were splashes and splotches of paint on her tanned feet, halfway up her arms, and in her bird's-nest blond hair.

"Make it eight o'clock and you've got a deal." He breathed in a waft of oil paint, turpentine, and the ever-present Chanel No. 19. "What's the occasion?" Not that she needed one.

"Celebrating finishing another work of art. Just dropped it off at the gallery. Not quite dry yet, but I couldn't bear to wait." She beamed. "It's magnificent, my best yet. Someone's going to snap it up."

"If they have any sense." When you were accustomed to speaking your mind and being up-front and honest, it hadn't been easy learning not to be. But sometimes it was necessary, and you just had to get on and do it. Crossing to the computer, Lachlan checked the bookings. "Table four OK?"

Table four was at the back of the restaurant.

"Stop it! Don't you know who I am?"

"Never seen you before in my life."

"We'll have my usual table." Of course she would: the one in the window, the best in the house. "And is that pork and prosciutto thing on the menu tonight?"

"No," said Lachlan.

"Well, I'd like it anyway. You know it's my favorite."

"I'll see what I can do." He loved her, but she drove him mad.

"*Bastard*." Peering out through the plate-glass window, Peggy gave a cry of outrage. "He's out there again! What's the *matter* with the man?"

The local traffic warden was the bane of her life, and was it any wonder? "You are parked on double yellows," Lachlan pointed out.

"That's not the point. It's the way his eyes light up when he sees my car. I swear he's fixed one of those tracker things to it. OK, I'm off." Racing to the door before the warden had time to issue a ticket, she raised a hand in farewell. "See you later. Oh, and we'll be wanting some of those raspberry macarons. Don't forget to make them!"

"What did your last slave die of?" said Lachlan.

Peggy jangled her keys at him. "Exhaustion!"

....

The first time Lachlan had set eyes on Peggy Smart, it could have gone very much either way. Luckily for him, he'd perfected a sublime new pear and Pernod dessert that morning and was in an excellent mood.

Which just went to show, being nice to a complete stranger definitely had the power to change your life.

It was a Monday lunchtime, one of the quieter times in the restaurant attached to the Elphick Hotel in Bloomsbury, which was why Lachlan had been left in charge of the kitchen while Jean-Pierre, the head chef, took his day off. When one of the waitresses approached him and said, "Table six have asked for a bottle of Heinz salad cream," she maintained a cautious distance. Well, he did have a sharp knife in his hand at the time.

"Ignorant peasants," said Lachlan. "I hope you told them to sod off."

"If you want them to sod off, it's your job to tell them."

And on another day, maybe he would have. Instead, he put down the knife, crossed to the door separating the kitchen from the dining room, and peered through the glass porthole.

Table six was occupied by a woman in her late fifties and a younger man who looked like a shy accountant. In his twenties, with neatly brushed brown hair, boyish good looks, and a nervous demeanor, he wore a suit that was well cut but slightly too big for him. He was listening attentively while his companion spoke, her hands gesturing wildly as she relayed some story or other. Her hair was blond and fastened in a doughnut bun with a bright pink ribbon tied around it. Her dress was an explosion of pink, orange, and yellow flowers, and she had scarlet Crocs on her feet.

At that moment, she came to the punch line of whatever she'd been saying and exploded with laughter. As she clutched the arm of her dining companion, he visibly flinched and leaned back in his chair. But Lachlan had pushed the door open an inch and could hear her now. She had a great laugh, the best, the kind that was genuinely infectious.

He'd always had a soft spot for people with a really good laugh, and there was just something about this one that captured his attention. He also loved that she found herself so hilarious.

"Pop over to the Tesco Express," Lachlan told the astonished waitress. "They'll have some."

She did an exaggerated double take. "Who are you, and what have you done with the real Lachlan?"

"Don't worry. We'll charge them enough for it."

Ninety minutes later, the waitress approached him once more. "Table six loved their lunch and would like to congratulate the chef."

Service was over, so Lachlan went out to accept their compliments.

"Oh, hello." The woman's eyebrows shot up. "You aren't Jean-Pierre."

"It's his day off." Some people felt cheated when they discovered their food hadn't been cooked by the chef they'd seen flipping omelets on Saturday-morning TV. Luckily this one didn't seem to mind.

"No worries. You're good."

"I know."

"Prettier too." She caught the oh-my-God look on her lunch companion's face and shook her head. "Not in that way, Benjie. I'm not flirting with the lad. It's just a statement of fact."

The squeezy bottle of salad cream was now sticking out of the woman's crocus-yellow Versace handbag, its cellophane seal around the lid still intact. Lachlan said, "You didn't use it in the end, then."

"Never planned to. Just wanted to see what you'd do."

"And if we hadn't obliged?"

"I'd have left."

He indicated the squeezy bottle. "Did you look at your itemized bill? We charged you twelve pounds for it."

"Which is why I'm taking it home with me." She shrugged. "Waste not, want not."

"So we passed your test. Now what?"

"Now I become a regular customer." Her blue eyes sparkled up at him. "Aren't you the lucky one?"

And she had indeed become a regular customer. Her name was Peggy Smart, she'd spent the last thirty years building up an international haulage business with her brother, and now the time had come to enjoy the benefits of all that hard slog. Having sold her share of the company, she persuaded Lachlan to prepare the food for her retirement party, to be held at her home in Bayswater. Over the course of the last year, they'd become friends…well, in an employee/employer kind of way. And when Peggy announced her plan that night to get out of London and relocate to Cornwall, she also asked Lachlan if he'd consider moving with her in order to work as her private chef.

Under other circumstances, it would have been an incredible offer. But Lachlan turned her down. Catering for Peggy and her endless stream of guests would be an easy job, but working in restaurants was both his passion and what he needed to do in order to build his career. He thanked her for the offer, explained why he couldn't take her up on it, and asked whereabouts in Cornwall she had in mind.

"Who knows? So long as it's somewhere by the sea. I'm heading down this weekend to take a look at a few properties." Reaching for her phone, she gave it a couple of taps and brought up the short list she'd compiled from an upmarket real estate agency's listings. "There's one in Padstow…another place just outside St. Ives…or this one down on the south coast, not far from Looe."

"That last one's close to where I grew up," said Lachlan.

"Really? Do you know the house?"

"Know it? I got caught there one night, hiding in one of the outbuildings."

Peggy looked delighted. "Caught doing what?"

"Drinking cider, making out with a girl from school, the usual things sixteen-year-olds get up to."

"You wicked boy. Come down with me on Saturday. You can show me around."

But he couldn't. His job was here in London, and he had to work. Peggy had urged him to pull a sickie, then even attempted to bribe him with the promise of dinner at the best fish restaurant in Cornwall. It was somewhere he'd longed to visit for years, but he explained that he still couldn't go.

So instead she took along her son Benjie, the young dining companion who looked like an accountant but wasn't one.

Six months later, Peggy made a typically flamboyant entrance one evening at the restaurant where Lachlan was currently working, then insisted on taking him for a drink once his shift was over.

"So you're enjoying the new place?" he asked when they eventually sat down together in a pub off Tottenham Court Road.

"It's fantastic." Peggy hadn't chosen the big house outside Lanrock because of his connection with it; she'd bought it because it was the best one she'd seen. The property in Padstow had major parking issues, and the one close to St. Ives had turned out to have noisy neighbors. As she had observed at the time, if anyone was going to be noisy, she'd rather it was her.

That same day, having made one of her customary on-the-spot decisions, she'd bought Cliff House, and seven weeks later she had moved in. The style and size of the six-bedroom Victorian property suited her down to the ground, and the decor was subdued and minimalist, which wasn't remotely her taste but gave her carte blanche to transform it. What those elegant eau-de-Nil and ivory walls needed to liven them up was some fabulous art.

Peggy had promptly headed down the hill into Lanrock, prepared to support the local economy and spend a fortune on amazing paintings, only to discover that the two art galleries catered heavily for tourists and almost entirely sold seascapes, beachscapes, cliffscapes, and pictures of boats. If you loved artwork in endless dreamy shades of blue, green, and pale gray, there were literally hundreds to choose from. Whereas if you preferred something bolder, basically you were stuffed. You might as well buy some paints and canvases and do the job yourself.

Which was what Peggy, being Peggy, decided to do. Within a week, she'd discovered how she was going to spend all her newly acquired free time.

"I can't believe I've never done this before," she had exclaimed, displaying her hands like badges of honor, showing off the dark paint stains ingrained around her previously immaculate nails. "It's the best feeling in the world…like being head over heels in love! And the thing is, I'm so *brilliant* at it. All that talent I didn't even know I had!"

Now, like a proud mum, she showed Lachlan the photos of her creations on her phone, and he made all the right noises while inwardly marveling at her confidence. The previously empty walls of Peggy's new home were now covered in giant canvases daubed and splattered with paint in alarming shades of purple, burnt umber, bottle green, blood red, and black.

Like most people, he knew nothing about abstract art, but taste was an intensely personal experience, and what some people hated, others found irresistible. Maybe Peggy was as talented as she evidently thought she was, but as far as he was concerned, the paintings looked as if they'd been created by a toddler having a tantrum.

"They look…extraordinary." Was that a good thing to say? Purely to be polite, he continued, "So will you stop now that you've filled the house?"

"Are you out of your mind? Why would I stop? I'm going to sell them!" Peggy was clearly delighted with herself. "I've lined up appointments with a dozen of the most successful galleries in Devon and Cornwall, and I'm going to go with the three that offer me the best deals. By the way, have you changed your mind yet about coming to work for me?"

Since getting to know her, Lachlan had grown used to these zigzagging conversations. He suspected it was her way of trying to catch people off guard until they inadvertently blurted out the answers she wanted to hear.

"It's not that I don't want to," he explained, yet again. "But I need to build my CV, show people what I can do. Learn from the best and get my name out there. Ten years from now, I want to set up my own restaurant."

"I can't believe you're being so stubborn." Peggy tsk-tsked. "I'm offering you a fantastic opportunity."

"I know you are." He touched the rim of his whisky tumbler against her wineglass. "And it's truly appreciated. But it isn't part of my career plan."

chapter 5

THE DOZEN MOST SUCCESSFUL ART GALLERIES IN DEVON AND Cornwall, it turned out, didn't have the excellent taste Peggy had hoped for. As she explained during her next meeting with Lachlan three months later, the useless so-called experts preferred to stick to selling their wishy-washy seascapes to gullible tourists with zero appreciation of true art.

"So what are you going to do?" said Lachlan. It was a Saturday afternoon, he had two hours free between lunchtime and evening service, and they were sitting on a bench outside the Serpentine café overlooking the pond in Hyde Park. Peggy had treated him to pizza, fries, and a can of 7UP.

"Going to do? I've already done it. Bought my own gallery, haven't I!"

He blinked. "Seriously?"

"Damn right. When I decide something needs to happen, I don't hang about." She gave a nod of satisfaction. "Those other losers are going to regret turning me down, I can tell you. It's in the center of Lanrock, on Beach Street."

"Wow," said Lachlan, because Beach Street was right on the front, a prime location for any business. "Well, that's fantastic." He raised his can to her across the wooden table. "You're still a mover and shaker. Good for you."

"Once a businesswoman, always a businesswoman. Turns out I need to keep myself occupied."

"Nothing wrong with that."

Peggy said, "Nothing wrong with getting a haircut either. You should try it sometime. Look at you."

Lachlan smiled, experiencing a simultaneous pang of loss, because now she was sounding like May. Not that they were remotely similar; it was just the motherly way she'd said it. Had it really been a year and a half since May had died? God, it was still impossible to think she was no longer here. He missed her so much.

But Peggy was right about his hair, which was past shoulder length now. He raked his fingers through it. "I'll get Raffaele to sort it tonight."

"You two boys still getting along OK?" During the course of their conversations, she had learned all about his checkered past growing up.

"Of course."

"Still with the same girlfriend, is he?"

"Vee? Oh yes." Lachlan watched as a dragonfly landed on the table next to his plate.

"Driving you mad?"

He shrugged. "She's great. Things are just different now. When we were two single guys, it was easier." Three months ago, Vee had moved in with them, and the dynamic had, inevitably, changed. Vee was cheerful and brilliant company, an inspired joke teller, and always up for a night out or a party. He liked her enormously, but she was also forever leaving random clothes, bits of makeup, items of jewelry, and half-eaten slices of toast around the place. To add insult to injury, her favorite meal was a Bombay Bad Boy Pot Noodle mixed with chopped-up frankfurters and Jamaican jerk sauce.

Her presence had certainly made an already small flat seem a whole lot smaller.

"Ever thought of moving back to Lanrock? If someone made you the right offer?"

Lachlan narrowed his eyes at her. Peggy's tone was deceptively casual, which meant she was up to something. All of a sudden, he knew what the plan was.

No way on this earth.

"Look, it's kind of you, but I really couldn't. Cooking's all I want to do." And she knew that. How many times did he have to tell her?

Peggy looked at him. "What do you think I'm offering?"

"You've bought the art gallery. You need someone to run it. And maybe do a bit of part-time cooking for you on the side." He wished he hadn't pretended to like her paintings now.

But her eyes were bright. "Well, you jumped the gun and guessed wrong, smart-ass. I already have someone to work in the gallery."

"Oh." He glanced at his watch; it was nearly time to head back to work. "Sorry."

"OK, I'm going to level with you. There's a massive gap in the market down there in Lanrock. Fish and chips and takeouts galore. A couple of places that call themselves gastropubs, but that's only because they sprinkle cilantro leaves over everything. Hotels catering for the old folk who don't have any teeth left. Places serving pub grub." Peggy's upper lip did an Elvis curl of disdain. "There's one restaurant serving really good, Michelin-quality food, but the owners are miserable buggers, and the place has about as much atmosphere as a dentist's waiting room."

Lachlan nodded; as an assessment, this was harsh but fair. Run by a middle-aged married couple who loathed each other almost as much as they appeared to despise their customers, Morgano's was known locally as the Morgue. Then again, it was entirely likely that Peggy had turned up with a bunch of outrageous friends one night and ended up getting kicked out for being too drunk and noisy.

"Did they bar you?"

"Maybe. But I wouldn't have wanted to go back anyway. Grumpy fuckers."

He grinned. "Speaking of going back, I need to leave soon."

"Could you take a quick look at something for me before you go?" She dug around in her lime-green handbag, its oversize designer logo glinting in the sunlight, and passed him some folded sheets of paper.

Lachlan read the real estate agent's details in silence. After his last wrong guess, he wasn't going to make another one. Finally he said, "Who's this for?"

"You, if you want it."

"I can't afford a place like this." Not that it was anything lavish; the small building was situated on one of Lanrock's narrow backstreets, a one-bedroom flat above business premises that had last seen service as a burger and milkshake bar.

"I know you can't. But I can."

He put the details down on the table. "Peggy, this is… I mean, *why*?"

"Oh come on, use your head." Diamonds flashed rainbows of light in the sunshine as she began counting on paint-stained fingers. "One, I'm an atrocious cook. Two, it's driving me mad not having anywhere nice to go out to dinner. Three, you've had a tough start in life, and I think you deserve a break. Four, I'd want my own table, and if I ever need private catering for parties at my house or at the gallery, you'd provide that too. Five, the property would be mine. If you leave, I'll resell it. And six, you will always, *always* have potatoes dauphinoise on the menu." She stopped counting and eyed him beadily. "Well, what's the verdict? Yes or no?"

Inside his chest, a cloud of locusts appeared to have taken flight. Lachlan glanced again at his watch. "Can I think about it?"

"No, you bloody can't. Take it or leave it." Impatiently, the consummate businesswoman pursed her pink-lipsticked mouth. "Makes no odds to me if you turn it down. I'll just find someone else."

Would she? Or was this her version of a deal-clinching double bluff? Lachlan considered it for a long moment. Finally, he said, "You must be a really shocking cook to be this desperate."

Peggy nodded gravely. "You have no idea."

He held out his hand, and they shook on it. "In that case, let's hope I never have to find out."

There was a glint of triumph in her kohl-lined eyes. "So we have a deal. You've seen sense at last. Good lad."

No wonder she looked smug; he had no doubt she'd get her money's worth out of him. He'd turned down her offer to work as her private chef, but she'd ended up getting what she wanted anyway.

Then again, so had he.

"Also," she added as an afterthought, "if my friends and I are rowdy, you're never allowed to chuck us out."

Someone close by threw a handful of bread crumbs into the air, and there was a flurry of beaks and wings as several gulls swooped down to hoover them up. *Back-back-back* clacked one of the gulls as, waiting for more food, they eyed their audience with regal impatience. *Back-back-back.*

Back to Lanrock, thought Lachlan. Back to the place and the people who'd rescued him and helped make him into the person he was today. He had no doubt that between them, Teddy and May had saved his life.

And now, thanks to Peggy Smart, this was happening. It was a hell of an opportunity, that was for sure. Only time would tell if it turned out to be a good idea.

chapter 6

Teddy Penhaligon was sitting out on his cabin balcony, the reflection of the sun bouncing off the Aegean Sea as the luxury ship left Mykonos. He was still dazzled and pinching himself, because the last couple of weeks had been such a revelation.

Until coming away on this holiday—and he'd only reluctantly agreed to make the booking because Amber had nagged him half to death about it—the future had felt like an ordeal to be struggled through, like wading through cold, waist-high mud. He'd still missed May so much, every minute of every day. He also knew, because she'd told him so herself, that she wanted him to find happiness again. With someone nice, so he wouldn't be lonely. When she'd said it, he'd nodded and agreed that maybe eventually he would consider it, while knowing in his already fractured heart that it was never going to happen.

And it hadn't.

Until now.

Oh, it was definitely happening now.

Hearing a light tap on his cabin door, his heart lifted, and he called out, "It's on the latch. Come on in!"

Seconds later, Olga stepped out onto the balcony, and his heart lifted further still, because she was just *so* stunning. Her long blond hair was pulled back into a braid that was in turn coiled into a bun and decorated with pink silk flowers. She wore lipstick to match, a pale-green dress that clung to her curves, and delicious rose-scented perfume.

"You look amazing," Teddy told her as she planted a light kiss on his mouth, then rubbed the tip of her finger over his lower lip.

"Sorry, there, all gone. And you do too, very smart. Most

distinguished. Anyway, I have a surprise for you." She revealed the plastic bag she'd been hiding behind her back. "Only a small one, but I thought you'd like it."

"You shouldn't have." Teddy opened the bag and took out a stuffed toy bear wearing a jaunty tasseled hat and waving a Greek flag. Maybe some men might have thought *no, you really shouldn't have*, because it wasn't remotely to their taste, but as a foster parent, he'd had plenty of practice over the years with being given an eclectic selection of homemade cards and presents. For someone who'd never owned a cuff link in his life, he'd received more than his share of wonky hand-painted clay pots to keep cuff links in.

"Remember when we were having lunch today in the taverna on Mykonos and I said I needed to pop across the road to buy something from the pharmacy? That was a white lie. I bought you this instead." Olga stroked the furry bear's arm. "A teddy for my wonderful friend Teddy, you see? To remind you always of our first cruise. He has a kind face and a dear little paunch, just like you!"

"That's because the food's been too good on this ship." Teddy patted his stomach, then checked his watch. "Speaking of food, it's almost eight. We should be heading down to join the others."

"And after dinner, I thought of something else we could do." Slipping her hand into his, Olga said, "You shouldn't leave your cabin door in the latch for me."

"*On* the latch," Teddy corrected her, but only because he knew she wanted to be corrected. She prided herself on her excellent English, but there were still a few colloquial terms capable of tripping her up.

"On the latch. You never know who might slip into your room while you're out on the balcony. They could steal anything they wanted, and you wouldn't know."

He patted her arm, charmed by her concern. "What are they going to make off with, my hairbrush and wash bag? I don't have anything worth stealing."

"You do now. You have your teddy bear. Anyway, after dinner, I think we should go to reception and ask for another key card for me, so you don't have to leave the door unlocked." She paused, searching his face. "Unless you don't want me to have my own key."

It made sense. Olga had a tiny inside cabin five decks down, which naturally meant that they met up at his, where it was possible to sit out on the spacious balcony.

"No, forget I said it. I'm being too forward." She shook her head. "I'm sorry. You'd rather keep your privacy. I understand…"

"It's fine. Of course we can get another key for you," Teddy said hastily. "You're right. It's a great idea. We'll sort it out as soon as dinner's over."

"Only if you're sure."

"I'm more than sure."

"Well then, that's good." She gazed at him, her huge eyes locking onto his. "And sorry again if I'm too…forward. When I think something, I say it straightaway. Maybe sometimes I scare people by doing this."

"You don't scare me," said Teddy.

"I'm glad. I can't help it. It's just the way I am. And I forget that we've only known each other for a couple of weeks. When I'm with you, I feel as if we've been together for years."

Over dinner at the table for ten, they shared stories about the day with their new friends and discussed plans for tomorrow's stop at Heraklion on Crete. After the main course had been cleared away, one of the ship's photographers came around to each of the tables in turn, offering to take photos for those who wanted them.

"Oh, we should have one!" Leaning against Teddy on her left, Olga rested her hand on his arm, and they both smiled broadly as the flash went off.

"Anyone else?" said the photographer when theirs had been taken.

Bernard, seated to Olga's right, cleared his throat. "Could we have one taken together as well?"

"Bernie, of course! With the three of us, you mean?"

He reddened. "Well, maybe just you and me? If that's OK?" And when it was done, he said, "Now I'll have something to show my friends once I'm home. With a bit of luck, my ex-wife'll get to hear about it. That'll make her sit up and take notice!"

Olga said, "I can't believe she left you, Bernie. A handsome man like you."

"I know. Me neither."

"Why did she go? Were you mean to her?" Her eyes widened. "Were you unfaithful?"

"Definitely not. I just played too much bridge. That's what she said, anyway."

"And she didn't like that? Maybe she should have learned to play too."

"That's what I told her! I even offered to teach her myself. She just wasn't interested." As he gestured in disbelief, the sleeve of his smart jacket slid back to reveal his watch.

"Oh my goodness," Olga exclaimed. "Bernie, is this new? Did you buy it today? It's amazing!"

He beamed, evidently delighted it had been noticed. "Treated myself. Well, can't take it with you, can you?"

"Why can't you take it with you?" She looked puzzled. "Where are you going?"

"It's just a saying," Betty explained from across the table. "Meaning you can't take your money with you when you die."

Olga looked shocked. "Oh, Bernie, are you ill? Are you definitely going to die?"

"We're all going to pop our clogs one day. I'm hoping for a few more years yet though." Bernard held out his wrist so she could admire the watch in all its shiny glory. "Not bad, eh?"

"It's a Breitling Chronomat Evolution." Olga tilted his wrist this way and that so the diamonds glittered in the overhead lighting.

"Well done." Bernard was visibly impressed. "Not many people would know that."

"I love beautiful watches. One day, I hope to have one of my own," said Olga.

"Well, mine's a Sekonda," Teddy joined in cheerfully. "Forty quid from Argos, and it's not let me down yet."

"A watch like this is a thing of beauty and a joy forever." Olga reverently touched the face of the Breitling on Bernard's hairy wrist. "It's a feat of miraculous engineering. Each minute you're wearing it, you appreciate every aspect and feel special, am I right?"

"She knows," Bernard agreed, nodding with pride.

"If I ever have one of my own," said Olga, "I'll love it until the day I die." She pressed the flat of her hand against her tanned cleavage. "When I was ten years old, we didn't have enough food to eat, and I was always hungry. Now I can afford to eat delicious meals like this one, and every day, I appreciate that luxury so much. And the clothes I wear, they are quite cheap to buy, but I do my best to make them look good. Because it's nice to have dresses that aren't made out of old curtains, you know? So I try to look stylish. Also, this is my first proper holiday, and I've met all of you…" She gestured expansively around the table. "And you're all such lovely people. Getting to know each one of you has been so wonderful, *so* very wonderful… Oh no, I'm getting overemotional now. But I mean it from the bottom of my heart. I can truly say this has been the happiest time of my life."

"Oh my gaaaad." Millicent from Milwaukee was dabbing at her eyes with a linen napkin. "You're starting me off now. Honey, we love you too."

"Thank you." Olga's voice broke as she managed a wobbly smile. "You're all so kind."

"Had me worried when we first saw you, mind," Millicent went on. "Walter's eyes near popped out of his head, and I thought, *whoa, Nelly*, gonna have to watch out for this one!"

"Oh no! Why did you think that?" Olga's eyebrows rose in dismay.

"It was when you climbed out of the swimming pool in your red bikini."

"Really? Is red unlucky for you? Goodness, I'm so sorry. I won't wear it again, I promise."

"Honey, no worries. I'll admit it now, I felt a tad threatened at the time. Walter and me were getting along so well, I just thought what if you decided he was the one that took your fancy? But you didn't. You chose Teddy instead. So it's all fine."

Teddy took care to maintain a straight face, because Millicent from Milwaukee was in her late seventies and Walter from Texas was eighty-two, twenty years older than himself.

"I didn't set out to choose Teddy," Olga explained. "When I came on this trip, I had no plans to choose anyone. But when I saw him across the room at our first cocktail party, my heart went *boom*. It made the decision for me." She broke into a wide smile. "And fingers crossed, made the right decision."

"My heart went boom once," cackled Phil, a retired dairy farmer from Wiltshire. "Ended up having a triple bypass and six days in coronary care."

"But now you're here, alive and well." Olga raised her glass. "We're all here, having the most wonderful time, and I think we should celebrate still being alive!"

She was amazing, incredible, more of a woman than Teddy could ever have hoped to meet. He reached for his own glass and held it alongside hers. To his unexpected new friends—and one in particular—he said with feeling, "I'll drink to that."

....

"Where's it gone?" The woman was sitting bolt upright on her padded sun lounger, agitatedly searching her silver carryall. She pushed her Ray-Bans to the top of her head, her voice rising in panic as Teddy approached. "It's vanished. It was in here, and now it's disappeared. Oh my God, where *is* it?"

Today on the ship, they were having a day at sea. Following lunch together, Teddy had headed off to a lecture in the theater on the subject of serial killers, while Olga had chosen to sunbathe by the pool up on the top deck. Now he found her with her earbuds in, listening to music and reading a book while the woman continued to panic-search on the sun lounger next to her.

When Olga looked up and saw him, she smiled and removed her earbuds. "Hello! Was it fun? Did they teach you how to become a serial killer?"

"It was great." Teddy turned to the other woman, who was wearing a pale-blue kaftan. "What is it you've lost?" He couldn't help himself; if he encountered any kind of problem, he felt the need to try to solve it.

"I haven't lost it. It's *gone*." Her glasses slid off and clattered to the ground, and Teddy bent to retrieve them. "Which rather implies that someone has taken it." As she said this, the woman glanced sideways at Olga.

"Oh! Are you accusing me?"

"I'm not accusing anyone. I'm just saying my bag was down there." The woman pointed to the narrow gap between their sun loungers. "And I don't know how anyone else could have possibly reached it."

"Wow," said Olga. "I don't even know what you're talking about."

"It's a wide platinum bangle studded with diamonds and sapphires." The woman addressed Teddy. "I didn't want to leave a tan mark, so I took it off, put it into my bag, and zipped it shut. Because, like an idiot, I assumed it would be completely safe in there."

Olga's eyes blazed. "Did you see me with your bangle? No, because I did not touch your bag."

"I was asleep," the woman retorted.

"Oh, well, in that case, you'd better search me." Leaping off her sun lounger, Olga stood in front of her accuser in her striped yellow bikini and held her arms outstretched. "Here I am. Start searching! Although I'm telling you now, if I had stolen your stupid bangle, I'd probably have moved away and found a better hiding place."

Teddy was appalled by what was happening in front of him. Olga was trembling, her jaw set. Still glaring at the woman on the sun lounger, she went on, "Actually, maybe we should call the ship's captain so he can see what I'm being accused of. If I'm guilty, he can arrest me and throw me in the hold for the rest of the cruise."

All around the pool area, people were watching avidly, enjoying a show that didn't involve them.

"Hurry up," Olga instructed. "I'm waiting to be searched, and I don't have all day."

The woman heaved a sigh and backed down. "I'm not accusing you.

I'm just… It's an expensive bangle. My husband's going to go berserk. Look, sorry, OK?"

"And once again, I didn't take your bangle." Olga bent down to collect her bag, book, and phone, then gave the woman a final furious stare. "Maybe next time, you should think before you speak." Raising her eyebrows at the empty glasses on the tray beneath the other sun lounger, she added icily, "And if you didn't drink three cocktails, perhaps you wouldn't fall asleep and snore."

Teddy took her back to her cabin.

"I'll be all right. I just need time to calm down." She shook her head.

"It's horrible, but try not to let it spoil your day." He hated to see her so upset. "If she goes to the security office, they'll be able to check through the CCTV, see what really happened."

"You think they have it all over the ship?" A muscle was jumping in her jaw.

"I'd imagine so. Then she'll really have to apologize to you."

"I don't want her apology," said Olga. She massaged her temples with trembling fingers. "I've got a headache. I'm going to have a shower and a rest."

Teddy gave her a brief kiss, but she was too distracted to respond. As he was leaving to make his way back up to his own cabin, Olga called after him, "When I was twelve and very poor, a man accused me of stealing his wallet from his pocket. I was cold and I was hungry, but I hadn't taken his wallet. It's the worst feeling in the world, being found guilty when you're innocent. It left its mark on me."

His heart went out to her. "I'm sorry."

"Me too. I ended up wishing I *had* stolen it." Olga let herself into her cabin and closed the door.

chapter 7

WHEN LACHLAN MCCARTHY HAD FIRST ARRIVED IN LANROCK, HE'D
been thirteen years old and pretty much a fireball of frustration and
rebellion. He'd also been aware that he was running out of chances,
which only made him more intent on pushing the boundaries to their
very limits.

His mother, sixteen when she'd given birth to him, had struggled
on for four years before realizing she couldn't cope with motherhood
any longer. No one knew who his father might have been, least of all
her. Having signed Lachlan over to social services, she'd disappeared six
months later.

The intervening years had been tricky, with plenty of well-meaning
help being offered by social workers, caregivers, teachers, and various
foster placements. But they couldn't compete with the confusion, the
resentment, and the anger experienced by Lachlan, who was baffled by
the unfairness of it all. He was endlessly told that he needed to behave
well, work hard, and consider his future, but he failed to understand
why. What could his future possibly hold anyway? He had nothing to
look forward to and no one to love. Nor was there anything he wanted
to do.

This was the Lachlan who was delivered to May and Teddy, with a
warning to them that he would undoubtedly prove to be a handful. At
thirteen, he was startlingly good-looking and both intelligent and charismatic when he wanted to be. But those brief periods were interspersed
with long silences, outbursts of temper, and overbearing restlessness as a
result of the gaping hole of boredom inside him.

In his first few weeks at 19 Wood Lane, Lachlan spent hours alone in
his room, got into a fair few fights at school—because his fellow pupils

were *idiots*—and gained the dubious distinction of having received six detentions in a single week.

It took a couple of months before he calmed down enough to realize that he might be cutting off his nose to spite his face. And that this came about was all thanks to May.

"What were your parents like?" He asked the question one day while May was cradling a sleepy Ginny on her lap. Ginny was nearly five and had multiple disabilities: she crawled rather than walked, her speech was garbled, and she still wore diapers.

"Mine? Oh, well, I'm sure my mum was lovely, but she died when I was three, so I don't really remember her." May smiled at him and tapped the tip of Ginny's nose to make her laugh. "*Boop!*"

Lachlan wondered if anyone had ever playfully booped *his* nose. He had no memory of it having happened. Had his mum done it to him when he was a baby? Who knew?

"What about your dad?" he asked.

After a couple of seconds, May said gently, "Well, he did his best. In his own way. We kind of muddled through together. He found life… hard, I guess you could say."

"Hard in what way?"

She shrugged and stroked Ginny's fine hair. "He drank. A lot. He'd disappear every so often for a few days at a time. When the drink took over. And then he died."

"What did he die of?"

"He didn't want to live anymore." May took a tissue out of the box on the coffee table and tenderly wiped a ribbon of drool from Ginny's cheek. "He took his own life."

"Fu—wow." Lachlan was learning not to swear in this house. He was used to hearing about other children's traumatic life experiences, but it had never occurred to him that May might have been through bad times too. She just didn't seem the type. "How'd he do it?"

She shook her head. "It doesn't matter. It wasn't a pretty sight."

"You saw him?"

"I found him." May rocked Ginny, who had fallen asleep.

"How old were you?"

"Same age as you are now."

Fuck. "What happened to you after that?"

"I was taken into foster care, sweetheart. Looked after by kind people."

Lachlan remembered the searing sensation inside him. "Did it make you want to break everything?"

She smiled briefly. "Oh my word, yes. But the trouble with that is, it doesn't do any good. You either have to try and fix whatever's broken or learn to carry on without it."

"You can break stuff that belongs to other people. Then it doesn't matter."

May said mildly, "Well, it matters to the other people."

Various adults over the years had made similar comments, but coming from May, it felt like an observation rather than a lecture. Because it was something she'd been through and figured out for herself.

"Is that why you and Teddy became foster parents?"

"Paying it forward, you mean? I think so. I just felt as if it was something I wanted to do."

"Even when we're a pain in the neck?" His own temper outbursts were coming back to haunt him; he'd been so convinced she couldn't possibly understand.

"Even then," May said simply.

"Sorry about your roses last week. It was me who pulled the heads off."

"I know. And look, here we are," she told him with a smile. "I still love you."

"You can't *love* me." Lachlan felt his chest tightening with emotion; he was pretty sure no one had ever loved him.

"Hey, I wouldn't say it if it wasn't true. Do you know how many children we've had come to us here?"

"No. Well, I know it's loads."

"Seventy-three so far. Sometimes they stay for a few days. Other times, they're here for months or even years. But I've loved every single

one of them. It's like giving birth but without the pain. I see a face and—
ding!—it happens." Her voice softened. "Because you don't have to share
love out like candies. That's the thing. You don't divide it up so everyone
gets a tiny amount. Love grows, sweetheart. Everyone can have as much
as they need. OK, could you wait here while I take Ginny up for her nap?
I'll be back in two minutes."

Lachlan waited.

When May returned, she said, "Now, is there anything else you want
to ask me?"

He nodded, finally brave enough to say it. "Could you give me a hug?"

"Of course I can, sweetheart." She opened her arms to him. "Come
here. If I say so myself, I'm good at hugs."

It felt like being wrapped in a warm blanket of happiness. Lachlan
closed his eyes and felt like a much younger version of himself. When
it was finally over, he knew this was a hug he'd never forget. He opened
his mouth to speak, then realized how idiotic it would make him sound.

"What is it?" prompted May.

He had to ask. It came out as a whisper. "Could you boop my nose?"

Her face softened. She did it twice, *boop boop*. "And one more for
luck." She did it again. "There you go."

"Thanks," said Lachlan. "Don't ever tell anyone, will you, that I
asked for that?"

"No worries. I won't breathe a word." She smiled. "Although I can't
promise I won't do it again."

Three days later, it was Ginny's fifth birthday. When Lachlan arrived
home from school, he found May in the kitchen making a cake.

"What's the matter?" he said, because she was wincing as she lifted
the bag of flour over the weighing scales.

"Oh, all my own silly fault. I slipped on the path as I was taking the
washing out, landed on my hand, and sprained my wrist. And now I
don't know how I'm going to make this cake."

"Ginny won't mind if you can't do it." Lachlan doubted if Ginny
was even aware it was her birthday. "She'd be just as happy with a plate
of cookies anyway."

"Rule number one in this house." Tipping the bag of flour, May managed to spill a fair amount onto the table. "If anyone has a birthday, they get a proper homemade cake with decorations and candles… *Ow.*"

Lachlan helped himself to a glass of black currant punch, gulped it down, and left the kitchen. Thirty seconds later, he returned carrying one of the dining chairs and placed it next to the worktop.

"Sit down," he told May. "If you tell me what to do, I'll make the cake."

"Sweetheart! Have you ever made one before?"

"No. But if you trust me to try, I'll give it a go."

It took three hours altogether. Lining and greasing the tins, mixing the ingredients, baking the layers, then waiting for them to cool before sandwiching them together with buttercream and jam. Then came the icing on top, the flowers made from individual sugar-paste petals, and *Happy Birthday Ginny* written in bright green icing by wielding an icing bag with a tiny nozzle that fit onto the end of it.

Finally, they added the candles. The cake looked a tiny bit lopsided but…amazing.

"We need to take photos of this," said May. "It's the best cake I've ever seen."

Lachlan suspected this was something of an exaggeration, but he couldn't help feeling proud anyway. It was pretty good for a first attempt, and May was suitably impressed, which made him feel so happy he could burst.

"It'll probably taste like crap," he said to flatten her expectations.

Everyone had gathered in the garden, the candles were lit, and the cake was carried out. Ginny babbled and beamed as they all sang "Happy Birthday" to her, then more photos were taken by Teddy before the cake was ceremoniously cut.

And it didn't taste like crap. The cake was light and delicious. Lachlan found himself receiving genuine compliments for the first time in his life, and it was just the best feeling in the world. Ginny ended up smearing most of her slice over her face and arms, but he didn't mind; it was her birthday, and she could do whatever she liked with it.

When the birthday party was over, he helped with the cleanup and asked May if she'd teach him how to make the cottage pie she always made on Fridays, because it was his favorite.

After that, he was unstoppable. Every evening and each weekend was spent in the kitchen, learning from May and soaking up information. He fell in love with cooking and with the joy of serving people dishes that surprised and delighted them. Cooking programs were watched, endless books were taken out of the local library, and as the months went by, Lachlan's passion continued to grow. He learned to taste a new sauce and work out the individual ingredients that had gone into it. He taught himself to use knives correctly to slice and dice at the speed of light. He collected quite a few cuts and gashed fingers along the way.

"This is it," he told May and Teddy. "This is what I want to do for the rest of my life."

"I know." May hugged him. "I'm so happy for you."

"I never had anything to look forward to before. Whenever I pictured my life, I just thought it'd be drugs and stealing and going to prison, then getting out again, on an endless loop."

"It doesn't have to be like that," said May. "You can decide to be different. It's what I did. You can do it too. You already are."

chapter 8

AND NOW HERE HE WAS, EIGHTEEN YEARS LATER, SWITCHING OFF the lights and setting the security alarm as he prepared to leave the restaurant after another busy evening's service. The love hadn't faded, and the novelty of having his own name over the door hadn't worn off yet.

Ginny's birthday cake had been the start of it all, and it wasn't until his own eighteenth birthday that May had come clean.

"Little confession, sweetheart. Remember the day I hurt my wrist and you made that first cake for little Ginny?"

"Ye-es." He wasn't likely to forget it.

"Well, I *did* slip and fall. But I didn't hurt myself. I was fine. When it happened, though, I wondered how I'd manage if I really had sprained my wrist and couldn't make the cake." Her cheeks flushed. "And I thought I'd have asked you to help me. So when you came home from school, that's when I pretended I couldn't do the job myself. Just to see if you'd want to help."

"May. I'm shocked."

"I know. It was one of those spur-of-the-moment ideas. I knew you needed some focus in your life and I just wondered if baking might be the thing to provide it. I did feel a bit guilty about that." With a smile, she said, "But I can't be too sorry, when it did the trick."

Out in the street now, the church bells were chiming eleven, but it was the summer season, and the tourists hadn't gone to bed yet. After an evening spent cooking at warp speed in the kitchen, Lachlan still had plenty of adrenaline in his system. Maybe some chefs could make themselves a mug of tea and go to bed, but he needed time to wind down.

He headed to the beachfront and made his way through the tables outside Bert's Bar. Inside, the locals greeted him, and Polly served him his usual glass of pinot noir. Polly was blond, curvy, and always cheerful, and she and Lachlan had an uncomplicated relationship that suited them both: whenever either of them fancied a bit of no-strings sex, they exchanged a certain playful look, and that was that, it happened.

As far as Lachlan was concerned, work came first, and relationships weren't currently a priority, so this arrangement suited him just fine. Occasionally things got tricky though. Like now. The door to the ladies' loo swung open, and Ella emerged, her eyes lighting up when she saw him.

Ella was an athletic brunette dental hygienist with whom, pre-Polly, he'd had a similar arrangement last winter. It had been great, both enjoyable and mutually beneficial, until Ella had decided that what they needed was to be in a *proper* relationship. "Because why not?" she'd exclaimed, as if it was the most brilliant plan ever and made absolute sense. "We're perfect together! We get along well, and the sex is amazing. It just seems crazy not to be a real couple… Think how much fun we'd have!"

Lachlan's heart had sunk, because the last thing he wanted to do was hurt or upset anyone. He'd been up-front and honest from the start, and Ella had agreed with him, stating that this was all she wanted too, and for the first few weeks, it had been fine…until the sense of ownership and wanting more had come creeping in.

It had happened with Ella but hopefully wouldn't happen with Polly. "Lachlan! I wondered if we'd see you in here tonight. How *are* you?"

"Good, thanks." At least Ella was smiling this evening. Since the tricky breakup, whenever they bumped into each other, she'd alternated between making barbed comments and whispered offers. You never knew what you were going to get.

"The funniest thing happened this afternoon," she continued. "I got off the train and was on my way out of the station when I passed a woman talking on her phone and heard her mention your name, so of course I had to stop and listen. Don't worry. I was discreet!"

After a long pause, Polly said, "What was she saying, then?"

"Basically, that Lachlan's losing his touch." Ella looked smug. "Apparently she came to interview him today, and he was flirting with her like crazy, trying to persuade her not to leave so he could see her after work. He told her she could stay at his place tonight and go home tomorrow—"

"Hang on, I didn't—"

"She said it was hilarious, he was really pulling out all the stops, but she wasn't interested. Oh dear, poor *you*." Ella looked at Lachlan. "Being turned down and left with no one to keep you company tonight. I guess that's why you came here instead, to see who else you might be able to hook up with." She grinned, glanced for a final moment at Polly to see her reaction, then said, "Bye!" and sauntered off to rejoin her friends in the back bar.

"OK, that didn't happen," Lachlan said firmly.

Polly gave him a cool look. "Sounds as if it did."

"She was the one who made all the running. I turned her down." As if to make amends for never offering the full boyfriend experience, he at least remained monogamous for as long as each arrangement lasted.

"It's none of my business what you get up to." A cloud of steam flew out of the glass washer as she opened it and began rapidly hanging up the pint mugs and wineglasses. "But just to let you know, I'm not used to being second choice."

"You aren't second choice. I came here tonight to see you. Either the journalist was lying to whomever she was talking to or Ella was. Because I wasn't interested. And I can prove it!" Belatedly it occurred to him that he had a witness. "Amber was there. She heard everything. All you have to do is ask her!"

"Oh, of course I do, because that's someone I can really believe." Polly rolled her eyes. "We all know Amber will say anything you tell her to say."

"But I haven't told her to say anything. We can call her right now." Taking out his phone, Lachlan saw the time and hesitated. "Except she might be asleep."

"Don't bother. I won't be coming back to yours tonight anyway."

This was Polly's way of taking her revenge because Ella had got one up on her. Given a couple of days, he knew she'd come around and forgive him for something that hadn't been his fault in the first place, but right now, his night wasn't going to end in the way he'd hoped.

"No worries." He knocked back the rest of his wine and gave her a rueful smile. "I'll head over to the Dolphin. See you."

As he reached his flat above the restaurant, a text pinged up on his phone:

Don't go to the Dolphin. I'll come to yours. See you in twenty minutes. X

He paused, considering the offer without enthusiasm. The adrenaline rush had worn off now, and he was no longer in the mood. Spotting the arrival of an email, he saw that it was from Teddy and opened the attachment.

Another photo of the two of them, Teddy with Olga, taken by a third person. They were looking happy together up on deck, with decorative lights behind them. Olga's arm was snaked around Teddy's waist, and her turquoise dress was split to the thigh. She was trouble, he knew it. You could just tell.

Lachlan sent a text back to Polly:

Sorry, already home and falling asleep. Pretty shattered. I'll call you tomorrow. X

Ten seconds later, she replied:

Please don't go to the Dolphin. Xxxxx

Five kisses. His heart sank. The last thing he wanted was to hurt her, but if she was on the brink of getting emotionally involved, the kindest thing would be to end their arrangement.

His phone began to ring.

Oh no, not again.

But this time it wasn't Polly. It was Amber.

So she was still awake after all.

"Hi, are you at home?"

"Just got in." He made his way up the stairs. "Did Teddy just send you the same photo?"

"He did, and I think they look great."

"Hmm."

"You're obsessed. Are you alone, or d'you have company?"

"Alone. Polly thinks I came on to that journalist this afternoon, so she's punishing me."

"Ha, it'll do you the world of good."

He laughed. "So vy are you calling, eef not to tell me I'm right about Evil Olga?"

Unless it was to offer herself up to him as a replacement for Polly…

OK, it wasn't going to be that.

"If that's your attempt at a Russian accent, it's terrible. And they look so happy together!"

"They do," Lachlan conceded, "and I'm glad Teddy's having a fantastic time. I'm just being wary on his behalf."

"Anyway, never mind that now. Get yourself into bed this minute, and switch on the TV. Go to the plus-one channel. You won't believe the people they've got in this episode."

Lachlan broke into a grin, because he knew at once what it was. Five weeks ago, they'd discovered a new series called *Cooking for the Enemy*, a show that was simultaneously awful, fascinating, and completely addictive. They'd watched the first episode twice, and it had instantly become their nonguilty pleasure because, as he'd told Amber, if it was a pleasure, there was no need to feel guilty about it. Since then, they'd taken to watching it together from their separate beds in their separate flats, either live or later on-demand, chatting on their phones and exclaiming at the idiocy, the awfulness, and the bizarre cooking skills of the contestants aiming to impress their worst enemy enough to win them over with the meal they'd produced.

"Found it." Lachlan kicked off his espadrilles and launched himself onto the bed. "How much have you seen?"

"Only five minutes. I wanted to wait for you. Brace yourself," said Amber as the opening titles rolled. "The guy in the red sweater had an affair with his ex-girlfriend's daughter, and his ex slept with his best friend for revenge."

"And what are they cooking?" He was inevitably more interested in the food.

"Sole bonne femme from him. Fried haggis with kidney casserole from her. Oh my God, she hates him so much."

"Look at his hairy neck."

"Look at her kitchen!"

"Whoa," they both roared in unison as the man in the tight red sweater boasted that he wasn't afraid of a bit of spice and the camera cut away to reveal his ex-girlfriend slicing up a Carolina Reaper chili.

"That'll kill him," Amber gasped as the woman smirked at the cameraman.

"They wouldn't let her do it," said Lachlan.

"Hello, have you seen which channel we're watching? They might."

As the show continued on its comical malevolent way, they commented on the rival contestants, picked sides, and took bets on the final scores. Lachlan drank a bottle of Corona and Amber opened a can of Diet Coke, he ate salt and vinegar chips while she polished off a package of cashews, and as they carried on chatting companionably, he realized he'd far rather be here like this, watching TV with Amber, than in bed having sex with Polly from the pub.

chapter 9

MALTA WAS HOT, GOLDEN, AND MAJESTIC. TEDDY AND OLGA HAD taken a two-hour walking tour of the tiny capital, Valletta, with its narrow limestone streets and tightly packed buildings. Stopping at a café, they sat outside in the shade to drink iced orange juice and eat pastizzi, the tiny golden pastries stuffed with ricotta that were a favorite snack on the island, while watching the passersby.

"Right, what's the time now? After this, shall we visit St. John's Co-Cathedral?" Olga leaned sideways to check his watch, then continued reading from the cruise ship's city guide. "Or there's the Grandmaster's Palace…or the Lascaris War Rooms. You choose, my darling. Which would you prefer?" She looked over at him, saw the look on his face, and covered her mouth. "Oh, I'm sorry! I said darling! I didn't mean to do that! I was thinking it in my head, and it just slipped out."

Teddy pulled a handkerchief from his pocket and mopped his brow, because beads of perspiration weren't attractive. As he gazed at Olga's smooth, perfect face, untroubled by dampness, he was overcome with emotion. She was so lovely and so honest. With Olga, what you saw was what you got.

"Don't be sorry." He reached for her hand. "I never thought anyone would call me darling again. To hear it from you is…well, it's like a miracle."

"Oh, Teddy. And it's the same for me. I can't believe I've met someone as wonderful as you." She stroked his fingers and broke into a dazzling smile. "I tell you what, it's a good job I'm not the kind of person who cries, because otherwise I might. You make me so *happy*."

He reached across and kissed her on the cheek, until Olga turned her head and her cheek became her mouth, and here they were, in public, with people sitting around them and others walking past. Maybe it only lasted a second or two, but Teddy knew he would never forget this moment for as long as he lived. It was perfect.

"Come on. Let's go." He rose to his feet. "Before we get arrested."

"Where shall we visit? The palace?"

He tucked her arm through his. "It's a surprise."

Ten minutes later, they reached Republic Street, hung with flags, crammed with shops, and buzzing with life. They walked along it until he saw what he was looking for. He drew Olga across with him until they were standing outside the door of the upmarket jeweler's.

"My goodness, are you treating yourself to something? This place looks *expensive*."

Teddy rang the bell, and they were buzzed in, to be greeted by a welcome blast of air-conditioning and a man in a smart suit.

"We're looking for a watch," Teddy announced with pride. "A nice watch, for my…friend."

"Teddy!" Olga gasped and gazed at him, wide-eyed. "You can't do that!"

"Why not? I want to. You don't have a watch, and you need one, if only to stop you always having to look at mine."

"But yours is so cheap," she exclaimed. "And I don't think they sell cheap ones here." She turned to address the salesman. "Do you sell very inexpensive watches too?"

The salesman winced as if she'd asked him about his sex life. "No, madam, we do not."

"Relax," said Teddy. "We can't have Bernard being the only one at our dinner table showing off a fancy new watch, can we? Let me buy you something you'll be proud to wear."

Olga still wasn't convinced. "But…are you sure you can afford it?"

Did he love her? It was far too soon to say it out loud, but he felt as if he did. Since meeting her on the ship, he'd felt forty years younger. "Of course I can. Remember the other day when you bought me a present? Well, now it's my turn to buy you one."

"Oh, Teddy…"

"Shall we start looking?" He gestured toward the glittering glass cabinets with their artfully angled lighting. "How about these? I might not be an expert, but they look pretty good to me."

"I should think they would look good." Olga's green eyes lit up as she followed his gaze. "They're Cartier."

chapter 10

APPROACHING THE OLD BARBERSHOP ON RIVER STREET, LACHLAN saw Raffaele outside on the hot, dusty sidewalk, deep in discussion with the delivery men who were unloading chairs from the back of a precariously double-parked van. As a family squeezed past, their small son dropped his red-and-yellow ball and let out a wail as it rolled into the gutter. Raffaele instantly reached down to retrieve the ball and handed it back to the boy. The sight took Lachlan back to the day their friendship had first begun.

Not that this had happened on the first day they'd met. Oh no. Back then, it had been suspicion at first sight. He'd been fifteen years old, as had Raffaele when he'd arrived at May and Teddy's house. Everyone had seemed convinced that with only three weeks between them in age, they were bound to bond in an instant.

But Lachlan had taken one look at the new arrival and recognized a rival when he saw one. Now that he'd discovered cooking and become less of a liability—to quote his relieved teacher—he'd made friends, and thanks to the way he looked, plenty of girls were keen to attract his attention.

It didn't help that Raffaele was a couple of inches taller than him and possibly even more good-looking, furious though it made Lachlan feel to have to admit this. Plus the newcomer had the kind of charming, easy manner that meant adults took to him right away. May and Teddy were delighted to have someone so laid-back and helpful around the house, and Lachlan felt a squeeze of jealousy inside his chest, because what if they preferred this new arrival to himself?

At home, he largely ignored Raffaele. At school, he didn't speak to him at all.

Luckily, Raffaele's popularity there didn't extend to the other fifty percent of the pupils. The ninth-grade boys in particular despised the effect he had on the opposite sex, and when Raffaele got friendly with the girl generally acknowledged to be the ultimate catch, the vitriol was ramped up on a daily basis.

Lachlan made sure he kept out of it; he wasn't going to give anyone a chance to send *him* away from here. All he wanted was for Raffaele to decide Lanrock wasn't for him and that he'd rather move somewhere he didn't get taunted and bullied every day.

The situation remained unchanged for the next couple of months. Lachlan either observed from a distance as Raffaele was submitted to the usual new-boy hard time or heard about it thirdhand. Until one day on his way home from school, he turned a corner and saw a group of boys piling onto Raffaele on the ground, wrestling his backpack off him, and sending it flying through the air until it crash-landed in a flower bed.

Dale Jenkins was the one who'd thrown it, the ringleader of his gang, and he'd left his own sports bag on the sidewalk in order to be able to concentrate on beating up the new kid. Even from this distance, Lachlan could see the blood dripping from Raffaele's nose. Unzipping the abandoned Nike bag, he took out a ball and threw it hard at Dale's head. Luckily, hand-eye coordination was one of his skills, and the impact caused Dale to yell out and roll off Raffaele.

Still on the ground, Dale bellowed, "What the *hell*?" before twisting around and spotting Lachlan. "You! Whose side are you on, dickhead?"

"Not yours." Lachlan remembered being cornered by Dale Jenkins during his own first weeks at school two years ago, being taunted that his mother was a hooker and a smack-head. What the kids hadn't known about his past, they'd gleefully made up. Over time, they might have stopped saying it, but as far as they were concerned, Raffaele was just the same, another victim to be publicly humiliated.

Control or be controlled. Across the road, Raffaele had now slid out of his attacker's reach and jumped to his feet, blood dripping onto the sidewalk. Lachlan raced over, landed on Dale's chest, and wrestled with him for a few seconds before finally managing to pin him down. He glared with such ferocity at the other boys that they backed away in fear. Then, pinging his finger against Dale's forehead in time with each word, he said, "Leave. Him. Alone. You. Ugly. Little. Twat."

"*Ow*. Get off me, you bastard."

With a cool smile, Lachlan squeezed Dale's earlobe. "Leave him alone from now on, or you'll regret it, and that's a promise." He climbed off Dale, pinged his forehead once more for good measure, then said, "Off you go."

"Thanks," said Raffaele as they made their way home together. "You didn't have to do that."

"I know. But that lot really piss me off." Lachlan shook back his overlong hair. "They're dicks."

"You're going to have a black eye."

Lachlan touched the bruised side of his face; Dale had managed to land a couple of punches before being brought under control. "He got lucky."

"Let's just hope it doesn't ruin your good looks."

Lachlan smiled briefly, because Raffaele had the kind of dry humor he liked. "Well, I reckon yours are wrecked. He's definitely broken your nose."

Blood was still dripping onto Raffaele's white shirt. He shrugged. "Wouldn't be the first time."

The way he said it, Lachlan understood. "How old were you?"

"Five, six? Thanks, Dad."

Growing up in foster care meant they were both accustomed to hearing such stories. Lachlan kicked a stone into the road. "Bastard."

"Yeah, well. He's dead now. So I guess I won."

Wow. "Did you kill him?"

Raffaele laughed. "No, the drugs did that. But it was the best news ever. Better than Christmas. Mind you, that's not saying much when most of them have been shit. Better than other people's Christmases, where everyone's happy," he amended. "You know, like the ones in the ads on TV."

It was October, the leaves were falling around them, and heavy drops of rain had begun to spatter the sidewalk. Lachlan said, "May and Teddy do a brilliant Christmas. If you're still here then."

Raffaele paused to take a packet of chewing gum out of his pocket. He offered it to Lachlan, who hesitated, then took one. "Might have to make sure I am."

When they arrived home, Teddy was still out at work, and May had too much experience dealing with teenage boys to fly into a panic. As Raffaele stripped off his shirt so they could try and get the blood out, she looked at Lachlan. "Did you do this to him?"

Which was a fair enough question, seeing as it was the most likely scenario.

Lachlan shook his head. "Not me."

"It wasn't him," said Raffaele. "He came to my rescue."

"Like Superman," said Lachlan.

"Except if it'd been the real Superman, he'd have stopped them before my nose got broken."

"Fine. Next time, I'll just leave you to die in a ditch." But Lachlan was grinning now.

"He's been telling me about the Christmases you have here." Raffaele turned back to May. "Says they're really great."

"Oh, well, we do our best. Now, let me have a good go at this shirt." May bustled through to the utility room with a tub of Vanish before calling over her shoulder, "What are we having to eat tonight, chef? Chicken pie or beef stroganoff?"

Raffaele was wiping the blood from his face and neck with a piece of kitchen towel. "I'd better get in the shower, clean myself up."

Before he headed upstairs, Lachlan said, "Which one d'you like best?"

Their eyes met across the kitchen table, Raffaele's brief smile acknowledging the olive branch. "I really like both of them. But the stroganoff's my favorite."

Lachlan nodded and said casually, "Cool. We'll have that."

From that day on, the bond between them had remained rock-solid. They'd forged an alliance, discovered that being friends rather than rivals made life infinitely better, and supported each other in every way. May and Teddy called them "our boys" and took pride in each and every one of their achievements. As a pairing, they were an unstoppable force at school. Best of all, they formed an unbreakable code so that if either of them had their eye on a particular girl, the other one stepped back and allowed them free rein.

Thanks to May and Teddy, Lachlan had found the brother he didn't know he needed. It was a good feeling, he'd discovered, to have someone who was entirely on your side.

Now, as he reached the barbershop, Raffaele gave him an appraising glance. "You could do with a trim."

"Thanks so much."

"Just letting you know it's time. I can do it now if you want." Raffaele was grinning; he couldn't help himself. He cared about these things. It really bothered him when ends needed tidying up.

"Let's do it." Lachlan went into the shop, collected one of the just-delivered chairs, and carried it back outside. Raffaele fetched a towel, a spray bottle of water, a comb, and scissors. And there on the sidewalk, Lachlan sat on the chair and allowed Raffaele to do his thing.

Just like old times.

It was a purely practical solution to a tricky dilemma that, having begun quite by chance, had ended up changing Raffaele's life.

Lachlan had moved around the country, working in different kitchens in order to build his CV. Eight years ago, he'd been taken on by a five-star hotel in London and discovered just how much it cost to live in the capital. But Raffaele had made the move two years earlier, renting a grim basement flat in Peckham with a fellow hairstylist who was, serendipitously, leaving to return home to Bradford. Lachlan replaced him, and there they were, sharing a home again. Even if it was a pretty unappealing one.

The carpet in the flat was faded and threadbare, but at least they had one, whereas a vacuum cleaner was a luxury they couldn't afford. This was why, whenever Raffaele cut his friends' hair, they carried a chair outside rather than have to sweep up the clippings with a dustpan and brush.

He'd been sorting out Lachlan's hair one evening in late spring when a middle-aged man from the local homeless shelter, who'd been watching them for a while, asked if Raffaele could do the same for him. The man's name was Christopher; he was going for a job interview the next day and was worried that his straggly graying locks would put any future employers off. He'd tried to cut them himself with blunt scissors a few months ago, and it had all gone horribly wrong.

Raffaele agreed and gave him a neat short back and sides. The next day, the interviewing employer offered Christopher the job. By the end of the week, word had spread, and a dozen or so guests from the shelter had turned up at the basement flat.

Lachlan informed Raffaele he was a soft touch who was getting massively taken advantage of, but Raffaele, who was a far nicer person than Lachlan, carried on regardless. And a couple of months later, passing by one Friday evening on his way to a party in Dulwich, a TV morning show host was intrigued enough to stop and ask the homeless woman on the chair surrounded by her belongings what was going on.

When she told him, the TV host knew he'd struck gold. Raffaele was an unknown twenty-three-year-old with the appearance of a model, giving up hours of his time each week to help those less fortunate than himself. By Monday morning, he found himself being filmed by a TV crew, cutting hair outside the flat before being whisked off to the studio for a live interview with the man who'd discovered him and his clearly besotted female cohost. She wasn't the only besotted one either; the viewers at home fell in love with Raffaele's striking good looks, charm, and altruism. More TV appearances and newspaper interviews followed, and actual celebrities began calling up the salon where he was working to be seen by him.

Lachlan was forced to have a serious conversation with himself during this period; he was of course delighted that such a fantastic opportunity had arisen for Raffaele, but it was hard not to also feel a bit jealous. It took a while, but he managed it, after a long late-night phone call with Amber during which she reminded him that he might want to be a brilliant chef but he most definitely didn't want to be so famous that he'd be recognized in the street.

This was true. Annoyingly, Amber had a talent for being right. Having his culinary skills admired by other chefs and customers who enjoyed his food was one thing, but Lachlan couldn't imagine anything worse than being a familiar face to complete strangers; he was too volatile and might react badly if they saw him in the street and yelled out something he didn't want to hear. Telling them what he thought of them wouldn't do his career any good at all.

Here in Lanrock was OK though; he could cope with this lower and less intrusive level of recognition. It was different and felt safe; it was largely people he knew.

Whoops, like Polly over there, coming out of the bakery opposite and pretending not to have seen him, marching off up the sidewalk with an I'm-so-busy look on her face. He'd said he'd text her and hadn't, and this was her way of teaching him a lesson. *Snip-snip-snip* went the scissors as Raffaele concentrated on tidying up the ends of his just-washed hair.

"What have you done to upset Polly?"

That was the thing about Raffaele; he never missed a trick.

"I didn't sleep with her."

"Who did you sleep with instead?"

"No one."

"Were you sick?"

"Just tired." No need to mention watching the TV show with Amber; it was irrelevant anyway. Sometimes it was easier to leave certain details out, especially where Raffaele was concerned.

"And now she's getting her own back."

OK, he was talking about Polly, not Amber. Lachlan nodded and earned himself a sigh of exasperation.

"How many times have I told you? Don't *nod*."

But Raffaele was a fast worker, and the trim only took a few minutes. As Lachlan lifted the chair to carry it back inside, Peggy drew to a halt in her Range Rover and bellowed out the window, "Table for two around seven, OK?"

He nodded. "No problem."

"How's the refurb coming along?" She turned her attention to Raffaele in the doorway.

"Still on course to open next week. How are you, Peggy?"

"Marvelous, as always! Just off to the gallery. Reckon a bit of a pep talk's in order. OK, *OK*." She shook her head in despair, because the string of drivers backed up behind her were having the temerity to toot their horns. "God, the people around here are so impatient! See you later."

"Wouldn't want to be on the end of one of Peggy's pep talks," Raffaele said drily.

"It's only Benjie." Lachlan brushed a few snipped ends off the shoulder of his black polo shirt. "He's used to it."

chapter 11

OF ALL THE JOBS IN ALL THE WORLD, BENJIE SMART STILL WISHED
he hadn't ended up being landed with this one. He wasn't suited to it and
was fairly sure his mum knew this, but she remained adamant that the
only way to overcome his misgivings was by doing more of it for longer,
thereby getting better as time went by.

Benjie had googled and devoured countless articles online over the
years, with titles such as "How Confidence Can Be Yours!" and "Banish
Shyness Forever!" But all they'd done was frighten the life out of him. It
was OK for people like his mum to tell him to get a grip, but she couldn't
begin to understand. Peggy Smart had never known for a single second
how it felt to be paralyzed with fear because what if you tried to say
something and it came out all wrong? Or it wasn't the right thing to say
and the other person demanded to know why you were burbling such
rubbish?

This was how he'd ended up becoming such a figure of fun at Framley
Hall. At the first sign of weakness, the teasing by the other boys in his class
had intensified, causing his slight stammer to worsen, and after that, it
had been a slippery slope. They'd mocked him for everything, from wearing the wrong kind of sneakers to being a member of the chess club. He'd
been prepared to endure the bullying and wait for it to lose its novelty
value, then hopefully fade away of its own accord. And this might even
have happened if another concerned mother hadn't heard about it from
her daughter and taken it upon herself to tell Peggy what was going on.

It was the worst thing that could have happened, and Benjie still
felt faint with horror at the memory of the day he'd left school at the
usual time only to spot his mother waiting at the school gates alongside
a pimped-up stretch limo and a uniformed chauffeur who was holding

up a card bearing the names of the five main culprits. Bedazzled by the unexpected surprise, the boys gleefully made themselves known to the chauffeur, whereupon Peggy Smart proceeded to tell them who she was and exactly what she thought of them for being cruel to her son. Frozen to the spot thirty meters away, Benjie had wanted to die. Pretty much the entire school was watching and sniggering by now. But the sniggers weren't directed at the bullies, were they? Oh no, they were all for him.

Then, when his mum had finally finished giving his classmates a piece of her mind, she called out to him, beckoning him over to join her. "Benjie, come along. We're out of here. And I hope you bunch of absolute brats have learned your lesson."

The sound of everyone in the school laughing at him as the limo pulled away was something he would never forget. From then on, he'd no longer been B-B-Benjie Not-so-Smart. The mocking, jeering comments had become far worse.

As had his stammer.

When the art gallery was empty, as it was now, Benjie found himself with plenty of time to sit at his desk, think back over the past decade, and wonder if there had been any opportunity he could have taken that might have changed the course of his life for the better. The limo afternoon had been the most agonizing incident, he knew that. And a couple of months later, when the teasing and bullying had become unbearable, his mother had removed him from that school and planted him in another. But by then it was too late; teenagers had the ability to smell weakness in a new arrival, and in no time at all it was happening again, a self-fulfilling prophecy destined to make every day an ordeal.

With school finally behind him, university turned out to be not so bad. He might not be stunningly handsome, but he knew he had an OK physique and the kind of everyday good looks that made people smile and relax when they first met him. A couple of the kinder girls in his halls of residence had told him he had a cute face and puppy-dog eyes, which should have sounded flattering but somehow hadn't done him much good. He'd even allowed them to set him up on a few dates, but those hadn't worked out. All in all, the three years had turned out to be a lonely experience, given that by this time, he'd completely lost both his confidence and the knack of making friends. And once he'd gained his degree in history and set about applying for jobs, he'd discovered that this too was a lot harder than other people made out. Prospective employers seemed to like his CV, but as soon as he was sitting in front of them being interviewed, he could feel their interest fall away.

After several months of rejections, Benjie began work in one of the offices belonging to his mother and uncle's haulage company. It wasn't exciting, but it was peaceful and hassle-free. His fellow workers knew who he was and accepted him. They were all in their forties and fifties and didn't mind that he was quiet. He was content there, if still a bit embarrassed that he hadn't been able to find himself a job. When Peggy had decided to move down to Cornwall, he'd been happy to stay on in his rented flat in Birmingham…

That was until she'd taken up painting with a vengeance, decided she was the best thing since Banksy, and on a complete whim bought the Lanrock Gallery to sell her art to an enthusiastic public.

Except neither the first person his mother had employed to work there nor the public had turned out to be enthusiastic.

With typical verve, Peggy had headhunted a smartly dressed, smart-talking young woman from a gallery in St. Ives. At the end of the first week, when none of her paintings had sold, she'd invited Benjie down for the weekend and sent him into the gallery to masquerade as a potential buyer. The young woman promptly informed him that the big splashy paintings weren't even worth looking at before steering him over to the work executed by other artists, two of whom subsequently turned out to be friends of hers from St. Ives.

Benjie wasn't there when his mother stormed down to the gallery and sacked the woman on the spot. Twenty minutes later, she returned to the house and offered him the position instead. Although it was more of an order than an offer.

"Benjie, think about it." She gestured wildly, indicating just how ridiculous it would be for him to refuse. "What do you have to lose? Your job up in Birmingham is no great shakes, is it? And the other people in that office are as dull as ditchwater! Why not rent out your flat and move down here instead? You can have the top floor of the house, a self-contained apartment just for you. And what could be nicer than living in Lanrock? The people are friendly, the sea's on your doorstep, and you can make new friends. It'll be a whole new start!"

His mum had the knack of being persuasive and not giving in until she'd gotten what she wanted. It was why her nickname at the haulage company was the Pit Bull. Benjie tried to picture himself working in the art gallery, being charming to strangers while persuading them to part with their hard-earned money. He said, "I don't think I'd be very good at…you know, s-selling paintings."

"But, sweetheart, at least you'd *try*." Peggy's huge earrings jangled as she shook her head. "Not like that two-faced witch, only interested in flogging her friends' rubbish. After I told her to get out, you should have heard the things she said to me about my art!"

Benjie could imagine. The woman had made one or two cruelly dismissive comments while he'd been studying his mum's paintings; he just hadn't shared them with her. The thing was, Peggy might be the Pit Bull when it came to the haulage company that had made her fortune, because that was purely business. But the paintings were different; they were personal. She loved each and every one of them, poured her heart into creating them, and the slightest criticism was like a dagger to her chest. Even now, just thinking about the parting remarks from the woman she'd sacked, the pain was evident in her eyes.

She gazed at him imploringly now. "Please, Benjie. Say yes. You'd love it here."

How could he say no? He'd agreed in order to protect her. If he was in charge of the gallery, he could ensure she didn't get to hear any more potentially hurtful comments. But it wasn't until he'd actually been working there for a couple of weeks that he'd realized quite how many of them there were.

Visitors to Lanrock loved to have a good look around the shops and galleries while they were on holiday, and as a rule, they didn't bother lowering their voices while sharing their opinions of the various items they found for sale. It was one thing, Benjie soon discovered, overhearing families in the craft market making fun of the miniature Cornish cottages constructed out of seashells, but it was quite another when they entered the gallery, eyed his mum's huge canvases with bewilderment, then cracked up laughing when they got close enough to see the price tags. Only yesterday, a middle-aged couple had sniggered and pointed at Peggy's favorite painting, commenting that it was the kind of art Ben would produce. It wasn't until the wife spotted Benjie's name badge and marveled at the coincidence that he discovered Ben was the family bulldog.

Abstract art was always open to criticism. Neither Benjie nor the vast majority of the customers knew much about the skills required to create it…or even whether any skills were involved. Everyone had their own views on what they liked or didn't like, however, and sadly most of the visitors to the gallery felt these bold, brash creations weren't their cup of tea.

Needless to say, the gallery rarely sold any of the Peggy Smart originals, but Peggy outright refused to soften her uncompromising style. Luckily, the more conventional paintings and sculptures proved popular, which kept the business afloat. Every now and again, Benjie bit the bullet and bought one or two of her canvases under a made-up name before anonymously donating them to charity fundraisers a safe distance away. He knew it was a crazy thing to do, but it meant the world to his mum, who adored hearing his stories of the people who'd wandered into the gallery and fallen head over heels in love with her work. Really, it was the least he could do.

Speak of the devil…

No, not the devil. She was his mum, and he loved her to bits. Feeling his pulse begin to quicken as the Range Rover pulled up outside, Benjie just wished a family hadn't chosen this moment to enter the gallery. They were already noisily poking fun at the big splashy yellow and maroon canvas in the window, comparing it with the time their teenage son had thrown up all over the floor after three bowls of blackberry crumble and custard.

"Ah, fantastic, one of our artists is here!" This was his method for warning people not to say anything awful in front of her. Holding open the door so that his mum could bring the meter-square canvas inside, Benjie said extra jovially, "Peggy Smart, how wonderful to see you! And what's this you have for us? Another m-masterpiece?"

His stammer always revealed when he was lying.

"I do, I do. Hot off the easel!" Peggy beamed at the family and propped it up against his desk so everyone could admire it. This one was more of a mint-chocolate-chip color palette with a terrifying deep-red smear in the top right-hand corner that hinted at a violent murder followed by hasty removal of the body. "There! What d'you think? I'm *so* pleased with it!"

The visitors were gazing at the canvas, slack-jawed.

"It's m-m-marvelous." The added stress made Benjie's stammer worse, but he battled on. "You've done it again! The colors…the balance…the m-mood it creates…"

Peggy nodded smugly. "I know. It's one of my best."

The younger son of the family said, "How much is it?"

Peggy laughed. "More than your pocket money, I'm afraid! But it would be a wonderful investment for the future. No, don't touch it. The paint's still wet…"

"We'll hang it in pride of place in the w-window." Glancing outside, Benjie had never been more relieved to see the traffic warden making his way down the street. "Peggy, if you don't disappear, you're going to get another ticket…"

"Oh, that dreadful man. He drives me mad! Doesn't he understand I'm an artist? You'd think they'd give me a free parking pass, wouldn't you? It's not so much to ask!" She beamed at the family again, vigorously shook each of their hands in turn, then dashed outside just as the traffic warden reached the shop. With a flurry of apologies and a swirl of her topaz silk scarf, she clambered into the vehicle and disappeared in a cloud of kicked-up sand and dust.

The small boy, his eyes like saucers, said, "I never met a real artist before."

"Well, you have now." With his mother safely out of the way, Benjie felt the muscles in his shoulders begin to relax.

"Is she rich?"

"Yes."

The boy gazed around the gallery. "I'm good at painting. Mum, can I be an artist when I grow up?"

The family didn't buy anything, but Benjie hadn't expected them to. An hour later, an older couple came in and chose a small but sweet print of fishing boats in the harbor, painted by a popular local watercolorist. Then a delivery arrived from a framing company, and Benjie hauled the taped-up case through to the back room. He was battling to break through the securely fastened layers of cardboard when he heard the gentle *ting* of the bell above the door outside. Leaning to the right to see who it was, he glimpsed curly auburn hair and a green-and-white-striped canvas shoulder bag and ducked back out of sight to regain some equilibrium, because it was her, Jo, the girl from Lachlan's restaurant.

Sadly, the box cutter had carried on cutting while his attention was elsewhere, and the next moment, a zing of pain made itself felt. Looking down, he saw that he'd managed to slice through the web of flesh between his left thumb and index finger, and blood was now pattering down onto the lid of the cardboard case.

Benjie went into panic mode; he had a customer out in the shop and an injury he wasn't sure how to deal with without drawing attention to himself. It was Jo, which didn't help. Worse still, the sight of more blood than he was used to seeing was making him feel weirdly light-headed.

"Hello?" she called out politely. "Is anyone there?"

Panicking, Benjie dropped the box cutter on the floor and clutched his left wrist in a feeble attempt to use his right hand as a tourniquet. Staggering slightly, he bumped against the box and called out, "Sorry, um… Oh God…"

"Are you OK?"

The air in the office appeared to be turning misty gray, and blood was dripping onto the floor. Mortified, he mumbled, "Not really…"

"Right, I'm coming in." He heard footsteps cross the shiny floor, then Jo pushed the door properly open and stopped dead. "Whoops, get down!"

In his befuddled state, Benjie thought maybe a bomb was about to go off. "What?"

But she already had her arms around him and was guiding him away from the edge of the desk while simultaneously lowering him to the floor. Which was just as well, seeing as his vision had blurred and his legs no longer seemed to be working.

"There. You'll be fine," Jo reassured him. "You were about to pass out. I thought I was looking at a ghost! Now, let me hold your arm up in the air. Good job this floor isn't carpeted. What a mess! Do you have a first-aid box around here?"

He'd nearly fainted. How embarrassing. This had never happened to him before in his life. Closing his eyes, Benjie murmured, "Bottom drawer of the desk, on the left."

"Good. Keep your arm up. Take deep breaths. Hang on, here's the wastepaper bin in case you throw up."

He was lying on the floor, being looked after by a girl who had no idea he'd had a crush on her for months. The thought of puking into a bin in front of her was even more appalling. Luckily he wasn't feeling sick, just woozy. But the blood was returning to his brain, and his vision was clearing. He watched as she located the first-aid kit, cleaned his hand, and surveyed the cut before padding and wrapping it securely in gauze swabs and a bandage.

"There," she said when it was done. "I don't think it needs stitches, but we'll see what it's like in a bit. These cuts bleed like anything, so they look scary. Better now?"

"I think so." Well, no longer light-headed, but still mortified. Fainting at the sight of blood was hardly a macho-man thing to do.

"Want to try getting up?"

"OK."

She helped him into a sitting position. "There, how does that feel?"

It was on the tip of his tongue to say "Lovely." Luckily, he didn't. But the sensation of her bare arm supporting his shoulders was one he knew he wouldn't forget in a hurry.

"I'm good." He nodded, still unable to meet her gaze. "Thanks."

"Hey, no worries."

"Lucky for me you came in when you did. Otherwise…"

"They'd have found you tomorrow morning dead on the floor in a giant pool of blood. Sorry, that was a joke. Of course it wouldn't have happened. Sometimes I say things and people think I'm serious." She grimaced. "And other times, I'm trying to be serious but they think I'm joking. Life can get very confusing."

Benjie levered himself to his feet. "Well, I'm glad I'm not dead. And you m-made a good job of bandaging me up."

"I did a first-aid course a few years back. Been searching for injured people ever since. You're the first one."

"I'm honored."

"I'm glad I found you. I was starting to get tired of waiting. Oh, that sounds like—" She stopped abruptly and shook her head. "Like a princess in a fairy tale. See what I mean? Never mind. Anyway, d'you want some help cleaning up the crime scene?"

"Sorry?"

"This." She pointed to the blood-spattered black-and-white vinyl flooring.

"Oh, no. I'll take care of it." As the feeling of normality returned, so did his shyness. "Anyway, you came in here for a reason."

"Oh yes, so I did! I wanted to buy the painting in the window, the one with all the black and red swirls."

"Really?" Benjie's eyes widened in amazement.

Jo grinned. "Sorry, that was another joke. I mean, Peggy's great, but her stuff's a bit out of my league. I was actually looking for a card for my nan. It's her birthday on Saturday."

Of course it had been a joke. Benjie mentally kicked himself for being so gullible. "You can have one," he said. "On the house."

"Did you really think I was going to buy the painting?"

"I thought it was unlikely." He managed a rueful smile, then felt himself get embarrassed all over again because she was so nice, and if he were the confident type—like an actor on TV or someone like that—now might be the perfect moment to say casually, "Look, if you ever fancy going for a drink, just say the word."

But he wasn't an actor on TV, he was only himself, and it would probably all come out wrong anyway, or else she'd look horrified and say, "God, are you mad? Why would I want to do *that*?" So he didn't say anything at all.

They headed back through to the gallery, and he pretended to busy himself with a pile of glossy brochures instead while feeling his armpits prickle with shame at having had the temerity to even think such thoughts. Biting his lip, he endured the awkward silence until she'd selected the card she wanted.

"This one. It's lovely." She held it up to show him, then dug into her bag and brought out her purse.

"No, no, just take it." He waved her away. "Your reward for saving my life."

"OK, thanks." Jo slipped the card into her striped canvas bag. "So, better be off. I'll see you tonight!"

What?

Had he invited her out? Had his mouth uttered the words while his brain was otherwise occupied?

"S-sorry?"

"Seven o'clock. Don't be late!"

OK, had it actually happened? It didn't help that his tongue had glued itself to the roof of his mouth.

"You look confused," said Jo. "Peggy's booked a table for the two of you. Didn't she mention it?"

At the restaurant. For dinner. *Oh, phew.*

Except also *not* phew, because wouldn't it have been amazing if he had asked her out for a drink and she'd accepted without him even having been aware of it?

"Right, no, she didn't. But...yes. Well, see you later."

"Bye! Oh, one more thing."

"Yes?" Benjie's heart began to thud.

"It's going to be a lot easier to clean that blood up," Jo told him, "if you do it before it dries."

chapter 12

"YOU'RE LOOKING SMART TONIGHT. THAT BLUE SHIRT SUITS YOU."
Peggy regarded her son fondly and gave an approving nod. "Brings out
your eyes."

"Mum." Benjie shook his head slightly; he'd never been comfortable
receiving compliments.

"Here she is, then! I hear you came to the rescue this afternoon."
Peggy beamed as the pretty waitress approached their table.

"Oh, it was nothing." Jo turned to Benjie. "How are you feeling
now? Better?"

"He's never been keen on the sight of blood. Good job you're not
squeamish, love!"

Jo grinned. "No chance, not working here. Lachlan's forever collect-
ing cuts and burns. Now, what are you two having tonight? The turbot's
fantastic."

"You mean he's ordered too much of it? No, I'll have the lamb.
Benjie, how about you?"

"I think the…t-turbot."

"Great choice. And how's the hand? Did you get it looked at?"

Benjie shook his head. "No. I'm sure it's fine."

Jo said, "Well, make sure you keep it clean. You don't want it getting
infected. If it starts feeling hot and sore, take yourself off to the doctor's."

When they were alone once more at her favorite table by the window,
Peggy said, "She's a lovely girl."

Benjie's ears reddened. He examined his cutlery.

"Don't you like her?"

"She's OK. Mum, please don't."

Honestly, and she was being so subtle. Peggy held up her hands, palms out. "I won't say another word. Now, tell me about the rest of your day. Any other interesting customers?"

Dinner proceeded in the busy restaurant. Peggy's lamb was sublime, cooked just as she liked it. Hopeful holidaymakers could be seen hovering outside the entrance, studying the menu displayed in its glass case. Those who ventured in and hadn't prebooked were gently turned away. Others, yet to be seated, waited at the bar. For the millionth time, Peggy congratulated herself on having had the foresight to buy this place. She adored coming here and always being able to get a table, and she enjoyed chatting with the waitresses and other diners. She especially loved seeing Lachlan working away in the kitchen, visible through the wide stone archway that separated it from the dining room. He'd been appalled at first by the idea that everyone would be able to see and hear him, but Peggy had insisted the punters would love it. And she'd been right. They'd had to put up a notice warning that diners might occasionally want to cover their ears, but those sweary moments were infrequent enough to feel like a prize worth having. Lachlan was a cheerful, witty chef who dealt well with stress in the kitchen. And when his work was done at the end of the evening and he came out to greet everyone, his audience enjoyed his presence even more.

As did Peggy. She took a sip of wine, watching him now as he flambéed a pan of oysters with a flourish. The table who'd ordered them began to cheer, and Lachlan acknowledged their applause with a brief nod and a smile while keeping his attention on the job. His hair might have been trimmed by Raffaele, but it was still long and tied back. With his dark eyes flashing and those expressive eyebrows, he looked wonderfully piratical. A table of women, paying close attention as he called out instructions to Paolo, the sous chef, exchanged raised eyebrows of their own and pretended to swoon. Since opening the restaurant, Lachlan had acquired something of a fan club. Well, it would be weird if he hadn't, when you looked at him.

Peggy hadn't admitted it to a soul, but she felt almost as proud of Lachlan as if she were his mother. Much as she loved and adored Benjie— and she did, of course she did, with all her heart—his personality was the exact opposite of hers. He was a lovely boy, quiet and thought-ful, good-hearted and utterly dependable. Whereas in Lachlan, she'd instantly recognized how like her he was: driven, hard-working, and endlessly ambitious. He was mercurial, quick-witted, plain-speaking, and impatient. Bringing up Benjie, she'd so often wished he could have been more confident and outgoing, but it wasn't something she was able to make happen. He was who he was, and that was it, and she loved him anyway.

But if she *could* have chosen certain qualities for her son, she would have tried to mold him into more of an extrovert. The first time she'd spoken to Lachlan, it had been like meeting a kindred spirit. As they'd gotten to know each other, it had also felt like being given a wonderful opportunity to help the kind of boy she'd have chosen as another son.

And really, was there anything wrong with that? Lachlan had had a rotten start in life, but he'd worked incredibly hard to overcome it. And he'd never asked her for anything, either. She admired him for that.

Anyway, here was Benjie returning from the bathroom, carefully edging past the other waitress, then glancing over at Jo, who was serving coffee to table eight.

"Mum, are you OK here if I head back? I'm pretty tired."

"Of course, off you go." Peggy tilted her face so he could give her a kiss on the cheek. Once dinner was over, he tended not to linger, prefer-ring to go home and chat with his online friends, whereas she liked to stay on and talk to actual human beings. "See you later, love."

As he was leaving, she caught him glancing once more in Jo's direc-tion, but she was still busy. The next moment, she looked up and called out, "Bye, Benjie," causing him to jump out of his skin and almost close the door on his own face.

"Oh, b-bye…"

Peggy's heart went out to her boy. If there were a confidence-boosting magic medicine she could buy for him, she'd do it in a flash, no matter what the cost. But apart from cocaine and alcohol, there didn't appear to be anything else that would be up to the job.

Speaking of alcohol. She raised her hand to attract the other waitress's attention and said, "Could I have another glass of the Fleurie, my darling, when you've got a minute? Thanks so much."

Peggy left before eleven o'clock and sat on the bench just up from the restaurant until Jo came out ten minutes later, finished for the night and on her way home to the cottage she shared with her grandmother on the other side of Lanrock.

"Oh, hi." Spotting Peggy in the pool of lamplight, Jo added, "Waiting for a taxi?"

"Waiting for you, actually. I wondered if we could have a little chat."

Jo hesitated. "Is this about my nan's birthday card? I did offer to pay for it."

"Oh shush, it's nothing like that. Shall we take a walk along the beach?" Peggy was already on her feet, keen for their conversation not to be overheard.

They headed down the street and made their way onto the dry sand. There was a thin crescent moon in the sky, and the stars were bright overhead. Peggy listened to the rhythmic swish of the waves as they reached the shoreline, then broke the silence between them.

"You're a great waitress. I notice these things. Everyone likes you."

"I like working there." After a moment, Jo said, "Is this about the restaurant then?"

"Not really. It's about…"

"Another job?"

"No. Although I suppose it would be, kind of." Peggy realized she hadn't gotten her answers in the right order. "Look, can I ask if you're seeing anyone at the moment?"

"You mean, like a boyfriend? No."

She'd thought not, but it had seemed prudent to double-check. "Good."

In the darkness, it was just possible to make out the bafflement on the girl's pale, freckled face. "Why's it good?"

"Because I have a proposition for you. But first, I need you to promise to keep this between us. Which I'm pretty sure you would, because you're a good person. If you weren't, I wouldn't be asking you in the first place."

"OK." Jo nodded. "Better tell me what it is though. I'm curious now."

"It's Benjie. You've seen him several times in the restaurant. And today in the gallery. You know the kind of boy he is."

"Quiet, you mean?"

"Quiet, shy…he doesn't socialize. Since he moved down here, he hasn't managed to get to know anyone his own age. He sits at home on his computer, talking online to people he's never met in real life, and it's just not…helping. What he needs is a chance to get out and about. He needs a friend, someone to help him build up his confidence." Peggy paused, took a breath. "And I wondered if you'd be his friend."

There, she'd said it.

"Oh, except," she added hastily, "I'd pay you, of course!"

Jo did a double take. "Are you serious?"

"Would I be here if I wasn't? I want to help my son, make life easier for him. It's hard enough for anyone moving to a new town, but it's harder for Benjie because of his shyness. And you're so relaxed, I just think maybe he could learn from you, open up a bit."

"Wow," said Jo. "When you say you want me to be his friend…what exactly do you mean?"

"Oh, I'm not asking you to be his girlfriend, nothing like that." Peggy shook her head. "And definitely no sex, I promise!"

"Right," Jo said faintly.

"I just thought a normal kind of friendship, that's all I'm suggesting. It would help him, give him the boost he needs. How much do you earn per hour at the restaurant?"

"Um…"

She was hesitating, not yet convinced. Leaping in, Peggy said, "Whatever it is, I'll match it. Plus expenses, of course. How many shifts do you work each week?"

"Four lunchtimes, three evenings, usually." Jo was still sounding cautious.

"So that's perfect. You can still do those and meet up with Benjie during your time off. You could go into the gallery again, buy a couple more cards, have a nice chat, then ask him if he'd like to go along with you to some music thing or whatever, say you've been given two tickets… All you have to do is invoice me for everything. I'll set up a direct debit so it's all covered."

"The money thing seems weird." Jo bent down to pick up a flat pebble and spun it into the sea, watching as it skip-skip-skipped across the surface of the water before sinking without a trace.

Peggy looked at her. "Would you do it for free?"

Silence.

"Exactly," said Peggy. "It's a big ask. You hardly know him. Treat it like a job, and don't worry about it. Benjie's never going to find out, is he? Not unless you tell him. Because I certainly won't."

Another pebble was selected and spun into the waves rippling onto the shore. Finally Jo said, "What if he thinks I'm doing it because I fancy him? That two-tickets business is what they always tell you to do in advice columns when you don't know how to ask someone out."

"Be up-front! Just come out and say it. Tell him you like him as a friend but that's all. He wouldn't pester you, if that's what's worrying you."

"No, he's not the type." Jo nodded in agreement. Yet she was still hesitating. "The thing is, I'm leaving in September. Did you know that?"

"I didn't. Where are you going?"

"Traveling. My belated gap year while my nan's well enough not to need me. Thailand, Australia, New Zealand, all the usual places."

"Nice," said Peggy. "So some extra cash would come in handy."

"Lachlan told me you never take no for an answer."

"He was right."

"Are you going to keep at me until I say yes?"

"Of course I am. I love my son, I want to help him, and I reckon this would be a great way to go about it. Someone like you could be just what he needs to bring him out of himself."

A warm breeze ruffled Jo's coppery curls. Finally she broke into a smile. "OK, deal."

"Good girl. Thank you." Peggy shook her hand. "I have a feeling you're going to be the making of Benjie."

"I'll do my best."

She was adorable. What a terrific plan this was going to be. Buzzing with delight at having sealed the deal, Peggy said, "And as another thank-you, I'm going to give you one of my paintings. For free!"

"Wow," said Jo. Then she shook her head. "That's really kind, but I can't let you do that."

"Of course you can. I'll let you choose your favorite out of all of them, whichever one you want, as big as you like!"

"And if Benjie comes over to my nan's house once we're friends, how would I explain the fact that one of your expensive paintings was up on our living room wall?"

"Ah. Good point."

"I know. So thanks for the offer," said Jo, "but best not."

....

Benjie always looked forward to meeting up with his friends online, mainly because it didn't involve having to speak and wonder what kind of sounds might come out of his mouth.

When he was typing online, he didn't stammer. He could say whatever he wanted to say, via the comforting medium of the keyboard. There was no need to panic, because there was no pressure to get it right the first time. And having gotten to know these friends through a shyness forum he'd joined six months ago, there'd been an agreement from the word go that none of them would ever suggest they use Zoom.

This was Benjie's favorite time; it was his way of socializing, and it was blissfully hassle-free. He could be himself, but a better version, without the fear of people being disappointed when they heard him speak or met him in real life. He liked all of them—they were a group of eleven in total—and they liked him in return.

But Dani was the one he'd truly connected with. She was the one who caused his pulse to quicken, who always made him laugh, and who would make him blush and stammer in real life, because he had the most almighty crush on her.

Luckily this wasn't real life. It was far better, and this was the way they both preferred it.

She was already online, waiting for him. Hey, about time too.

We went out to dinner. I left Mum down there. Wait till you hear what happened to me at work today.

What? Tell me!!

And when he'd finished relaying the story—in the kind of witty, self-deprecating way he could never have managed if he'd had to speak the words—Dani typed back, Oh now I'm jealous of the waitress because she got to look after you.

It wasn't romantic. It was really embarrassing.

Still jealous though. What's she like?

Nice.

Pretty?

Curly red hair and freckles. Dani had long silver-blond hair, big brown eyes, and the loveliest little pouty mouth. Her figure was neat, she liked to wear shorts and slogan T-shirts, and her teeth were amazingly white. She wore quite a lot of makeup and had confided in Benjie that this was because she was worried her face might not be good enough without it. Even though it would have been, of course. But she preferred to hide behind her mask, and he understood that. If he could get away with it, he'd do it too.

Well, don't go falling in love with her, that's all, she typed now.

He grinned, because this was a game they liked to play. I won't, I promise.

And don't let her fall in love with you either. She can't have you. You'll just have to tell her you've already found your future wife.

It was only a joke, of course, but it made him happy to play along. I probably won't see her again for weeks. But when I do, I'll let her know. Have you found the perfect church yet?

Still narrowing them down. There's a gorgeous one on the island of Santorini. I'll send you a photo, hang on…

He waited. A few seconds later, the photo popped up on his screen, of a traditional Greek church, painted dazzling white, with a cobalt-blue domed roof and bright pink bougainvillea framing the sturdy wooden door.

I like it, he typed. Add it to the short list.

This Jo. Is she prettier than me?

No one's prettier than you. You're going to be my beautiful bride. It was a fantasy; it was harmless. He pictured Dani arriving at the church, wearing a simple white dress and a lacy veil…

And you'll be my handsome husband. He knew that while Dani was sending her reply, she would be smiling as broadly as he was, because it was fun to pretend.

I will, he typed back. Can't wait.

....

"Here's to us." Teddy raised a glass, his gaze encompassing everyone around their dining table. "To new friends. And new beginnings."

"New friends and new beginnings." They all joined in with gusto, clinking glasses and beaming at one another. It was the last night of the cruise. Tomorrow, they'd be going their separate ways. But there would be meetups in the months and years to come.

"And you never know," said Millicent from Milwaukee. "Some of us might have to buy ourselves a new hat."

"Oh no!" Olga looked horrified. "Did you lose yours? The beautiful one with the pink ribbons? I loved that hat!"

"I haven't lost it, honey. It's kind of a jokey saying when you think a couple might be tying the knot. Getting married," she explained when Olga shook her head in confusion. "If things carry on going well for you and Teddy, you never know what might happen. And if it does, you'd have to invite all of us along, wouldn't you? To the wedding!"

Olga laughed. "I understand, I think. But what is it that you tie into a knot?"

"You don't want to know." Walter nudged Millicent and waggled his eyebrows.

"Anyway, we aren't going to lose touch," Teddy promised.

"I really hope you won't lose touch with me," Olga teased him. "That would be horrible."

"Not going to happen." Teddy clasped her left hand.

"How long will it take you to drive home to Cornwall in the morning?" said Phil. The ship was arriving back in Southampton at seven, and they were hoping to have disembarked by nine.

"We're not going straight down there," said Olga. "I need to pick up more clothes from my place, so we'll be heading up to Reading first."

"Bet everyone's looking forward to meeting Olga," Phil said to Teddy. "Or haven't you told them yet?"

"Of course I've told them." Bursting with pride, Teddy gave Olga's fingers a reassuring squeeze. "They can't wait."

"You're a lucky chap, I'll say that for you." On his other side, Bernard gave him a nudge.

"Actually, he isn't. I'm the lucky one." The new watch glittered on Olga's elegant wrist as she returned Teddy's squeeze. "I'm the luckiest person in the world."

chapter 13

"Here we go," said Lachlan the following afternoon as they saw the car pull up outside number 19. "The moment of truth."

"We're giving her the benefit of the doubt," Amber reminded him.

"I know." He flashed her a reassuring grin. "We're going to be lovely. But we also need to stay alert."

"Nag, nag, nag."

"And try not to throw yourself at her like an overexcited puppy."

"Stop teasing her," Raffaele chided as Amber pinched Lachlan's wrist.

"Will you look at that?" said Lachlan. "She's waiting for him to open the car door for her."

"Teddy always used to open the door for May," said Amber.

"Only to help her when she was ill. Oh wow…"

"Being lovely means being kind," said Amber, although he sort of had a point. It was three o'clock on a drizzly gray Saturday afternoon, and Olga had poured her curves into a stretchy white lace bodysuit cinched at the waist with a bright orange belt. She was also wearing silver high-heeled sandals, tasseled earrings, and an orange flowery headband in her hair.

"Maybe she's representing her country in the Eurovision Song Contest—*Ow*," murmured Lachlan as Amber gave his arm a bigger pinch.

"Look at Teddy. See how happy he is. And that's what matters."

"We're on the same side, remember," Lachlan told her. "I want him to be happy too."

Amber opened the front door, and they spilled out of the house to greet them. "Hi, you're back! We've missed you so much!"

The introductions were made. Close up, Olga was even more

beautiful. "I've heard so much about all of you," she exclaimed, greeting each of them in turn in her crisply accented English. By the time she reached Amber, the zip at the front of her lace jumpsuit had undone itself by a couple more inches, and a flash of lime-green bra was visible. "Oops, better do myself up. My bosoms are excited to see you!" She hugged Amber with enthusiasm. "You smell wonderful! Do I smell nice too? I'm wearing Diorissimo because it's Teddy's new favorite—we chose it in the duty-free shop on the ship!"

"It's gorgeous." Amber beamed.

"I'm delighted to be here. So this is Teddy's house. Wow, it's so big!" Stepping back to admire it, Olga reached for his hand. "I mean, it looked amazing in the photos he showed me, but it's even better in real life."

Amber couldn't bring herself to look at Lachlan. As they all helped to carry the luggage inside, she saw him exchange a glance with Raffaele. When everything was lined up in the hall, Raffaele said lightly, "Wow, six cases. That's a lot."

"I love clothes. And shoes. And shopping. All of it, really." Olga spread her hands expansively. "We drove back to my place to collect enough to keep me going while I'm down here."

"How long d'you think you'll be staying?" Lachlan's tone was easy.

"Ah, who knows?" Her green eyes sparkled. "As long as Teddy wants me here, I guess. Maybe by Tuesday, he'll be fed up and ask me to leave!"

"You know I'd never do that." Teddy gave her a loving look. "Now, shall we all have a cup of tea? We've had quite a journey today."

"You've had quite a journey for the past three weeks," said Lachlan.

"It's been the most wonderful three weeks of my life," Olga announced. "And now we're here, it's going to get even better. I think we should be celebrating with champagne."

"Definitely," said Teddy, beaming.

In the kitchen, a bottle was opened and toasts were made. Then Teddy showed them more of the photographs he'd taken during the cruise. Amber was doing her best not to be suspicious of Olga's motives, but it was hard when Olga kept talking about money; she wasn't doing herself any favors.

"Oh, I almost forgot, I bought presents for each of you!" Disappearing out to the hallway and rifling through one of her cases, she returned with three bags. "I've been so looking forward to meeting you that I wanted to bring you something… I hope you love them!"

Raffaele received a comb in the shape of a cruise ship. Lachlan was presented with a fridge magnet depicting a bowl of paella. Graciously, they thanked her.

"Oh, it's fantastic!" When it was her turn, Amber admired the large multicolored plastic ball attached to a key ring.

"You have to turn it on. There's a tiny switch." Olga leaned forward, giving them all an excellent view of her cleavage. She found the switch and the lights came on, flashing red, yellow, and green like a hyperactive traffic light. "You see? Teddy told me about your stained-glass shop, so I knew you'd like something bright and colorful! Do you love it?"

"I do!" Help, and she'd have to add it to her already hefty bunch of keys… Hopefully the battery wouldn't last too long.

"And I know how annoying it is when batteries run out, so I bought extra ones. They had them in the service station when we stopped for gas!"

"That's so thoughtful." It *was* thoughtful. Amber was touched by the gesture.

"I just wanted to give you a little something. I chose them specially, to go with your jobs," Olga explained. "Teddy's so proud of you all. He loves you very much." She clapped her hands with delight. "And now he loves me too!"

....

"Did you notice anything else about her?" said Lachlan when they left the house forty minutes later. Teddy was tired after the early start and long drive, and Lachlan needed to get back to the restaurant to prep for the evening ahead.

Raffaele nodded. "She was holding his hand practically nonstop."

"Some people are just like that. They like to hold hands." Amber still felt the need to defend Olga in order to counterbalance Lachlan's suspicions.

"That's not what I'm talking about." Taking his phone out of his jeans pocket, Lachlan scrolled through his emails until he found the one from Teddy with photos attached. "OK, here she is…and here…and here." He whizzed through a few more. "Then here we are in the last week of the cruise."

Amber peered at the photos. "I don't even know what I'm meant to be looking at."

He tapped the screen. "Before, she wasn't wearing a watch. Then she suddenly starts wearing one."

"So?" Amber frowned. "She's allowed to buy herself a watch."

"I couldn't zoom in far enough on the photos, but she was wearing it today," said Lachlan. "And I'm pretty sure Olga wasn't the one who paid for it."

"You don't know that."

"Not for sure, no. But they cost a few grand."

"Maybe it's a fake from the market." Amber was aware she was grasping at straws now.

Raffaele, many of whose clients in his Chelsea salon wore expensive watches, shook his head. "It wasn't."

She winced. "Oh God. He's so happy though."

"Teddy's just not used to dealing with women like that. He's never been targeted before." Lachlan paused. "If he is being targeted. But I think maybe you should have a chat with him."

"Me? Why me?"

"If we all pile on, he's going to feel ganged up on." Lachlan's hand in the small of her back propelled her across the road as a motorbike came racing down the hill toward them. "We'll keep an eye on her, obviously, as far as we can. But we do need to warn Teddy, and we need to do it in the right way. And that's better coming from you."

There was a gap between the hem of her top and the waistband of her skirt. The sensation of his fingers against her bare skin sent a quiver of…something down Amber's spine. Flustered, she turned to look at the disappearing motorcyclist. "He was going too fast. What an idiot."

"Probably a hit man, hired by Olga to mow us down." Lachlan

winked at Raffaele. "Put us out of the picture before we can stop her fleecing Teddy of every last penny he has."

....

Back at her flat, Amber stripped off and jumped into the shower. As she reached for the shampoo, the sensation of the hot water streaming down her back reminded her of the touch of Lachlan's hand, and she gave a huff of exasperation, because wasn't it about time she got these ridiculous feelings for him out of her system? They had to be past their sell-by date by now, surely?

Lachlan was one of the people she loved most in the world, and the bond of friendship between them was unbreakable. The only thing that could ever wreck it was if they were to overstep that friendship line and… No, don't even think it, because the repercussions would be too hard to bear. Just because she knew she'd want it to last forever didn't mean it would. Going by Lachlan's track record, it would be a miracle if it lasted longer than a few weeks. She suspected it had to do with his tumultuous early years, but now his career was all-important to him, and he simply didn't do serious romantic relationships. If he was hungry, he helped himself to a slice of toast. If he was in the mood for sex, he met up with someone who was happy to provide it. And that was enough; he needed nothing more from a partner than that. If the girl in question was keen to have sex *and* make him a plate of toast afterward…well, that was a welcome bonus. But it was still about as emotionally involved as Lachlan wanted to get.

Out of the shower, she wrapped herself up in a towel. As she began combing her wet hair, she looked at the two photographs on her bedside table. In the first, she and her mum were having a picnic on the beach, and the dark blur in the top left-hand corner belonged to the out-of-focus wing of a gull that had just swooped down and made off with the sausage roll she'd been about to eat. It was Amber's favorite photo; in it, she and her mum were both wide-eyed and laughing at the bird's brazen theft. Even better but sadly not captured on camera, several seconds later, the gull had lost its grip on the sausage roll, which had fallen through the air and landed on a bald man's head.

It had been a happy, sunny day. They'd been on Bovisand Beach, not far from their home in Plymouth, and had asked a passing stranger to take the photo for them. Amber had been sixteen, and her mum had still been well enough for them to make the trip; it wasn't until almost two years later that the cancer had stealthily spread and the symptoms had returned with a vengeance.

She touched the glass-covered photo with an index finger; it was eleven years ago now that she'd lost her mum. She'd worried at the time that all those joyful memories would fade and be lost, but this hadn't happened. They were as clear and bright now as they'd ever been, perfectly preserved. At will, she could conjure up the emotions, the sounds, and the scents of those days.

She knew too how incredibly lucky she'd been. Her mum had died when she was eighteen, which meant she was out of the foster care system, yet at the same time motherless and more in need of care than ever.

That was when May and Teddy had stepped in and rescued her. She'd carried on writing to them since her first stay four years earlier, and they'd attended the funeral in Plymouth. Some of the hugs Amber received that day were tolerated rather than welcomed, but when May's comforting arms had folded around her, she'd never wanted them to let go.

May and Teddy said she was welcome to come to Lanrock to see them at any time, but wary of seeming needy and desperate, Amber had stayed away, choosing to grieve privately instead until the worst of it was out of her system. Four months later, in November, May called and asked if they were ever going to see her, and overcome with yearning, she caught the train down to Lanrock the next day. It was wonderful to be with them again, cocooned in the warmth of their welcome, and at their insistence, she ended up staying for the weekend.

On the Sunday afternoon, Teddy said, "Now, not long until Christmas. And obviously it's going to be a tricky one for you, but we'd be so happy if you'd spend it with us."

"Really?" Amber had been dreading it. One of her friends in Plymouth had said she could go to them, but she'd seen the friend's parents exchange a glance and had sensed they weren't wild about the idea.

"Sweetheart, you're part of the family." May hugged her. "Of course we'd love to have you here. The more the merrier!"

As she was preparing to leave on Sunday evening, the phone rang.

"Lachlan!" May's face lit up. "How are you doing, my lovely boy? Now listen, we've just persuaded Amber to stay with us for Christmas this year. Are you going to be able to make it down here too?"

It had turned out to be an unforgettable Christmas. As everyone had kept reminding Amber, her mum wouldn't have wanted her to be miserable. She'd slipped off to her room a couple of times for a quiet weep, but all in all, those few days had ended up being a hundred times better than she'd expected them to be. Raffaele had made it back too, and it had been brilliant to see him again. There was a pair of five-year-old twins with mild cerebral palsy, who were excitable and wildly energetic. And there was Lachlan McCarthy, who had left Teddy and May's care just before Amber's own arrival four years earlier. She'd seen photos of him before, around the house and in the many photo albums May kept in the living room, but they hadn't conveyed the astonishing energy of the person he was. Meeting him for the first time, she was struck by his vitality, the brightness of his eyes, his quick wit and irreverent humor. He was so confident it was almost intimidating.

Having taken over in the kitchen as soon as he arrived on the afternoon of Christmas Eve, Lachlan was busy, busy, busy, chatting endlessly while he worked, relaying stories of the restaurant where he was currently employed in Oxford. He was twenty, two years older than she was, and Amber knew he'd had a difficult upbringing, but he seemed so much more grown-up and in control of his life than she did. His hair and eyes were so dark they were almost black, and he was wearing a thin black sweater and jeans, but somehow he gave the impression of being in technicolor.

After playing with the twins for an hour, Amber ventured back into the kitchen for a glass of water. Lachlan, glancing over his shoulder, said, "Do me a favor? Could you pass me that knife?"

There were several knives on the table. "Which one?"

"The seven-inch."

Momentarily flustered, she chose a knife and held it out to him.

His eyes glinted with amusement. "Oh dear, is that how long your last boyfriend told you seven inches was? Sorry to break it to you, but that's the five-inch."

Amber blushed, handed him the correct knife, and left the kitchen, deciding she didn't much like him after all.

Dinner that evening was annoyingly delicious. Afterward, several of May and Teddy's friends came over for drinks and an impromptu party. Music was playing, people were chatting and dancing, and Amber was passing around a plate of canapés. Then the familiar opening chords of "Last Christmas" filled the living room, and the loss of her mum hit her in the chest like a watermelon.

There was a group of people at the foot of the staircase in the hallway, and she couldn't face battling her way through them to get upstairs. Instead, she slipped outside and headed to the wooden bench at the far end of the garden, where Teddy always liked to sit and feed the birds.

She'd heard the song playing on the radio most days in the last month and been OK, but tonight was different. Every year on Christmas Eve, she and her mum had sung this song to each other, then shared homemade pizzas on the sofa and watched *The Holiday*, their favorite film, together.

That had been their tradition, and now it was never going to happen again.

Wrapping her arms around herself, Amber wept silently in the darkness and wondered if the ache in her chest meant that one day soon, her heart might actually break in two. A couple of minutes later, she heard the crack of a dry twig snapping underfoot and saw someone in the shadows making their way across the lawn.

"Oh, it's you." Her heart sank when she saw that it was the man in black himself, Lachlan McCarthy.

She didn't want him to sit down next to her, but he did anyway.

"You don't have to be here," she muttered. "I'm OK."

"Except you're not, are you? So what you're saying is you'd rather I left you to cry on your own. Even though your face is a mess and you don't have any tissues."

"How do you know I don't have any?"

"Because if you did, you'd be using them by now."

He had a point. The non-waterproof mascara had been a big mistake. Still, talking to him had stopped the tears, for the time being at least. And she was going to have to head back inside at some stage. With a flicker of hope, she said, "Do *you* have a tissue?"

"No."

"Helpful."

"But I have a sleeve, and you're welcome to use it."

He was still wearing his thin black crew-neck sweater. It would absorb mascara stains far more readily than her red wool dress, but still she hesitated.

"And look, I'm sorry about earlier," said Lachlan, "making fun of you in the kitchen. I can be a bit of a dick sometimes. I say stuff without thinking." He nudged his knee against hers in a friendly way, and she burst into tears all over again. "Oh God, what have I done now?" He looked dismayed.

Amber shook her head. "You apologized. It makes me cry when people are kind to me. It's all right. I'll stop in a minute."

"Here, help yourself to my sleeve. I insist." Nobly, he held out his arm, causing her to make a noise that was a cross between a sob and a splutter of laughter.

It was a strange sensation, wiping your eyes on someone else's sweater, especially when their warm arm was still inside it. But she did it anyway and discovered that the soft jersey material smelled faintly of cinnamon and mince pies. When she'd finished, Lachlan said, "Better now?"

Amber nodded. "Thanks."

"What was it? The George Michael song?"

Another nod. "Most of the time, I can hear it and be OK. But tonight…not so much."

"It's Christmas, and it just got to you."

"Mum and I used to sing it while we were making pizzas on Christmas Eve. Then we'd eat the pizzas and watch our favorite movie. It was our family tradition. We used to love it so much." Amber wiped her eyes again, this time with the back of her hand, then gazed up at the star-speckled night sky. "And now it's gone. We're never going to watch that film together again. Sorry." Belatedly she remembered that he'd had to endure far worse, had been taken into foster care when he was only four. "I'm being selfish. You've had a crappy time too."

But Lachlan shook his head. "Never mind me. I've had years to get over it. Anyway, listen, the thing about traditions is you can always start new ones. Or just do them with different people. OK, you can say no if you want, but how about if we watch the film later tonight? Tell me what you'd most like to eat. And I'll make it for us. We could have mini pizzas or baby burgers or—"

"Hang on, why are you doing this?" She eyed him with caution in case it was a trick. "Why are you being nice?"

"O ye of little faith. To make up for earlier. And because you've had a rough few months." He shrugged. "It's May and Teddy's fault, if you must know. They forced me into becoming a better person. I never used to feel guilty about being bad, and now I do. Well, some of the time."

Touched by the admission, Amber said, "OK, that'd be good. You might not like the film though."

"What is it?"

"*The Holiday.*"

"Oh God, are you serious? Jack Black and Cameron Diaz? Kate Winslet playing air guitar in her pajamas?"

It was dark, but she could see the pained expression on his face.

"You hate it."

"I was kind of hoping you and your mum's favorite film might have been *Goodfellas* or *The Terminator*."

They heard the sound of a door opening and closing, then more footsteps.

"There you are." Raffaele appeared out of the darkness. "What are you two doing out here?"

Amber said, "I had a bit of a moment."

"Want to watch a film with us later?" said Lachlan.

"I'd be up for that." Raffaele shrugged. "What kind of film?"

"Oh, you'll love it. It's this hilarious romantic comedy called—"

"No, it isn't," Amber interrupted firmly. "We'll go through the DVDs, find something we all like."

And they did. After the guests had left and Teddy and May had retired to bed, the three of them sprawled out on the living room sofas with mini pizzas and watched *The Blues Brothers*. It wasn't remotely romantic, but it was a classic comedy with a giant car chase, killer punch lines, and wildly catchy songs that they all joined in with.

"That's decided then." When it was over, Lachlan tapped his bottle of Sol against each of their drinks. "From now on, this is our new Christmas Eve tradition." He looked at Amber. "I mean it. Deal?"

She no longer wanted to cry. It was 1:30 on Christmas morning. In the corner of the room, the colored lights on the overdecorated tree were still twinkling away. Her mother might no longer be here, but she still had so much to be grateful for: a life to live and a future to look forward to.

She nodded. "Deal."

"And remember," Lachlan added, "you've always got us if you need a friendly sleeve to cry on."

Looking back, was that the moment she'd felt the first spark of attraction?

Possibly, though she was pretty sure she'd refused to acknowledge it at the time, because it was her first Christmas without her mum and it felt all kinds of wrong to be experiencing feelings of a non-grieving kind.

Anyway, that had been then. This was now, and she needed to be getting a move on. She instinctively reached for the second framed photograph on her bedside table, because she could never look at one and not the other.

This one was of May and Teddy in their living room, sitting side by side on the squashy brown sofa on the day they'd celebrated their silver wedding anniversary. It was their beaming smiles as they gazed into each other's eyes that made it her favorite photo of the two of them. May had been recuperating from surgery when it was taken, but still they'd radiated pure joy.

When May had died, they'd all wondered if it was even possible for Teddy to get over such a loss. Yet here he was, three years on, having found someone who was bringing much-needed happiness back into his life.

Lachlan and Raffaele might have their suspicions, but none of them had any idea how this brand-new relationship with Olga might turn out.

chapter 14

New salon, new life. Raffaele stepped back and studied the signage that had gone up this afternoon. *Raffaele & Co.* was written in dark-blue cursive script over a bronze background.

Next to him, shielding her eyes from the sun, Amber said, "Fabulous."

He led her inside, where the wallpaper was the same shade of midnight blue overlaid with bronze vines climbing the walls. Vintage-style light bulbs with golden filaments illuminated the interior, the full-length mirrors were in ornate distressed-gold frames, and the seating in the waiting area was upholstered in deep purple velvet.

He looked at her. "Well? What do you think?"

Amber was already nodding emphatically. "I love it. Nothing like the London salon."

That had been the idea. In London, the salon was all silver and white with sleek lines and space-age spotlights. He and Vee had chosen the decor together. "I know. I wanted a complete change. Come and have a look upstairs."

The flat above the salon hadn't been a priority; all he needed was somewhere to sleep. He'd had it repainted throughout and furnished with the basics.

"Bit empty," said Amber.

"That's why I'm showing it to you. If you see anything you think will brighten the place up, let me know." Hastily he added, "Well, unless it's one of Peggy's paintings."

"I'll keep an eye out."

"No cushions. I hate cushions."

"All men hate cushions." Amber crossed the living room and picked a framed photo off the windowsill to examine it more closely.

Raffaele instantly wished he hadn't put it there. "Vee gave it to me for Christmas a couple of years ago. It's a nice frame."

"Nice photo too."

It was. Taken by a friend at a pre-Christmas party, it had captured him and Vee dancing, laughing as they shared a joke neither of them could remember. That was back when they'd been happy, of course, and always joking and laughing together. Before it all, bafflingly, went so wrong.

Raffaele thought he'd been doing a pretty good job of pretending to be absolutely fine about the breakup, because that was the best way to get over things. Fake it till you make it was the system he was going with. He said casually, "I'll keep the frame, change the photo. Got any good ones I could use?"

"Of me? Hundreds." Amber mimicked a starlet pose. "I'll draw up a short list."

He took the photo from her and placed it facedown on the windowsill. "Maybe one of all of us."

Amber said, "Do you still miss her?"

"Who?"

"Vee, of course."

"No. Not really. Maybe a bit." Male pride battled with wanting to be honest with Amber. "But it's over. I miss the old Vee, the way she used to be, the fun we used to have. I don't miss the Vee she turned into."

Nor did he understand how or why it had happened.

"We didn't get to see that side of her."

Raffaele shrugged. For the first two years of their relationship, Vee had come down with him to Lanrock all the time, and everyone had loved her. Since it had all started to go wrong, she'd refused to make the journey. And now she was out of their lives for good. "You were lucky," he said.

....

That night, not yet used to sleeping in the new bed, Raffaele lay awake and restless for an hour before giving in and getting up again. He threw on a sweatshirt and jeans and left the flat; taking a walk was the best way to beat insomnia.

It was midnight, the air outside was still warm, and the streets were quiet. Walking always worked. London was behind him now. As he made his way down to the beach, he concentrated on mentally picturing the months ahead, in a brand-new salon and working with a radically different clientele.

It wouldn't always be easy, but only an idiot would expect it to be. Compared with his early years, this was Disneyland. And compared with so many of the kids he'd known growing up in foster care, he'd been amazingly lucky. He would never let himself forget that.

He paused, memories of those days stirring like ghosts. The other thing he knew he'd never forget was the sensation of being a nuisance, unwanted and in the way.

Rejection. It had been tough. At times, he'd felt as if he were facing a mountain that was too big to climb. He remembered being yelled at and shooed out of rooms by his parents. Later on, once he'd been removed from their care and had grown more aware of their situation, he'd told himself they'd been doing it to help him, trying to protect him from seeing what was going on and maybe stepping barefoot on a discarded needle. They hadn't meant to make every day an ordeal; they just couldn't help themselves, because the drugs were stronger than they were. Heroin had them in its thrall.

OK, don't think about that now; it all happened a quarter of a century ago. They tried, they died. Maybe they'd even loved him for a while before discovering a drug they loved more.

He reached the beach and sat down on the dry sand. He watched as a succession of froth-tipped waves reached the shoreline, sliding up, then gracefully receding before being overtaken by the next one to come along. The gentle *swoosh-swoosh* was hypnotic. Lanrock might not have the all-night bustle and bright lights of London, but it had the sea.

Raffaele closed his eyes, allowing his imagination to conjure up the next memory, preferably a cheerful one this time.

And here she was, making her presence known as he'd suspected she would, smiling that playful smile of hers. Not that he'd seen too much of it in recent months.

His phone vibrated inside his pocket a split second before it began to ring. Above the sound of the waves swooshing onto the shoreline, he heard Vee say, "Can't sleep?"

As if thinking about her had conjured her up out of the ether. He ran the flat of his free hand over his scalp. "It's not that late."

"Pretty late to be down on the beach." Her comment made him realize she'd tracked him through the location app they'd both installed on their phones last year. "What's going on?"

"Nothing at all."

"That's the kind of thing you always say. It's so annoying."

"It's the kind of thing I say when it's true."

"Got someone with you?"

He could exactly picture the expression on her face. "No."

"Or are you just saying that?"

Raffaele exhaled slowly. Why, *why* was she doing this? He said, "Is there a reason for this call?"

"I want the rest of your things out. All these boxes cluttering the place up…the mess is doing my head in. And don't tell me to book a courier," she went on dismissively. "I don't have time to deal with it, and it's not my job anyway. So if you don't want it chucked into the street—"

"I'll come and collect it tomorrow." Cutting her off, he wondered how it had come to this. The old Vee would never have spoken to him in such a way. The familiar emotions of frustration and regret spiraled up, because a year ago, the idea that they could be sniping at each other like this would have been unthinkable.

"What time?" Her tone was spiky.

"How about midday?" Matching spikiness with sarcasm, he added, "Would that suit you?"

"Perfect. I'll make sure I'm out." She hung up.

This was what their relationship had come to. Raffaele stood up, dusted sand off his hands, and walked the length of the beach, then back again. As he was making his way home along Tresilian Road, the door of the Sailor's Rest swung open, and several girls came tumbling out. The Sailor's Rest was well known for its late lock-ins. One of the girls did an exaggerated double take and said, "Honestly, story of my life! We spend all night not finding any gorgeous men, and the moment we leave, we find one practically on the doorstep. Hi, Raffaele, remember me?"

He did. Her name was Polly, she worked at Bert's Bar, and she was wearing a bright red sash with *Birthday Girl* printed on it. He'd met her a while back, when he'd been in there with Lachlan. "I remember."

She beamed. "It's my birthday!"

"I'd never have guessed. Happy birthday. Have you had a good night?"

"Brilliant. Well, apart from the lack of decent men. Where's Lachlan?"

"No idea. At home, I guess."

"Hiding from me, more like. Anyway, never mind him. Now we've got you instead." Polly slipped her arm through his. "Want to go for a drink?"

She'd already had many, many drinks.

"Thanks, but I need to get home too."

"I could come with you." Polly waggled her sash. "You can help me celebrate!"

"I wouldn't do that, though. You and Lachlan are kind of…you know."

She gestured dismissively. "We're not a couple, if that's what you're saying."

"Still, it wouldn't be right."

"Boring," said Polly.

"It's an agreement we have."

One of Polly's friends said brightly, "I've never slept with Lachlan."

"Not for want of trying," snorted one of the other girls.

"Just saying, I'm young, free, and single." Polly's friend gave Raffaele a saucy wink. "And so are you, now you've split with Vee and moved down here. I'm easy to find, if you ever fancy some company."

"You're easy, full stop," said Polly.

Raffaele made his escape and headed back to the flat above the salon that smelled of new furniture and fresh paint. Unlike Lachlan, he'd never gone in for casual relationships. Since breaking up with Vee, he'd had no desire to sleep with anyone else; instead of taking his mind off things, it would just make him feel worse.

As he was undressing for the second time, a text arrived:

Did you pick someone up or are you on your own?

Vee had carried on tracking him, he realized, all the way back from the beach.

He typed Irrelevant and pressed Send.

Then he deleted the tracker app from his phone.

chapter 15

"I'm liking the look of this stuff." The visitor had been making his way around the workshop while Amber prepared slices of colored glass for her next commissioned piece.

She glanced up from her work. "Thanks. Glad to hear it."

He removed his mirrored sunglasses and surveyed her with amusement. "I like the look of you too. Can you talk and work at the same time, or is that annoying? Am I allowed to ask questions?"

He was around forty, Amber guessed, with tanned skin and surfy, sea-salty white-blond hair. He was wearing cut-offs, a faded Maroon 5 T-shirt, and a silver dog tag on a chain around his neck.

"It's OK. I can multitask." She was used to people chatting to her while she worked; they liked to hear about the methods of cutting and putting together the glass, creating the items she sold in the studio.

"So what's your story?"

"Sorry?"

"You. Here, doing this. I'm curious. I like to find out about people. Did you grow up wanting to work with stained glass? Was it always your dream? Who taught you how to do it?"

"No, no, and a woman called Suzanne."

"I like more detail than that. And confession time," added the man, "I already know some of your story."

Amber continued filing the edges of a shard of sapphire-blue glass. "You mean you looked at my website?"

"Better than that. I'm a friend of Peggy's. My name's Dom Burton." He was admiring one of the lampshades she'd recently made. "I'm staying with her for a few days. She mentioned you when I met her for lunch earlier, and you sounded interesting, so I thought I'd come over and check you out."

"Why?" Amber was curious. There was a hint of Essex in his accent, and his clothes weren't expensive—well, as far as she could tell—but he exuded the kind of confidence you generally found in wealthy people.

Plus he was friends with Peggy.

"Because I'm always on the lookout for a good story. Here, just so you know I'm legit." He pulled a battered wallet from his back pocket and handed her a business card.

Dominic Burton, the Burton Hotel Group.

She'd heard of them; they were boutique hotels, quirkily styled to appeal to arty, creative types.

"It doesn't prove you're legit," she pointed out. "Just that you have access to a good printer."

He grinned. "Excellent point. Peggy told me I'd like you. She was spot-on, as usual. See the octopus up there?" He pointed to the window. "Could you make one six times bigger than that?"

The three-dimensional glass octopus was thirty centimeters in diameter. "I could," said Amber.

"How much would it cost?"

As a rule, this was the moment people visibly lost interest. But when Amber told him the price, he said, "And if I wanted more, I'd get a discount?"

"You'd get a discount." She nodded, still wondering if he was playing a game with her.

"Thirty percent off?"

"Twenty."

"I'm seeing the head and tentacles lit up from the inside, stretching out and winding across the ceiling." He came over to her workbench, pulled up one of the high stools. "And if you're wondering if I'm serious, I am. They'd look amazing in my hotels. So Peggy tells me you were in foster care here. That's how it all started. When your mum was ill."

He was direct, she'd give him that. But in an open, genuinely interested way. And since there were no other customers around, there was no reason not to tell him. As she worked, Amber ran through the story of her first stay in Lanrock, and Dom listened attentively.

"My mum had taken out life insurance when I was little. We only had a small terraced house in Plymouth, but when she died, the mortgage was paid off."

"Good for her." He nodded his approval. "Lucky for you."

Lucky. It wasn't the first time Amber had heard this. She said, "I'd rather have had my mum back."

"God, I'm so sorry. I'm an idiot." He clapped a hand to his heart. "Of course you would. Please forgive me."

It was hard to resist such a heartfelt apology. She went on, "So I stayed in Plymouth for the next couple of years, working in an office, but the work was boring and my boss was gropy. Then I came down here one weekend to see May and Teddy—my foster parents—and they told me their friend Suzanne was looking for someone to run this shop." Up until that point, Suzanne had been managing to work and deal with customers, but the constant interruptions had driven her to distraction; in the end, she'd realized she needed to hire some help. Amber said, "May recommended me, and Suzanne took me on. And every chance I could, I'd watch her at work. She started showing me how she did things, then after a while let me have a go myself."

"And were you still living in Plymouth?"

Amber shook her head. "I sold the house and bought a tiny cottage just down the road from here. It was the best thing that could have happened. I had a job I loved and a boss who didn't grope me, plus May and Teddy were close by."

Dom gave a nod of satisfaction. "I like this story. What happened next?"

"Well, Suzanne didn't have a website, so I built one for her, which did wonders for the business, especially out of season. We started taking orders from all over the world. And I learned more about the creative side, started making my own stuff and selling it too. Then, after three years, a customer walked into this studio one day, and Suzanne fell in love."

"Always up for a love story. What was he like, as good-looking as me?"

"Actually, she was a dentist called Tamara, down here from north Wales on holiday. She dropped in every afternoon, and they flirted with each other." Amber smiled at the memory; it had been such a joy to witness, she'd looked forward to it about as much as they had. "Well, it went on from there. In the end, Tamara persuaded Suzanne to move to north Wales because it would have been harder for her to give up her dental practice. Suzanne asked me if I wanted to stay on, and of course I did. So she sold me all her tools and equipment, and I took over the lease on this place. That was six years ago, and I've been here ever since. Here, you may as well take one of these." She passed him one of her own business cards. "See? You're not the only one with access to a color printer."

"I'll treasure it," Dom said and grinned, laid-back and confident. "Will you email me a detailed drawing of your design?"

"I can do that tonight." She had to double-check. "Are you really serious about this?"

"Absolutely. A giant stained-glass octopus is the kind of thing our clientele will go nuts for. And you'll be featured in our brochure too. Guests like to know about the people behind the artwork."

This sounded good. Something else occurred to Amber. "Do you have Peggy's work on display in your hotels?"

"Peggy's great." He paused. "Can I trust you?"

"You can trust me."

They were alone, but he lowered his voice anyway. "They're not my style."

Feeling guilty, Amber did a tiny shrug and a nod. "Nor mine."

"Look, maybe they're good, I don't know. She persuaded me to buy one last year, and because I love her to bits, I didn't have the heart to say no." Dom pulled a face. "When she comes up to London, she always stays in our Notting Hill hotel. So now, as soon as we know she's on her way, we get the painting out of storage and hang it in her room. The moment she checks out, it goes back into storage. And if you ever tell her that, you'll break her heart."

"If I ever tell her that, she'll break your neck," said Amber.

After Dom had left, she sat down and began to sketch out ideas for the octopus. It was a warm, sunny afternoon, and the hordes of visitors to Lanrock were down on the beach, giving her time to concentrate.

But first, it made sense to give Peggy a call.

"Just had a visit from your friend Dom," she said.

"Thought you might." Peggy chuckled. "I was telling him about you and the boys this morning."

"He says he wants to commission me to make some pretty expensive chandeliers for his hotels."

"Sounds like Dom."

"He'll definitely buy them, then?"

"Oh yes, love. I know he acts like a chancer, but he's a man of his word, knows what he's doing. Hang on, I've got a text coming through… Ha, it's from him."

"What does it say?"

"Where are my specs? Let's have a look. It says, 'When Amber calls, tell her to stop being so suspicious. She needs to learn to trust me.'"

Amber laughed. "Why would I trust someone I don't know?"

"Did he flirt with you?"

"I don't think so. I didn't notice. Maybe a little bit." She had a history of sometimes not noticing when it was happening. "Is he single?"

"Broke up with his wife before Christmas. Hasn't wasted much time since."

Amber had another think. "I'm pretty sure he wasn't flirting with me."

"Don't you worry," said Peggy. "He will."

chapter 16

BENJIE FELT HIMSELF START TO GO RED THE MOMENT HE SAW JO cross the road toward the gallery.

She pushed open the door and said cheerfully, "Hi, how are you?"

It was a shame she wasn't asking this question online. If she had, he'd have been able to type back, All the better for not having blood gushing out of my hand! which would have made her laugh and resulted in him feeling instantly more relaxed. The jokey comment was there in his head, but his mouth found it just too complicated to say, so instead he replied, "I'm good, thanks. How are y-you?"

Boring, boring. God, why couldn't he lose the anxiety for just one minute? Was that really too much to ask?

"You're looking well! How's the hand? Better now?"

"Yes." He held it up as proof.

"Oh, I had to come and tell you, my nan absolutely loved her card. She says it's so beautiful she's going to keep it up on the mantelpiece all year!"

"That's great." Benjie winced inwardly; he sounded so *lame*.

"She asked me to come over and pick up another one for her friend's birthday next week. So here I am. I'm even going to pay for this one!"

She was such effortless, easy company. They were interrupted at that point by a woman coming in to choose a framed print, which made Benjie wonder if Jo would give up and leave, but she didn't. When the other customer finally departed, she was still happily going through all the cards, choosing the very best one for her nan's friend.

"This one," she announced when they were alone once more.

"Excellent choice." Benjie had been practicing this in his head.

"What can I say? I have great taste. Now, I've had an idea, and feel free to say no if you don't want to." She took a deep breath and for the first time looked nervous. "If you're not doing anything else tonight, there's a band playing at the Dolphin. I've got a couple of tickets, and I wondered if you'd like to come along with me. Not as a date," she went on hastily. "Just as friends. But if you're not interested, that's absolutely fine."

Benjie's mind was quietly boggling; what an invitation to come out of the blue! He stared at the wall behind Jo, trying to formulate some kind of intelligible response.

"Come on. Help me out here," she prompted. "I plucked up the courage to ask you. Don't leave me hanging."

"I…er…that sounds great. Um, I'd like to see the band. Who are they?"

"So that's a yes?" Visibly relieved, Jo waggled her hands. "Yay! They're an indie band called Greyfox. I've heard they're pretty good. Kind of edgy, you know?"

Benjie could imagine. He might not have an edgy bone in his body, but he was capable of admiring it in others. Well, from a safe distance at least.

In his head, he imagined saying "Edgy is my middle name." In reality, he said, "Sounds pretty good," then instantly wanted to kick himself, because that was how Jo had described the band.

Would he ever get anything right?

"Cool." She nodded happily. "Meet you outside the Dolphin at eight?"

"Eight. Cool." Oh, for crying out loud, he'd done it *again*. What was he, a parrot?

....

By seven, Benjie had tried on several different outfits, and none of them were right. No way could he go along to see the band dressed like a bank manager.

When he told her he wouldn't be online for a few hours, Dani typed, What's this? Is my future husband going on a date?

Not a date, he typed back. A friend invited me along to see a band at a local pub. But I look like a nerd.

OK, let me help. Send a photo.

And when she'd seen what he was currently wearing—the blue shirt his mum liked, paired with smart gray trousers—she replied, Take those off! Wear jeans and an old T-shirt with a casual shirt over it, unbuttoned.

Much better, she replied once he'd sent the second photo. Now ruffle your hair so it doesn't look combed. Don't fold the shirtsleeves up so neatly. Just relax and have fun. Are you sure this isn't a date??? It had better not be! Xxx

Benjie felt all warm and happy. It was nice to feel wanted. He replied, It isn't, I promise.

The pub was packed, the band was loud, and the beer was warm. The huge rugby-sized lads behind him were jumping up and down, cider sloshing out of their pint glasses and landing on the back of Benjie's shirt.

But he stuck it out and tried to look as if he was dancing too, in a muted kind of way. At least the ear-splitting music made it impossible to talk or hear what anyone else might be saying.

"Well?" said Jo when they'd escaped to an outside table during the band's break. "Enjoying it?"

"Great," said Benjie with an overly enthusiastic nod.

She lowered her voice and leaned across the table toward him. "Really? My brain feels as if it's about to explode."

"Don't you like the band?"

"Not really, if I'm honest."

Oh, the relief. Benjie whispered back, "Nor me."

"Shall we leave?"

"Yes, let's." He grinned, and they finished their bottles of Peroni.

Twenty minutes later, they were sitting side by side on the harbor wall, eating battered cod and chips from the best takeout in Lanrock. Benjie listened to the gentle creaking of the boats tied up below them, the slap of the water against their wooden hulls. Above them, clouds scudded across the darkening sky. As he ate another chip and licked granules of salt from his fingers, he heard a drunken male voice in the distance yell, "What a top night, mate!"

He couldn't agree more.

"Honestly, sorry about that," said Jo. "Serves me right for not listening to their music first. My nan's friend gave me the tickets because her grandson's the drummer."

"The guy with the giant spider tattoos on his face?"

"That's the one. He's actually a sweet guy, loves his Siamese cats. But I can't say Greyfox is ever going to be my favorite band."

"Hey, doesn't matter. We gave them a try. And it was still fun." Look at that, no stammer. Sitting side by side on the harbor wall made it easier to talk. Possibly the three bottles of lager had helped too. Kicking his heels gently against the wall as he selected another chip, Benjie said, "I've enjoyed this evening." *Understatement of the year.*

"Good. So have I." She smiled at him.

He had to ask. "Why did you invite me? Why not one of your other f-friends?"

"Honestly?" Jo shook her auburn curls out of her eyes. "Most of them around here are coupled up. And my university friends are spread all over the place. I liked chatting to you in the art gallery the other day. It's just a question of being brave and making the first move, isn't it, when you meet someone who you think could be a new friend. Not a boyfriend," she emphasized for the second time. "Just someone to get to know, so you can relax and hang out together. It's how you meet new people, isn't it? What's the worst that can happen? They can only say no. And if they do that, it's not such a massive deal. You just move on. Their loss, not yours."

Benjie said, "You make it sound so easy."

She shrugged. "It isn't complicated. It's nice to have friends to do stuff with. Even if the stuff sometimes turns out to be a bit rubbish."

"I'm glad I didn't say n-no."

"Me too." Jo threw a strip of batter into the air, and they watched as a gull swooped down and made off with it. "So does that mean you'd be up for another adventure sometime?"

"Why not?"

"Well, I'm free on Wednesday evening."

"Me too." It was a heady sensation, someone who knew him in actual real life wanting to get to know him better. Benjie said, "What shall we do?"

"Do you paraglide?"

Help. "Um…no…"

"Don't worry. Leave it with me." Jo pinched an extra attractive chip from his bag and admired its crunchy golden edges. "I'll think of something."

It was 10:30 by the time Benjie arrived home. Dani was online, waiting for him.

You've been ages! How was it?

Brilliant. The band was horrendous. We had a great time.

How did you say goodbye? Was there kissing?

Noooo.

Did you tell her about me?

I mentioned you, yes. And showed her a photo too.

Oh God, which one?

You're out in the garden, wearing your yellow dress. She said you look gorgeous.

Is she prettier than me?

No. She's pretty, but you're better.

Did you take a photo of her?

Benjie hesitated, because while they'd been sitting on the harbor wall, Jo had taken a selfie of the two of them together. Then she'd looked at it and exclaimed, "Oh, this is a good one. Give me your number, and I'll send it to you."

No, I didn't, he told Dani. Which was technically true.

What if she falls in love with you?

Not going to happen. She's only here until September. As soon as the summer season's over, she'll be off traveling on her gap year. We're friends, that's all.

I'm sorry. I can't help feeling a bit jealous.

Benjie pictured Dani sitting cross-legged on her bed in her parents' bungalow, with her blond hair tumbling around her shoulders and her toenails painted bright orange. In his imagination, she was wearing a sky-blue sweatshirt and striped shorts and her favorite daisy-shaped earrings.

No need to be jealous. I love you.

There, he'd finally said it. Well, written it at least. Was it true? He certainly loved the idea of her. Over the last six months, they'd spent many hundreds of hours in each other's virtual company. He knew everything about her. They'd exchanged endless confidences. He looked forward to their online conversations every single night. He even knew what she smelled like, because when he'd asked her which perfume she wore, he'd gone to the out-of-town superstore days later and surreptitiously sprayed himself from the tester bottle, committing the scent to memory. Now, every time he imagined it, he felt close to her.

Surely that was love?

Benjie watched the screen on his laptop and realized he was holding his breath. What was Dani thinking? Maybe he shouldn't have said it.

Finally her reply appeared:

Crying here. Oh Benjie, I love you too. Xxxxxx

chapter 17

SUNDAY WAS THE HOTTEST DAY OF THE YEAR SO FAR. FOR LACHLAN, after a sixty-hour week in the kitchen while everyone else was outside enjoying the sunshine, the weather on Sundays was usually a letdown.

But not today. He and Amber had come down to the beach and played an energetic game of volleyball with a group of friends before going for a swim and racing each other to the end of the bay and back. Once out of the water, Amber had stretched out on her towel and announced that it was his turn to go and buy the ice cream.

By the time he'd returned from the ice cream shop on the seafront, it was too late; she'd fallen asleep. Lachlan said her name, gave her foot a nudge with his own, and finally declared that if she didn't open her eyes, he'd be eating both ice creams himself.

When Amber didn't wake up, he carried out his threat, sitting with his back to the sun in order to give the ice creams enough shade so they didn't melt before he could finish them. Even when he allowed a drip to land on her leg, she didn't stir.

Lachlan knew she'd been up until three this morning, starting work on the mad chandelier Dom Burton had asked her to make for him. God, though, she looked adorable when she was asleep. He took in her flawless complexion, still slightly flushed from the heat and their race across the bay. Her hair was drying fast, curling up at the ends. Her gold-tipped lashes didn't so much as flicker when a small child close by let out a billion-decibel shriek.

It wasn't often he got the chance to observe her uninterrupted. Her mouth was fractionally open, her head had fallen slightly to one side, and she was wearing silver hooped earrings that brushed her neck. One hand was resting across her torso. The pale scar on her left forearm was the result of a careless moment in her studio last year involving a soldering iron. Her long legs were tanned and smooth, apart from the small birthmark on her right thigh. The birthmark was shaped like South America, and Lachlan had never touched it because that would have been incredibly inappropriate. Although he'd always wanted to.

Resisting the temptation to kiss Amber that night on the beach four and a half years ago remained the single proudest achievement of his life to date.

It was also his biggest regret. Because being noble and self-sacrificing was all very well, but it was also pretty bloody frustrating. He hadn't done it, which meant he'd missed out on something he'd wanted to happen more than anything. And where was his reward? Apart from Raff, nobody else knew about his completely heroic act, so no one had even thanked him.

Then again, maybe this was his reward. Sitting here on the sand alongside Amber, whom he loved more than anyone else in the world. Well, he also loved Teddy and Raffaele. But they didn't fall into quite the same category.

An overly enthusiastic golden Labrador came hurtling out of the sea and bounded back to its owners. It shook itself vigorously, and droplets of water arced through the air, spraying both Amber and himself.

"Sorry!" called the owners.

Lachlan raised a hand to reassure them it was fine. Nature's way of telling him he could probably do with a cold shower.

Oh, but that night four and a half years ago would forever be etched indelibly into his mind. It had been the Sunday before Christmas, the first time Vee was coming down with Raffaele, though because of work commitments they wouldn't be arriving until the next day.

May, still in good spirits but clearly unwell, hadn't been up to venturing out to Lanrock's pre-Christmas fireworks celebrations on the beach, but she and Teddy had insisted Lachlan and Amber shouldn't miss it on their account.

Seeing Amber again had had its usual effect on Lachlan's emotions, but he'd grown used to it by then, accustomed to chucking a metaphorical bucket of cold water over himself whenever his thoughts began to stray in that direction.

Had it seemed different this time? Had the attraction felt stronger? Had he given himself away, or was it that Amber had begun to feel it too?

They'd reached East Beach early and found a good spot on the sand where they were sheltered by rocks and away from the main crowds. He'd asked Amber how May was really, and she'd updated him with the latest results of the tests and treatments. The doctor had already warned them that the spread of the cancer meant May's time was limited. Hopefully she had another year, maybe eighteen months, but it would be unrealistic to expect anything more than that.

"She never complains," Amber told Lachlan. "She's amazing. They both are."

"So are you." He knew she visited the house every day without fail, helping to look after May. "You went through it with your mum, and now you're having to do it all over again with May. Can't be easy."

"We've been so lucky to have her. I'm just trying to make things easier for them, that's all. Thanks." Amber reached for the hip flask he was offering her and took a mouthful of Jack Daniel's.

"And how have things been with you?"

She flipped back her hair and turned her head to look at him, and he saw the flames from the bonfire further along the beach reflected in her eyes. She sighed. "Honestly? Not great."

Amber was hard-working and endlessly optimistic; he wasn't used to hearing her sound resigned. He put a comforting arm around her shoulders—*comforting, nothing more*—and said, "What's wrong? Is it Calvin?"

She shrugged. "Kind of. Not in that way."

Calvin was the guy she'd been seeing back in the summer. He was probably a nice guy and had always been friendly enough, but Lachlan had met him a few times and taken an instinctive dislike to him, possibly because he was jealous, or maybe because Calvin was just one of those people who seemed so in control of his own life. He was a real estate agent who worked for his wealthy father's chain of agencies and drove a gleaming silver BMW. He also wore expensive suits, fastened his silk ties with a flashy tie pin, and liked to show off about all the money he made and the exotic holidays he took.

Anyway, they'd broken up in September, and Lachlan had been delighted.

But since Amber was clearly unhappy, he put on his solicitous voice and said, "Do you miss him?"

"No."

"Is he pestering you? Making a nuisance of himself?" He brightened; nothing would make him happier than to confront Calvin and tell him to back off.

Amber made a *pfft* noise. "No."

"What is it then?"

"I think I just don't understand why I finished with him."

Well, that was an easy one. It was because Calvin was a smug prat.

"Why did you?" said Lachlan.

"He was fine. He was lovely to me. And nice-looking. Good job, great car. He didn't do anything wrong." She uncapped the hip flask and took another swig. "But it just wasn't enough."

"That's an excellent reason to dump him. Are you feeling guilty? Is that it? For hurting his feelings?"

"Not even that. I just wonder *why* he wasn't enough. On paper, he ticked every box. And it's not like I'm Beyoncé. I'm nothing special, so what gives me the right to find someone like Calvin not good enough? I should have been grateful he liked me. I tried so hard to be happy with him, but it just wouldn't happen, and it's so"—she spread her hands in frustration—"*so* annoying!"

How could she even think she was nothing special? Then again, maybe that was what made her special. Feeling his heart beat faster beneath his thick padded jacket, Lachlan said, "You have high standards. Don't knock it. That's a good thing."

Their eyes locked, and for a moment, it felt as if Amber was gazing into his very soul. He found himself unable to look away. What was going through her mind right now?

Then she started to laugh. "Unlike you, who doesn't have any standards at all."

The smell of woodsmoke from the bonfire hung in the air. Lachlan had been imagining kissing her, drawing her closer and meeting her warm mouth with his own. He wanted it to happen, more than anything, but knew it mustn't. Luckily her laughter broke the tension, and it was as he was giving her a look of mock outrage that the sky lit up and the first machine-gun bursts of fireworks exploded into the night sky overhead.

The crowd whooped and applauded, and Lachlan felt Amber shiver beside him. He took off his red woolen scarf and added it to the white one she was already wearing around her neck.

"I didn't know it was going to be this cold." She spoke through chattering teeth, and he pulled her closer to his side. When she touched his hand, she said, "How can you be so warm?" and he closed his fingers around her icy ones.

Pow, pow-pow-pow went the fireworks, and *pow-pow-pow-pow* went Lachlan's heart, banging away inside his rib cage, because something was happening that absolutely mustn't happen. Inside his jacket pocket, Amber's thumb was curling against the back of his hand, gently stroking his knuckles. She was gazing out to sea rather than up at the fireworks, and her head was tilted to one side, resting against his shoulder. He could see the puffs of condensation with each breath she took, and now she was turning to look at him again, her face moving closer to his. She murmured, "I probably shouldn't be doing this, but…" and she edged closer still, enabling him to breathe in the mingled scents of Jack Daniel's and the strawberry jelly sweets they'd shared on their way down to the beach.

When Lachlan heard the words coming out of his mouth, it was as if they were being spoken by someone else. He shifted away and said, "We definitely shouldn't do this…sorry…"

Pow! Pow! Pow-pow! Giant chrysanthemum bursts of blue and gold and crimson and green filled the night sky, overlapping each other as they formed the ear-splitting climax of the display.

"Oh *God.*" Amber shrank back and buried her face in her hands. "Oh God, I'm such an *idiot.*"

"Hey, stop it. You're not." He had to raise his voice to be heard above the applause from everyone else on the beach. "You're great, and I love you. You know I do. It's just there's too much at stake if it went wrong. We'd be—"

"Don't, *don't* say any more. I'm so embarrassed." She twisted away from him, every inch of her cringing. "Please go away. Leave me alone."

"No, I'm not going to do that." In that moment, Lachlan knew he couldn't tell Amber he felt the same way about her. It might be the truth, but it would make the situation between them agonizing; it would be unbearable. And sooner or later, the inevitable would happen.

Because the inevitable always did.

What he needed to do now, he realized, was put the issue to bed—irony of ironies—once and for all. He took hold of her wrists and drew her hands away from her face. "Look at me. And listen. Sometimes you meet someone and know you're going to be best friends for life. That's what happened to me when I saw you for the first time. And it was the same for you, I know it was. It's *better* than the other kind of love because it lasts forever. Nothing's ever going to come between us. Right?"

Amber swallowed, nodding fractionally, still looking sick. "I suppose."

"No suppose about it. What we have means a million times more than some casual hookup. And trust me." He pointed to his own chest. "As the king of the hookup, I know what I'm talking about."

There was still anguish in her eyes. "But I just feel so—"

"No need to feel anything," Lachlan interrupted firmly. "We're going to be best friends forever, and nothing's going to change that. And if you don't nod and say 'Yes, Lachlan,' I'm going to tickle you until you can't breathe."

"*Wah!*" Amber let out a shriek as he made a playful grab for her ribs. "Yes, Lachlan. Nooo, don't tickle me!"

He held her, and there were the flames from the bonfire reflected in her eyes once more. "No awkwardness, no need to be embarrassed. We're going to have the best Christmas ever, you hear me?"

"Yes, Lachlan."

"Say it like you mean it."

"*Yes*, Lachlan!"

And there it was: against all the odds, he'd done it, had both resisted the ultimate temptation *and* come up with an excellent reason why it should never happen again. What a total hero; he deserved a medal. "Good." He leaned forward, gave her a brief best-friend kiss on the cheek, then stood up and hauled her to her feet. "Come on. It's freezing. I need a burger and a beer. Let's get out of here."

Amber dusted dry sand off her jeans. "One last thing. You won't tell Raffaele about this, will you? I don't want him to know."

"Hey, I won't say a word." Lachlan held a hand over his heart. "And that's a promise."

Which would have been fine, if only Raffaele hadn't arrived with Vee the next day and been so unnervingly on the ball.

"What's happened?" he said to Lachlan that evening once they were alone. "What's going on between you and Amber?"

"Nothing." Lachlan knew he wasn't the one who'd given the game away. It was Amber, doing the best she could to behave normally but not quite managing it.

"Don't give me that. Something's happened." His light-brown eyes narrowing, Raffaele said, "If you've slept with her…"

"I haven't, OK?"

"You mean you tried it on and she turned you down? That's even worse. I *knew* you wouldn't be able to resist."

Lachlan had promised Amber he wouldn't blurt out her embarrassing moment, but this was on another level entirely. For the first time, he'd done the right thing, the honorable thing, and now he was being accused of trying to seduce her anyway.

Which was why he'd been forced to tell Raffaele what had happened and explain to him that for once in his life, he'd behaved like a total bloody hero.

When Raffaele had heard the whole story, he'd nodded and said, "Well, you make sure you stick to it."

chapter 18

AND NOW HERE THEY WERE, FOUR AND A HALF YEARS ON, LYING ON the beach less than a hundred meters away from the spot where their first kiss had so nearly happened. In a parallel universe, maybe it had. But back here in this one, he'd stuck to his principles for the greater good so could only continue to imagine what it might have been like.

Lying on his side with his head propped up on his hand and his elbow resting in the warm sand, Lachlan watched as a scarlet ladybug landed just to the left of Amber's belly button and began making its leisurely way up her rib cage.

Lucky ladybug. He found himself observing her again, watching her eyes moving beneath her closed eyelids. Was she dreaming? Who did she dream about? What if four years ago he'd made a terrible mistake and missed his chance? How was he going to cope when Amber met the love of her life and settled down, had children, maybe moved away? He knew it was crazy; this was something he couldn't prevent, but he dreaded it happening. What if it was someone he absolutely knew wasn't right for her? How could he stand back and let—

"Hey," said a voice as a shadow fell over the sand, and Lachlan jumped.

"Jesus." He twisted around to look up at Raffaele. "You nearly gave me a heart attack."

At that moment, a gull wheeling overhead dropped a deposit from a great height. It landed with an audible splat on Amber's breastbone, and the ladybug flew off in disgust. Amber's eyes snapped open and she yelped, "What was *that*?" She stared over at Lachlan and the open can of Coke in his hand. "Did you just chuck some of your drink at me?"

"You wish," said Lachlan as she tried to see what had landed just below the base of her throat. "Don't touch it—"

Too late; Amber smeared it with her hand and let out a wail of despair. "Oh, for God's sake. I got gull bombed yesterday, and now it's happened again! It's not funny!"

Lachlan was still laughing as she pretended to wipe it across his arm. "It is quite funny. As far as seagulls are concerned, you're irresistible."

"Eurgh, and now it's dripping down…" She scrambled to her feet and raced off down the beach to the water, dodging dogs and toddlers along the way before wading through the breaking waves and plunging into the sea to wash off the mess.

"What?" said Lachlan, because Raffaele was giving him a measured look.

Raffaele shrugged. "Nothing."

"Shame we couldn't have caught it on video." Lachlan lay flat, shielding his eyes from the sun as he gazed up at the cloudless blue sky. "That was hilarious. Heard any more from Vee?"

"No." Raffaele lowered himself onto the sand and helped himself to a swig from the can of Coke. "Why? Has she been in touch with you?"

Lachlan shook his head. "Just wondered how things were going. You said she called you the other night." It was a shame; they'd all loved Vee until the relationship had gone wrong and her difficult side had shown itself.

"Haven't heard from her since." A muscle was jumping in Raffaele's jaw. "And I can't think of any reason why I'd see her again, not now I've cleared all my stuff out of the flat." The Coke can gave a metallic crunch as his fingers tightened around the sides. "It's over now. No going back."

One of the things Raffaele loved most in life was when you were reading a really good novel, engrossed in the story, and then out of the blue, an ingenious twist stopped you in your tracks, making you gasp and rethink the entire plot.

What he'd just witnessed was exactly like one of those moments. Only not in book form, in real life. And it wasn't so much an ingenious plot twist as a sudden realization.

He'd spotted Lachlan and Amber on the beach from a distance, lying side by side on the sand. As he'd been making his way toward them, he had assumed they were chatting to each other, but when he came closer, he saw that Amber had fallen asleep with her head tilted in Lachlan's direction. Lachlan, lying on his side with his left arm supporting his own head, was watching her, studying her face while she slept. And when Raffaele had altered trajectory in order to get a better view, it was the expression he'd seen on Lachlan's face that provided the twist he hadn't known existed.

He had stopped dead in his tracks. They'd been best friends for sixteen years; he knew Lachlan's face as well as he knew his own. Better, possibly, because he'd seen it more often over the years. And the expression he knew best of all was the one when Lachlan was eyeing up a girl who'd piqued his interest.

It was a winning look, that was for sure, and a successful one too. The tiny playful smile happened quite naturally whenever he observed his next conquest, the dark eyebrows lifted a fraction, and his eyes emitted some kind of magic spark that rendered him irresistible to anyone who happened to be captured by it.

And it always, *always* worked.

This wasn't that look, though. Observing from a distance of ten meters away, Raffaele saw that this was a whole different kind of look, one that was in another league to the I'm-going-to-seduce-you-then-never-see-you-again one.

This was soft. And serious. And filled with genuine longing. Raffaele saw Amber's chest rise and fall and a tiny insect land on her hip. He saw the fingers on Lachlan's right hand instinctively reach up, as if to move it away, before he hesitated and drew back, because physical contact with her bikini-clad body was too intimate a move to make.

Sitting on the sand beside Lachlan, Raffaele smoothed the dent out of the Coke can he'd gripped too tightly. It wasn't jealousy he was experiencing now. It was dread. He'd long feared that one day, Lachlan would decide to set his sights on Amber, which would be fine, he could easily accept that, if only Lachlan wasn't who he was. But he *was* Lachlan, mercurial and capricious and with all the romantic staying power of a mayfly.

And yes, he'd known something had nearly happened between the two of them a few years back. He also knew that it had been instigated by Amber and prevented from happening by Lachlan. But clearly, now, Lachlan's curiosity had been aroused, and his feelings for her had grown.

If he made his move, Amber wouldn't be able to resist him.

Which meant, because Raffaele had seen it happen so often before, that as soon as that curiosity had been assuaged, Lachlan would lose interest and move on to the next willing conquest. Leaving Amber heart-broken and the friendship between the three of them in pieces, possibly never to recover.

Raffaele knew he was right. He also knew, because he'd witnessed it so many times over the years, that when Lachlan was caught out in any way, he dealt with it by closing down the conversation and swiftly changing the subject. Maybe he even thought he was developing genuine feelings for Amber, but they both knew how disastrous that would be. Inevitably, because Lachlan couldn't help the way he operated, she would end up being just another box to be ticked.

It mustn't happen.

Amber was now emerging from the sea, wringing out her hair as she made her way back up the beach toward them.

"All clean. No more gull poo." She threw herself down on her beach towel.

"Until the next one comes along." Raffaele indicated the gulls screeching and circling overhead.

"Urgh, don't say that. Ooh…" She rolled over to haul her ringing phone out of her bag. "Hi, Olga!"

Lachlan grinned. "Probably after the code to Teddy's safe."

Amber listened to Olga for a bit, then said, "Of course I can do that. I'd love to. It'll be fun!"

When she'd ended the call, Lachlan said, "Helping her pick out the best life insurance policy for a wealthy man in his sixties?"

"She's invited me to go shopping with her tomorrow in Plymouth."

"She's probably after a smart black outfit that might come in useful in the near future."

"She's just being friendly." Amber threw a pretzel at him. "It's nice. You should try it sometime and stop being so suspicious."

Raffaele saw the fleeting quirk at the corner of Lachlan's mouth. He and Amber both knew it was shorthand for *And you need to stop being so gullible.*

No one mistrusts another person, Raffaele reminded himself, more than someone who knows they can't be trusted themselves.

....

After a week of cooking and tasting restaurant food, on Sunday evenings Lachlan invariably craved pizza. At eight, after more swimming and another ruthlessly competitive game of volleyball, they left the beach and headed over to Giovanni's, bagging one of the outside tables overlooking the harbor.

By 9:30, Amber was ready to leave. On Mondays, she didn't open the studio until two, but tomorrow's jaunt to Plymouth with Olga meant she needed to put a couple of extra hours in this evening on the stained-glass octopus.

"Want us to walk you home?" Lachlan offered.

"No need." She drained her glass and grabbed her beach bag, then gave each of them a hug. "I'll let you know how it goes with Olga tomorrow."

Raffaele was pointing at her bag with his slice of Sicilian pizza. "And don't forget to put that flashing traffic light thing on your key ring."

Of course Raffaele had said it; he was the kind, thoughtful one.

Amber patted him on the shoulder. "And that's why you're my favorite."

"I should probably head off too," said Lachlan when she'd disappeared from view.

"Not yet. Stay." Raffaele reached for the bottle of Montepulciano and refilled both their glasses. "There's something I need to talk to you about."

"What is it? The salon? You don't have to worry. Everything's going to be great." It was opening tomorrow, albeit quietly and without fanfare because Raffaele didn't want any fuss.

"Not the salon." Raffaele ran the flat of his hand over his close-cut hair, gleaming golden-brown beneath the hundreds of white solar lights strung up over the terrace.

It didn't take a genius to work it out; Raffaele had to be more cut up over the breakup than he'd been making out. "Vee then?"

Raffaele took a swallow of wine, then dropped the last crescent of pizza crust onto his plate. Finally he said, "No, it's over. I knew that weeks ago. Vee's out of the picture for good." He paused again, swirling the Montepulciano around in his glass. "The thing is, there's someone else."

"*What?*" Talk about a bolt from the blue. "You're seeing someone already? In London or down here?" Lachlan shook his head in amazement, because Raffaele had never been the type to bounce from one girl to the next. Unlike himself. "Bloody hell, you kept that quiet!"

"OK, I'm not *seeing*-seeing her. Not yet. Well, not in that way." Raffaele looked up, directly into Lachlan's eyes. "But I know how I feel about her, and I want it to happen. More than I've ever wanted anything before."

All around them, people at neighboring tables were eating and drinking, talking and laughing. Lachlan, returning Raffaele's steady gaze, suddenly felt as if he were at the epicenter of a tornado, surrounded by roaring noise but experiencing only ominous silence. Something about the way Raffaele had said it told him what he was about to hear.

"Who is it?" A rhetorical question, but maybe, just maybe, his oldest friend might say, "It's Janine who works in the bakery next to the salon. I've been going in there to buy sausage rolls six times a day."

No such luck.

"It's Amber," said Raffaele.

Fuck. Fuck. *Fuck.*

chapter 19

LACHLAN'S HAND TIGHTENED AROUND HIS GLASS. "Wow."

"I know. It's a wow for me too."

"It never occurred to me… Well, I never thought…"

"Me neither." A faint smile lifted the corners of Raffaele's mouth. "Not for all those years, until I was down here a couple of months ago, and something just *happened…*"

"What?" Lachlan felt as if he'd been jabbed with a cattle prod. "You mean it's been going on since then?"

"No, no. I didn't do anything." Raffaele shook his head, then pressed his clenched fist to his chest. "It was in here. All of a sudden, I just knew. She's the one. And that's not an exaggeration. I mean it."

"And what about Amber? How does she feel about this?" It was taking all of Lachlan's self-control to sound normal.

"She doesn't know. I haven't told her yet. That's why I wanted to speak to you. I think I've managed to keep my feelings under wraps. I mean, you didn't notice anything, did you?"

Still numb, Lachlan shook his head. "No."

"So the thing is, do you think I should tell her? I want to, but I'm worried it's too soon after Vee. Amber might think it's just one of those rebound things and not take me seriously. I mean, *I* know it isn't a rebound thing, but it might bother her." Raffaele gestured helplessly. "What do you reckon? Should I go ahead and make my move? Or be patient and give it a few more weeks?"

Some questions didn't need thinking about. "That one," said Lachlan straightaway. "Be patient and wait. Definitely give it a few more weeks."

"Really? I don't *want* to wait, obviously…"

"But you should. You have to. This is how you feel now, but you might change your mind."

"I won't."

"You might."

"But I won't, because I'm not like you, am I?" Raffaele fixed him with a steady gaze. "I don't do that. This is going to be long term. I know it is."

This was what Lachlan was afraid of. Deep down, he'd always known that one day, Amber would fall in love with someone else and settle down with them. But how could he cope if that someone else was Raffaele? Seeing them together all the time and having to keep his own emotions completely hidden, day after day, year after year… Oh God, it would be agonizing, unendurable; he just wouldn't be able to handle it. Feeling sick, he said, "OK, but I still think you need to hang fire for a few weeks. Maybe a couple of months. Because otherwise, it's really going to look like an overlap. Everyone'll think there was something going on before you and Vee broke up." Thinking fast, he played his trump card. "And that would make Amber look bad. People would think she was the one who caused it."

"Right. OK," Raffaele said. "Didn't think of that."

"She'd hate it. Give yourself some time." Lachlan was painfully aware that he was the one needing time. In all honesty, he knew he wouldn't be able to stave his best friend off indefinitely, but right now, the best he could do was persuade Raffaele to wait in order to give himself a while to get used to the idea. Plus—and he knew he was clutching at straws now—there had to be a slim chance that Raff might change his mind.

Raffaele nodded slowly. "OK, I guess you're right. Suppose I'd better hang on for a few weeks."

"Or a few months," said Lachlan. "And don't tell Amber. Don't make any kind of move. There's no rush, is there?"

"I'll leave it until summer's over. It might kill me, but I'll manage somehow."

"Good." Phew, that was something at least.

"Do you think we'd make a good couple though? We would, wouldn't we?"

Lachlan looked at his best friend, sitting casually on his chair with his left ankle resting on his right knee. He was laid-back, good-looking, and big-hearted. Unlike himself, he was also monogamous, emotionally calm, and an indisputably good bet.

He said, "Of course you would," and felt an almost physical ache in his chest, because it was true.

"Thanks." Raffaele grinned and raised his glass. "Here's to me and Amber then. Cheers."

"But not yet," Lachlan reminded him.

"Fine, not yet. Cheers!"

Forty minutes later, Lachlan pushed open the door to Bert's Bar and saw the look of relief on Polly's face. The other week, they'd sparred, she'd rejected him, and then, when she'd changed her mind, he'd in turn rejected her. Not having seen him since, she'd evidently been worried he might not be back.

And now he was. As he reached the bar, she said perkily, "Fancy seeing you here!"

Not in the mood to play games, Lachlan said, "I'll have a San Miguel, please." And when she'd flipped the cap off the bottle, he added, "Want to come back to mine tonight?"

Polly couldn't conceal a triumphant smile. "Well, I was going to head over to the Dolphin for a late one with the girls, but—"

"OK. Doesn't matter."

"No, it's fine. I can cancel them." Hastily, before he had a chance to duck out, Polly called to her friend, "Meg, no need to wait. I'm not going to bother with the Dolphin. You and the others go on without me."

Meg looked at Lachlan and started to smirk. Coming over to join them, she said, "Now I wonder what happened to change your mind. Got a better offer, by any chance?"

"Maybe." Polly was vigorously polishing the wooden top of the bar.

"Mind you don't wear yourself out. Need to keep your strength up." Outspoken Meg turned and gave Lachlan a nudge. "Haven't seen you in here for a while."

He took a swallow of San Miguel. "I've been busy."

"You missed Polly's birthday last Wednesday."

Had he? "Sorry," he said. "Happy birthday for last Wednesday."

Polly said carelessly, "Thanks. We had a brilliant night down at the Dolphin. Should have joined us."

"We bumped into Raffaele as we were leaving," Meg chimed in. "Polly invited him back to her place to finish up the birthday celebrations."

Lachlan knew what Meg was trying to do. She was making the point that he ran the risk of losing Polly if he didn't buck up his ideas, that she might decide to go off with someone else and then he'd be sorry.

Well, he might be sorry if only they had an actual romantic attachment.

But they didn't.

Only mildly interested, he looked at Polly. "You invited Raff back to yours? And did he say yes?" *Surely not.*

"He wanted to, you could tell," Meg interrupted once more. "But he said you and Polly had history together, so he couldn't do it."

Lachlan exhaled. There it was, the unbreakable pact that had been in place for the last sixteen years, the very one that now meant he had to stand back and allow Raffaele free rein with Amber.

"It's sweet that he's such a good friend to you," Meg concluded, ever loyal to her own friend. "If it had been any other bloke, they'd have said yes in a flash."

....

Lachlan had been hoping Polly would say she needed to get back to her own place last night. Instead, she'd insisted on cuddling up, repeatedly kissing his neck and telling him how much she'd missed him, before falling asleep and leaving him to lie awake thinking about Raffaele and Amber.

Which meant he'd only managed to get an hour or two of sleep himself. And now it was morning, with the sun streaming in through the windows along with the sound of the gulls crying overhead. By the time he opened the door to see Polly out, it was almost eight o'clock. It was also, predictably, the moment Amber happened to be passing by on her way down to the beach for her morning run.

Spotting her, Polly waved enthusiastically and called out, "Look, there's Amber. Hiya!" while running a possessive hand across Lachlan's torso.

Amber waved back and carried on jogging, her blond ponytail bouncing from side to side and her eyes shielded from the sun by the Ray-Bans Lachlan had bought her last Christmas after she'd accidentally sat on her own much cheaper sunglasses and broken them.

"I need to be getting started in the kitchen," said Lachlan, polite-speak for letting Polly know it was time to leave.

She stroked his shower-damp hair. "Did you and Amber ever sleep together?"

"No."

"Why not?"

"It's not like that between us." It had been on the tip of his tongue to say he liked Amber too much to mess her around, but he managed to hold back, because it wouldn't be fair to Polly.

She gave his earlobe a playful squeeze. "Maybe Amber's boobs just aren't big enough." She'd always been proud of her own pneumatic breasts. "Right, I'm off. See you soon." She planted a lingering kiss on his mouth. "And don't leave it so long next time. I missed you."

Lachlan had been pretty much ready to end their easy arrangement. But now the Raff-and-Amber bombshell had crash-landed in his life. If a harmless friends-with-benefits scenario managed to take his mind off it, where was the harm in keeping it going?

He might as well.

....

It was like going shopping with a whirlwind. Having collected Olga at nine, Amber had driven to Plymouth. She needed to open the studio at two, so they had to be done by one, which meant they only had three hours in which to find the perfect outfit for Olga to wear when Teddy took her along to the golf club dinner in order to introduce her properly to his friends. So far, she'd tried on fifteen different outfits.

"He wants me to look amazing," she explained. "So I need something to knock them off their socks!"

Amber wondered if she'd been invited along as the voice of reason. If Teddy had suggested it in the hope that Olga might come home with a smart navy two-piece suit, he was out of luck.

Then again, maybe Teddy didn't want Olga to dress like an office manager; he seemed perfectly happy with the way she wore her clothes.

"Now this I like a *lot*." Emerging from the changing room in one of the charity shops on Cornwall Street, Olga did a joyful twirl. The dress was canary yellow, tight-fitting, and above the knee, with silver tassels all around the neck and hemline. She followed the twirl with a shimmy. "We've found the perfect one, hooray! And it's only six pounds fifty!"

"Are you sure you don't want to look in any other shops?" said Amber, because Teddy had given Olga a hundred and fifty pounds to buy herself something special.

"No, this is the one. I'll get some shoes to go with it and make Teddy proud. If there's money left over, I'll buy him something nice. A tie, perhaps, to match my dress! Wouldn't that be chic?"

And against all the odds, in another charity shop farther down the road, she did manage to find a tie, paler lemon-yellow and with a row of squirrels dancing across it. Amber had never seen someone so delighted with a discovery. "So cute! And only two pounds, hooray!"

Once the shoes had been bought—high, crystal encrusted, and decorated with silver butterflies—Olga hugged her and said, "I've loved shopping with you. Come on. Now we have time for a lovely lunch!"

Ten minutes later, they were installed in a smart seafood restaurant overlooking the marina that Olga had found yesterday on Google.

"Nice, eh? The reviews are excellent. I checked. Choose whatever you want. My treat!" And when she saw Amber hesitate because it felt wrong to be using Teddy's money, Olga shook her head vigorously. "No, no, I will give Teddy back the amount I didn't spend on clothes. I do have some money of my own, I promise, from when I was working in the beauty salon."

"So you left there just before the cruise?" Amber felt guilty for asking, but Lachlan had wanted to know. When he'd tried to find out before, Olga had deftly changed the subject.

"Oh, the manageress was a cow! She hated me because her daughter worked there but all the clients preferred to be seen by me. When she got cross about it, I told her it was because I was the best. Then I knew she was about to fire me, so I walked out. Awful woman. Oh, thank you, darling!" Olga beamed up at the waiter bringing their menus. "What do you recommend? Is the sea bass good?"

When they'd placed their orders, Olga took photos of the marina and said, "Just think how much some of these boats cost! Such an expensive hobby. I wonder if some of the owners are here in this restaurant right now."

And when lunch was over, she paid the bill, then excused herself and disappeared to the ladies'. Waiting to leave, Amber saw her stop on the way back to chat animatedly with a couple of men over by the bar.

"Who were they?" she said when Olga returned to the table.

"Oh, the older one is called Derek. I complimented him on the beautiful shirt he was wearing. And guess what? It turns out he owns one of the boats in the harbor. He was charming and *so* friendly." Olga gave the two men a little wave as they left the restaurant. "I think people are friendlier here than in London. He offered me a ride on his boat!"

Amber blinked. "Are you going to go?"

"No, because they're sailing down to Brittany this afternoon, and I know you have to get back to work. It would have been nice, but never mind. Oh, you look shocked!"

"I was just wondering about Teddy…"

"But Teddy wouldn't mind. He's not jealous! Is that what you're thinking?" Olga laughed. "Listen, I love Teddy and he loves me, but we aren't joined at the ankle! When he wants to go and play golf, I don't mind, so why would he care if I went for a sail on a boat? Come on. Let's take a photo of us at the end of our first trip together… Big smile! There, hasn't this been great?"

chapter 20

Raffaele had decided against a flashy opening ceremony, but when the doors of Raffaele & Co. opened on Tuesday morning, there was a bit of a party atmosphere anyway. He was renting out the chairs in the salon to a number of stylists, who'd arrived with silver and blue helium balloons, plastic glasses, and bottles of prosecco. Nosy tourists were out on the street peering in through the windows, and a journalist from the local paper had turned up, along with a couple of locally based Instagrammers and paparazzi.

"So, it all looks great," exclaimed the young male journalist. "Small, though! Not what you're used to in London."

"I've worked in all sorts of salons over the years," Raffaele replied equably. "And I've liked all of them."

"Yeah, but the one in Chelsea was pretty glitzy, full of celebs, all that kind of thing."

"I'm more interested in the hair than how famous my clients are. It was time for a change."

The journalist nodded eagerly. "Time to come home."

"And I'm very happy I did."

"Feels like a nice relaxed atmosphere in here." As he said it, one of the stylists refilled his plastic glass, and he took an enthusiastic gulp before the fizzing had a chance to die down. "Bet you're looking forward to it staying that way!"

"Meaning?" Raffaele raised an eyebrow, silently daring him to mention Vee.

"Nothing at all!" Hastily backing down—because this was the *South Cornwall Gazette*, not the *Daily Mail*—the journalist babbled, "And you must be looking forward to meeting your new clients."

"I am. In fact, we need to get started. Can't keep people waiting…"

"Hi, it's me. I'm first!" A tall, faintly familiar brunette jumped up from the purple velvet sofa over by reception. Greeting Raffaele with a determined kiss on the cheek, she said, "It's good to see you again. I've been so looking forward to this!"

She was wearing a low-cut top and tight jeans, and her hair was already blow-dried. In the nick of time, Raffaele remembered where he'd seen her before. "You were with Polly when she was celebrating her birthday."

"That's right! And what a celebration it was." She bounced into her chair and beamed at him in the mirror. "I'm Meg."

The journalist said, "Meg, OK if we get a couple of photos of you and Raffaele together?"

"I'd love that. Snap away!" Meg wriggled with delight as Raffaele fastened the black cape around her.

Raffaele said, "And what kind of look are you after?"

"Entirely up to you." Meg's lashes fluttered, her gaze meeting his in the mirror. "You can do anything you want with me."

"Wahey!" Two speedy glasses of prosecco at ten in the morning were clearly doing a happy dance in the young journalist's bloodstream. "Sounds like you've got quite a fan there!" Glancing around the salon and out through the window at the women gathered outside, he went on, "In fact, I reckon there's a lot of ladies glad to have you back in Lanrock."

"Well, I'm single," said Meg, "and I'm definitely glad he's moved down here." Beckoning to Raffaele to move closer, she added in a stage whisper, "Plus I've never had a fling with Lachlan."

"Does that make a difference?" One of the guest stylists looked interested.

Meg nodded, evidently delighted to be able to impart this information. "They stick to their boy code."

"Oh, bad *luck*." The stylist gave Raffaele a comical look. "If you're only going to sleep with girls who haven't slept with Lachlan…well, there's not much left to choose from, is there? Poor you!"

Benjie gazed down at himself. He looked like a seal. It had taken a while to squeeze into the black neoprene wetsuit, but now that he was zipped up, it actually felt good. Fascinated, he flexed his arms and legs and surveyed the elongated shadow his body was casting across the wet sand in front of him while the late-afternoon sun warmed his back.

He'd never surfed before, simply because he hadn't had anyone to go surfing with. But it was Wednesday, this was his next just-friends date with Jo, and joining the beginners' surfing class on the beach had been her idea. All they'd had to do was rent boards and wetsuits from the surf shack and book an hour-long lesson. It wouldn't have occurred to him to do it on his own, but now he was here, he was really looking forward to it.

"Ready?" Jo's eyes were shining as the instructor prepared to begin the lesson.

"Ready." There were eight of them in the class, and one couple had to be in their seventies, which was boosting his confidence at least.

"You look great," Jo told him. "Like a secret agent."

"I'm probably going to look like a s-secret agent who falls off his surfboard a lot."

"So? Everyone has to start somewhere." She grinned at him, her springy red-gold curls glowing in the sunlight. "Even secret agents. And I bet I fall off more than you do, but who cares? We're going to have fun."

"OK, are we ready to start?" The instructor clapped his hands. "Pay attention, you two young lovebirds at the back."

Mortified, Benjie said, "Oh, we aren't l-l-lovebirds!"

But the instructor wasn't interested in excuses. He said, "Now watch me and lie down on your boards like *this…*"

....

Three hours later, Dani had just written: So you enjoyed it?

Talk about understatement. Still buzzing with adrenaline, Benjie typed back: It was so cool. I never thought I'd be able to stand up, but I did. People on the beach were applauding! Here…

He uploaded the two photos taken by Jo that showed him in the most flattering light. In the first, he'd been laughing as he strode out of the water with his board tucked under his arm. In the other, he was actually surfing. Only for a couple of seconds before he'd tipped off and disappeared beneath the waves, but Dani didn't know that. Jo had managed to capture the moment, and he looked great.

Oh wow, amazing! And you look so happy!

She was right, Benjie realized. His whole face had been lit up. He'd felt so enthralled, there'd been no time to be self-conscious. The sea spray, the still-warm air, and the sense of freedom had been completely exhilarating.

It was great, he typed, admiring the way he looked in the two photos. When you and I go on holiday, I'll have to teach you how to surf too—I'll be an expert by then!

Can't wait. Maybe when we're on our honeymoon.

What did you do this evening?

Went to the mall to do some shopping. Bought myself some glittery eyeshadows. Want to see?

Of course!

The photo popped up a few seconds later, filling the screen. There was Dani, smiling at him as she sat cross-legged on her bed, holding the eyeshadow palette up to the camera. Her eyelids glittered pink, lilac, and sapphire, and her lip gloss was a vivid shade of fuchsia.

Benjie typed, You're so beautiful.

She typed back, And so sparkly!

He replied, Very sparkly. This was a reference to a line in *Rain Man*, a film they both loved and had watched together several times.

Dani typed, Ooh, we could watch it again if you like. Fancy doing that now?

It was a long film. Benjie hesitated before replying, Maybe another time. I'm pretty tired.

You must be, after all that surfing. When are you going to see Jo next?

Not sure. Maybe at the weekend.

Right. You must be looking forward to meeting up with her again. She sounds like lots of fun.

Uh-oh. Benjie could sense how Dani was feeling right now. He said, She's a friend, that's all.

If he'd needed to say those words out loud, he knew he'd have been stuttering by now.

Silence. The screen on his laptop didn't alter. His pulse began to quicken. Finally, the next line from Dani appeared: I love you so much.

Benjie hesitated, then wrote, I know. I love you too.

Well, what else could he say? Anyway, it was true. Kind of.

The next line flashed up: Who do you like best? Jo or me?

He looked at the photo of himself emerging from the sea in his black neoprene wetsuit, with his hair wet and tousled and his huge smile making him look relaxed and happy in a way he seldom felt.

It was Jo he'd been looking at as she'd taken the photo on her phone. She was the one who'd been whooping and applauding from the shoreline when he'd managed to stay upright on his surfboard for maybe three whole seconds.

Feeling torn, he carefully tapped out, You, of course. Xxx

chapter 21

Last night had been Benjie's second evening spent with Jo. This morning at breakfast, he'd definitely seemed cheerful. Peggy had heard him singing in the shower, and when he'd left for work, he had planted a kiss on her cheek. He was wearing more aftershave than usual, she couldn't help noticing, and had attempted to spike his hair up with gel. It didn't entirely suit him, but it warmed her heart to see him making an effort.

Welcome to the real world, my lovely boy.

Later that evening in the restaurant, Peggy waylaid Jo on her way back from serving a table in the tiny outside courtyard. She murmured, "I've paid the money into your account. How did things go last night?"

"Thanks. Really well." Jo glanced furtively behind her to make sure they couldn't be overheard. "The surfing was a brilliant idea. He loved it."

"Good. What's the plan for the next meetup?"

"I was thinking maybe a trip to the theater."

"Boring. We need something more fun than that."

"OK, let me have a think. I have to get back to the kitchen now." Jo slipped away.

Peggy returned to the table in the window, where Dom Burton was studying the wine list. Dinner was over, but he clearly wasn't ready to leave yet. As she sat back down, he said, "I just called Amber. She's on her way."

"You've got that look in your eye." Peggy and Dom had been friends for years, since they'd lived next door to each other in West Kensington; she knew him so well. "What is it you're really interested in? The stained-glass octopus or the artist?"

"Oh, Peg, what do you think?" Dom flashed a smile. "Can't I be interested in both?"

It was growing dark outside when Amber reached McCarthy's. She could see Peggy and Dom through the lit-up window. Pushing open the door, she breathed in the amazing cooking smells and waved at Lachlan in the kitchen, visible through the stone archway at the far end of the restaurant.

She greeted Peggy and Dom, then slid into the empty chair. "Sorry I couldn't meet you earlier. I had a commission to finish. All done now."

"So you're saying a commission's more important than meeting me?" Dom's tone was genial. "I'm not sure my ego can cope with that."

"This one was short notice, for a golden wedding celebration. Tomorrow morning, it's going to be collected and driven all the way to Poole in time for the party."

"But I'm your favorite client." Dom poured her a glass of red. "Go on, admit it. You know you want to."

"You're definitely the client who sends me the most emails." After meeting him last week, Amber had received at least a dozen while he'd been visiting Copenhagen, Amsterdam, and Berlin on business trips. Now he was back in Cornwall for a few more days, as shy and retiring as ever.

"I like to know how things are going. Will you definitely have it finished in three weeks?"

"I said I would, so I'll make sure I do." Who needed sleep anyway?

Dom winked at her. "That's what I like to hear. You missed an excellent dinner tonight by the way. This place is a hidden gem."

"Don't even think of trying to headhunt Lachlan," Peggy warned. "You're not stealing him away to work in one of your hotels. I discovered him, and he's staying right here where he belongs."

Thirty minutes later, Lachlan's stint in the kitchen was over for the evening. At Peggy's request, he came over to join them. Another chair was pulled up, and more drinks were ordered.

Dom said, "Peggy was just telling me more about Teddy and the new woman in his life. Sounds like she's set on turning him into a new man."

Lachlan said, "We just have to hope he doesn't end up a poorer one."

"Oh, but what about Monday?" Amber was finding herself increasingly torn between liking Olga as a person and acknowledging that she could be unpredictable. "She bought that dress in the charity shop and gave the rest of the money back to Teddy."

Lachlan said mildly, "Have you never heard of the double bluff?"

"Yes, but—"

"And she practically invited herself onto some random guy's boat in the marina."

Amber had deliberately not mentioned this to him. She raised her eyebrows. "Who told you about that?"

"She did! I dropped some bread rolls off at the house yesterday, and Olga was in the middle of telling Teddy!"

Amber spread her hands. "So that proves it was innocent."

"Or a triple bluff."

"Well, now I'm curious," said Dom. "I need to know what she looks like."

"Tall, blond, very striking…" Amber began, but Lachlan already had his phone out; the prospect of trying to describe a person with words was evidently so last century.

"Here she is." He found a photo and showed it to Dom. "That's her and Teddy together on the cruise. I mean, I know Amber thinks I'm being too suspicious, but can you blame me? All I'm trying to do is look out for Teddy."

Irritated because Lachlan was showing him the photo that showed Olga at her most flamboyant, Amber opened her own phone and found the selfie of the two of them in the restaurant on Monday. It was much more flattering and normal.

"She sent me this one of us, from when we were in Plymouth."

Dom had been looking at Lachlan's phone. Now he studied hers and started to laugh. "So this is Olga? I thought I recognized her. I've seen her in her gold bikini, causing a kerfuffle down on the beach."

Oh, what? Amber purposely avoided Lachlan's gaze, because she just knew he'd be looking triumphant.

Clearly delighted, Lachlan said, "Well, that sounds about right. What kind of a kerfuffle?"

"Well, I don't mean she was yelling at people and starting fights. But she was definitely the center of attention. Doing yoga or Pilates, one of those bendy activities. Striking poses and looking pretty spectacular, I have to say."

Amber could imagine. "And she was on her own?"

"Only to begin with. Once she started, heads were turning, I can tell you. Before long, there were kids and dogs joining in, and a fair few holidaymakers… It turned into quite the circus, but Olga didn't seem to mind. She was chatting and laughing with everyone, helping people with their poses. I've seen her down there a couple of times now. Only from a distance," Dom added with a grin. "I didn't join the class."

"See what I mean?" said Lachlan.

Amber sighed. "Yes, how dare she exercise on the beach and be nice to the people who join in?"

"While wearing a gold bikini? That's just attention-seeking."

"So what do you think people should be wearing on the beach in June? A giant dressing gown and a couple of thermal vests?"

Lachlan shrugged. "I'm just saying we need to protect Teddy. Don't we owe him that much at least?"

"You know what you need to do, then," Peggy announced in her usual forthright manner. "If you think Olga's only with him for his money, you want to find someone who's got more of it than Ted has."

"Actually, that's not a bad idea," Amber conceded.

"It's a genius idea." Lachlan nodded in agreement.

"What?" Dom sat back, belatedly realizing all eyes were now upon him. He put down his drink. "Why are you looking at me like that?"

....

"I feel like a spy," said Amber the following morning.

Next to her on one of the wooden benches overlooking West Beach, Lachlan said, "That's probably because we're *being* spies."

It was ten in the morning, the sun was already blazing down, and Olga was fifty meters away on the sand, doing her thing. She was wearing a fringed turquoise bikini today, glittering with crystals, and her long blond hair swung around her shoulders as she bent and stretched and performed an advanced yoga routine with strength and grace. As Dom had described, she was surrounded by children, joyfully attempting to replicate the various moves and shrieking with laughter when they lost their balance and fell over. A red setter on an extended lead was bouncing around too. And over there to the right, observing Olga with undisguised interest, was Dom Burton.

"Let me have a go," said Amber.

Lachlan passed her the binoculars. "He's looking richer today."

He was. Dom might still be casually dressed, but there was an expensive gold watch glinting on his wrist, designer dark glasses perched on top of his head, and the keys to his Porsche dangling from his fingers.

Twenty minutes later, the yoga workout concluded and the children dispersed. Olga sat down on her towel, applied sun cream to her face and shoulders, then leaned back on her elbows to survey the scene and enjoy the sunshine. Having called Teddy this morning and casually asked the question, Lachlan had learned that yes, Olga liked to perform yoga on the beach every morning, and no, of course it didn't bother him. Why shouldn't she want to keep herself in shape?

Amber's phone rang and she answered it.

"Well?" It was Raffaele, fully booked in the salon and unable to join them. "How's it going?"

"She's only just finished the yoga. Oh, here we go. Dom's heading over now. He's talking to her…she's talking to him…he's laughing…"

Next to her, having grabbed the binoculars back, Lachlan said, "Oh, she's definitely interested. She can't take her eyes off him. You should see the way she's smiling up at him—*Ow.*"

Almost garroting him with the binoculars strap, Amber took another look herself. "She's just being friendly. That's the same way she smiles at me!"

"OK, my client's waiting. I need to get back. Keep me updated," said Raffaele before hanging up.

"She's spotted the key ring, and now she's asking him about his Porsche." Lachlan was smug. The next moment, they ducked their heads as Dom swung around and pointed to his car in the little beachfront parking lot.

They carried on watching as Dom sat down next to Olga and the conversation continued. "He's got the knack, hasn't he?" Amber marveled. "I wouldn't know what to say if I had to chat up a complete stranger on the beach."

"It's easy enough." Lachlan shrugged.

"Easy enough for you, maybe. But how do you even start?"

"Make a funny observation. Or pay them a compliment, but not in a sleazy way. Smile as if you're old friends sharing a joke. Then just take it from there."

"So if we didn't know each other and you wanted to get to know me, how would you do it?" Amber couldn't help it; she was intrigued. Flirting was something she'd always been rubbish at.

Lachlan turned to look at her, as if deciding what to say. Then he shook his head. "No, I can't. It has to be the real thing. It'd be too weird to do it with you."

She hid her disappointment; it would have been nice to hear what he might have said if they were strangers, what kind of non-sleazy compliment he might have paid her. She wasn't even sure what her best features were or how Lachlan saw her as a member of the opposite—

"Smooth move." He was watching Dom and Olga through the binoculars again. Olga had risen to her feet, shrugged on a semitransparent sapphire-blue kaftan, and was now rolling up her towel. "He just passed her a business card, and she's slipped it into her bag. They're still chatting. She's definitely interested. If he's asked her to meet up with him and she's agreed, we've got her. Oh, there they go… This is perfect, working out even better than I expected."

Laughing together, deep in conversation, Dom and Olga made their way back off the beach, climbing the steps that led to the parking lot. When they reached Dom's car, they halted and carried on talking. Finally, Olga turned and headed for home. After sitting in the driver's seat of the Porsche Carrera for a few minutes, Dom climbed out once more and walked over to the two of them on the bench.

"Well?" said Lachlan.

"You weren't kidding. She's a firecracker."

Oh no. Amber's heart sank. "And?"

"I don't know. I just can't tell. And that's not like me at all." Dom spread his hands. "I always know."

"Did you ask her out?" said Lachlan.

"Yes, I told her I was free this afternoon, offered to take her out to lunch over in St. Austell." They'd chosen today because Teddy was away, taking part in a golf tournament in Devon; if Olga was interested in seeing more of Dom, Teddy would never know she'd spent hours away from Lanrock.

Amber said, "So did she say yes or no?"

"Neither. I offered to show her the new hotel. Happened to mention my palazzo in Venice. I was *so* charming." He grinned at her. "Like, completely irresistible."

"Look, you were in full view of everyone," said Lachlan. "Olga's only been here a couple of weeks, but the locals already know who she is. And she's not stupid."

Dom nodded. "I know. That's why I gave her my card. Now we just have to hang fire and see if she gives me a call."

chapter 22

In the salon over on River Street, Raffaele was blow-drying the hair of a girl called Penny who worked as a nurse at the local hospital. Having put down her copy of *Hi!* magazine, she was now scrolling through the latest news on a gossip site on her phone.

"Oh!" When she jerked her head upright, for a split second Raffaele thought he'd burned the back of her neck.

But he knew he hadn't. He switched off the dryer. "Everything OK?"

"I'm fine. Sorry, it just caught me by surprise, sitting here with you doing my hair and this coming up on my phone."

She lifted it to show him, and he saw the photo of Vee. When he read the accompanying headline, he said, "Oh God, what now?"

"Haven't you seen it?" She grimaced. "Sorry, I thought you'd have known."

But that was the thing about online gossip—the column of shame was capable of flashing up new stories literally within minutes of them happening. Raffaele put down the brush and hair dryer and together they read the piece, titled "Sandwiches at Dawn":

The extensions were flying this morning when reality star Dawn Kerrigan confronted celebrity hairdresser Vee Harper in her Chelsea salon. After a disastrous haircut, Dawn protested that her life was over and no longer worth living, according to an anonymous client who witnessed the interaction and took these photos. The two women were yelling at each other and insults were exchanged. Speaking to one of our journalists afterward, Dawn stated, "She did my bangs wonky. I couldn't believe it and told her she was a useless cow, and that's when she really lost her temper. Vee Harper called me all sorts of names, which I thought was shocking because there were old people of, like, forty or fifty having to listen to her terrible abuse of me. Then I said a couple of very mild replies and left the salon, but she ran after me. By now in fear for my life, I tried to hide in the sandwich shop across the road, but she followed me inside and started throwing packets of sandwiches at my head. Seeing as I'm allergic to cheese, I was especially appalled to discover that one of the sandwiches contained Brie."

When we approached Vee Harper for a statement, she said nothing but responded with a rude gesture.

Were you in the sandwich shop when the altercation happened? We pay good money for videos. Contact us at the number below.

"To be fair," said Penny when they'd finished reading the piece, "that Dawn Kerrigan is a nightmare. If anyone deserves to have sandwiches thrown at their head, it's her."

Maybe so, but Raffaele's stomach had tensed, because what in God's name did Vee think she was playing at?

Screaming matches with clients were horrifically unprofessional, no matter how tempting it might be to retaliate. Knowing Dawn Kerrigan's appetite for drama, it was a wonder Vee hadn't been arrested. Becoming known as a stylist who was capable of hurling sandwiches at clients had to be terrible publicity for the salon.

He might no longer be involved, but it didn't stop him feeling as if he was.

He shook his head. "She shouldn't have done it."

"D'you think it's because she's struggling to get over the breakup? She must have been devastated when it happened."

"No idea." Raffaele shrugged, switched the hair dryer on again, and got back to blow-drying Penny's hair. He might have been the one who'd left London, but it was Vee who'd ended their relationship.

....

Vee's trouble in the sandwich shop was nothing compared with the latest episode of *Cooking for the Enemy*. Lachlan was watching a mother-in-law who looked like a belligerent flamingo pitted against her son's wife, and the vitriol was real. The older woman was scathing about her daughter-in-law's ability to prepare meals, clean the house, and raise the children, and every time she said something awful, the younger woman mimicked her by squawking loudly and stalking around the kitchen in a flamingo-y way.

"Imagine meeting your perfect other half and falling madly in love with them," said Amber, "then being introduced to their mother and discovering she's a living nightmare."

She was watching the show from her own bed a quarter of a mile away, and Lachlan was lying on his with the duvet kicked off because who needed one during a heat wave? They had their phones propped up and were using FaceTime to chat about the show as it unfolded in all its horror on their TVs.

"Marry me and you won't have to worry about it." Lachlan grinned. Not having any parents had its advantages.

"What's that sausage roll you're eating?" Amber peered suspiciously. "Did you make it yourself?"

"No. Greggs." He showed her the paper bag bearing the famous logo.

"Don't blame you." Mischievously she said, "They're better than yours."

On the TV, the mother-in-law announced with a huff, "That girl can't cook to save her life. She'd eat takeout toast if she could get it delivered, lazy cat."

"If Teddy ends up marrying Olga," said Amber, "she'll be like our stepmum."

"Don't."

"But she would!" She was really teasing him now. Olga hadn't responded to Dom's earlier offer, and Amber was gloating as if it proved beyond all doubt that she'd been right. Lachlan still didn't agree and had asked Dom to give it another go tomorrow. Dom, ultracompetitive and shocked that he'd failed to mesmerize Olga with his good looks, many hotels, and unassailable charm, had vowed to up his game.

Idly, Lachlan said, "If you didn't know Dom and he chatted you up on the beach, then asked you out, would you say yes?"

"I might."

"Would you? Really?" That gave him a jolt; he hadn't expected her to say it.

"Yes, but it's not the same, is it? I'm single. Olga's with Teddy."

"Never mind Olga. I'm just asking, if Dom introduced himself and offered to take you out to dinner, you'd go?"

"In theory. Why not? He's good fun... What's wrong with that?"

What was wrong with that was the way it was making Lachlan feel. He wasn't liking the idea one bit.

First Raffaele, now this.

"He's a womanizer." As he said it, he experienced a wave of jealousy. "Short attention span."

"Kettle," said Amber. "Pot."

"Seriously, you wouldn't want to get involved with someone like Dom."

"One, I know. Two, it hasn't happened. Three, it's pretty unlikely." She was laughing at him. "You're getting carried away here."

He wasn't; he just didn't want to consider the possibility of it happening. The thought of Dom Burton turning up and whisking her—

Click.

It wasn't a loud noise, but it was enough to make Lachlan sit up and turn to see what had just hit the glass.

"What is it?" said Amber.

"Something knocked against the window. Might be kids messing around outside. Hang on."

Amber said, "Take me with you," and he scooped up his phone.

The left half of the window was closed. As Lachlan crossed the bedroom, a second tiny pebble flew through the open window on the right, hitting him in the face.

"Ow." Rubbing his left cheekbone, Lachlan peered down into the street below.

"Oh God, oh God, I'm so sorry." Polly let out a wail. "I was trying to aim for the glass. I didn't mean it to go through!"

"And you were trying to hit the glass because…?"

"I wanted to see you! I left three messages on your phone, and you didn't call back."

"Who is that?" said Amber from the windowsill. "I can't see."

"It's Polly," said Lachlan.

"I saw your bedroom light was on, so I knew you were in there." Peering up suspiciously, Polly said, "Who are you talking to?"

"Why didn't you call her back?" said Amber.

"I was watching the TV show with you."

"Have you got someone in there with you?" Polly demanded.

He nodded. "Yes, I'm with Amber."

"Don't you dare say that!" Amber was outraged. "Now she's going to think I'm in your bedroom!"

"Does it matter?" Lachlan touched his face where the pebble had hit him.

"Of course it matters! She'll tell everyone I was up there with you."

And would that really be so terrible? Evidently it would. Lachlan sighed and shouted out of the window, "No, that wasn't true. Amber isn't here with me."

Polly yelled back, "Now I know you're lying to me. Of course she's in there."

"This is crazy," said Amber. "There's only one way to prove it now."

"How?"

"Invite her up."

"I don't want to invite her up. I'm watching TV with you."

"Well, we're missing the last bit. It's nearly over now anyway. She's desperate to see you. And have wild sex with you, at a guess. So you may as well do it. Then at least she'll know I'm not secretly hooking up with you myself."

From the pavement, Polly bellowed, "If you're shagging Amber, just be honest and admit it."

"Right, that's it. I'm not having her spreading rumors about me," Amber said crossly. "Let her in."

The line went dead; she'd ended the call.

On the TV behind Lachlan, the presenter on *Cooking for the Enemy* purred, "So there we go. That's all for tonight. I think it's safe to say none of us would want to be invited along to *that* family reunion! Bye for now, until next week..."

"Lachlan, will you *answer* me?" Polly was getting upset now. "It's not fair to treat me like this."

Oh God. Amber would be furious if he didn't prove that she wasn't in here with him. Lachlan pressed the buzzer to open the front door. "Come on up."

....

"I shouldn't be phoning you. Why am I phoning you?" Vee's voice was hoarse; he guessed she'd been crying. "I suppose you've heard..."

Raffaele said, "Just a bit." It wasn't as if he'd had any choice; practically everyone he'd ever met in the hairdressing world had either called to let him know or texted a link to the latest online piece about this morning's contretemps. He'd been fending off journalists' requests for a statement since midday.

"It's so unfair. It's like people are *trying* to make me lose my temper."

"And the more often you do, the more fun it is for them."

"Don't take their side, please. Those bangs weren't even lopsided. I swear she got home and blow-dried it to make it look uneven. Or cut it herself. She'd pull out her own teeth for a bit of attention. What a cow."

Raffaele closed his eyes. "Don't say that publicly."

"I know. But she is. Have people been pestering you to say something?"

"Yes."

"And did you?"

"No."

"Good. Thanks. Oh, what a bloody awful day."

Silence fell. He heard her sighing and licking her lips, as she did when she was lost in thought.

Finally she said, "What's happening to my life? Everything's going wrong."

"You need to get some rest. Go to sleep now. It'll blow over."

"Oh, will you look at that? Some troll's just left a message on my Instagram telling me I deserved to lose you because I'm such an evil witch." He heard her give a muffled scream of frustration. "What is wrong with these people? What do they get out of it?"

"Don't engage. Just block them."

"Or you could go on there and tell them they're the loser."

"No way. That's what they want," Raffaele reminded her. "I'm not getting involved."

"Thanks a lot. You're a great help," Vee snapped and hung up.

....

"I don't understand. What's going on?" Polly had been trying to unbutton her green flowery shirt, but Lachlan put out his hands and stopped her. She looked confused. "Is this a joke?"

He couldn't blame her. Doing buttons back up wasn't exactly what he was known for.

"It's not a joke. Look, it's been great. We've had fun. But I think it's time to call it a day."

"*Why*, though?" She gazed down in disbelief as he refastened the final fiddly mother-of-pearl button. "I'm here now! You like sex, I like sex, so why can't we just carry on doing it together?"

"I only asked you to come in so I could show you Amber isn't here. She didn't want you thinking she was in my bedroom with me. But she's nothing to do with how I'm feeling now. I just don't think it's fair to you."

"So instead you're going to make me stand back and watch you take home a string of other girls…"

Lachlan shook his head. "Honestly? I don't think that's going to happen. The casual hookups aren't really doing it for me anymore." He picked up her shoulder bag, hanging over the back of a chair, and passed it to her. "But we don't have to fall out over this, do we? We can still be friends."

Polly snatched the bag from him. "No, I don't think we can. And I'm not falling for that bullshit about no more hookups either. Because a leopard doesn't change his spots, Lachlan." Evidently set on making a soap-opera exit, she yanked open the door. "And trust me, you're a leopard through and through."

Keeping away from the window this time, Lachlan heard her heels clicking on the pavement as she fairly stomped up the street. What he'd said to her had been how he felt now, but time would tell. It would be interesting to see which of them turned out to be right.

He checked the time; it was only twenty minutes since Amber had hung up on him. Maybe he could call her back and they could watch the last section of *Cooking for the Enemy* on demand.

But when he tried to get through, Amber's phone was switched off for the night.

Damn. And how typical. Couldn't *anything* ever go according to plan?

chapter 23

THE ENVELOPE WAS HANDWRITTEN WITH JUST HIS NAME ON IT. Picking it up from the mat along with the rest of the Monday mail that had been delivered to the salon, Raffaele opened it first. At a guess, it would contain a request for a raffle prize for some local charity fundraising event. Which was fine, he was happy to oblige; this was what returning to Lanrock was all about.

It wasn't a request for a raffle prize.

Dear Raffaele,

I hope this doesn't come as a shock to you. To be honest, I'm not even sure if I should be doing it. But I'd like to give you the option of meeting me. If you don't want to, that's fine, I understand. And if I don't receive a text from you, I promise not to bother you again. I'm currently on holiday down here in Charlestown, so if you think you'd like to meet for a coffee, I'd be very happy to see you.

OK, time to explain. My name is Eamonn Johnson, and I was a good friend of your mother, Jan. We grew up next door to each other on Parsons Road in Glasgow. We were at school together too. She was a lovely girl, and I have fond memories of her. I was so sorry when I heard she'd passed away.

Anyway, I've followed your career over the years, ever since that time you appeared on the TV breakfast show. Not in a stalkerish way, I promise. Your name was instantly recognizable, and as soon as I saw you, I knew it was you.

You've done so well, Raffaele. Jan would have been incredibly proud of you and everything you've achieved against the odds. I don't know how interested you might be to hear stories about her and the way she was before she fell in with the wrong crowd, but if you'd like to meet, I'm happy to drive over to Lanrock any time this week that suits you.

And just so you know a bit about me, I'm here on holiday with my wife, Mandy. She works as a nurse, and I'm a senior paramedic. We've lived in Edinburgh for many years, our daughter works as a teacher in Newcastle, and our son is in the army.

Well, that's it for now. I hope you'll get in touch. It would be good to see you.

Very best wishes,
Eamonn

P.S. I have a photo of me and your mum. You might like to see it.

Raffaele reached the end of the letter, then read it through again. His mother and father were dead, and he had few memories of them. In one way, this had seemed like a good thing, because other children with bad memories had found it harder to deal with them. But the prospect of meeting up with someone who'd known his biological mother before the drugs had taken hold was something else, an enticing offer he already knew he wasn't going to be able to refuse.

How could he not want to listen to a voice from the past who was capable of filling in even a tiny segment of the void?

Without giving himself time to think or change his mind, he pulled out his phone and sent a text to the number Eamonn Johnson had written at the top of the letter:

Hi, Raffaele here. Thank you, I'd like this very much. I'm happy to drive to Charlestown. How about the Pier House Hotel this evening? Would 7 p.m. work for you?

He pressed Send.

A minute later, the reply came through:

Perfect. See you at 7.

The door to the salon flew open, and Anna, one of the stylists working today, burst in. "Can you believe it? Bloody raining! Look what's happened to my hair—total frizz bomb—and some madwoman in a white Range Rover just drove through a puddle and splashed my skirt! If this is what today's going to be like, I should've stayed in bed." She looked at Raffaele and saw the phone in his hand. "Oh God, what's wrong? What's happened now? If it's that crazy ex of yours, playing silly buggers again, just ignore her."

"It's not Vee," said Raffaele. "And don't call her my crazy ex."

"Sorry, ignore me. Have a Malteser." Anna offered him the packet. "Either way, looks like it's going to be a bad day all around."

It was a busy one. Raffaele worked without stopping for a lunch break and carried on through the afternoon. Finishing just before six, he showered and changed, then set off for Charlestown.

He parked, then walked down the road that ran alongside the elongated narrow harbor and led to the Pier House Hotel. The last time he'd come here had been with Vee, back when they'd still been happy. This morning's heavy rain had passed, and a watery sun was now setting low in the sky, bringing the tourists out with it.

A man in a pale-blue sweatshirt and faded jeans was standing on the sidewalk outside the entrance to the hotel, watching intently as he approached. And that was the moment Raffaele knew. Drawing nearer, he saw the man's face in more detail, recognized the way Eamonn Johnson was so visibly waiting to see what his reaction would be.

His pulse quickened. The door to the hotel burst open, and sounds of music and laughter spilled out along with an emerging couple and their small children.

"Raffaele, hi. Good to meet you," said Eamonn Johnson. "You're looking well. It's pretty busy in there. Lots of noise. I thought maybe…"

"One of the outside tables, yes." Raffaele indicated the ones at the side of the hotel, facing the small pebbled beach with the calm sea beyond it.

A couple of minutes later, sitting down with their drinks, Eamonn clinked his glass against Raffaele's. "Well? What are you thinking?"

"Quite a lot of things." Raffaele took a steadying breath. "The weirdest one is, it almost isn't a surprise."

"I didn't know how to do it. Didn't seem right to put it in the letter. I didn't know if it would have been a good time or a bad time to read it." Eamonn opened his wallet and laid a photograph on the table. "That's me and Jan when we were both sixteen."

Raffaele's hand trembled as he slid the photo closer. He'd seen several of his mother before, knew what she'd looked like later, after the addiction had taken hold, but still he concentrated on her first, taking in the center-parted blond hair, the plump cheeks, bright eyes. She was wearing a shiny purple bomber jacket over a denim dress and looked as happy as it was possible to be.

Then he turned his attention to sixteen-year-old Eamonn Johnson and saw what he'd somehow known he'd see: himself as a teenager. If he'd ever worn a Rolling Stones T-shirt, navy Adidas shorts, and a pair of red plimsolls. There was also a badly drawn tattoo of the Stones' famous tongue logo on his left forearm. Raffaele silently pointed to the tattoo and raised his eyebrows.

"I know. Embarrassing." With a familiar lopsided smile, Eamonn pulled up the sleeve of his blue sweatshirt to reveal an untattooed left arm. "I thought it'd be a good idea to draw it on with felt-tip pen. To make me look cool."

Raffaele studied the face in the photo that so eerily resembled his own, from the narrow light-brown eyes and close-cut dark-blond hair to the straight nose and defined cheekbones.

"How long were you together?"

"As friends? For years. As a couple?" Eamonn paused and shook his head. "Never. Unless you count the one weekend she spent with me after running away from the Spanish guy."

"Was he the one who got her into drugs?"

"Oh yes. Jan was crazy about him. He was all she ever wanted. And it used to just kill me, because he treated her like dirt but she loved him anyway."

"And you?"

"I loved her. But I couldn't compete. I'd been friend-zoned for years. She was enthralled by him. And by the drugs. It broke my heart, but there was nothing any of us could do to stop it happening. Until she turned up at my place one night. They'd had a massive fight because she'd caught him with another girl. Jan told me she'd had enough, she needed to get her life back. She also told me I was the one she wanted. I was gullible and desperate enough to believe her. It was the best—the most magical weekend of my life. We made plans for the future…and then on Monday, she went back to his flat to pick up the rest of her things. She thought he'd be at work, but he was there. He begged her to go back to him." Eamonn shrugged. "And of course she did."

Not far from their table, a gull and a magpie were tussling over a discarded sandwich crust on the ground. Finally, knowing when it was beaten, the magpie conceded defeat and flew off, leaving the gull to triumphantly gulp down the crust.

The irony didn't escape Raffaele.

"There wasn't anything I could do to change her mind," Eamonn went on. "I did try, but he was the one she wanted to be with. Jan made me promise that if he ever asked me if we'd slept together, I'd say no. He never did ask though. I went back to university, and she stayed with him. Six months later, I heard she was pregnant. Then that Christmas, I bumped into them in the street. She was pushing you in a stroller. They seemed…happy. He said, 'Want to have a look at my son? Raffaele junior. Pretty cool, eh?'"

Raffaele's heart contracted. "What did I look like?"

"Just…like a baby. You were asleep, bundled up against the cold with a hat over half your face. You didn't seem as dark-haired as him, but then Jan was blond… I thought if they'd named you after him, maybe that meant you were his after all."

"And how did she look? Jan?"

"Beautiful. Healthy." Eamonn nodded reassuringly. "She stayed clean all through the pregnancy and for almost a year afterward. I was away, but friends at home kept me updated. It wasn't until after that that it all started to go wrong."

Raffaele had been told this by social services, but it was good to hear it from someone who'd actually been there. His mother had loved and cared for him, for that first year at least.

He gazed across the table at his biological father, the man who could have given him an entirely different life. It wasn't Eamonn's fault that he hadn't been able to alter his mother's decision. If he had been, hard drugs most likely would never have featured in Jan's life. They might have stayed together, could still have been a couple today... A whole different future would have unfolded for all of them. In this potential parallel universe, Raffaele could have grown up to be a driving instructor or a doctor or a civil servant called Steven or Marcus or Tom.

Then again, who knew? Maybe as a teenager, he would have fallen hopelessly in love with a girl who persuaded him to try heroin, just once, to see what it was like. Who was to say that he wouldn't have been the one found dead in a squat with a needle hanging out of his arm?

No one was immune to potential tragedy, and there was no telling how anybody's life would turn out. Sometimes one poor decision was all it took.

No regrets, no regrets. Teddy was a gift he hadn't expected to receive.

Raffaele looked at Eamonn. "So you didn't really know for a long time."

"No, I moved away, lost contact with the people back home. Then later, I heard Jan had died and that you'd been taken into foster care before that. Obviously I was upset, because I'd loved her. But there was nothing else I could do. Eventually I met Mandy, we had the kids, life went on. It wasn't until years later, when I saw you on breakfast TV, that I realized you hadn't been the Spaniard's son after all."

The Spaniard. He was deliberately not calling him by his name. Raffaele appreciated the gesture. Nodding, he said, "Must have been quite a shock."

"It was. After that, I watched you, read up about you in the papers and online. I wanted to contact you, but all of a sudden you were famous, everybody's favorite, and I didn't want to look as if I was crawling out of the woodwork, jumping on the bandwagon like some people do." Eamonn paused and looked at him again. "Plus whenever you were interviewed about your past, you always seemed so laid-back about it. You had amazing foster parents, and you'd come through it all so well. I decided it was better not to get involved. For your sake," he emphasized. "Not mine."

"Does your wife know about me?"

"Of course she does. She's looking forward to meeting you. If you want to, of course."

"I'd like to." Raffaele nodded. "How about your children?"

"I called them last night. They're fine about it too."

Raffaele glanced down once more at the photo lying between them on the table, then up again. He smiled slightly. "Hello, Dad."

Eamonn's smile mirrored his own. "Hello, my boy. It's good to meet you properly at last."

Raffaele placed his hand on top of his father's and held it there. It should have felt strange, but it didn't.

Eamonn said, "Shall I tell you where I was when you sent me that text this morning? Parked in my car just across the road from your salon."

"Seriously?"

"I put the letter through the door fifteen minutes before you opened it. When I saw your reply, I nearly came bursting in. But that wouldn't have been fair to you." He gave Raffaele's fingers a squeeze. "I had to hold myself back, give you time to get used to the idea of meeting someone before you found out who I really was."

"You said in the letter that you had a photo, but you didn't put it in the envelope," said Raffaele. "I had no idea, obviously. But it did make me wonder if there was a reason why you'd want to save it until we met."

"Smart lad. Clever." Eamonn gave a nod of approval. "Like your mum."

Raffaele felt as if he'd been holding his breath for hours. "Tell me more about her," he said. "And then tell me all about you."

chapter 24

THE FOLLOWING EVENING TURNED OUT TO BE FULL OF SURPRISES. As Amber was working on the giant octopus, Raffaele appeared in her studio and said, "Come on. That's enough. We're going over to see Teddy."

"What for?"

"Tell you when we get there."

Neither of them was expecting the sight that greeted them when they made their way around the side of the house.

"When I called, Teddy said they'd be in the back garden," Raffaele explained. The next moment, he stopped dead. "Bloody hell, and this is why."

"Here they are! Come on over! Isn't this the best thing ever?" Calling to them across the lawn, Olga enthusiastically beckoned them over.

"Join us!" Teddy beamed.

"It's amazing," cried Peggy, sparkling wine splashing out of her glass as she waved with abandon. "I'm going to get one too!"

The hot tub was huge, rectangular, and bright turquoise, filled with bubbling water and three overexcited adults. Teddy, trim and tanned, was wearing knee-length shorts. Olga was bursting out of a sunflower-yellow bikini, and Peggy had abandoned her multicolored kaftan on the grass and jumped into the hot tub in her black bra and underpants.

"Have a drink!" Olga indicated the bucket stuffed with ice cubes and bottles. "Join us!"

Amber didn't dare glance at Raffaele; unnervingly, the group in the hot tub looked like a sixty-something couple in a TV sitcom who'd been joined by a racy younger neighbor. She said, "Thanks, but I don't have a swimsuit with me."

"I didn't either." Peggy gaily pinged her bra strap. "And I didn't let it stop me!"

Peggy never let anything stop her from doing anything.

"This is brilliant!" Teddy had never looked happier. "We ordered it two days ago, and the company installed it yesterday!"

"There were hot tubs on our cruise ship," Olga chimed in. "We loved sitting in them, chatting away with our friends. It's so sociable!"

"Honestly, I'm fine here." Keen to get down to the reason for their visit, Raffaele dragged a padded chair across the terrace toward them, then collected a second one when Amber said, "Me too."

"Raffaele has something he wants to tell us," Amber explained when they were settled with drinks, then saw that he was shaking his head slightly.

"It's OK. Maybe another time."

"Oh, don't say that! We're interested now!" Peggy exclaimed. "We all love a bit of gossip, don't we?"

When Peggy had moved down to Lanrock and she and Teddy had struck up a friendship, Amber and Lachlan had secretly wondered if it might develop into something more. But it hadn't happened; much as they enjoyed each other's company, that was as far as it went. And now it looked as if Peggy and Olga were getting along like a house on fire too.

"Is this about Vee?" said Teddy. "It's OK. We saw all that stuff online about the sandwiches. It'll blow over. Don't you worry."

Raffaele hesitated. "This isn't about Vee. It's something else."

"Good news or bad news?" Teddy began to look concerned.

"Surprising news. But good. It's quite…personal."

"Oh, and you weren't expecting me to be here." Peggy pulled a face. "I'm in the way. I'll leave!"

"It's OK. No need for you to go." Raffaele shook his head, evidently having made up his mind. He turned and smiled at Teddy and Amber. "I wanted to tell both of you together. Yesterday, I met my dad."

It took a couple of seconds for his words to sink in. Peggy said, "But Lachlan told me your father was dead."

"The man I was named after is dead. Turns out he wasn't my father after all." Smiling, Raffaele said, "And now the real one's gotten in touch."

"Oh my God! But why now, after all this time?" Olga's eyes were wide. "Is he after your money?"

....

The last time they'd spoken, Vee had hung up the phone. Now, at almost midnight on Tuesday evening, she was calling him again.

"I had another argument." She sounded blunt and annoyed.

Raffaele closed his eyes. "With Dawn Kerrigan?"

"No, with most of my staff. But mainly Marina. It wasn't even my fault. She called me a liability and said the salon was going to end up going down the drain because of me."

Marina was the assistant manager. She was usually supremely patient. "Is it true?"

Vee ignored the question. "She told me to take the rest of the week off to get my act together. She said I need to see a doctor."

"I think that's a good idea. You're under a lot of stress."

"What can a doctor do? Tell me to take some deep breaths and calm down? Big deal."

"Maybe they could prescribe something."

"Tranquilizers? No thanks. You know I won't take anything like that."

Raffaele did know. One of her aunties had gotten addicted to sleeping pills, and Vee had witnessed the agony of her trying to wean herself off them. Painkillers for headaches was as far as she went.

"Make an appointment," he said. "They might be able to help. What have you got to lose?"

"Not much. Most of it's already gone. Oh God, sometimes I just feel so…as if I want to *burst*."

"Look, you've got a few days off work. Just relax, get plenty of sleep, stop thinking about other people, and concentrate on yourself."

"I don't like myself." He heard the despair, the confusion in her voice. "I don't like what I'm turning into."

"You could try yoga. Olga does it every morning on the beach. She says it's fantastic for focusing the mind."

"So Olga's still around, is she? I thought she might have disappeared off into the sunset by now." Vee had heard all about Olga but not met her.

"She's still here. Someone else is here too." Stretched out across the sofa in his flat, Raffaele couldn't help himself; he had to tell her.

"Don't tell me. You've got a new girlfriend?"

"There's no new girlfriend."

"Who then?"

"My dad."

"What, Teddy?"

"I mean my biological father."

"*What?*"

By the time he'd finished relaying the whole story, Vee was in tears.

"Why are you crying?"

"I'm just so happy for you."

Sometimes, she could still be her old self. "Well, thanks. It's been pretty amazing."

"And I'm also mad at you," said Vee.

Raffaele's heart sank. "Why?"

"Because you didn't call and tell me before now. You weren't even going to mention it. This is massive news, and if I hadn't called you tonight, I wouldn't have known."

"I'm sorry." It mattered to her too, he realized now. Even if their relationship was over. "I did want to tell you. I just thought…you know."

"That I wouldn't care? Oh God. What am I, a monster?"

"I'll send you a copy of the photo he gave me."

Silence. He heard her chewing her lip and knew she was deep in thought. Finally he said, "Vee?"

"Yes?"

"What are you thinking?"

"I'm thinking I'm off work. I could catch the train down tomorrow, get away from all the crap going on up here, see Amber and Lachlan and Teddy again. I'd love to meet Eamonn…and Olga…"

"I'm not sure." He was torn. They were no longer together. Surely it would only confuse matters?

"I'll be good. It won't be awkward. And I won't yell at you, I promise.

You said I needed to relax," Vee begged. "Let me come down, please. Maybe a few days in Lanrock will do the trick."

He'd missed her, missed her like crazy. But they'd broken up for a reason.

"I won't try to crawl into your bed, if that's what you're worried about. I'll sleep on the sofa. Please, Raff. It'd be so great to see everyone again. And I want to meet your dad!"

....

Moose was in his element, flinging himself around like an-out-of-control helicopter. Launching himself into the air, he caught the purple Frisbee in his mouth.

"Good boy! Over here!" Benjie crouched down and clapped his hands.

"Moose, no, bring it to *meee*!" Sticking her fingers in her mouth, Jo gave an ear-splitting whistle.

Moose eyed each of them in turn, his tail wagging madly as he decided which way to go. Mind made up, he hurtled toward Benjie, skittering plumes of dry sand in his wake.

"Moose, you traitor!" Jo threw up her hands in despair. "How could you?"

"*Very* good boy." Benjie triumphantly rubbed Moose's ears as the dog dropped the Frisbee at his feet.

"I can't believe you won," Jo wailed.

"What can I say? He just loves me more. It's my magnetic personality." Benjie hurled the Frisbee back into the air, and Moose took off like a rocket once more, chasing it into the sea.

Jo joined him on the sand and nudged his foot with her own. "He really does like you. Moose doesn't take to just anyone, you know."

"I like him too." Moose was an eclectic mix of King Charles spaniel and some kind of terrier, with long floofy ears, a waggly tail, and an enduring passion for playing Frisbee on the beach. He belonged to Jo's grandmother, but Jo was always happy to take him for extra walks. In the last week, they'd fallen into the habit of bringing him down to the beach for the hour between Benjie finishing at the gallery and Jo starting work in the restaurant.

He'd discovered that being recognized and adored by a dog was one of the best feelings in the world.

The other discovery had been that it was an awful lot easier not to stammer when you were talking to a dog.

Because Moose didn't care either way; it didn't bother him one bit. So long as someone was paying him attention, he was happy; he would gaze longingly into your eyes, push his cold nose into the palm of your hand, then do a dip and tilt of his head to remind you to give his ears a rub.

Here he came again now, tearing back out of the water following a playful tussle with a golden Labrador, his beloved Frisbee in his mouth.

"Shower time. Brace yourself," said Jo as Moose dropped the Frisbee at her feet and gave himself an almighty shake. She checked her watch. "I need to get ready for work. See you tomorrow?"

"Great." Tomorrow was her evening off, and they were meeting up at seven. "Where are we g-going?"

"It's a surprise. You'll just have to wait and see." She grinned and leaned forward to clip Moose's lead back on. "But it'll be fun, I promise."

He knew it would be.

"Stay like that." Reaching for his phone, Benjie took a quick photo of Jo with her eyes bright, her auburn curls bouncing around her shoulders, and Moose next to her, dripping with seawater and with his pink tongue hanging out.

She pulled a face. "Did I blink? Do I look OK?"

"No idea," said Benjie, "but Moose looks great."

She laughed and gave him a playful shove. "Oh well, so long as *he* does, that's the important thing."

Benjie was already looking forward to tomorrow. One way or another, this was turning out to be the best summer of his life.

....

"Not being funny, mate," said the big man in the Union Jack shorts, "but do the punters actually buy this stuff?"

Benjie took a long inward breath. It had happened before and it would happen again, but it would never happen without him fantasizing about taking one of those sideways flying karate kicks at the person who'd said it, sending them sailing through the open door and out onto the sidewalk.

"S-sometimes they do, yes."

"Blimey, takes all sorts. More money than sense, some people. What's this one meant to be, then?" The man pointed to the square canvas on the wall in front of him, carefully spotlit for maximum impact.

What would Jo say?

"It's indicative of the drudgery of day-to-day life, scrolling on into the oncoming weeks when all you can see ahead is darkness and d-disappointment." Benjie gestured expertly with his hand. "And then you notice the lines over there, top right, with the white cloud in the distance? That's the sensation of forgetting the endless misery and deciding to leave it behind you while you pack your cases and set off on holiday... See that splash of b-blue? That's the first glimpse of ocean...and those black rectangles are your worries, floating away..."

The man was staring intently at the canvas. He turned to look at Benjie, open-mouthed. "Like...heading into the light?"

"Exactly like that."

"Whoa, that's amazing. And all those dots of white over there, on top of the black and gray..."

"Yes, well done." Benjie gave him an encouraging nod. "Go on."

"It's, it's like they're dancing in the dark!"

"Spot-on! Signifying hope for the future, better times ahead. Once you take it all in and completely understand it, you feel...?"

"Like, uplifted?"

"You've got it. Brilliant."

"Fuck me," said the man, still entranced by the canvas in front of him.

Well, I'd rather not.

Aloud, Benjie said, "It's an incredible feeling, isn't it? When you genuinely connect with a painting like that?"

The man nodded, his face reddening. "It's quite emotional."

"It's a powerful piece of art."

"I could carry on looking at this forever."

"Well, we close at five. But you're welcome to stay until then."

"I'm really feeling it." The man slapped his hand to his chest. "In here."

OK, please don't have some kind of coronary event. Benjie said, "Take as long as you like. I'll leave you to it."

Minutes later, the man approached his desk. "I want to buy it. It's, like, outside my price range though. Could I pay in instalments?"

Benjie said, "The artist takes her work very seriously."

"Oh, sorry. I didn't mean to—"

"But when other people genuinely connect with her paintings, that makes her happy. How about if we halve the price *and* remove the gallery's commission?" Benjie scribbled the numbers on the sheet of paper in front of him, crossed them out, then showed the man the final, much-reduced figure.

"Really? That's amazing." The man looked as if he might burst into tears. His face reddening once more, he clasped Benjie's hand across the desk and shook it. "Mate, you've got yourself a deal."

"You won't regret it," said Benjie.

You see? Sometimes the magical connection was made. It was just a shame it couldn't happen more often than it did.

chapter 25

I've got a confession to make.

Benjie's stomach tightened. Confessions were never a good thing. He typed back, What is it?

I'm jealous of Jo.

Why? You don't need to be.

He told himself he wasn't lying. He might be attracted to Jo, but she was showing no sign of returning his feelings. They were friends, that was all. She'd said as much from the outset, and that was fine. It was a lot better than nothing.

I saw a photo of her. She's really pretty.

What? How? Had he accidentally sent Dani one of the ones he'd taken on the beach? He typed, Where have you seen a photo?

I looked up McCarthy's restaurant on Tripadvisor. Someone posted a review and a photo of himself in the restaurant with the best waitress in Cornwall.

Benjie opened another tab on his laptop, found the page, and saw the review, posted by his mum's friend, Dom Burton. There he was sitting at the table by the window, showing off the food in front of him while Jo stood to his left, clearly having been lured over. At a guess, seeing as it was a bit lopsided, Peggy had been the one who'd taken the photo.

Dom's accompanying review declared: *Exquisite food. If I lived in Lanrock, I'd never eat anywhere else—Lachlan McCarthy is a genius. And my thanks to Jo, the best waitress in Cornwall. How many stars out of five would I give this meal? At least fifty.*

That was it: short, sweet, and typically expansive. In the photo, Jo's curly hair was tied back, and she was wearing no makeup, but her smile was genuine, and she looked like someone you'd want to get to know.

Sorry, Dani typed. I didn't know there was going to be a photo of her. I just wanted to see where she worked, and there she was.

It's OK.

And you're meeting up with her again tonight. Where are you going?

No idea. It's a surprise.

Benjie had begun to wonder if it would be easier not to mention his evenings out with Jo, but Dani would only want to know where he was anyway, if he wasn't chatting online with her.

Well, have fun. But not too much! Will you message me when you get in?

Of course I will.

Love you. Xxx

Love you too. Xxxx

Love you more. Xxxxx

....

"I bought you something," Benjie told Jo when he'd finished relating the story of this afternoon's encounter in the gallery with the man in the Union Jack shorts.

"What d'you mean?" She looked confused, then slightly alarmed when he pulled the small gift-wrapped box out of his jacket pocket.

"Don't panic. Nothing m-major. Just something I thought you'd like."

Her expression was wary. "Why?"

"As a thank you for helping me sell the painting."

Jo said, "I wasn't there."

"I know, but I channeled you. Remember how you made up a story last week about one of Mum's canvases, the blue and gray one with the splashes of green? And you said you could see caves in a forest? Well, that's what I did. I pretended I was you and just went for it. And I didn't even stammer. It was like you said—if you sound as if you know what you're talking about, people will listen and believe you."

"Maybe I gave you the idea, but you're the one who did it. I wish I could have been there to see you. And confidence builds confidence," Jo reminded him, her smile causing his heart to do a flip.

"Anyway, open it." He passed her the box and watched as she pulled off the wrapping paper, then opened the lid.

"Benjie, you can't give me these."

"I can. I think I just did."

They'd seen the earrings last week, in the window of a jeweler whose tiny shop was next door to Amber's studio on Leopard Lane. As they'd been passing, Jo had spotted them and exclaimed, "Oh, look at those! I love moonstones…they're so glowy!"

They'd stopped to admire the earrings, and he'd said, "Are you going to buy them?"

She'd hesitated, then said firmly, "No, saving my pennies for the big trip."

Maybe she hadn't given them another thought since then, but Benjie had. He'd always enjoyed picking up clues and remembering what people liked. The earrings hadn't cost pennies; the amount of work the jeweler had put into creating them was reflected in the price, but the result was both simple and effective.

"I can't accept them, Benjie."

"You have to. They don't let you return earrings for pierced ears." He gave her a look, because she was clearly still mortified. "Hey, you said you liked them. I wanted to buy them for you. You can take them with you on your gap year. They'll look great on you. And you can't give them back to me," he concluded with a shrug. "They wouldn't suit me."

Jo hesitated, looking at him with an expression he couldn't interpret. Finally she said, "Well, if you're sure."

"Of course I'm sure. That's why I b-bought them."

She ran her fingers over the moonstones. "Thank you, Benjie. I love them."

"Thank you for…being here." That came out sounding wrong, but oh well. Changing the subject, he said, "So come on then. Where are we g-going tonight? What's the surprise?"

"OK, I'm warning you now, you might not like the sound of this. But once it's over, I promise you'll feel so proud of yourself."

Benjie pulled a face. "My mum used to say that when she took me to the d-dentist."

Oh God. When he saw the sign forty minutes later, his heart plummeted.

"Remember what I said." Jo slipped her arm through his, her tone encouraging.

He dug his heels in. "I'm not doing that."

"Have you ever tried it before?"

"Are you mad? *No*."

"I'm not asking you to swim with sharks. It's only karaoke."

"I'd rather swim with sharks."

"Well, I'm going to do it, and I can't sing to save my life."

"Fine, you do it. I'll watch."

She gestured around them, at the hundreds of trailers and chalets, the children racing around on the grass outside the social club where the evening entertainment was held. "It's a holiday park where no one knows you, hardly the London Palladium."

"Still no."

She grinned. "Or we could come back tomorrow."

The sign outside the entrance proudly announced that tomorrow evening was the competition to crown this week's Mr. Lanrock, alongside a photo of last week's winner, a beaming, bronzed bodybuilder type with fluorescent white teeth and a tattoo of a naked Kardashian on his chest.

"Maybe not," said Benjie.

"Good, because I have to work tomorrow night. Come on. Let's get a drink."

Inside, the club was crowded, but the atmosphere was relaxed and casual. There were children of all ages on the dance floor in front of the stage, paying rapt attention to the middle-aged woman currently warbling her way through Adele's "Make You Feel My Love." Neither the woman nor her audience seemed to mind that her voice was reedy and off-key. When the song ended, she bowed extravagantly, and people cheered and applauded as if they'd just been serenaded by Adele herself.

Benjie drank a beer quite fast and listened to the next guy on the stage bellow his way through an Elvis number. Out of the corner of his mouth, he said, "He's not as bad as the woman."

"His voice isn't as good as yours," said Jo.

"I can't sing."

"Of course you can. We sang in the car on the way here, didn't we?"

That was when he hadn't been aware of her fiendish plan for this evening. Except it wouldn't be a successful fiendish plan, because he wasn't going to do what she wanted him to do.

Jo spoke to the DJ in charge of the karaoke machine and added her name to the list. Ten minutes later, she was called up onto the stage and threw herself into a performance of "Live and Let Die." Her voice wasn't the best, but she gave it all she had, and everyone clapped madly in appreciation.

"They loved you," Benjie told her when she rejoined him afterward.

Her eyes were bright. "I was so scared. But now I feel *amazing*."

"You weren't scared."

"Oh, I was! And now I've done it, that's something else I can tick off my bucket list."

He looked at her, pink-cheeked with exhilaration. "I still can't get up there."

"You could if you wanted to. You just don't want to."

She was wearing the moonstone earrings he'd given her. She looked beautiful. With a surge of adrenaline, Benjie realized how much he liked her, how much he owed her, and how wonderful it would feel to impress her.

If he did it, she would cheer for him the way she was now cheering for the trio of girls screeching along out of time to "You're the One That I Want" from *Grease*.

He could if he wanted to.

He imagined Dani's reaction later tonight if he was able to go home and tell her he'd sung on stage in front of hundreds of strangers.

He imagined Jo shrieking with delight, throwing her arms around him, and exclaiming, "Oh my God, you were brilliant. I can't believe you actually did it!"

How would that feel?

Would it make her like him more?

Would she kiss him?

How would *that* feel?

Behind him, he heard a middle-aged woman say to the man next to her, "Gonna put your name down, then?"

"No way. Wouldn't catch me going up there."

"God's sake, Jerry." The woman's tone was dismissive. "You're pathetic."

The more nervous he looked, Benjie knew, the worse it would be. This was how boys at school knew who to pick on. So he did some more channeling and settled on the older guy who'd sung the Elvis track while appearing to love every second in the spotlight.

His heart raced, his mouth was dry, and he wished he'd had time to down a couple more beers, but never mind that now. The oh-so-familiar opening bars of Bon Jovi's "Livin' on a Prayer" filled the vast room, and he concentrated on following the prompts on the screen in front of him…three, two, one…

"You did it!" Jo yelled, clutching his arms and jumping up and down. "That was amazing! *Well done!*"

In a daze, Benjie wondered if she was about to kiss him. It didn't happen, but for a swooping slow-motion moment, he'd thought it might. The most terrifying experience of his life was behind him, the challenge had been completed, and adrenaline was making his whole body zing. Plus…

"I didn't stammer." It somehow didn't happen when he sang. Then again, he'd never sung in front of other people before tonight.

"Everyone loved it. They were all clapping and joining in, singing along with you!" Still holding his arms, Jo shook her head. "I'm so proud I could burst. How do you feel?"

"Happy. Times a hundred."

She pulled him to her and gave him a huge hug. "I'm so glad you don't hate me."

Benjie breathed in the clean apple scent of her shampoo, felt her soft curls brush against his cheek. She'd burst into his life like a genie out of a bottle, and he couldn't begin to explain how glad he was that it had happened. "Of course I don't hate you."

Their faces were close; maybe now the kiss was going to happen after all. What if he was waiting for her to make that first move, while she was holding back, waiting for him to be the one to take the lead?

"And now, next onto the stage we have Eddie from Swindon, and he's going to be singing 'New York, New York'!"

"Woo-hoo!" Jo released her grip on Benjie and began to applaud as Eddie from Swindon took over the microphone and waved to his grandchildren on the dance floor. "I love this one!"

"Did you take any photos of me?"

"Are you kidding? I took loads. And some video too."

Up on the stage, Eddie from Swindon had started spreading the news. Benjie said, "Can you send it to me?" He wanted to show his online shyness group tonight; they'd be astounded when they saw what he'd achieved.

He especially couldn't wait to show Dani.

....

Benjie was still buzzing with adrenaline when he arrived home. Following the sound of music blaring out, he found Peggy in her art room, bopping along to the *Hamilton* soundtrack while throwing glossy maroon paint onto a canvas.

"Darling! Which do you prefer?" She pointed to the canvas on the easel in front of her, then to a turquoise one propped against the wall. "Which one do you think is *better*?"

"Um…I like both."

"Choose!"

"OK, the one against the wall."

"Ah, shame. The pre-drinking one." She took a slurp of red wine from the goblet in her hand. "I wanted to see if it'd loosen me up, free the inhibitions, allow my talent full rein!"

"I think if you drink every time you paint, your liver might explode by Christmas." Listen to that, not a stammer in sight.

"True. I just feel so inspired, though, after you sold that painting this afternoon. I might have to carry on working all night!" Loading a clean brush with emerald-green paint, Peggy said, "D'you think he might want to buy this one too?"

"I don't know. Mum, guess what I did tonight?" Benjie couldn't help himself; he took out his phone and pressed play on the video.

"Who's that? He looks a bit like you! Oh…" Peggy's mouth dropped open, and she grabbed the phone from him, spattering green paint. "*Is it you?*"

He turned down the volume on *Hamilton* and observed his mother's face as she gazed raptly at the screen.

"Don't cry," he said when a tear rolled down her cheek. "It's not that b-bad."

She was still watching, enthralled. "Oh my baby, *look* at you! What happened?"

"Everyone clapped and cheered. It felt…fantastic."

"Was this Jo's idea?"

He nodded. "I'd never have done it if it wasn't for her."

"She's doing you the world of good. I'm so glad you're friends."

"Me too." The memory flashed into his mind of wanting to kiss Jo, of thinking for an exhilarating moment that she'd wanted to kiss him too. "We have a great time together."

"I'm so glad. She's a lovely girl… Whoops, sorry!" A dollop of paint had flown off the end of Peggy's paintbrush and landed on the front of his shirt. "Don't worry. If it doesn't wash out, I'll buy you another one. Fancy some wine?"

Having made his excuses and escaped upstairs to his apartment, Benjie opened his laptop and saw that Dani was already online, waiting for him.

She typed, Did you have a nice time?

He'd never heard her speak, but in his head, he could clearly imagine her saying the words aloud.

It was great. I've got something to show you. He posted the video and waited for it to upload. She hadn't heard him speak either, for obvious reasons, but this was singing, which was different. It was safe. And she would be so impressed.

The video had finished uploading. He knew Dani was watching it now. At one point while she'd been recording the performance, Jo had briefly turned the camera onto herself in order to shake her head in amazement and mouth, *Wow.*

When he knew it was finished, Benjie wrote, Well?

The reply popped up seconds later. I'm crying. You're amazing. So proud.

He typed back, I still can't believe I did it. Never thought I could, not in a million years.

People are always telling us we can do anything we want to do. And now you have. All thanks to your friend Jo.

Benjie paused. He knew he'd developed feelings for Jo. But he had this incredible connection with Dani too. He didn't want to hurt her. Maybe he should stop talking about Jo, pretend they were no longer going out and having adventures.

He typed, You don't have to worry. I'm still here for you.

Dani replied, It's just I love you so much.

He looked at the last photo she'd sent him, of herself smiling and holding up the plate of bacon sandwiches she'd just made after he'd told her they were his favorite late-night snack. She'd written jokingly, When we're married, we'll have bacon sandwiches together every night!

Benjie was torn. Pretending they were a couple was all very well, but it was never going to happen, was it?

He couldn't imagine someone as gorgeous as Dani being interested in him in real life.

....

The last client of the day was someone Raffaele hadn't seen for fifteen years.

It wasn't a surprise; he'd seen the name on the list of appointments and marveled at the chutzpah of his old enemy.

Dale Jenkins swaggered across the salon as if they'd been friends forever. "All right, mate? How're ya doing? See?" He turned to address the skinny woman who'd followed him in. "Told you I knew him! We were at school together, me and Raff. Used to have a right laugh. This is my girlfriend, Tonya," he went on. "She's, like, a big fan of yours so I said I'd introduce you."

Tonya was thin and plainly dressed, with her hair styled in a neat bob. Dale had put on several pounds in weight and was doughy-faced, with grubby fingernails and too-tight jeans.

"Hi, good to meet you too." Raffaele shook Tonya's hand, because it wasn't her fault she was involved with an idiot. Once Dale was seated in the chair and ready for his haircut, he went on, "I wouldn't say we were friends, though. You were the school bully, remember? You and your little gang made my life a misery for a few weeks."

"What? That was just banter, mate. Havin' a laugh, like. I wasn't a bully."

"Weren't you? Are you sure? Every day, you mocked me because my parents were dead," Raffaele reminded him. "You told everyone it was my fault they hadn't wanted me." He reached for his comb and scissors, aware that everyone else in the salon had fallen silent.

"But I… No, it wasn't like that," Dale blustered. "I didn't *mean* it…"

"You broke my nose. That wasn't an accident." Taking a sharp snip out of Dale's hair, Raffaele met his terrified gaze in the mirror. "You must remember that. There was blood everywhere."

"Look, mate, it was just a bit of fun—"

"For you, maybe. No, don't move. Keep your head still. We don't want any more bloodshed, do we?" And in the ensuing minutes of silence, Raffaele proceeded to give Dale Jenkins the best haircut he'd ever had in his life.

When a chastened Dale had left the shop with Tonya in tow and his throat intact, Anna the stylist said, "You didn't even charge him! What's all that about?"

"I embarrassed him in front of his girlfriend. That was enough." Checking his watch and realizing he needed to get to the train station, Raffaele added, "Besides, getting my nose broken was the reason I found my best friend. So in a way, it was worth it."

"If it was me," Anna's client said robustly, "I'd have booted him out of the salon."

"Ah well." Raffaele reached behind the till for his keys. "He caught me in a good mood. It was his lucky day."

....

He couldn't help the way he felt; when Raffaele saw her step off the train, his stomach flipped just as it had all those years ago when they'd first started seeing each other.

Vee's closely cropped hair was still bleached white, but there was a newly added tint of pink. She was wearing a strappy lilac vest, khaki shorts, and purple espadrilles, and her long brown limbs gleamed in the sunlight. Having not seen her for a few weeks, he experienced a jolt of attraction that it was no longer appropriate to feel. Being apart from her was easier than this; he could control his emotions better when she was a couple of hundred miles away.

"Raff." She came toward him, her long silver earrings swinging as she dragged her overnight case along the dusty platform. "Looking good."

"You too." The vintage choker around her neck had been his birthday present to her; he'd bought it in the vast flea market at Clignancourt while they'd been on holiday in Paris last year, not long before everything had started to go horribly wrong.

Vee curled her free hand around his neck and gave him a brief kiss on the cheek. "You smell nice."

Raffaele took the wheelie case from her. Had he deliberately chosen the bottle of Aventus she'd given him last Christmas?

As they threaded their way along the narrow streets busy with holidaymakers, Vee said, "Are you glad you moved back down here?"

He nodded. "I am. It's different. Good to be home."

"With the family. And now you have more family. Does it feel amazing?"

"It does. Weird but great. He looks like me. We couldn't stop staring at each other."

"And this is why you never looked Mediterranean. You're not half Spanish after all." Her eyes danced. "Now we know why you hate olives."

She was in a good mood. Why couldn't it always be like this? Raffaele said, "I can't wait for you to meet him."

"Me neither. Looking forward to seeing Teddy again too. And Amber and Lachlan." She hesitated, searched his face. "Have you told them terrible things about me? Does everyone hate me now?"

"I haven't told them terrible things. Nobody hates you."

Vee grimaced. "Tell that to the staff at the salon. Most of them seem to." As they came to the pharmacy on Long Street, she said, "Let me just pop in here. There's a couple of things I want to pick up."

When she reemerged minutes later, Raffaele said, "What was it you needed?"

"Oh, don't start." Vee rolled her eyes and firmly zipped up her shoulder bag. "It's not actually any of your business."

This was what she'd been like for months: up and down for no reason he could fathom. Despite her vehement denials, he was starting to wonder if there was some kind of drugs issue after all.

chapter 26

By ten in the evening, the little party was still going strong out in the garden. Eamonn and his wife, Mandy, had driven over from Charlestown, reaching Teddy's house at eight. Raffaele had introduced them to Teddy and Olga, Amber, and Vee. Lachlan was stuck at work but would be leaving the restaurant early and hopefully here soon.

As far as Raffaele was concerned—and to his relief—the evening couldn't have gone better. Everyone had exclaimed over the similarities between himself and Eamonn. Photos were taken and many stories told. He'd worried that Vee might be tetchy and difficult, but she hadn't been at all, which was great, obviously, but just made him wish she could be like this all the time. She had hugged Amber, exclaiming how much she'd missed her. She'd also taken an instant liking to Olga, resplendent in a peacock-blue satin jumpsuit and dramatic false lashes.

And now here she was, giving an impromptu speech, thanking Eamonn for being brave enough to make contact with the son he'd never known.

"None of us with parents can understand how it feels to grow up without them," Vee continued, "but most of us here have known Raff long enough to understand how much this means to him. I'm just so happy for him. And Eamonn's a lovely person…well, we knew he'd be lovely…" She hesitated, licked her lips, then fiddled with the collar of her gray silk shirt, distracted and evidently losing track of what she'd been about to say next.

"I know, I have this effect on women." Lachlan stepped out of the shadows and joined them, prompting laughter. "Sorry I'm late. I got here as soon as I could." He gestured to Vee. "Sorry, carry on. Didn't mean to interrupt."

She blinked and shook her head. "It's fine. I'm done. How are you?"

Raffaele watched as Lachlan wrapped his arms around her. "I'm OK. Good to see you again."

"You too." Vee returned the hug. "Still cooking your fancy-pants food?"

"I am. Still eating Pot Noodles with chopped-up frankfurters and jerk sauce?"

"All the time."

"You're disgusting."

"You should try putting it on your specials board. Give those customers of yours a real treat."

Lachlan laughed. "Right, that's enough insults. You aren't the only one I'm here to see." He turned to survey Eamonn, who'd been drawn into a conversation with Teddy and Olga. "He looks even more like you in real life than he did in that photo you sent me."

"I know." Raffaele was glowing with pride. "Come on. Let me introduce you."

Shortly after eleven, Eamonn and his wife left to drive back to Charlestown. Everyone had liked them both and enjoyed meeting them. While Vee and Amber were talking to Teddy and Olga, Raffaele found himself being taken to one side by Lachlan.

"So what's going on with you and Vee?" Lachlan kept his voice low.

What indeed? Raffaele shook his head. "Nothing's going on."

"Not so far. But it's looking like it could happen. She seems keen."

"Sometimes she's like this. The next minute, it goes the other way."

"Maybe she's having second thoughts. You moved down here, and now she realizes how much she's missed you. Maybe she regrets getting stroppy and losing her temper and from now on is going to make a real effort to be nice."

"I don't know…"

"If she wants you back and promises to change, would you be up for that?"

Belatedly, Raffaele figured out what Lachlan was driving at, why he was so interested. He shrugged. "I can't say. It's just…complicated, you know?"

"How are you feeling about Amber now?"

And *bingo*, there it was. He didn't enjoy not being honest with Lachlan, but it was for all their sakes that he needed to keep the story going.

"That hasn't changed. I still want her. This is why it's so confusing." He frowned. "I know you said I shouldn't tell Amber how I feel about her, but maybe I should say something—"

"No, I don't think you should. Not yet at least." Lachlan shook his head. "It wouldn't be right. I told you, it's too soon. You need to wait until you're properly over Vee. If that even happens. Because I don't think you *are* over Vee."

"OK." That was something he still wasn't sure about either. "You're probably right."

"Trust me, I am," said Lachlan.

....

Raffaele had made up a bed for Vee on the sofa. Twenty minutes after retiring to his own room, there was a tap at his door.

Oh God, the temptation. But no, it wouldn't be a good idea. He didn't reply.

Then the door creaked open, and through almost closed eyelids, he saw her dark outline enter the bedroom. Remaining absolutely still, he closed his eyes and felt the duvet lift as she slipped beneath it.

She was behind him. A minute or so later, she rested her hand on his waist. "You're awake," she murmured, her breath warm on the back of his neck. "I know you are."

He stayed silent.

"Raff, I can always tell when you're pretending to be asleep."

He smiled slightly. "I'm not pretending. I am asleep."

"I've missed you. So much." She moved closer, her warm body pressing against his.

He'd missed her too; the aching loss had been unbearable. But they'd broken up for a reason. He couldn't sleep with her now, not on her first night down here. They needed to see how they got along together first.

"We mustn't," he said quietly. "It wouldn't be right."

"Are you kidding me?"

"Not kidding."

"You want me to get out of your bed and leave you in peace?"

"Yes."

Silence. Then she hissed, "You absolute loser. You should thank your lucky stars I offered."

"Vee, don't." *Oh, here we go. This is familiar.*

"Don't you tell me what to do." Her voice rose. "Nobody tells me what to do, least of all you." The switch had been flipped; she was out of the bed in a flash, yanking the duvet to the floor and stalking out of the room. The door slammed shut behind her, and he heard something hit a wall and shatter—a mug, from the sound of it.

"I hate you, I hate you. I'm so glad we broke up," Vee bellowed.

"Go to bed and get some sleep. You're supposed to be destressing."

Furiously, she yelled, "How can anyone destress when they have to cope with someone like you?"

....

"Oh, hello." Amber looked up in surprise. "I thought you were in Italy."

"That was yesterday. Now I'm back. Can't stay away." There was mischief in Dom's blue eyes. "Had to come and see my favorite stained-glass artist. By the way, are you free this evening?"

She blinked. "I am. Why?"

"I've booked a table at McCarthy's. Thought you might like to join me."

"I still don't understand. What for?" Belatedly, she realized he was laughing at her.

"It's called having dinner together. Enjoying each other's company. Maybe a bit of flirtation. Play your cards right, and there could even be some holding hands under the table."

Amber had been expecting it to be something business-related. She raised her eyebrows in confusion. "Do you mean we'd be going on an actual date?"

"I do." Dom grinned at her look of surprise. "Did you not realize I fancy you?"

"From what Peggy says, you fancy pretty much everyone."

"No law against it, is there? I enjoy good female company." He thought for a moment, then said, "Including Peggy's, but I don't fancy her. Can I see how things are going with my octopus?"

Amber took him over to the table where she'd been soldering together some of the sections that made up the tentacles.

Dom admired what she'd done so far. "You're very talented."

"I know." She ran a hand lovingly over the first completed section; it had been wonderful to work on something so over the top.

"Could you make a giant dragonfly for the St. Ives hotel?"

"You tell me what you want and I'll do it."

"Steady on." He gave her a playful look. "In that case, I want to take you to dinner tonight."

Should she? He was an inveterate ladies' man. But she didn't have to take him seriously, did she?

"Go on, say yes. It'll be fun."

It would be fun. And didn't she deserve some? Plus it would take her mind off Lachlan, which could only be a good thing.

"I'd love to," said Amber.

Dom mimed huge relief. "Thank God for that. After getting rejected by Olga, my ego couldn't cope with being turned down again."

....

Lachlan was plating up at top speed in the kitchen when he glanced through the whitewashed stone archway into the restaurant and saw a splash of turquoise that reminded him of Amber's favorite dress. A split second later, he realized it *was* Amber's dress, with Amber inside it. Then he saw who she was with, heard her laugh at something Dom Burton had just said, and felt a jolt of jealousy, because they were being seated at a table for two.

"Are those for table four?" Jo was waiting at the pass to collect the plates he'd been working on.

"Sorry, yes." He carried them over to her. "All done."

"You've forgotten the toasted hazelnuts."

Shit, concentrate. He remedied the omission and gave an apologetic nod. "Thanks."

But for the next two hours, he couldn't help glancing across at them, hearing their bursts of laughter over the hubbub of the rest of the room. Amber had her blond hair fastened up with silver combs and was looking stunning, her face lit up in the reflected glow from the candles on the table. Dom, meanwhile, was relaxed and expansive, clearly enjoying her company.

Lachlan certainly wasn't enjoying having to watch them together. Dom was a player, a ladies' man…and yes, it took one to know one, which just made it all the more infuriating. And Amber already knew what he was like, so why on earth was she having dinner with him? Not to mention clearly having such a great time?

They'd started with Perrier-Jouët champagne. Then Dom had ordered a bottle of Chablis Premier Cru Vaillons. Earlier, he'd fed Amber one of his scallops from his own fork. Now the meal was almost over, and he was still doing it, persuading her to try a spoonful of his raspberry and cassis sorbet. As Lachlan watched, he saw the wolfish grin and the faux-accidental brush of his hand against Amber's wrist. Dom was moving in for the kill, supremely confident as to how this evening would end, because when you were a brash, successful businessman with a powerful effect on the opposite sex, it was how all dates ended.

Please let Amber have more sense than to fall for his little game.

Because it *was* a game. Lachlan knew that better than anyone. It was one he himself had played for years.

"You OK?" Paolo the sous chef was looking concerned.

"Me? I'm great." His jaw tense, Lachlan added, "Never better."

By eleven, the restaurant was finally empty. Jo said, "Well, Peggy's friend Dom Burton is my all-time favorite customer."

"No accounting for taste," Lachlan murmured under his breath. Well, nearly under it.

"Oh, come on. He's lovely! And he thinks you're brilliant."

"I am brilliant."

"He's funny," Jo protested, "and so charming."

And so full of himself, thought Lachlan. He was being unfair, he knew that; up until this evening, he'd really liked Dom.

"He's one of the best tippers we've ever had. Did you see how much he left us tonight?"

"Come on. Let's get this place cleared up. I want to be out of here."

Minutes later, he heard Jo whisper to Paolo, "I don't know what's up with him. He's not usually this grumpy. I reckon it's because he and Polly have broken up."

If only it were something as completely irrelevant as that.

Forty minutes later, Lachlan watched the opening titles of *Cooking for the Enemy* from his bed. Having seen the trailer, he and Amber had been looking forward to this week's episode, in which a woman was cooking for her ex-husband's mistress.

He picked up his phone and counted to ten in order to slow down his breathing. This was crazy; it was like being sixteen years old again, plucking up the courage to ask out the prettiest girl in school. Except he'd never needed to pluck up the courage back then, because the possibility of rejection had never been an issue.

He counted to ten a second time, then called Amber's number. She should definitely be home by now.

Her phone rang out. She didn't answer. After six rings, he listened to her voice telling him she couldn't get to the phone right now.

Oh, and why is that? Are you too busy having sex with a lecherous man who'll get what he wants then not even bother to see you again?

Or worse still, will *want to see you again?*

Lachlan didn't leave a message. He hung up, then switched off the TV. He wished he could as easily switch off the unwanted thoughts spiraling through his brain.

Feeling like this was no fun at all.

....

The Rupert Hotel was a stylish five-star on the clifftop overlooking Lanrock's West Beach. By midnight, Amber and Dom were the only ones left in the bar, and she'd just stifled a yawn for the second time.

"You're gorgeous." Dom clinked his glass against hers. "Even when you're doing your best not to yawn."

"It's your fault I'm tired. All those extra hours I've been putting in on that octopus."

"I'm entirely to blame. And now I'm kicking myself." He put out a hand as Amber reached for her bag and began to lever herself up from the velvet zebra-print sofa. "You don't have to leave."

"I do. It's late."

"I have an incredible room just upstairs. I'd love you to stay."

Amber looked at him. They'd had a brilliant evening. Dom was great company. If he wanted to see her again, she'd say yes. But she also knew that if she'd really wanted to sleep with him tonight, she wouldn't be having to fight the urge to yawn like a hippo.

Her body was saving her from possibly making a big mistake, and she was grateful to it.

"I'm going. Thanks for a lovely evening."

He gave in with good grace. "I'll walk you home."

"You don't need to, honestly. I'll be fine."

"Hey." He rose to his feet and took her hand. "I'm not doing that. Come on. Let's go."

Leaving the hotel, they made their way along Angel Street, which bordered the west side of the river that divided Lanrock into two halves. A cool breeze had sprung up, and when Amber shivered in her strappy turquoise dress, Dom put his arm around her shoulders as they headed for the bridge. It felt nice, and she found herself leaning into him. He might be a player, but he was an entertaining one, full of fun and disarmingly honest.

"…and after Carla, there was Paulette. She was a firecracker." He shook his head.

"What went wrong between you and Paulette?" She was being given a crash course in his long list of past relationships.

"She had a schnauzer called Peeboy who was completely un-housetrained and peed everywhere. I mean, I love dogs, but it was a nightmare. When he peed in the car and all over my phone on the same day, that was enough. They both had to go. Does that make me a terrible person?"

"You're not terrible."

Dom dropped a playful kiss on her temple. "Thank you. I'm not terrible in bed either. In case you were wondering."

Amber laughed and wondered if she should kiss him properly when he dropped her at her cottage. She wasn't yearning to, not like how she secretly imagined it would feel to kiss Lachlan in that way. But maybe she should give it a go.

"You shouldn't laugh," he murmured into her hair. "I'm very shy. No confidence at all." But he was smiling as they resumed their walk. "I say, we're being put to shame here. Look at that."

"What?"

Dom pointed to the centuries-old stone bridge that crossed the river up ahead. "Talk about romantic. It's like being in Venice."

The water glittered beneath the arched bridge, reflecting the street-lights above it. In the very center, Amber saw the outline of two people kissing, their arms wrapped around each other.

For a moment, she was tempted to capture the scene in a photo, then show it to the couple and offer to send it to them as a happy reminder of their holiday. Then she remembered that in all the excitement of getting ready tonight, she'd forgotten to charge her phone.

As they drew nearer, the couple continued to kiss, in between break-ing off to laugh and talk to each other. It wasn't until they'd almost reached the bridge that Dom said, "Oh my God, look who it is. I almost didn't recognize her with her clothes on."

Amber peered through the gloom, then did a double take. Blond hair tumbling down her back, pink-and-white-flowered trouser suit, a pair of familiar white platform shoes…

"I prefer the gold bikini," said Dom.

There was no other way to get home; the bridge led to the other side of Lanrock. Amber heard Teddy's laughter. Would they be embarrassed when they realized she'd seen them kissing? She murmured, "Maybe they'll be too busy to notice us."

But at the sound of their footsteps, Olga turned. "Oh, hello! Look, darling, it's Amber!"

"Hi." Amber gave a little wave as she and Dom reached them. "It's late…just on my way home."

"You look so beautiful," Olga exclaimed. "I love your dress! Teddy and I have been out to dinner with friends of his from the golf club. Quite boring really. They kept talking on and on about golf. But we were just having a romantic moment here on the bridge, under the stars and the moonlight!"

When you saw the person you thought of as a father figure doing this kind of thing in public, it was slightly weird. Amber said hastily, "Well, we should go—"

"And how about you?" Olga interjected cheerfully. "Have you had a good evening?"

"Wonderful," said Dom. "We had dinner at Lachlan's."

"Oh, very nice," said Teddy with pride. "He really is a tremendous chef."

Amber smiled at Teddy, then at Olga. "We're off then. Night!"

....

Amber was working in her studio the next morning when Olga came to see her.

"Hello, darling! How funny to run into you last night." She gave Amber a heavily scented kiss on each cheek. "Can I ask about the man you were with? Is he your new boyfriend?"

Amber put down the slice of magenta glass she'd been filing into shape. "No, it was a first date. He's commissioned me to make a chandelier."

"So it's not serious?"

"Not serious at all. Why?"

Olga looked relieved. "Well, that's good news. But I needed to come and check with you, to make sure. He seems like a charming man. And he is very rich, am I right?"

"I think so. He owns a few hotels, according to him." Feeling like a rookie double agent, Amber wiped her prickling palms on her jeans. "Do you know him then?"

"No, but last week, he talked to me on the beach. He was watching me doing my yoga session, then approached me afterward. I mean, he was handsome and seemed very nice, and I'm always happy to speak to anyone I meet, but he was a bit forward. Chatted me up, then invited me to have lunch with him that afternoon! And made a big point of showing me his expensive sports car. A red Porsche, and so proud of it. Anyway, I just wanted to warn you that he's the kind of man who would flirt with a stranger on the beach and ask her out."

"OK. Well, thanks for letting me know." Oh God, what would Olga say if she ever found out the beach meeting had been a setup?

"I mean, he could still be nice. I'm sure he is! But I just thought I should let you know."

Yet more guilt. "What did you say when he asked you out to lunch?"

"I told him no thank you, of course! Then he gave me his business card and said to call him if I changed my mind. Which I didn't, because why would I change my mind? As soon as he'd driven off, I threw the card away."

Amber said jokily, "Even though he has a Porsche?"

"Darling, a man driving a flashy sports car is most likely to have a tiny penis. Not saying your friend does," Olga added hastily. "It might be huge. I don't know!"

Still struggling to keep the conversation on track, Amber said, "So you weren't even tempted to go for lunch with him?"

Olga looked baffled. "But there would be no reason to do that. Not when I have Teddy. Why would I want to meet up with someone else?"

"Well, that's nice to hear." Oh, the relief.

"And at least I know that Teddy doesn't have a tiny—"

"*Lalalalala!*" Amber clapped her hands over her ears in the nick of time. "*Can't hear you, lalalala!*"

....

Lachlan was adding drops of aged balsamic to strawberry puree in the restaurant kitchen when he heard a voice that made the hairs stand up on the back of his neck.

The next moment, Olga poked her head through the stone archway and said, "Hello, we're here to surprise you! Can you squeeze us in for lunch?"

Did that mean she was with Teddy? "Um, it's a bit late…but of course I can."

Olga clapped her hands. "Hooray, thank you so much!"

"See?" said another familiar voice. "I told you he didn't hate you."

What? Not Teddy then. Lachlan broke into a smile as Vee appeared alongside Olga. "She thinks you don't like her," Vee explained. "I said of course you did. Why wouldn't you? She's great!"

"Right. Jo, can you take them to table three?" He'd been hoping to close early, seeing as the two people who'd booked for 1:15 had failed to turn up. No-shows were always infuriating, but this afternoon, there was a new recipe he wanted to experiment with before evening service.

"We'll be quick, I promise." Vee had caught the glance at his watch. "Not being funny, but I'd kill for an egg and fries."

"She said that to me!" Olga pulled a face. "I called her a heathen."

Lachlan said drily, "She is a heathen. I'm used to it. And yes, I can do an egg and fries."

"You're my favorite chef!"

"I'll have the crevettes," said Olga, "with the asparagus and parmesan sauce. Because I'm not a heathen," she added proudly. "I have an excellent palate."

When Lachlan took their food out to them fifteen minutes later, curiosity got the better of him. "So this is a surprise, seeing you two out together."

"A happy accident." Vee was clearly in a cheerful mood. "Raff's at work, obviously. Olga and I just happened to bump into each other on the beach."

"And Teddy has another golf tournament," Olga chimed in. "So we thought, why not come and enjoy your beautiful cooking? Oh, I forgot to tell you." She turned to Vee. "Teddy and I saw Amber out on her date last night. She looked so lovely and seemed to be having a great time, but I really hope he isn't going to break her heart… Oh my God, these crevettes are *amazing*."

"Not as amazing as my egg and fries." Still admiring her plate, Vee beamed up at Lachlan before returning her attention to Olga. "When the three of us were sharing the flat in London years ago, I used to beg this one to do homemade fries almost every night. And he always did, even if he didn't get home until really late."

Lachlan said good-naturedly, "Only to stop you living off those bloody Pot Noodles of yours."

"They were good times, weren't they?" Vee's huge brown eyes swam with tears, and she gave an involuntary honking sob, like a goose. "We were all so happy back then."

"Oh, darling, don't! You mustn't get upset." Olga leaned across the table and stroked her wrist. "We're having a happy time now, aren't we? The best time!"

"We are. Sorry." Vee sat back and pressed her fingers against her temples. "So much for trying to relax. I get these stupid tension head-aches, and crying just makes them worse." She took a blister pack of acetaminophen out of her bag and knocked a couple back with a gulp of water. "I'll be fine. I suppose the trick is not to get myself into a state just because my whole life's going down the drain."

"Here, tissue!" Olga produced a pack, Mary Poppins–style. "Does Raffaele know how upset you are? Maybe if I sit him down and have a talk with him, would that help?"

Vee's eyes were closed, and a muscle was jumping in her throat. She shook her head. Lachlan thanked the final table of departing diners and showed them out. When he turned back, he saw that Olga was now gently cupping Vee's face in her hands, murmuring reassurances and dab-bing with a tissue at Vee's cheeks.

As if they'd known each other for years rather than a couple of days. Was she determined to involve herself in all their lives? Already unsettled by her casual mention of Amber's date with Dom, Lachlan was half tempted to suggest that he should be the one to deal with Vee.

Before he could speak, however, the door burst open, and they all heard a shriek as a woman stumbled over the threshold. Clutching the doorframe, she snapped, "That's a trip hazard, for a start!"

"Sorry, we're closed," Lachlan announced. Drunk holidaymakers, fresh from the pub; just what everyone wanted.

The woman gave him an acerbic *you're wrong* look. "No, we've booked a table."

"Still closed." The next moment, he recognized the man behind her. Oh, great.

"Made the booking last week," said Gerry Walsh. "Thought it was about time we came over to check this place out."

Gerry Walsh, whose restaurant in St. Austell had won a Michelin star last year and who hadn't stopped banging on about it ever since. Gerry Walsh, whom Lachlan had called a dick during the course of that last newspaper interview. He might not have specifically named him, but the journalist had made it pretty clear. Years ago, before moving back down here, he'd worked in a hotel kitchen with Gerry, and they'd never gotten along. While undoubtedly a decent chef, Gerry had made a habit of pinching other people's ideas and passing them off as his own. He'd enjoyed bullying those members of staff below him in the hierarchy and constantly bad-mouthed his fellow chefs. He had also been furiously jealous when his advances were rejected by the female staff, who preferred to flirt with Lachlan rather than himself.

OK, to say they hadn't gotten along was an understatement.

"Well, thanks for thinking it was about time you came over," said Lachlan. "But I'm afraid that time was one fifteen. It's now"—he checked his watch—"almost two o'clock. And the kitchen is closed."

"Oh, come on. You're still here, aren't you? It's not our fault we got held up in traffic. Bloody tourists blocking the roads. Can't blame us for that."

He was breathing out great wafts of alcohol; Lachlan guessed he'd been held up in one of the pubs in Lanrock. "Sorry." He flashed a not-sorry smile. "Maybe if you'd bothered to call and let us know you'd be late. But you didn't book the table under your own name."

"God, you don't change, do you?" Gerry snarled. "I saw that interview in the paper, by the way. Calling me a dick."

Having watched the exchange, Olga said, "Is it any wonder? Listen to yourself. You're drunk, *and* you sound like a dick."

He rounded on her, then spotted the plate in front of Vee. "Fucking hell, is that the kind of food he's serving these days? Good luck with that then. Looks like we've had a lucky escape if an egg and fries is the plat du jour."

Vee snapped, "Not that it's any business of yours, but Lachlan's an old friend, and he made this for me as a favor."

Gerry laughed derisively. "Oh, he's a *friend*, is he? I suppose that means he shagged you once. Got a lot of female *friends*, has our Lachlan."

"I'm not your Lachlan. And this is getting boring. You can leave now."

"Are you kidding? I'm just getting started. Egg and fries, that is hilarious."

"I'm a friend who's never shagged him," Vee said icily.

Gerry looked from Vee to Olga and sneered, "Must be a pair of lesbians then." Taking out his phone, he lurched toward the table to take a photo of Vee's plate.

Olga's hand shot out and gripped his wrist so tightly he emitted a high-pitched yelp of pain. Removing the phone from his grasp, she said, "I don't think so."

"Oi, give it here." Gerry made a furious attempt to grab it back, whereupon Olga shook an admonishing finger at him, pulled open the V of her low-cut white shirt, and dropped the phone into the left cup of her violet lace bra.

Beaming at him, she said, "You can have it back when you leave. If you ask nicely."

"You're fucking mad."

"And you're still extremely rude." Her emerald eyes flashed.

"I wouldn't eat in this dump if you paid me."

Lachlan turned to Gerry's girlfriend. "You could do so much better than him."

In response, the girlfriend tipped her head to one side and eyed Lachlan with simmering resentment. "You don't remember me, do you?"

Shit. He hadn't, had he?

When he continued to look blank, she went on, "You think you're so great, don't you? I worked as a waitress at the Red Room when you were there. I really thought you liked me. So I invited you to my twenty-first birthday party at my dad's house in Hampstead."

Birthday party...Hampstead... OK, vague memories stirring.

"You didn't dance with me once, and you ended up getting caught kissing my dad's girlfriend in the downstairs loo."

Ah yes, that was it. In his defense, he'd had no idea she was anyone's girlfriend; for some reason, it hadn't come up in conversation.

"Anyway, you're lucky you didn't cook us lunch," the girl said now. "We were going to put hair in the food."

"Mind you," Gerry chimed in, "now we've seen the crap you serve, I'd have preferred the hair."

Whoosh went the contents of the water jug that had been on Vee and Olga's table. Expertly flung by Olga, the great wave of water and half-melted ice cubes flew through the air and drenched Gerry Walsh from head to foot.

"There," said Olga. "Lucky I was looking after your phone for you. Otherwise, it would've gotten wet."

"You're both crazy," Gerry yelled.

"Absolutely right," said Olga.

"I'm crazier than she is," Vee added. "If I'd had your phone, I'd have stamped on it."

"I could have you arrested." He jabbed a finger at them. "All of you."

"Actually," came a voice through the stone archway behind them, "that might not be the best idea." In the kitchen, Jo was holding up her own phone. "I've recorded everything you said."

"Oh, fuck off," Gerry Walsh snarled. "I suppose he's shagging you too."

"Leave her out of this." Jumping to her feet, Vee took Gerry's phone back from Olga and thrust it into his hand. "You're drunk, you're disgusting, and you're definitely a dick. And now you're out of here, before I really lose my temper."

Water was still dripping off him. For a moment, Lachlan thought he was going to carry on arguing with Vee. Then, evidently sensing her simmering fury, he turned to his girlfriend and muttered, "C'mon. We're going."

Vee held the door open for them. "Try sleeping it off," she advised as they passed her. "You're going to be so ashamed of yourself when you wake up."

"At least when I wake up, I'll still have a Michelin star." It was Gerry Walsh's final vindictive retort.

"You might not have a professional reputation for much longer though," Olga called out. "Not if people get to hear the things you've said in here today."

Gerry looked at Lachlan, and suddenly there was fear in his eyes. "You wouldn't do that."

"*He* might not," said Vee. "But I would."

When they'd left, Lachlan opened a bottle of wine and poured each of them a glass.

"Well done. That's brightened my afternoon." When they'd all clinked glasses, he said to Jo, "You'd better delete the video. I don't trust myself not to use it."

"I was lying when I said I'd recorded everything." Jo pulled a face. "I ran out of space on my phone just before it got to the bit about putting hair in the food."

"Good. He's an idiot, but he wouldn't have done it."

"You're too nice." Vee was diving back into her plate of egg and fries, unbothered by the fact that it was now cold.

"You were fantastic," Lachlan told her. Then he turned to Olga. "And you were great too."

"Throwing water at annoying people is one of my talents. I did a good job, I think."

"You did. A very good job."

"And he deserved it."

"Absolutely." He lowered his voice as Jo reappeared with a squeegee to begin mopping up the water on the floor. "And just for the record, I don't hate you."

"No? Are you sure?" She gave him a smile that was half-dubious, half-playful.

It was an odd sensation, realizing that you might be starting to like someone against your will. Lachlan said, "It takes me a while to work out whether or not I can trust people."

"I know. Believe it or not, I've noticed." Olga's green eyes glittered. "I also know there is nothing I can say to make you trust me. We'll just have to be patient and see how things go."

chapter 27

The house was always so much quieter when Peggy was away. This morning, she'd driven up to Birmingham to attend a shareholders' meeting, and the plan had been to stay on for another couple of days to celebrate a friend's birthday in style.

Benjie's phone rang not long after he'd arrived home from work to an empty house, while he was eating black-currant jam on toast in the kitchen.

"Darling, I've just been through my suitcase, and I can't find Magda's present. I wrapped it up in my bedroom before I left. Could you go and see if it's still in there somewhere?"

"No problem." Benjie was in a cheerful mood; tonight he was meeting up with Jo again. Tantalizingly, she'd already texted him with the message You won't believe what happened at work today! Tell you all about it when I see you. Don't be late!!!

As if he would ever be late. Taking his half-eaten slice of toast with him, Benjie bounded up the sweeping staircase to his mother's room. The cleaner wasn't due until tomorrow, and the bedroom was in its habitual state of chaos, with the bed unmade and the duvet all bunched up.

There was a half-empty water glass on the bedside table alongside a tape dispenser and a pair of scissors. Straightening the duvet, he uncovered a discarded belt, a necklace, a bank statement, and a roll of purple satin ribbon. Finally, lifting a pillow, he came across an empty crumpled envelope, an art magazine, and the neatly wrapped present, next to the remains of a sheet of wrapping paper.

"Found it," he told Peggy, who was waiting on the other end of the phone. "You left it on your bed."

"Oh, typical! How annoying."

"Yes, well, if you didn't leave your room in such a state, this wouldn't happen."

"Have I ever told you how much I love being nagged by my own son to tidy my room? No, I have *not*," said Peggy. "Because I don't love it one bit."

"I could put the present in the mail tomorrow morning."

"No, don't worry. It won't get here in time. I'll pick something else up for her in Selfridges. Are you going to be seeing Jo again any time soon?"

Just hearing her name spoken made his pulse quicken. "Yes, tonight. I'm meeting her in less than an hour."

Not that he'd been counting down the minutes like a child on Christmas Eve.

"Well, I'm sure she'd like the present, so why don't you give it to her instead? OK, have to go. At least I can stop wondering where it got to now. Did you sell any more of my paintings today, darling?"

"No. Sorry." A family from London had mocked them mercilessly this afternoon, but he didn't tell her that.

"Bloody hell, what's the matter with people? Right, have fun. See you soon. *Mwah!*"

And she was gone. Fitting the last piece of toast into his mouth before any of the jam slid off, Benjie straightened the duvet, gathered together the various abandoned items, and placed them on the bedside table. He wasn't remotely interested in the bank statement, but as he was in the process of folding it back up, a name jumped out at him. Freezing in mid chew, he tried to make sense of what he was seeing. But it continued to make no sense at all, because what reason could there possibly be for his mother to be making an online payment to Joanne Morton?

And not just one payment either. As his gaze slid down the page, with rising disbelief, he saw her name appear again…and again. The recipient of a modest—but not *too* modest—amount of money each time.

His chest muscles tightened, recognizing what his brain was refusing to take in.

Surely not.

But if not, what else could it conceivably be?

Then he recognized the significance of the dates the payments had been made and knew there was no other explanation.

The realization was crushing. *Oh God, please no, anything but that.*

....

They were due to meet at seven. Benjie was there by ten to. He watched the waves rolling in and the happy holidaymakers squeezing every last minute of enjoyment from the beach before heading back to their rented cottages and apartments to ready themselves for the evening ahead.

Then Jo came into view in the distance with Moose darting around her feet, exploring the strips of driftwood and tangled mounds of seaweed that had been washed up onto the sand. When she spotted him, she waved and said something to the dog, who lifted his head, then came racing across the beach toward him, ears flying.

Normally Benjie would have been overjoyed by the effusive waggytailed greeting. Not this time. As the dog launched himself at him, he wondered if, after this evening, he and Moose would ever meet again.

It would have been easier if he weren't here, bouncing around and being all cheerful, but too late now.

"Hiya!" Jo was beaming, her hair tied up with a pale-green cotton scarf that matched her sundress. "Have you been waiting to hear what happened in the restaurant today? I've been bursting to tell you!" She threw herself down onto the sand next to him and waggled her hands excitedly. "It was the craziest thing!"

"This is for you." Benjie handed her the small parcel wrapped in thick lilac embossed paper and tied with purple ribbon. He felt like a detective, minutely observing her reaction and on the lookout for clues.

"Why? Oh, Benjie, you don't have to do this. You mustn't! I don't need you to keep buying me things."

Was that a flicker of guilt in her eyes? Was it shame? Or greed, wondering what the gift could be this time?

"I didn't buy it. It's from Mum."

"What? Why's your mum giving me a present?"

This time, Jo definitely looked wary. She wasn't great at hiding her emotions, Benjie realized. Which was ironic. Moose placed a paw on his knee, and he shook it. "She just thought you might like it."

Carefully, Jo unwrapped the parcel, then the silver tissue inside it, and drew out a long velvet scarf, slinky and soft, in shades of apricot and burnt orange with streaks of yellow and green.

"This is amazing. It feels so…" She saw the designer label, and her eyes widened. "Oh my God, she can't give me this. It must have cost an absolute fortune."

Peggy's friend was a redhead, which was why she'd known the colors would also suit Jo. Benjie said, "Well, she w-wanted you to have it, so you must have done s-something right."

The faint flush on her cheeks told him all he needed to know. In that moment, fury and pain collided inside his chest. As he watched her stroke the expensive velvet draped across her knee, he said, "C-can I ask you a question? Why has my mother been paying money into your b-bank account?"

The waves continued to roll onto the shore, children were shrieking with laughter and running about, and a group of noisy teenage boys were playing football nearby. But in their invisible bubble, a tense silence reigned.

"Well? Nothing to s-say?"

Jo's face was crimson. She kept her gaze fixed on the sea. "Benjie, I'm sorry. It was never—"

"You just happened to need a f-friend, someone to go around with in your free time, and I just happened to f-fit the bill… What an amazing coincidence." Benjie blurted the words out in a rush. "I mean, it's *such* an amazing coincidence I can't believe I was s-stupid enough to fall for it. But there you go, that's me. Desperate and g-g-gullible."

"It wasn't like that. Oh, Benjie, I promise it's not like you think. Look at how well we get along. I love going on adventures with you. I want us to stay friends *forever*…"

"You mean even if you weren't secretly being paid for it?"

"Yes!" Tears were brimming in her eyes; she was mortified and hating every second of this. *Well, good.*

"I don't believe you." His throat contracted. "I wish I d-did, but I don't."

Jo exhaled a shuddery breath. "I'm so sorry. How did you find out? Was it Peggy? Did she tell you?"

Moose was nuzzling his hand, ever hopeful of a treat. Benjie shook his head. "No, she left her b-bank statement out on show. And there was your name." He paused, swallowed. "I wonder if you can imagine how that f-felt, once I realized what it meant."

"I know, I know it looks bad, but it was Peggy's idea... She just came up with it and insisted on paying me. I'll make her stop." A tear dripped off Jo's chin. She wiped the back of her hand across her face.

"Why are you c-crying? Because you've just lost your extra income?"

"I didn't want the money. She made me take it. Peggy knew I was trying to save up to go traveling and said she couldn't ask me to do it for nothing. And I didn't know you then, did I? You were just a customer in the restaurant. Your mum thought I could help you to get out and about a bit more, and she could help me at the same time. She was trying to do a good thing!"

"But it wasn't a g-good thing, was it? She's ended up making it worse." Bitterly, Benjie added, "Story of my life."

"I'll tell her not to pay me anymore," Jo pleaded again. "We can carry on meeting up, doing stuff, having fun—"

"She won't be paying you anyway, because you won't be w-working for her anymore."

"OK, I'll pay back all the money she's given me! I will! Oh, stop it, Moose." She pushed away the dog, who was oblivious to the drama and far more interested in trying to lick her face.

"Don't bother." Benjie wanted her to feel as miserable as he did. "If you repaid her, it'd mean you'd have d-done all that hard work for nothing."

"But that's the thing. It hasn't *been* hard work! I swear to you, our meetups are what I look forward to more than anything else!"

Benjie looked at her. The sea breeze was ruffling her curls, and the whites of her eyes were tinged with pink. She looked vulnerable and desperate. If circumstances had been different and this were a movie, it would be at this moment that he could imagine leaning across, tilting Jo's face up to his, and making everything better by kissing her so softly that it felt like a dream…and *whoosh*, just like that, all their problems would be cast aside, misunderstandings forgiven.

Except circumstances weren't different, and there was no way of forgiving a misunderstanding like this one.

"I never meant for this to happen." Jo reached for his arm, but he shook her off, too wounded to listen.

"Except it did. And I don't care anymore. We're not going to see each other again. Have f-fun traveling." Having risen to his feet, Benjie gave Moose one last ear rub, then turned and walked away.

It felt important not to look back.

chapter 28

BACK AT HOME, BENJIE MADE A START ON THE BOTTLES OF SOL that his mother always kept in the fridge for guests. Never much of a drinker himself, he gulped down the first in one go, then levered open a second, because the shame and disappointment were so overwhelming he was prepared to try anything. He carried two more bottles out to the garden and sat on one of the sun loungers, glad that the weather appeared to be matching his mood. As he watched, heavy clouds were rolling in across the sea, blocking the sun. Within minutes, the sky was charcoal gray, the temperature had dropped dramatically, and fat raindrops had begun to land *splat-splat-splat* on the terrace.

Benjie stayed where he was, steadily drinking and waiting for the next hour to crawl by. Dani was out at her Tuesday evening dance class and wouldn't be home until 9:30. She would be sympathetic when she heard what had happened but also secretly relieved, because he knew she regarded Jo as her real-life rival. *Had* regarded her. He pictured Dani's lit-up face; never mind relieved, she would be over the moon to have Jo removed from the equation.

The rain fell faster and harder, soaking through his shirt and trousers. Benjie's hair was drenched, the heavy drops hitting his face and running down his neck. If he and Jo had still been down on the beach, they'd have run for cover, laughing at how wet it was possible to get in under a minute. She hadn't had a chance to reveal what her plans had been for the two of them this evening. Nor had there been time for her to tell him about whatever mad thing had happened at lunchtime in the restaurant. A small part of him longed to hear about it, but a larger, more spiteful part was glad he hadn't, because Jo had been bursting to relay the story, and now she couldn't.

He knew her well enough by now to be aware that this would drive her mad with frustration.

Good.

Well, unless the secret sharing and giddy enthusiasm had all been an elaborate part of the act, and in reality she couldn't care less.

He blinked the drops of rain from his lashes and took another swig from the bottle in his hand. Once you got used to the bitter taste, lager wasn't that bad. A rumble of thunder rolled overhead. The rain ramped up to the next level, coming down harder than ever, and the next brilliant flash of lightning zigzagged down into the sea.

OK, being struck down dead wasn't the answer. He didn't want his mother coming home and finding his sodden body out here on the terrace.

Although it wouldn't be his mother, would it? It would be either the gardener or the cleaner.

Banging his knee on the edge of the sun lounger as he hauled himself off it, Benjie headed back inside. The weird thing about feeling as if you'd had too much to drink, he was discovering, was that it really made you want another beer.

....

He didn't need the alarm to rouse him the next morning. He was already awake, feeling far too unwell to stay asleep.

It might not be his first hangover, but it was the worst by several miles. Mouth dry, head banging, eyeballs feeling as if they were being gripped from the inside, Benjie slowly sat up and saw that the waste bin in his bedroom was filled with empty Sol bottles. He counted six of them in there. Not so bad, surely? But that was before he crawled out of bed and spotted more bottles lying on their sides like felled bowling pins on the carpet.

Not to mention the ones on the sofa in the living room. Jesus, how many had he had? He didn't even remember drinking them.

Nauseated and broken, he staggered into the shower. Swallowed painkillers and drank a pint of water. Forced himself to get dressed and to pick up both the empty bottles and the chess pieces that lay scattered on the rug alongside his upended chess board. Each movement took all his concentration, until he looked across at the desk over by the window and saw his laptop with the lid open. *Zap* went his brain, firing a warning shot across the bow. He'd been on the computer, he remembered, but that was as far as his memory stretched. Had he sent terrible emails to Jo? To his mother? A sense of foreboding was now creeping through his body. He approached the laptop with caution as if it were an unexploded bomb.

Check the sent emails first. Nothing, thank God. Twitter, no, nothing there either. Instagram, nope. Facebook, zero, zilch, not even on the shyness group.

OK, breathe. This was good news. He'd saved Messenger until last, because talking to Dani was the least alarming prospect. If he'd poured his heart out to her, she would be on his side. Clicking, he came to their conversation and saw that he had indeed poured it all out, presumably while at the same time pouring ice-cold lager in.

He scrolled back to the beginning of last night's chat. It took a while. He'd relayed every last detail to Dani, who'd been wonderfully sympathetic in return. She'd also told him it was Jo's loss, he deserved better anyway…blah blah blah, then:

Are you OK?

Not really.

Oh, Benjie, I wish I could put my arms around you.

I wish you could too.

I'd give you the biggest hug in the world.

That would be so nice.

Benjie, I love you.

Love you too.

I'd never let you down.

I know you wouldn't. That's why you mean the world to me.

You're making me cry now.

Don't cry.

I wish I was there with you. I'd hug you so hard and never let you go.

I wish you were here. I want to hear your voice.

Same.

Can I phone you?

What? Benjie did a double take; had he actually typed those words? Had he been so drunk and desperate that he'd wanted to break down the barrier that had stood between them for the last six months?

Apparently he had. And Dani had clearly been as shocked as he was now. She'd gone silent, and he'd had to type again:

Please, Dani. Let's do it. You're the one I love. I need to tall to you.

We're talking online.

It's not enough. I want to feel as if you're really here. Are you scared?

Yes, I'm scared.

Don't be. I'm scared too, but I want to do it. OK, I'll tell you the truth, I have a stammer. Does that lut you off me?

No!

Come on then, give me your number. Let's do if.

Benjie, you never make typos. That's three now. Have you been drinking?

Just a bit.

Little bit or big bit?

Litter bit. What's your numbness? I'll call you nob.

Sober and hungover, Benjie winced at the realization that in order to try and prevent the typos, he'd switched to predictive text.

No, Benjie. You're drunk. It's not fair to let you do it while you're like this. We can carry on talking on here though.

I love yob.

Shall we talk about meeting up one day?

I want tog meerkat you now.

Benjie?

Benjie?

Tired. Going toy sleek now.

OK. Love you. Night. Xxxxx

Benjie exhaled shakily. Thank God she'd had the sense to say no. In his emotional state, he might have wanted it to happen, but actually getting through to Dani and speaking to her could have been completely disastrous. Imagine slurring and stammering *and* being catastrophically shy; it would have been enough to put her off him forever.

Ting went his laptop, and a new message arrived:

Morning! How are you???

Hi. Terrible.

Did I do the right thing last night?

Yes. With bells on.

I'm off to work now. Don't worry. I still love you! Message me later.

Thanks, will do. And sorry about the typos.

I forgive you. Try not to think about Jo. You deserve better than her. Love you, husband. Xxx

Love you, wife. Xxx

Another *ping*, and a photo arrived, of Dani holding up a packet of aspirin and a can of full-fat Coke. She'd captioned it Hope you feel back to normal soon! Xxxxxx

Look at that smile. She was so beautiful and so kind. What would he do without her?

Benjie closed his laptop. She was his best and most loyal friend, the only person truly on his side.

chapter 29

IT WAS ALMOST MIDNIGHT. AMBER WAS IN HER STUDIO, WORKING to finish a stained-glass tabletop, when she heard a tap on the window.

Her heart still did that breaking-into-a-gallop thing whenever she saw Lachlan with no prior warning, but after years of practice, she'd grown adept at concealing her emotions. Letting him in, she gave him a quick hug. "You smell amazing."

"Thanks." There it was, that oh-so-fantastic crooked grin, because he knew what was coming next.

She inhaled slowly. "Let me guess. Garlic, shallots, white wine, and morels."

He passed her the sealed container of wild mushroom risotto he'd been hiding behind his back. "I had a couple of portions left over."

"I knew this little hobby of yours would come in handy one day. Are you on your way out somewhere?"

Lachlan shook his head. "Just felt like some company. What have you done to your eyebrows?"

"Nothing."

"You have. They look different."

"Good different or bad different?"

He was studying them closely. "Good. I like them."

"Well, thank you. Olga did them for me this morning. My first ever time. She tinted them and shaped them to frame my face!" She waggled her eyebrows at him like Groucho Marx. Although hopefully not too much like him.

"You'll have her supergluing false lashes on you next. How much longer are you going to be here tonight?"

"Nearly finished. Why?"

"I thought we could go back to yours. Share the risotto and watch *Enemy* together."

"Great, I'd love that." Amber began wiping down the almost completed table with a damp cloth. Then she frowned. "Well, most of it. Not so sure about having to share the risotto."

....

"You had an affair with the mailman when you were still married to my dad!" yelled the teenage stepson.

"You hid caterpillars in my shoes," his stepmother hissed back.

"You flirted with my teacher in front of all my friends. I was the laughingstock of the whole school."

"And you wrote that you hated me all over my car," the woman snarled at him. "With my best lipstick!"

"I'm on his side," said Amber. "Poor little boy."

Lachlan said, "Maybe she tried her best to win him over but he was determined to hate her."

She grinned. "Now why does that sound familiar?"

"Shush." He nudged her, and she felt the butterfly touch of the hairs on the back of his wrist against her forearm. Risotto demolished, they were sitting side by side on her bed, propped up by mounds of pillows. In a parallel universe, they could be a proper couple, in love and as happy in each other's company as it was possible to be.

But if this was second best, it was still brilliant. Lachlan had told her all about yesterday's to-do in the restaurant with Gerry Walsh. He'd even grudgingly admitted that Olga's spirited involvement had made him like her a bit more. And today was the end of a long day; if he hadn't come over, Amber would have had a bowl of cornflakes for dinner.

"Are you still awake?" She felt him give her another gentle nudge.

"Mmm." She nodded, distantly aware that her head was now resting on his shoulder. On the TV, people were still hurling insults at each other, but she could no longer see them because her eyes had closed.

Her foot was resting against Lachlan's. She gave it a little wiggle and felt him wiggle back.

Oh, it felt *so nice…*

....

Amber jerked awake at the sound of the doorbell, so confused for a second by the sensation of a warm leg in the bed that didn't belong to her that she let out a bat-squeak of surprise.

The next moment, it all came flooding back.

Lifting his head from the mound of pillows, Lachlan twisted around. "Was that the doorbell?"

"No, it's the band of the Coldstream Guards. Of course it's the doorbell." She sat up and gazed in disbelief at the amount of light streaming through the gap in the curtains. "What's the time? Is it *morning*?"

"You sound astonished. It happens every day."

Amber grabbed her phone. It was almost seven. "But you're still here! I can't believe we both slept through the whole night." She might be a sound sleeper, but she knew Lachlan wasn't. OK, so she'd dozed off during the *Enemy* show on TV, while they'd both been sitting on top of the duvet. Now they were both lying beneath it. Lachlan was still wearing the T-shirt and board shorts he'd arrived in, and she was in her white cotton top and leggings.

The doorbell shrilled again. Surely even delivery drivers weren't cruel enough to try and get you out of bed before seven. Amber crossed to the window, then jumped back in shock at the sight of the red Porsche parked outside and Dom standing on the sidewalk waving at her.

"Oh God."

"Who is it?"

"Dom!"

"You don't sound very pleased. I thought you liked him."

"I *do* like him." She glared at Lachlan, who seemed to be finding the situation amusing.

"So let him in."

"You'll have to climb out the kitchen window."

"What? I'm not doing that."

"You have to! What's it going to look like, him seeing you here at this time of the morning?"

He shrugged. "Come on. We haven't done anything wrong. We just fell asleep watching TV."

"*We* know that. *He* doesn't." Amber gestured despairingly. "Get out of bed, for crying out loud. It's not funny!"

"OK, OK." Raking his fingers through his bedhead hair, Lachlan grinned. "But you really should answer the door. The longer you keep him waiting out there, the more suspicious it's going to look."

Honestly, if she could have bundled him up and hidden him in a cupboard, she'd have done it. If only all her cupboards weren't already full to bursting with junk.

"Morning!" On the doorstep, Dom gave her a big kiss. "Thought for a minute you weren't going to let me in."

"I was asleep." Amber was glad she'd thought to swoosh mouthwash around her mouth. "What are you doing here?"

"Drove down from London. Got a big meeting later. Thought you might fancy some breakfast." He held up a couple of cardboard cartons. "You did tell me you were an early riser."

"I am. Eight is early. Seven's an abomination."

"Well, these should help. I picked them up from the deli on Beach Street." He wafted the cartons under her nose. They smelled like absolute heaven.

"Look, Lachlan's here. We were watching that mad cooking show last night, and we both fell asleep. That's all."

"Sure? No wild sex?"

"No!" Oh God, he was only teasing her, but here came the guilty rush of blood to her face thanks to some of the thoughts that were flashing through her mind. "Absolutely none."

"In that case, I'll leave my dueling pistols in the car," Dom said cheerfully.

It was almost insulting, the way he wasn't remotely bothered to find Lachlan there, making coffee and getting a third cup down from the cupboard.

Over breakfast, which was enough for the three of them because Dom had bought pretty much everything in the deli, they talked about Lachlan's restaurant, the hotel in St. Ives that Dom was refurbishing, and the staffing problems inherent in the industry. The conversation flowed. Amber could see the similarities between the two men. They were both driven, ambitious, and charismatic. Weirdly, Lachlan was acting almost as if he were her boyfriend and Dom was their guest. There was an under-current of friendly rivalry that made no sense but made her heart beat faster all the same, because what was Lachlan playing at?

Time, however, wasn't on his side. At eight o'clock, he had to leave in order to be back at the restaurant before the day's food deliveries started arriving. When the two men had made their cheerful farewells, Amber accompanied him to the front door.

"Why were you being like that?"

He looked innocent. "Like what?"

"You know. Playing games."

Lachlan said, "I think he's the one doing that."

Amber shook her head. "You're a nightmare."

"And you look after yourself." As he touched her arm, she felt a zing of adrenaline. "What are you going to do now?"

"Not actually any of your business." To punish him, she gave him a little smile that was hopefully superior and mysterious. "Anyway, you probably don't want to know."

"I'm just saying, be careful. I know what men like him are like."

"Of course you do." As he turned away, Amber added silently, *Because he's the same as you.*

....

There it was: she'd closed the front door, gone back inside. To rejoin Dom Burton. Lachlan reached the end of Leopard Lane and turned the corner so he was out of sight of Amber's cottage. But not out of mind. What was going on inside right now? Was Dom saying, "Jesus, talk about outstaying his welcome. I thought he'd never leave. Come here, you gor-geous creature. We need to get you out of those clothes…"

Eurgh, no, don't think about it.

Lachlan felt sick. It killed him that Amber thought he'd been the one playing games. He hadn't; he'd been deadly serious.

And now it was six minutes past eight. He really did need to get back to the restaurant, but his feet were refusing to move. This was crazy; his feelings for Amber were rising on an exponential curve. He'd managed to keep his emotions under control for all these years, but now they appeared to be determined to make themselves felt. He wanted to protect her from Dom, who was clearly up for a bit of fun but not interested in any kind of serious relationship. Then, too, there was the situation with Raffaele, who could well be up for a serious relationship but who'd currently been distracted by Vee's reappearance. If Raff and Vee were to get back together, that particular problem would be solved, although unless Vee drastically changed her ways, Lachlan couldn't see a reunion ending well.

And finally there was himself, battling with his own escalating feelings for Amber but terrified of getting it wrong and ruining everything. Because if it didn't work out, the danger was that their friendship would never recover.

He loved her, more than he loved himself.

Lachlan closed his eyes, feeling the warmth of the early-morning sun on his eyelids. Last night had been one of the best nights of his life, and he hadn't even taken his clothes off. When he'd realized Amber was falling asleep next to him, he'd scarcely dared to breathe for fear of alerting her and being reminded to go home. Obviously it would have been fantastic if something magical could have happened between them, but just being there was enough. He'd alternated between dozing and waking throughout the night, and every minute had felt like a gift. It might be a different kind of intimacy, but it was still wonderful and worth treasuring, even if—

Vroooooooom. The unmistakable throaty roar of the Porsche broke into his thoughts, filling him with relief. If Dom Burton had climbed into his flash car and was preparing to drive off, that meant he wasn't giving Amber the time of her life in bed.

Thank God for that.

As the noise level increased, Lachlan belatedly realized he was two seconds away from being discovered loitering far closer to Leopard Lane than he had any reason to be. Hastily whipping out his phone, he pretended to be engrossed in a conversation that was so important he couldn't walk and talk at the same time. The next moment, the crimson Porsche rounded the corner and slowed, pulling up beside him. The windows were already down, and Eminem was blaring out at top volume. Eminem, *oh please.*

His eyes hidden behind mirrored sunglasses, Dom turned off the booming music. "Hey, I can give you a lift if you need one."

Lachlan turned away slightly and said into his phone, "Sorry, excuse me for a second," in a brisk, businesslike voice. The effect was somewhat spoiled by the phone choosing this moment to start ringing.

Typical.

Predictably, Dom broke into a broad grin. "Whoops."

"I'm fine. I don't need a lift."

"No problem. Just thought I'd make the offer." Evidently finding the situation hilarious, Dom said, "Word of advice, my friend. Stick to cheffing. Whatever you do, don't take up poker."

Laughing, he turned the music back up to maximum volume and drove off.

Lachlan answered the call.

Dave the disgruntled delivery driver said in his ear, "Where the bloody hell are you, mate? I'm stuck here outside the restaurant with all your stuff."

chapter 30

It was happening again; Raffaele could sense it. When he'd woken up, Vee had been cheerful. Then, while he'd been in the shower, he'd heard her yelling at the toaster because it kept popping the bread up before it was done.

Out of the shower, he heard her let out a shriek of fury because this time, the toast was too brown. By the time he reached the kitchen, she'd hurled the slices out the window, to the unparalleled joy of several gulls, who hadn't expected such a treat and were now descending in a flurry of wings.

The toast wasn't even burnt. He said, "I'd have eaten that."

"Bloody toaster. It's doing it on purpose, trying to wind me up." Vee's eyes blazed as she put the butter back in the fridge and slammed the door shut.

Raffaele said, "It's OK. I'll make you some toast."

"Don't bother. I'm not hungry anymore. That's it. I've had enough."

"You haven't had anything."

"I'm talking about this place." She exhaled, at the end of her tether. "It's doing my head in. I'm going back to London."

"But we're meeting up with Eamonn and Mandy tonight. They're off home tomorrow."

"I've met them already. You're the one they want to see again, not me. What's the point of me staying down here? You'll be glad to see me gone anyway."

It was useless trying to reason with her when she was like this, full of arguments and irritation. Maybe he *would* be glad when she was gone. God knows, a week down in Cornwall hadn't managed to relax her as much as he'd hoped; she was still liable to fly off the handle for no reason whatsoever.

Bang went Vee's case as she dropped it onto the living room floor and began throwing her belongings into it. *Boof* went her makeup bag, followed by various clothes, toiletries, and shoes.

Two minutes later, the case was zipped shut. "Right, I'm off."

Raffaele knew what she was doing, silently challenging him to try and persuade her not to go. Since he also knew it wouldn't work, he didn't try. "Well, have a good journey."

Her eyes promptly filled with tears. "Why does it always have to be like this?"

He shook his head. "It doesn't."

"It just happens." She reached out her arms and moved toward him, kissing him full on the mouth, then clinging to him in desperation before finally letting go. "I know. You can breathe a sigh of relief now. I'll leave you in peace."

Peace. Their situation was as inexplicable as her outbursts of temper.

"I can walk you to the train station if you want."

"No thanks. You have to get to work."

She turned and left. Raffaele watched out the upstairs window as she wheeled her case across the road, elegant and long-legged, smiling at an elderly couple as she passed them on the sidewalk as if she hadn't a care in the world.

He still loved her.

Kind of.

If only she wouldn't behave like this and drive him mad.

....

After finishing work for the day, Raffaele drove over to Charlestown, to the cottage Eamonn and Mandy had been renting. When they opened the door to greet him, a delicious smell of curry wafted out.

"Come on in. It's so lovely to see you again." Mandy gave him an enthusiastic hug.

"Sorry, Vee couldn't make it." Raffaele felt guilty on Vee's behalf; he knew Mandy had made the chicken curry specially because Vee had said it was her favorite. Well, when she wasn't adding chopped-up bits of frankfurter to noodles in a plastic pot.

"Doesn't matter at all." Eamonn was pouring him a drink. "At least we were able to meet her. And how have the last few days been? She must have enjoyed the break."

"Yes, it was good."

"She's a stunning girl." Mandy looked hopeful. "Do you think you two might get back together?"

"Well…" Raffaele shrugged in an offhand way.

"What is this, twenty questions?" said Eamonn. "Give the boy a break. Come on. We have food to eat."

Over dinner in the cottage's tiny back garden, they exchanged more stories of their lives. It still amazed Raffaele that these two people, whom he hadn't met until a week ago, could now feel to him as if he'd known them for years. There was an effortless rapport between them, the kind of instant connection that scarcely ever happened in life. As the evening progressed, Mandy produced her phone and took photos of the three of them. Then she showed Raffaele her favorite of all those she'd taken at Teddy's house last week.

"This one's gorgeous. I must send it to you." She tilted the screen so he could see the unposed photo of himself in mid conversation with Eamonn and Vee, all of them on the verge of laughter at something Eamonn had just said. "You look so happy together!"

The earlier fib had been prodding at his conscience. Raffaele couldn't bear it any longer; how could he lie to his newfound family? "OK, I need to tell you the truth. Vee didn't have to be back in London today. She left early because we had an argument."

Mandy looked sympathetic. "Oh, I'm sorry."

"She's been under a lot of pressure. Everything was fine until about a year ago. Then we started working together, and that's when it all began to go wrong. Vee got stressed and started losing her temper. The more stressed out she got, the worse everything became. Then the tension headaches made her more irritable, and from then on, it was as if I couldn't do anything right. Whatever happened, she would get mad with me." He took a gulp of his drink and felt his memory spooling back like a ticker tape in reverse, recalling the many occasions when it had happened. "It would come out of the blue for no reason at all. Other times, the tiniest little thing set her off. When she was in a good mood, she told me she still loved me. But then it would happen again…and again. And that's the reason we broke up," he explained. "Because neither of us was happy anymore. It wasn't what I wanted, but it had to happen. Which is why I decided to make the break and move back down here. I'd always thought we'd be together forever, but sometimes these things just don't work out, do they? And yes, I did wonder if a couple of months apart might make Vee think again and realize what we had." He shook his head. "But it doesn't seem to have worked. She's still stressed, still losing her temper, still mad at me. Except now that I'm down here and she's in London, she has more opportunity to lose her temper with other people as well."

There, he'd told them everything. The silence was broken only by the sound of children playing in a nearby garden.

"And until a year ago, you say she was never like this?" Eamonn had put down his fork and was paying close attention.

"Never. She wasn't the type to get angry. We hardly ever argued. We had fun, we worked hard, we socialized with friends and laughed all the time…" It was almost painful to remember the old Vee, whom everyone had adored. "I looked at her Instagram before coming over here tonight, and she's picking fights with people she doesn't even know. It just isn't *her*."

Eamonn frowned. "Has she seen a doctor at all?"

"She won't." Raffaele's jaw tightened with frustration. "Says there's no point. She wouldn't take any medication anyway. Well, apart from the pills for her headaches. She takes plenty of those."

Mandy nodded. "I saw her opening a packet of ibuprofen the other evening. How many does she take?"

"Loads. After she left this morning, I found three empty blister packs in the bathroom bin."

"And what are her headaches like?" said Eamonn.

"She said they're tension headaches, it feels like her head's about to explode. I told her she takes too many pills." Raffaele grimaced. "She told me to mind my own business. Do you think they could be making the headaches worse?"

"Has she ever fainted? Had any kind of blackout?"

"No." Raffaele frowned.

"OK, I'm a paramedic, not a doctor. But I do think she ought to see her GP, run through her situation."

Raffaele looked at him. "Why?"

Eamonn shrugged. "It would be sensible to get herself checked out."

It was now growing dark out here in the garden. The solar lights had come on and were happily flickering away in among the shrubs and trees.

Raffaele said, "I told you. She wouldn't go."

Another pause, then Eamonn brushed aside a fluttering moth and rested his elbows on the table. "When we were in Teddy's garden, Vee stood up and gave a little speech."

"I remember."

"Then she lost her way, stopped speaking, and did something like this." Eamonn gazed off into the distance, made chewing movements with his mouth, and smacked his lips together while reaching up and fiddling with the front of his shirt.

Raffaele nodded. "She does that when she's distracted or trying to think of something to say. She lost her concentration when Lachlan turned up. That was all."

"Well, maybe. But I think she lost her train of thought a few moments before Lachlan appeared. Like I said, I'm not a doctor, but I have seen patients doing something similar before. If I'm right, Vee could be suffering from minor focal seizures. Also known as focal impaired awareness seizures, or FIAs."

"Seizures? You mean like epilepsy?" Raffaele was taken aback. "She's never had any kind of seizure, not that I've seen."

"But what you've seen could be one of these very minor episodes," Eamonn explained.

"And if it is? What would cause that?"

The man who'd come into his life a week ago was now choosing his words with care. "Well, there can be lots of reasons, but the thing is, you've told me there's been a significant change in personality. And there are headaches…"

"You mean it could be something in her head causing it?" Raffaele felt as if his own voice was coming from far away while his pulse raced and the implications hit home. "Like a brain tumor?"

"Not necessarily." Eamonn's tone was steady, calm. "And I wouldn't say that to Vee at this stage. But I do think she needs to get checked out."

chapter 31

LANROCK MIGHT NOT BE BIG, BUT BENJIE HAD MANAGED TO STEER clear of Jo so far. Yesterday he'd caught a glimpse of her making her way along the road, heading into work, but the moment she'd glanced in his direction, he'd turned away. The shame and the anger were still there inside him, as corrosive as acid. Last night, he'd dreamed they were on holiday together in New Zealand, having the best time bungee-jumping from a high bridge. Waking up with a start and finding himself in bed with his phone's charging cable wrapped around his arm had come as a crushing disappointment.

Life was back to resembling a landscape of gray nothingness; all he had to look forward to now were his nightly conversations with Dani. Meanwhile, he had another six hours of being stuck here in the gallery, having to be polite to bored tourists who thought they were being hilarious when they made fun of Peggy Smart's paintings. Honestly, if he had a fiver for every time he'd heard someone say "A five-year-old could do better than that," he'd have enough to…well, buy one of her stupid paintings.

He hadn't forgiven his mother yet for what she'd done either.

A lad in his midtwenties had come into the gallery now. Benjie could tell at a glance that he wasn't a potential customer; his hands were stuffed in the pockets of his sky-blue hoodie, and he was avoiding meeting Benjie's gaze. Benjie carried on fixing strong nylon cord to the back of his mother's latest canvas. When he'd finished tying the knots securely and snipping off the ends, he looked through the front window and froze at the sight of Jo's grandmother crossing the road with Moose trotting along at her side. The next moment, Moose spotted Benjie and let out a joyful bark of recognition.

Benjie longed to see him. It was ridiculous, the bond they'd formed in just a few short weeks. But he didn't want to have to speak to Jo's gran, whom he'd also liked very much the couple of times they'd met.

Moose had no such inhibitions. Tail wagging madly, he pulled on his lead with such enthusiasm that Jo's gran wasn't left with any choice but to lurch into the gallery after him.

"Oh, sorry… Moose, be gentle!" Apologetically she added, "He's excited to see you. Are dogs even allowed in here?"

They weren't, but it was too late now. Crouching down so that Moose could rest his front paws on his knees, Benjie said, "It doesn't matter. Hello there. Look at you!"

It was actually nice to have someone pleased to see him. He ruffled the dog's ears, and Moose gave happy snuffles of delight, not wanting the attention to end.

"I'm so sorry, love, about what happened."

Mortified, Benjie pretended to be too engrossed in Moose to have heard.

Jo's gran raised her voice. "You know, between you and our Jo. She's sorry too. It was just one of those situations. She was only trying to help!"

"P-p-please." He felt his face heat up. "It's not—"

"And she's mortified that you found out, of course. I mean, what were the chances, eh? Poor Jo. She only did it because she needed the money, but who'd turn down something like that, in all honesty? It's an offer you can't refuse, love. That's what it is!"

"I d-d-don't w-want to—"

"She does feel bad about it though. I know it must have been upsetting—"

"I need to get b-back to work," Benjie blurted out, standing up and gesturing vaguely in the direction of the only other person in the gallery. "There's a c-customer who needs help…"

"Oh, sorry, love." Jo's gran looked over at the young man, who was standing awkwardly at the other side of the room. "I'll leave you in peace. Just wanted to let you know how Jo's been feeling. Come on, Moose. Off we go."

"Bye, Moose." Benjie wished the dog wasn't gazing up at him like that with sad brown eyes and a slowly wagging tail.

When they'd left, he turned to the lad in the hoodie. "Sorry about that."

The lad shrugged. "S'OK."

"I know you don't need any help. I just said it to get r-rid of her."

"I figured."

Benjie lifted the canvas with the newly attached string and carried it over to the cleared spot on the wall. When he'd finished hanging and straightening the painting, he stepped back.

"I like it," ventured the lad in the hoodie.

"I do too." This was the standard answer. It wasn't true.

"How much is it?"

Benjie finished writing out the price tag and fastened it to the frame. The lad leaned forward to read what he'd written, then said, "Do you think it would be an investment? Like, about ten years from now, would it be worth loads more?"

Normally a question like this would receive only one answer. Still unable to forgive his mother for her subterfuge, he shrugged and said without enthusiasm, "Depends on the market."

"Oh." It clearly wasn't the answer the visitor had been expecting. "I still like it though." He hesitated, then said, "What's the artist like? Do you know her?"

"I do. I've met her m-many times." *Too many.* Benjie was still convinced the boy wasn't a potential buyer, but the guilt had kicked in. He selected one of the glossy leaflets they'd had printed and handed it to him. "Here you are. This is Peggy Smart."

"Thanks!" The lad looked as if he'd just been given an Olympic medal. He beamed, then said, "I'm going to need to go away and think about it."

Benjie knew from bitter experience that this was customer code for *I'm going to walk out now and you'll never see me again.* He nodded. "Of course."

"I have to talk it over with my sister. Maybe bring her along with me tomorrow so she can have a look, see what she thinks."

"That's f-fine."

"You don't… I mean, do you have a business card?"

"We do, yes." Reaching into his desk drawer, Benjie found one and passed it over. "These are our opening hours."

The lad took it and read it. "So you close at five tomorrow. OK, we'll probably come in just before then."

....

It was hot outside, which meant Benjie had to have all the windows open to circulate some air. But Peggy was throwing one of her parties this evening, and the garden was teeming with sixty or seventy of the friends she loved to gather together at every opportunity.

Most of this lot were over fifty; they were also loud and screechy, their bursts of laughter grating on his ears. Worse still, one of the guests, who was the lead singer in a country and western band, had not only brought his electric guitar along with him but kept bursting into song of the my-sweetheart-fell-into-a-sinkhole variety.

By nine o'clock, Benjie had had enough. Dani had already told him she'd be out at her auntie's birthday party this evening and wouldn't be online before midnight. Unable to bear being here any longer, he showered and changed, then snuck out through the back door so no one could spot him and try to persuade him to stay.

No, thank you. He was escaping and going out-out. Not to one of the local pubs either, where people would instantly notice that he was on his own. Jumping into his car, Benjie drove off down the road, then took the turn that led away from the seafront.

He reached the trailer park several minutes later. When he and Jo had come here before, it had struck him how relaxed and nonjudgmental the atmosphere in the entertainment block was. There were guests and visitors of all ages milling around outside the entrance, families and couples, groups of friends and people on their own, either popping in for a quick drink or preparing to settle in for the evening. The place was friendly and everyone was in a good mood, making the most of their week away from the daily grind. As he walked in, Benjie knew people weren't looking at him, wondering why he was alone. As far as they were concerned, he and his wife could be taking it in turns to come over while the other stayed in the trailer to look after the kids.

They were all here to have fun. No one knew him or cared either way.

And tonight might not be karaoke night, but there was always entertainment of one sort or another, before the evening disco started at ten. According to the poster outside the entrance, there was going to be a limbo contest starting at…ooh, right about now.

The resident master of ceremonies, a jolly comedian in tight black trousers and a bright pink waistcoat, had the audience in the palm of his hand, tailoring his jokes to each of the people who'd joined him on stage to take part. The first contender was Arthur from West Bromwich, who tipped over backward before even reaching the pole but managed not to spill a drop of his pint. Next, an elderly woman called Pauline proved to be surprisingly bendy and limboed lower than anyone was expecting.

Then the comedian called the third contestant out onto the stage, and Benjie's world tipped upside down, because the girl who appeared through the curtain was Dani.

He stopped breathing. He stopped understanding. Because it made no sense; it couldn't possibly be her. But it was.

The comedian was consulting the list in his hand, waiting for the applause to die down. And there was more enthusiastic applause this time, because Dani was looking stunning in a little peach dress that clung to her body and a pair of electric-blue stilettos. Someone in the audience gave a wolf whistle, and she laughed, waved, and did a little hip wiggle, evidently enjoying the attention.

Like, what?

"And here we have contestant number three, Bella! Going to have to kick those heels off, my darling! They're nice, aren't they? Ooh, what size d'you take? I wonder if they'd fit me? That color's great. Matches my varicose veins!"

What? Why was the man calling her Bella? Why was she calling *herself* Bella?

More to the point, why wasn't she cripplingly shy?

Dani-Bella was joking now with the comedian, offering to help him stay upright if he tried on her towering stilettos. Then she faced the wooden limbo set and cheerfully encouraged the audience to clap in order to spur her on. Tiny and lithe, she proceeded to limbo effortlessly beneath the bar, set three feet off the ground.

"There she goes, Bella's through to the second round! You wait at the side of the stage with Pauline, my darling. That's it. And now we have the next contestant… Ooh, look at those muscles—I didn't know we had the Rock staying in one of our trailers! Hope he splashed out on a luxury one. Come on then, let's give a warm welcome to…Darren!"

Darren was tall, tanned, and shaven-headed, with the physique of a serious bodybuilder. He was also winking at Dani-Bella, who was beaming back at him, her pink lip gloss shining beneath the stage lights.

"I say, look at this," the comedian exclaimed. "Do you two know each other?"

"We just met backstage." Darren smirked, flashing fluorescent white teeth. "But it's going pretty well so far."

Benjie put down the drink in his hand and watched as Darren's limbo attempt failed, his massive chest dislodging the pole. Turning to Dani-Bella, he said, "No worries. It was worth it to get the chance to meet you. Catch you later, yeah?"

"Definitely." She pouted prettily and waggled her fingers at him as he left the stage.

Benjie's brain was buzzing as if it were full of bees. He still couldn't work out what had happened. He wanted to leave, but he also wanted to know what was going on. Because this couldn't be the girl he'd been talking to for the last six months. But if Dani had found a photo of a beautiful stranger online and decided to use it, how much of a coincidence was it that the stranger was here now, in Lanrock?

No, that didn't work anyway. In her photos, she responded to the things he'd told her. If she saw him here, would she recognize him?

He was going to have to make her notice him, then go from there. Make her explain what was happening. Because something had to be, didn't it?

Or he could leave now, just walk out of here and drive home, then wait until she messaged him later this evening. It would be easier, so much easier to do it online.

Oh God. First Jo, now this. The two best things that had ever happened to him, crumbling into nothingness in the space of four days.

Benjie turned and walked out of the entertainment block. He made his way back to the parking lot and sat in the car for a few minutes. Tackling Dani online would be easier, but maybe—for once in his life—he needed to be brave and do it face-to-face.

The question was, whose face was it?

He climbed out of the car and headed back inside.

The competition continued for another twenty minutes. Standing at the very back of the crowded room, Benjie watched it progress. Having gotten through to the final round, Dani-Bella ended up in fourth place. As everyone left the stage, muscly Darren beckoned to her from his position over by the bar, and Benjie realized he had to move fast. Heart pounding, he moved forward to intercept her before she could reach Darren.

He stopped directly in front of her and looked her straight in the eye. For half a second, she returned his gaze blankly, then her eyes widened in recognition, and her perfect rosebud mouth fell open.

"Oh my God," said Dani-Bella. "It's you!"

chapter 32

Benjie's heart was racing faster than it had ever raced before. "D-Dani?"

She hesitated, then said, "Yes…"

But it was an unconvincing yes.

He said, "I d-don't know what's going on."

Silence. Benjie could sense the thoughts whirling through her mind. Finally reaching a decision, she nodded in the direction of the main doors. "OK, you'd better come with me."

"Hey," Darren yelled over the heads of the crowd separating them. "What's going on?"

"I'll be back," she called to him. "Wait for me."

Outside, she whipped her phone out of her bra and paused to send a quick text before leading the way along one of the maze of narrow paths that crisscrossed the trailer park. She stopped outside a trailer, unlocked it, and led the way inside.

"You aren't Dani," said Benjie.

"No, I'm Bella. Dani will be here any minute now. I'm going to put the kettle on. Fancy a cup of tea?"

The door opened a couple of minutes later, and Benjie felt the world move into slow motion. The next moment, a face he recognized came into view.

The young lad who'd come into the gallery earlier was looking pale and terrified.

Bella said, "This is my brother Danny. He's sorry. He never wanted to hurt you. And I'm sorry too, because it was my bright idea to come down here so he could meet you." She paused, then added, "But not that sorry, because it had to happen eventually, didn't it?"

Benjie felt sick. It was all just so surreal. The face of the girl he'd had a crush on for the past six months belonged to a stranger who knew who he was but didn't actually know him at all. And the girl he'd been talking to, sharing his hopes, dreams, and innermost feelings, was a boy called Daniel.

His face burned, remembering all the times he'd told Dani he loved her.

"He just wanted to see you, talk to you in person," Bella explained. "It's his birthday next week, and I didn't know what to get him, so I booked us into this place for three days. Oh, I came fourth in the limbo competition, by the way," she told her brother.

Daniel nodded miserably. "That's good."

"And I met this really fit guy too! He's back there waiting for me. I mean, if you want me to stay here, I will." She turned to look at Benjie. "If I leave now, are you going to go berserk and beat Danny up?"

Startled, Benjie said, "What, *me*? N-no!"

"Good. I didn't think you would, but it's best to ask, isn't it? OK then, I'm off. See you later!" And with another of those cheerful waves, she left the trailer.

"Sorry." Danny broke the painful silence, his knuckles shiny-white as he gripped his knees in torn jeans.

"So when you wanted to send me a photo, you'd tell your s-sister what to do, then take pictures of her. And she didn't m-mind?"

Danny shrugged. "She was trying to help me. She saw how happy I was when we first started talking and getting along well together."

"You joined the group as a g-girl."

"I saw you on there before, when I was Daniel. I spoke to you once during a group chat, but you didn't reply. And you'd put on your bio that you were straight. So I left the group and joined it again a few days later using Bella's photo. I thought maybe you'd take more notice of me if you thought I was her. And I was right. You did." He lifted his head and looked properly at Benjie for the first time. "It was amazing, the best feeling ever. We started talking, and it felt like there was this instant connection. You were interested in me. *Everyone* was interested in me."

"What? You've been doing this with other people too?" Weirdly, Benjie felt a surge of…what, jealousy?

"No, no one else. But I could have if I'd wanted to. People chatted to me all the time. They were friendlier. They liked me more. I knew it was cheating, and I did feel bad about that, but not bad enough to stop, because it felt so fantastic. I'd never been so happy, because every day, I had something to look forward to."

Benjie watched Danny's thin fingers curl and uncurl, betraying his misery and discomfort. Considering they were two excruciatingly shy people, the fact that they were managing to have this conversation was an achievement in itself.

Benjie said, "I'm not g-gay though."

Danny hung his head. "I know."

"I'm never going to change my mind and suddenly b-become gay."

"I know that too."

All those months of talking about being together and getting married… It had all been part of the online fantasy. "Were you really planning to buy one of my mum's paintings?"

"No. I couldn't afford it. I just wanted to see you and talk to you, that's all." Danny gestured helplessly. "None of this was meant to happen."

"You didn't like me going out and m-meeting up with Jo." Benjie remembered the comments he'd made.

"I thought if you found yourself a real-life girlfriend, you wouldn't have time to bother with me anymore. You'd lose interest."

"You must have been thrilled when I told you about my mum p-paying her."

"I was. But I felt sorry for you too. It was a rotten thing to happen."

"Have you ever had a b-boyfriend?"

Danny flushed and shook his head. "It's bad enough being shy. Try being shy *and* gay."

He had a point. It must be even more difficult, Benjie realized.

Outside, a gaggle of teenagers were shrieking and laughing, heading down the path toward them with assorted cans of cider and beer. They were so easy in each other's company, messing about, having the best time together, their high spirits in sharp contrast with the sad, strained atmosphere here inside the trailer.

Benjie said, "Where were you earlier when your sister texted you?"

Danny looked embarrassed. "There's a speed chess tournament going on in one of the back rooms of the entertainment block."

"You were p-playing?"

"No, just watching. I like chess though. I play online quite often."

"I never knew that! I love chess. Why didn't you ever tell me?"

"Because you thought I was my sister," Danny said simply. "Bella can't stand anything like that—she says chess is for losers. I thought if she told you she played, you might not be so keen on her."

"I'd have been *more* keen." Benjie realized he'd never mentioned his passion for chess for the same reason. He glanced at his watch. "Would it be too late to enter now?"

Startled, Daniel said, "Yes."

"Oh, OK."

"But we could still go up there if you want. They've got loads of chess sets. People can play without entering the tournament."

Silence inside the trailer. The next moment, loud music began to spill out of the one behind them, and the noisy teenagers started to sing along.

"Sounds like a plan," said Benjie. "Shall we do that, then?"

For the first time, he caught a glimmer of a smile. Danny said, "I'm pretty good, just warning you now. Will you be able to cope if I beat you?"

"You might be the one that gets hammered." Benjie rose to his feet and followed him out of the trailer. "Just so you know, I'm pretty good too."

....

"You missed a great evening," Peggy told him when he returned not long after midnight. The party was over, the guests had departed, and she was stretched out across the sofa, finishing up a tray of hors d'oeuvres.

"Actually, I didn't. I *had* a great evening. No thanks." Benjie shook his head as she offered him the tray. When he and Daniel had eventually left the chess room after three games of speed chess, they'd bought fish and chips from the on-site takeout.

"You look happy. Where did you go? Oh!" Peggy looked hopeful. "Did you and Jo make up?"

His smile faded. "No. Why would I? It's not as if she's a f-friend, is it?"

"Darling—"

"She was just one of your em-employees," Benjie reminded her. It had been humiliating enough that his mother had come up with the idea in the first place but worse still that Jo had been happy to go along with it.

"It wasn't—"

"Anyway, forget it. I'm not interested. I had a nice t-time this evening. With someone who actually likes me."

"Well, that's wonderful, sweetheart. I'm so glad! Who is it?"

She was still being extra nice to him in an attempt to make up for her gigantic faux pas. Benjie, who hadn't completely forgiven her yet, said, "Doesn't matter. No one you know. Right, I'm off to b-bed."

"Love you," Peggy called after him as he headed up the staircase.

He might be in a surprisingly good mood, but she still didn't deserve to be let off that easily. In a neutral voice, Benjie said, "Good night."

chapter 33

RAFFAELE HAD BARELY SLEPT SINCE SATURDAY NIGHT. IT WAS NOW Monday evening, and he and Amber had come over to the house to give Teddy and Olga an update on the Vee situation.

"The last thing she posted on Instagram was 'Why won't people mind their own business and leave me ALONE?'" He showed them the screenshot he'd taken on his phone. "Then she deleted her account. It's gone."

"You should call her again," said Olga.

"She's blocked my number. And she isn't answering calls from anyone else either. We've all tried. We've left messages. She's blaming me for scaring her." He rubbed his hand over the back of his neck in frustration. "The trouble is, she's a grown woman, and no one can force her to see a doctor if she doesn't want to."

"What about the people at work?" said Teddy.

Raffaele shook his head. "I called the salon at lunchtime. Apparently she went in this morning, picked an argument with a junior stylist, and walked out again. They told her to take another week off. From what I can gather, they're glad to see the back of her."

Amber said, "Would she take more notice if you went up there?"

"Right now, I'd say not. She hates me. I was going to try anyway," he went on, "but I've got a wedding booked for tomorrow, a bride and her bridesmaids. I can't let them down, so Wednesday's the earliest—"

"We could go." Olga turned to Amber. "Couldn't we? Actually, that would be better, seeing as Raffaele's the one Vee's blaming right now."

Amber frowned. "Would she take any more notice of us? I mean, is it likely?"

"I reckon we can do it." Olga sounded confident. "And we won't know until we try, will we?"

"It's Malcolm's funeral tomorrow," Teddy reminded them. Malcolm was a local character and an old friend of many years' standing. "Otherwise I'd have offered to drive you up there."

Amber said, "I'd need to close for the day. But that's OK."

"I have a better idea," Olga chimed in, and within two minutes, she'd called the restaurant, spoken to Jo, and arranged for her to hold the fort in the studio tomorrow. Putting the phone down, she gave a brisk nod of satisfaction. "See? All sorted."

"You're so efficient," Amber marveled.

"I'm a Russian. It's part of my job description," said Olga.

Raffaele had no idea if the plan would work, but he was overcome with gratitude at their willingness to give it a try. He gave Amber's hand a squeeze and said, "Thank you."

....

They left Lanrock at five o'clock on Tuesday morning, just before sunrise. Luckily, Amber was used to driving Teddy's car. It was also a good time to set off; four and a half hours and two hundred and thirty miles later, they were approaching the flat in Peckham.

Olga texted Raffaele to let him know they were almost there. Having reinstalled the tracker app on his phone, he'd discovered he was still able to find Vee's location. When he messaged Olga back, he said, She's in there. At least her phone is.

They parked around the corner and made their way to the building Amber had last visited eighteen months earlier, when Vee and Raffaele had still been the happiest couple she knew. Together they descended the stone steps to the basement. The flat had been smartened up considerably over the years, especially since Vee's arrival. There'd been redecoration as well as the addition of much nicer furniture and lighting. Velvet cushions had even been brought into the equation, despite Raffaele and Lachlan having regarded them with as much suspicion as if they'd been unexploded grenades.

Today, the curtains were drawn and there were no signs of life. Amber rang the doorbell and waited, then rang it again.

Finally they heard Vee, on the other side of the door, say shortly, "What?"

"Delivery," Olga called out in a husky voice quite unlike her own.

Slowly the door opened. The moment Vee saw them, she tried to close it again, but Amber already had her foot in the way. *Ow…*

"Oh God, I suppose Raffaele sent you."

"Actually, we volunteered." Olga's voice softened. "Because we want to help, and we think you need someone on your side. That's why we're here."

Vee looked irritated. "I'm fine. There's nothing wrong with me." Aware that she was outnumbered, she backed into the flat. "I wish he'd never met that bloody father of his now. Why did he have to stick his oar in and come out with all that medical claptrap? How *dare* he say there's something wrong with my brain? This is crazy. I can't believe you're here…and if you want a coffee, you'll have to drink it black, because there's no milk… OK, I just need the loo. Back in a minute." She showed them into the living room and disappeared.

The living room was a mess, dusty and airless. There were discarded mugs and plates on every surface and a half-eaten Pot Noodle on the coffee table alongside multiple packets of painkillers and a snapped-in-half lipstick. Amber saw Olga glancing around and murmured, "It never used to look like this."

They waited. After several more seconds of silence, Olga suddenly said, "Is there another way out?"

What? Oh no…

Amber hurtled out of the flat, up the stone staircase, and down the road. Racing along the lane that separated the back-to-back houses, she reached the basement flat just in time to see Vee slithering headfirst out through the narrow bathroom window.

"*Aaargh*," Vee yelped, landing awkwardly on her hands and ending up in a heap on the tiny weed-strewn paving area.

"Don't do this." Amber knelt down and wrapped her arms around her. "I love you. We're here because we want to help. I know you're scared, but we're with you now. All you have to do is be brave and get yourself checked out."

Vee's eyes brimmed. "I can't."

"You can! It might be nothing. Then you'll know and you can stop worrying."

But even as Amber was saying it, Vee was wincing with pain, pressing the flat of her hand against her temple. Tears rolled down her cheeks as she looked at Amber and said helplessly, "That's the trouble though. I don't think it is nothing."

....

"Cheer up. My babushka—sorry, my grandmother—tried to run away once from the secret police in St. Petersburg." Olga's tone was conversational. "They threatened to shoot her. So you see, we're not so bad really!"

The walk-in medical center was only a mile away, but they'd accompanied Vee by each holding one of her hands, to be on the safe side. When they'd arrived and been told how long they'd have to wait to be seen, they had sat on either side of her on hard plastic chairs and made sure she couldn't make another bid for escape. Amber had brought plenty of snacks to keep them going. Olga provided a stream of hair-raising stories about her early years growing up in the Soviet Union, followed by tales of how she'd learned to live by her wits in the UK.

Finally, some three hours later, Vee was called through to be seen by a nurse, and Amber went with her to explain why they'd come here this afternoon. Amber handed over the printed-out email Eamonn had written, detailing the episode he'd witnessed and suspected of being a focal impaired awareness seizure—an FIA.

The nurse made notes as Amber told her everything. Next to her, Vee quivered and wound her legs tightly together like a pretzel while picking at the frayed denim of her skin-tight purple jeans. She argued a bit with Amber before conceding that yes, she did find other people more annoying nowadays, but that wasn't her fault. It was theirs for being so annoying in the first place.

Then it was time for another prolonged wait before they saw a doctor, who wanted to perform a full neurological examination. When he suggested that Amber might want to stay outside, Vee clung onto her arm and said, "No, please, I need her with me."

Now it was reflexes being tested, arms and legs checked, lights shone in Vee's eyes, and many more questions put to her. The doctor made yet more notes, disappeared and reappeared, then finally sat down and explained to Vee that she'd made the right decision coming here today. He was going to make arrangements to have her admitted to the hospital for further urgent tests.

And Vee, who had spent the last weeks in a blind panic fearing that she could be seriously ill, turned to Amber and said, "I knew it."

"You're going to be OK!" Amber squeezed her hand and marveled that against all the odds, Vee wasn't in a blind panic now.

It was as if a switch had been flicked.

"Don't worry. I'm not going to run away." Vee tipped her head back and exhaled slowly, then sat up straight again. "Now that it's happening, it's actually a relief. I can stop trying to convince myself I'm OK." She held up a hand and studied her outstretched fingers. "Feeling a bit shaky though. I could be in shock."

"That's allowed," said the doctor.

"So do I have a brain tumor?"

"Let's get the scans done first, shall we? Before jumping to conclusions."

"But you think it's a tumor."

"It's a possibility. When I used the ophthalmoscope to look into your eyes, there were signs of increased pressure inside the skull. Which is why we're transferring you to the best people to get you checked out."

Amber swallowed; Eamonn had been right.

"Of all the ways I've ever thought I might die," said Vee, "I never thought it'd be this."

"Hey, who says you're going to die?" said the doctor. "You could have another sixty years ahead of you."

While he was out of the office making arrangements for her admission to hospital, Vee began to cry silently, tears dripping onto the knees of her purple jeans. "I deserve this. It's my punishment for being such a cow."

"Don't even think that." Amber's heart went out to her. "You heard what the doctor said. It's something going on in there that's making you…cow-like."

"Moooo," said Vee, wiping her face with her sleeve while laughing and sobbing at the same time.

"It's going to be all right." Amber hugged her tightly. "I know it is."

"I wish Raff was here. Oh God, I wish he could be here now."

"I'll call him. He'll come."

"No, he won't. It's over. He's sick and tired of me being a monster." She winced and clutched her head. "Ow, it *hurts*."

"He loves you."

"I'm a nightmare. He hates me."

"I bet you a million pounds you're wrong."

"You don't even have a million pounds." Vee pulled a tissue from the box on the desk and made a sobbing, honking sound into it.

"I don't need a million pounds," Amber told her. "Because I'm right."

The door to the office flew open, and Olga burst in. "The doctor said I could come through. I've got Raffaele on my phone wanting to know what's going on." She thrust it into Vee's hand.

Vee lifted it to her ear, her voice breaking as she whispered, "Oh, Raff…"

They all heard Raffaele say, "Do you want me to come up?"

Vee choked back more tears. "Only if you want to."

He didn't hesitate for a second. "I'm on my way."

....

Lachlan was in the restaurant getting ready for evening service when Raffaele arrived, pale but determined, to update him with what was going on.

"She's having the brain scan now. If it's what they think it is, they'll be operating tomorrow."

It was actually happening. Shit, poor Vee. Lachlan felt sick at the thought of how she must be feeling. "How long will you be up there?"

"As long as it takes." Raffaele was impatiently jangling his keys, clearly keen to be gone.

"What about the salon?"

"A couple of the other stylists are going to cover for me. If the clients don't like it, they can take a hike. Jesus, I *knew* there was something wrong. All this time, Vee's been struggling to keep going, and it wasn't her fault." The anguish was there in his eyes.

"Not your fault either," Lachlan reminded him. "Don't beat yourself up about it."

"I should have made her get herself checked out months ago. I tried, but she just refused to do it. If Amber and Olga hadn't practically kidnapped her, it could have been too late. Thank God they did."

Vee was all he cared about; that much was blindingly obvious. He still loved her as deeply as he ever had. It was hardly the time or the place, but Lachlan couldn't help himself; he had to know for sure. "So you're not interested in Amber anymore?"

"Amber?" There it was, the momentary look of confusion, because he'd genuinely forgotten. Then he remembered and half smiled, aware that he'd been caught out. "It was never Amber. Always Vee."

Having observed him closely over the last week, Lachlan had figured out as much. He said, "You lied to me."

"I saw the way you looked at Amber, guessed what could be about to happen." Raffaele gave a tiny shrug. "I did it to protect her. To protect all of us," he amended. "Because I'm telling you now, if you break Amber's heart, I'll never forgive you."

"I'd never forgive myself." Lachlan acknowledged the warning. "Anyway, you'd better head off. Give my love to Vee, and let me know what's going on. Any time of the day or night."

....

"Just got back," said Amber when Lachlan answered his door at one in the morning. "Sorry, were you asleep?"

"Of course I wasn't. I've been waiting for you." As he gave her a hug, he felt her body sag wearily against his. "Come on in. Have you eaten? What can I get you?"

Upstairs, she stretched out on the sofa, clearly exhausted after having driven almost five hundred miles in one day. Lachlan heated up the pasta primavera he'd saved for her, and Amber hauled herself into a sitting position in order to eat it.

"They showed us the tumor on the scan. It's in a part of the brain called the temporal lobe, which controls temper and behavior. It's been growing inside her head for God knows how long, causing all the headaches and outbursts. From what they can see, they think it's benign, but they won't know for sure until they operate. That's happening at some stage tomorrow."

"Thanks to you."

"And Olga. She was brilliant today. She *was*," Amber emphasized, intercepting his hint of an eye roll. "You should have seen her. Vee tried to kick off again when she was being admitted to the ward, but Olga managed to calm her down. And all the way home tonight, she made sure I stayed awake."

Was there anything more infuriating than being told over and over again how amazing someone was in an attempt to persuade you over to their side? "That doesn't make her a hero. She just didn't want you crashing the car while she was inside it."

"Well, I just dropped her home—"

"You mean you dropped her at Teddy's house." He couldn't resist pointing this out, even if just to tease her.

"Will you *stop* it? I dropped her off, and Teddy was out in a flash, and you should have seen them hugging… It's the real thing," said Amber. "He's crazy about her."

"Of course he is. That's not what I'm saying."

"And she adores him. She *does*. You just refuse to see it. OK, I'm too tired to argue with you." She looked at her plate and put down her fork. "Sorry, I can't manage the rest of this either."

"We won't argue. You can stay. You can have the bed, and I'll sleep on the sofa."

But she was already hauling herself wearily to her feet. "It's OK. I'd rather get back. Loads to do tomorrow. Thanks for the food anyway."

Lachlan exhaled; and now he'd managed to self-sabotage the situation. "I'll see you tomorrow. Give me a call in the morning."

"OK." Amber yawned and nodded. "Raff's going to let us know as soon as Vee's gone into surgery. Oh God, I hope it goes OK. She must be petrified. Thank goodness she's got him there with her."

Lachlan watched from the upstairs window as Amber made her way along the narrow street, her hair gleaming as she passed beneath the pools of golden light from the ornate streetlamps. His heart contracted with love for her, coupled with the knowledge that though tonight might not have been the right time, he was fast running out of willpower. And yes, of course it felt wrong to even be thinking this way while up in London Raff and Vee were facing something so major, but he couldn't help himself. He knew, beyond a shadow of a doubt, that he wanted to be with Amber for the rest of his life.

....

The neurosurgeon arrived on the ward at 6:30 the next morning, just as the breakfast carts were beginning to clatter along the corridor outside. "I'm afraid it's not going to be any time soon," she told Vee. "A patient's just been brought in from emergency, and they need to be operated on right away."

"OK." Vee nodded and managed a weak smile. "That's fine. Thank you."

But as soon as the surgeon had left, her face crumpled. "I don't want to do this anymore. I want to go home."

Raffaele pulled his chair even closer to the bed and stroked her arm. "Hey, it's OK. You can do it." It might be agonizing having to wait for several more hours, but he wasn't going anywhere, and neither was Vee.

"I'm scared." Her eyes were huge.

"I know."

"What if I die?"

"You're not going to die."

"What if I'm not me anymore afterward?"

"They're doing this to make you better. Back to being the old you," Raffaele reminded her.

She gazed at him, nodded slowly. "Thank you for being here. I'm sorry I've been such a pain. I love you so much."

It was as if an impenetrable curtain had been separating them for months. Now it had been swept aside.

Squashing down his own fears, Raffaele leaned forward and kissed her on the mouth. When he pulled back, he said, "Not as much as I love you."

....

Amber was in her studio by seven, putting the finishing touches to the giant octopus. It was done at last, and Dom was coming to check it over at nine, after which it would be securely wrapped in endless layers of bubble wrap and transported up to his flagship hotel in London. Hopefully still in one piece when it arrived.

Nine o'clock came and went. So did ten. It was almost eleven before she heard the familiar growl of the car pulling up outside. When she went out to greet him, she saw that he had company.

"Hi," said Dom. "Sorry we're a bit late."

She looked at her watch. "Quite a lot late."

The raven-haired beauty at his side said, "It's all my fault. I wouldn't let him get out of bed."

"Right." Amber hid a smile, because the woman was running her hand up and down Dom's arm, giving little proprietorial squeezes as if his bicep were an avocado she might want to buy.

"This is…Nicole." From the fractional pause, Amber guessed that Nicole was a recent arrival in his life. "Nicole, this is Amber."

"He told me about you." Nicole was wearing a winning smile, along with an elegant caramel wrap dress. "I can't wait to see your octopus!"

"Not a euphemism," said Dom, straight-faced.

Inside the studio, Nicole gave a squeal of delight when she caught sight of the completed chandelier. "Oh my God, it's huge!"

Amber had fed flexible light strips inside the tentacles in order to show off the colors of the glass; vibrant shades of ruby red, bottle green, and yellow ochre came to life when she plugged in the leads and switched them on.

"This is perfect," said Dom. "You've done an incredible job."

She grinned. "I know I have."

Dom took photos of the chandelier in the workshop with Amber standing beside her creation, then passed his phone to Nicole and said, "Can you take a few of us together? We'll be using them for promo."

"There." When she'd finished, Nicole looked at Amber. "How artistic of you, tying your hair up with an old pair of tights!"

"Oh God." She'd done it earlier without thinking, to keep the ends away from her soldering iron, and had completely forgotten that the paint-spattered blue tights were still tied in a jaunty bow on top of her head. Pulling them out of her hair, she said, "Can we take a couple more without the tights?"

"No, it's done now. You looked fine. Rustic!" Nicole leaned lovingly against Dom and stroked his face. "Shall we go?"

Dom nodded. "Just give me a couple of minutes. Could you wait in the car?"

Her jaw tightened a fraction. "Fine, if I have to. But don't be long."

Nicole sashayed out of the studio. Dom waited until they heard the clunk of the car door, then said, "Sorry about that. She insisted on coming along."

"Not a problem." Amber smiled.

"Still." He gave her the kind of rueful, semi-apologetic look that said everything: he was an attractive man who liked a lot of women and quite often slept with them, simply because he could. "I met her a couple of days ago."

"Honestly, you don't owe me any kind of explanation. But I think Nicole thinks she's won the lottery."

He broke into that trademark easy grin of his. "It won't last, of course."

That went without saying. "She's very beautiful."

"So are you. But you don't flaunt it." Dom touched the discarded blue tights on her workbench. "In fact, you anti-flaunt it. And if you'd really liked me, you'd have dressed up a bit more today."

"This is what I wear when I'm working here in the studio. And I do like you," Amber told him. "Very much. As a friend."

"I'll take that. And I understand why. It's fine." He moved forward to give her a hug or a kiss, then visibly checked himself and gave her shoulder a pat instead. "See? A *friendly* pat. To prove what a good loser I am." His mouth twitched. "And I'm not used to losing, by the way. So my congratulations to the winner."

"Except there is no winner."

"Oh, I think there is."

She felt her scalp warm up. "Are you thinking it's Lachlan? Because it really isn't. There's nothing like that going on between us."

"Is that really what you think? Take it from one who knows." There was a twinkle in Dom's eye. "You might not feel that way about him, but he definitely has feelings for you."

"Not *that* kind of feelings." Startled, Amber shook her head. "I'd know if it was true."

He looked amused. "OK, if you say so."

Nicole reappeared in the shop doorway, no longer smiling. "Dom, you said two minutes, and that was four and a half minutes ago."

He glanced at her. "I'm having a conversation, Nicole. I'll be out when I've finished."

When they were alone once more, Amber said, "Plus Raffaele's his best friend. If there was anything to notice, he'd have spotted it. Raffaele always knows what's going on."

Dom raised his hands. "Hey, you don't have to believe me. I'm just saying what I saw. Maybe Lachlan works harder to hide it when he's with people he knows well. Whereas with someone like me, it doesn't matter so much. Easier to let your guard down, that kind of thing." He checked his watch. "Anyway, time I was gone. Just something for you to consider. I look forward to seeing how it all pans out." There was that easy, sunny smile again. "And please email me your ideas for the next chandelier, because I'm definitely going to want another one."

"Do you always get what you want?" Her mind buzzing with more information than she knew what to do with, Amber resorted to flippancy. Then she saw the look in his eyes.

"Not always," said Dom.

....

"So sorry about this," said the nurse, arriving at Vee's bedside. "They've had two more emergencies come in, so you've been bumped down the list. Looks like you won't be going into surgery for a while yet."

They'd been waiting five hours already. Reaching for Vee's hand, Raffaele fully expected her to kick off.

"OK," said Vee. "Any chance of a gin and tonic?"

The nurse smiled. "Best not."

chapter 34

"Any news yet?" Amber blurted out when Raffaele picked up.

"You can keep on calling me," Raffaele sighed, "but it's not going to make it happen any sooner."

"Sorry." She'd been messaging him all day, enduring the agonizing delays along with him and Vee, until Vee had finally been taken into surgery at the end of the afternoon. Now it was 10:30 in the evening, Vee was still in there, and Amber was finding the waiting increasingly difficult to handle. "If it feels like this for me, I can't imagine what it's like for you."

"Well, I'm spending most of my time answering texts and calls. Everyone's desperate for an update. Look, do me a favor," said Raffaele. "Lachlan's supposed to be cooking in the restaurant, and he's sending messages every five minutes. Tell him to stop, will you? As soon as I hear anything at all, I'll let you both know, I promise."

Amber's original plan had been to get to bed early and catch up on all the sleep she'd missed out on last night. In an ideal world, Vee would have been out of surgery by now, with the doctors hopefully convinced everything was fine.

But that hadn't happened, and there was no way she could sleep. For more than one reason.

She was still half wondering if Dom had been joking earlier, playing some kind of game with her for his own amusement.

She fired off a message to Lachlan:

Still no news. Raff says can you stop calling and texting him? It's doing his head in. He'll be in touch with us the moment he hears anything.

Lachlan messaged back thirty seconds later: Just getting rid of the last customers now. Want to come over?

Amber's pulse quickened. She typed, No.

His reply flashed up almost instantly: Fine, I'll come to you.

Her hair was still wet and tangled from the shower. She dragged a comb through it and changed out of her short nightdress into a T-shirt and shorts instead.

No perfume though. No makeup. And certainly no plans for anything to happen. God, no; hadn't she tried that once before, that Christmas on the beach? And been gently but firmly rejected? Her skin crawled with fresh shame as the memory of it came whooshing back. The humiliation had never faded, was installed permanently in her DNA.

Her phone went *ding* and another message lit up the screen:

Salted caramel mousse or pineapple parfait?

She typed back, What a ridiculous question. Bring both.

He arrived twenty minutes later, and she downloaded the next episode of *Cooking for the Enemy*. They tried to watch the show—next-door neighbors who'd been fighting for years over a bigamous cat who'd been dividing its attention between both adoring families—but it was impossible to concentrate. As the minutes ticked by, the tension escalated.

"Stop it," said Amber, when she saw Lachlan googling *How long does it take to remove a brain tumor?*

"They should have finished by now. It's been hours. What if something's gone wrong?"

This was what had been going through Amber's mind. Thanks to too many seasons of *Grey's Anatomy*, her overactive imagination was conjuring up all kinds of panic-inducing scenarios. The longer the silence continued, the more likely it seemed that something terrible must have happened and—

They both jumped a mile as her phone rang.

But it wasn't Raffaele; it was Olga. "This is killing us. Have you heard anything yet?"

"No." Amber's stomach was in knots. "We just have to wait."

Time continued to crawl by. Their favorite TV show had ended, but when Amber said blankly, "Who won?" Lachlan shrugged.

"No idea."

Something must have happened. Maybe they had broken the bad news to Raffaele and he was in no fit state to speak to anyone. It was almost midnight now. Lachlan finished his vodka tonic and disappeared into the kitchen to make another. Amber took a sip of her own drink, then almost knocked her teeth out on the glass as her phone burst into life once more.

This time, it wasn't Olga.

"She's fine," Raffaele blurted out. "It took longer than they were expecting because of a technical issue, but it's done now. They got it all out. And everything's looking good." His voice cracked with emotion. "The surgeon said it has to be checked by histology, but as far as they're concerned, it's an absolutely classic benign meningioma, and the operation couldn't have gone better."

Lachlan was standing frozen in the kitchen doorway, watching her. When Amber promptly burst into tears, he said, "*No…*"

She shook her head at him. "It's OK, it's good news," and the look of relief on his face was just indescribable.

Taking the phone from her, he heard the story again from Raffaele, then said, "Give her our love. This is the best news. Thank God."

When the call was over, he looked at Amber. "She's going to be all right. Why are you still crying?"

Which was the kind of question only a man could ask.

Her breath catching in her throat, Amber wiped her cheeks with the back of her hand and wailed, "Because I'm ha-ha-*happy*."

And just as neither of them earlier had been able to say how their favorite TV show had ended, neither of them ever knew how what happened next had begun. Amber found herself in Lachlan's arms, clinging to him like a rock in a storm. They were hugging and hugging as the pent-up anguish overflowed and spilled out of them, and it just felt so right, because they loved Vee and they loved Raffaele and everything was going to be all right and she loved Lachlan too…

The next moment, they were already kissing, and Amber had no idea which of them had made the first move. Like magnets, the draw was simply too powerful to resist. Lachlan's warm mouth was on hers, his fingers were sliding through the still-damp hair at the back of her neck, and every centimeter of her body was on fire, clamoring for more. She could feel his heart thudding against her rib cage, hear the sound of his breathing, inhale the scent of his skin, which was tantalizingly familiar because she'd known it before, but never this close up.

Oh God, this was an utterly magical experience, as mesmerizing and spectacular as the northern lights. For years, she'd worked so hard to suppress her feelings for Lachlan because they hadn't been reciprocated, but now it was happening at last, and she didn't know why, but neither could she say no. Because how could this be wrong when nothing—*nothing*—had ever felt more perfect in her life?

Then Lachlan was drawing back, shaking his head slightly, his eyes darker than ever and his breathing ragged. "We shouldn't be doing this."

"Why not? Don't you want to?" Amber blinked, petrified he was going to stop.

"Of course I *want* to, but…we mustn't." He looked so conflicted.

"Because you're seeing someone else?" Right now, she didn't even care if he was.

"No! I mean, I'm not seeing anyone. It just…wouldn't be right."

"I think it would."

In response, Lachlan closed his eyes and drew a slow breath. "You're not making this any easier for me. You know that, don't you?"

"Good. I don't want to make things easier." She could feel him trembling beneath her hand as it rested on his chest. "Can I ask you something?"

Lachlan's eyes slowly opened, and he gazed at her with such naked longing that it took her breath away. As he nodded, her phone began to ring. The next second, his own followed suit.

"It's Olga." Amber glanced at her screen, crashing back to earth with a thud.

"And Teddy," said Lachlan, looking at his.

Olga was sobbing. "Did you hear? Oh, the relief! Isn't it the best news?"

"Did Raffaele call to let you know?" Teddy was clearly overjoyed.

"He just did," said Lachlan.

"Who's that?" Olga had heard the voice.

Amber said, "It's Lachlan. He's here too."

"Oh, that's wonderful," Olga exclaimed. "You must both be as happy as we are—I hope you're going to celebrate!"

Amber locked eyes with Lachlan, who was still on the phone to Teddy. With a squiggle of reckless excitement mixed with anticipation, she said to Olga, "I'm sure we will."

The moment both their calls had ended, they were back in each other's arms, and this time, there was nothing to stop them. No questions asked, no answers given, no hesitation in going for what they both wanted more than anything else in the world. Their stars had collided. Amber had made up her mind, and she definitely wasn't going to give Lachlan the chance to change his.

Today was a good-news day, life was for living, and they were going to celebrate in the best possible way.

....

Lachlan's breathing was slowly returning to normal. Lying on his back on the left-hand side of Amber's bed—for the second time in less than a week, but this time with an entirely different outcome—he ran a hand over his torso, felt the sheen of perspiration on his skin, and wondered if he'd just made the most monumental mistake of his life.

The thing was, it didn't feel like a monumental mistake. If it hadn't been completely amazing, the subsequent excuses would have been so much easier to make. But this had felt perfect, which made it that much more complicated.

"Oh dear," Amber murmured, lying next to him. "You're not happy."

"I am."

"You don't look it. What's wrong? Was I rubbish?" She said it flippantly but with a faint undertone of fear.

"You know you weren't." Reaching for her hand, he entwined her fingers with his.

She tilted her head sideways to look at him properly. "But you're regretting it. Can I ask you that question now?"

"The one you were going to ask before we were so rudely interrupted? Fire away."

"That time before, when I tried to kiss you on the beach…you didn't want to. You pulled away, made me stop." She left the rest unspoken, and Lachlan sensed how much it had cost her to say that. He also knew he had to stay strong now and sound entirely believable.

"I had to," he replied simply. "Because I didn't want you to stop."

He saw Amber's eyes widen. "What?"

"Oh, come on. What man in his right mind would turn down a kiss from someone like you? That's just basic biology. Who'd refuse an offer like that? You're not exactly repulsive."

She absorbed this. "But you did turn me down."

"Because it was the right thing to do. I was uncharacteristically noble and heroic. And you know that too. You know what I was like back then. It could never have ended well. And nothing's changed. I'm still the same person. It's in my genes. I see a pretty girl, I sleep with her, and sooner or later, I get bored and move on to the next one. That's me. It's what I do, what I've always done. And the reason I never got bored with you is because we never did sleep together." Lachlan paused; he was forcing himself to sound more flippant, more offhand, and way less emotionally involved than he was currently feeling. More like his public persona and less like the one that, beneath the bravado, was floundering way out of its depth.

"Until tonight," said Amber. She blinked. "We crossed the line."

"We did. Well and truly."

"We weren't thinking. We were…celebrating."

That was one way of putting it. Lachlan shook his head. "And that's fine. It's done now. It was just sex, nothing more. But it mustn't happen again. We can't take the risk of it ending up wrecking what we already have. God knows, I wish I wasn't the way I am, but I know I'm never going to change. I couldn't bear to make you unhappy…and I *really* couldn't bear it if we weren't friends anymore. That would just—"

"OK." She stopped him in his tracks.

"OK what?"

"You're right." Amber turned onto her side so she was fully facing him. "Everything you've said, it makes sense. Tonight's a one-off. We needed to celebrate, and we got carried away. But it mustn't happen again."

Lachlan felt as if a rug had been pulled out from under him; he'd meant it, but he hadn't expected her to so readily agree with him. It was almost as if she was only too well aware of where his faults lay. Except of course she was; she knew him as well as he knew himself.

He nodded. "Right. Well, good."

"Never again," Amber insisted.

"Exactly." This was going to be torture.

Her fingers were still interlocked with his. The corners of her mouth curved up into the merest hint of an innocent smile. As she ran her bare toes lightly over his foot, she murmured, "So we're agreed, we're never, ever going to do this again. After tonight."

And there was his resolve, swooping and swirling like a playful ghost out through the open window, because there were hours of the night still to go. Overcome with relief and renewed lust, Lachlan drew her against him. "Sounds like a plan to me."

chapter 35

Benjie and Danny were walking along the shoreline together. It was 6:30, and at this hour of the morning, the beach was still practically empty. Lacy wavelets slid up the sand, glinting in the pale sunshine as the two of them made their way barefoot along East Beach.

It was their last chance to spend time together before Danny and Bella had to leave Lanrock and head home.

"I know this didn't turn out the way either of us was expecting," said Danny, "but it's still ended up being the best holiday of my life."

Benjie nodded in agreement. Considering he'd been catfished and Dani no longer existed, the situation had turned out surprisingly well. He had someone new in his life now, a boy called Daniel who knew him so well it was as if they'd been friends for years. "It's crazy. I mean, it'd be even more perfect if I was gay. I wish I was, but I'm just not."

"It's probably better this way. We can be friends forever. Nothing can spoil it. And we can still chat every night, can't we?"

"Definitely." They'd spent every available minute in each other's company since Sunday night, and the conversation had continued to flow. Neither of them had mentioned it, but Benjie knew he was stammering less often, and he was sure Danny had noticed too.

"The park still has trailers to rent in September," Danny said now. "I can come down again then."

"You don't have to book a trailer. You can stay at mine. Bella can too, if she wants." Bella had spent the last couple of days plunged into an enthusiastic fling with muscle-bound Darren, who hailed from Blackpool.

"Thanks, that's—"

"Oh God," Benjie blurted out, because what, seconds ago, had been nothing more than a dot in the distance had now turned into a rapidly approaching dog. For some reason, Moose appeared to find him completely irresistible, which had been flattering before but was just plain awkward now. And this time, he wasn't accompanied by Jo's grandmother.

"Hi. Sorry," Jo panted when she caught up with the dog. "He's just excited to see you."

She was glancing over at Daniel. Benjie wondered if she'd sent Moose over deliberately. He concentrated on ruffling Moose's ears and said, "Hello, boy."

"So how have you been?" Jo was doing her best to sound casual, but he could detect the underlying tension in her voice.

"Great. Never better." Straightening up, he took a step back. "Well, we n-need to get back. Bye."

"Oh, bye." She looked crestfallen. "It's good to see you again anyway."

"Is it?" Benjie couldn't help himself; the urge to make her feel bad was more than he could resist. "Or did s-someone pay you to say that?"

When Jo and Moose were safely out of earshot, Danny said, "I know why you did it. But you can see how guilty she feels."

"Good." He was glad. He'd related every last humiliating detail, and Danny had been sympathetic—of course he had. But now Benjie realized he was being given a bit of side-eye. Impatiently he said, "Why are you looking at me like that?"

Danny shrugged. "Felt a bit sorry for her, that's all."

Benjie was outraged. "Sorry for *her*?"

"It wasn't her idea, was it? Your mum was the one who came up with the plan. But you're speaking to *her*."

"I am now. I told her how mad I was though. It's what she's like. She comes up with stupid ideas without bothering to think them through. But she's my mum. And she means well. She gets it wrong, that's all."

"Maybe Jo meant well."

Benjie's lip curled, because Danny clearly didn't understand. "She pretended to be my friend. For m-money. That's different. It's deception."

"OK, but it still wasn't her idea."

"Why can't you understand how it made me feel? I *liked* her."

"I know. I'm just saying, from what you've told me, her life is a bit different from yours."

Were they having their first argument? Benjie couldn't believe Daniel was actually giving him a lecture. "So?"

"You live in a massive house on top of a cliff overlooking the sea. It's worth millions. You have your own apartment on the top floor and a great car and a job—"

"That I *hate*," Benjie interjected.

"Fine, you hate it, but it's still a job loads of people would love to have. And you've been on fantastic holidays. Basically, you don't have to worry about money…paying the bills…"

"That's not my f-fault."

"Didn't say it was." Daniel bent to pick up a flat pebble and skimmed it across the surface of the water…bounce, bounce, bounce, until it sank. "But it's not Jo's fault either that she grew up like most of us, scrimping and saving for treats and having to economize so we can pay for our phones and our trips to McDonald's. Because we're happy to do that, don't get me wrong, but if some Good Samaritan is going to appear out of the blue and offer us money to do a really easy job…well, I'm saying not many people would turn it down. I certainly wouldn't."

Seized with horror, Benjie stopped walking. "What does that mean? Did she pay you too?" Because if his mother had somehow gotten into his laptop and secretly made contact with Danny, he was definitely never going to speak to her again.

"Don't be daft. Of course she didn't. I'm trying to explain why Jo went along with it." With a faint smile, Danny said, "I can't believe I'm defending her, considering how jealous I used to get when you first started going out together. But that was before I met you, when you still thought I was a girl. I suppose now that we really know each other, I'm being more sensible."

Benjie sidestepped a crab scuttling across the sand in front of him. "So if I feel like a bit of company after you've left, you're saying I should give Jo a call and offer her the j-job back? Oh yes, sounds like a great idea. I'll definitely d-do that."

They'd almost reached the steps leading up from the beach. It was time for Danny to make his way back to the trailer park and for Benjie to get ready for work. Danny raked his fingers through his already breeze-ruffled hair. "Look, I don't want us to fall out."

"I know. It's OK. We're not going to." Benjie couldn't bear for that to happen.

"It's just you forgave your mum for doing what she did. And you've forgiven me for lying to you for months."

"I know where you're going with this." He shook his head. "Don't say it."

"OK, I won't. So long as you promise to think about it." There was that faint smile again, lighting up Danny's face. "That's good enough for me."

chapter 36

"Hey," one of the nurses called out as Raffaele accompanied Vee back along the hospital corridor to the ward. "We love your friends! Can you thank them for us?"

"Which friends?" said Vee.

"Hang on. I'll show you what they sent us." Diving into the office, the nurse, whose name was Dina, reemerged with a big basket of individual cakes wrapped in multicolored ribbons and crackling cellophane. "It just arrived! Isn't that gorgeous? Hang on. I'll show you the note…"

Raffaele read aloud, "'To all you wonderful NHS angels looking after our precious Vee—we're so grateful to you! With much love from Teddy and Olga.'"

"Oh, that's so lovely," said Vee.

"Olga called me last night to ask what the staff would like," Raffaele told Dina. "I took a wild guess."

"You did well." Dina turned to Vee. "And you're looking amazing too."

"Thanks." Vee did a little curtsy, then lightly touched the stapled-together craniotomy scar on the right side of her head. "Feeling good, considering Frankie just broke the news that I mustn't bleach my hair for the next six weeks!" Frankie was the seventy-three-year-old blond bombshell of the ward, currently recovering from surgery following a cerebral hemorrhage, and was busy ordering ornate wigs on eBay in preparation for resuming her career as a Dolly Parton tribute act.

"Ah, you look fabulous anyway," said Dina. "Whatever color your hair is. And listen, my daughter doesn't know you're one of our patients, but she's a huge fan of yours, been following you on Instagram for years. Last night, she was wondering why you'd deleted your account and wishing you'd bring it back."

"Oh, that's so lovely! What's her name?" said Vee. "I'll track her down and follow her on there. Would she like it if I sent her a message?"

"Her name's Tallulah Blue, and are you serious? You'd make her year!" Dina flushed with delight. "Vee, she's crazy about you. You've always been her favorite. She'd scream the house down if she knew I'd been looking after you here."

"Helping me put on my support stockings, you mean?" Vee laughed. "Bringing me a bedpan after the op when I couldn't get out of bed? Look, let me get my Instagram back up and running first. Once that's done, we'll have a photo together, then I'll write her a letter, and you can give it to her tonight."

It had only been four days since the surgery, but the change in Vee had been astonishing. Raffaele still couldn't get over the transformation. The anger and irritability had disappeared, vanished like early-morning mist, and the old cheerful Vee was back. She was still tired, obviously, and concentrating on building her strength back up, but it had been an absolute joy to witness the improvement. Miraculously, she was herself again.

"How about this one?" Frankie showed them the box that had been delivered while they were off the ward. "It's called the Marie Antoinette. Dolly enough for me, d'you think?"

Vee, back on her bed, clapped her hands. "Frankie, it's amazing. You're going to look more Dolly than Dolly herself! And don't forget what I told you about calling the salon if you ever need any help with your hair or your wigs. I'll always sort you out."

After lunch, with her phone charged up for the first time since she'd come into the hospital, Vee reinstated the Instagram account she'd previously deleted. Raffaele saw her wince, reading back through her final posts and seeing the anger in her words. "I knew it was bad, but this is worse than I thought. Everyone must hate me."

"They don't." He shook his head.

Vee gave him a don't-bullshit-me look.

"And if they do," he went on, "it's only because they don't know what you've been through." Only Vee's family were aware, and they'd been sworn to secrecy.

She spent several minutes scrolling through the messages sent and received over the course of the last few weeks, viewing them now with fresh eyes. "I was horrendous."

"It wasn't your fault. And you aren't horrendous anymore." Last night, they'd been paid a visit by the consultant neurosurgeon, who'd come to let them know that the results from the histology lab were back and that the meningioma was, as had been confidently predicted, one hundred percent benign. With no evidence whatsoever of malignant cells, she explained to Vee, there was no reason to worry that anything more alarming could crop up in the future.

After thanking her—yet again—Vee had said, "So does this mean that from now on, I'm always going to be calm and happy?"

"Well, fingers crossed." The surgeon turned to Raffaele with a smile. "Although I can't promise she won't get a bit annoyed if you forget when it's your turn to put the bins out."

Now, sitting cross-legged on the bed in a plain gray T-shirt and shorts, Vee passed her phone over. "Can you take a quick photo of me? Not loads, just one."

Raffaele took the photo. If she was going to post it online, her sizeable audience of followers was going to get a shock, but to him, she had never looked more beautiful. The still-fresh scar, held together with metal staples, was there on her scalp for all to see. She was wearing no makeup, and there were dark shadows beneath her eyes, but she was smiling broadly as she held up one hand to wave at the camera.

By the time he returned from the coffee shop twenty minutes later, Vee had already written what she'd wanted to write and posted it on her account along with the photo. Raffaele took out his own phone and read the post:

Hi everyone. Well, what can I say? I'm so sorry. For the past few months, I've been feeling increasingly unwell and cranky and angry. (You probably noticed.)

As many of you will know, I also lost my wonderful boyfriend, my dignity, and most of my friends. But five days ago, a couple of the last remaining people who still cared about me drove hundreds of miles up to London and forced me to seek medical help.

I've now had surgery to remove a benign tumor from my brain. It had been affecting my mood and my behavior in a very bad way. Basically, it turned me into a horrible person. I can't tell you how much better I feel already. Hopefully from now on, I'll be back to my old cheerful self.

Anyway, sorry again from the bottom of my heart to everyone I've been mean to. Every single argument has been my fault and no one else's. I've been a hideous bitch, I'm mortified by the way I behaved, and I just hope you can forgive me.

The staff here at the hospital have been fantastic, by the way. I can't believe how lucky I've been. Oh, and if you happen to be reading this, @TallulahBlue, your lovely mum Dina has been extra brilliant at looking after me. (Are you screaming? She said you would!)

"Does it sound all right?" said Vee when Raffaele had finished reading.

He nodded, swallowing the lump in his throat, because her words were so honest, so *her*. "More than all right. It's perfect."

"I haven't looked. Have there been any comments yet?"

"Are you serious?" Raffaele held up his phone so she could see for herself. There was a fast-moving torrent of replies scrolling up the screen, hundreds of them already.

Vee made a funny little squeak of fear in her throat. "Do they think I'm just making excuses?"

He wasn't supposed to be on the bed, but Raffaele sat down beside her and wrapped his arms around her. "They don't think you're making excuses. They love you. Even Dawn Kerrigan loves you."

"Wow." Vee rested the unshaven side of her head on his shoulder. "She's still a nightmare though."

Raffaele gave her a reassuring squeeze. "Everyone knows that."

She tilted his face so she could give him a kiss. "I'm so glad you're here."

He returned the kiss. "Me too."

"Nurse? Nurse!" From the next bed, Frankie waved her walking stick to attract attention. "These two are getting frisky over here. If someone doesn't draw the curtains around that bed, they're going to end up getting arrested."

....

It was like being a secret agent. Amber was living a lie, playing a role, pretending to be a different person, and loving every minute while at the same time acutely aware that at any moment, it could all come crashing down around her ears.

Not could. *Would.* Inevitably it was going to come to an end; she knew that. The accidental one-night stand that had happened a week ago had left her breathless and desperate for more. Like being given a taster of the world's most wildly addictive drug, she'd been powerless to resist when, the very next night, Lachlan had turned up after work with a rum-and-cherry cheesecake.

"We really shouldn't." He'd made an extremely half-hearted attempt to stop her when she'd greeted him at the door with a deliberately seductive kiss.

"The thing is," Amber had blurted out, "everything you said last night was true, except it's only going to cause a problem if I'm crazy about you. But I'm not! Not in a romantic way! So if neither of us wants that kind of relationship, which we definitely don't, there's no problem, is there? We're friends, we're both single, and we like having sex with each other. Which makes me think it would make perfect sense for us to be two single friends who like having sex with each other."

She had been breathing a bit raggedly by the time she'd reached the end of the proposal, silently praying that Lachlan would be on board but terrified that he might not be. She'd spent all day refining the argument in her head and practicing being all nonchalant about it. So long as Lachlan had no idea how she really felt about him, hopefully he'd agree. And really, she should be able to carry on hiding those feelings, shouldn't she? She'd had enough years of practice.

But then she'd seen him hesitate, and panic had set in. Gesturing wildly, she'd exclaimed, "Oh, come on. Don't be so boring! What's the matter with you? It's not as if I'm going to start crying and telling you I love you, is it? Can't we just have a fantastic no-strings shag?"

The look on Lachlan's face had been unreadable at that point. Amber had found herself holding her breath.

Then she'd seen the glint of mischief in his dark eyes, and the next moment, he pulled her into his arms. "Oh well, if you absolutely insist."

And that had been it; after that, they'd become friends with benefits.

Fantastic friends with out-of-this-world benefits. Inside Amber's head, she might be calling it making love, but as far as Lachlan was aware, it was simply joyous, brilliant, absolutely-no-strings-at-all sex.

He'd been coming over to her cottage every evening, under cover of darkness, and no one else knew what was going on; it was their secret.

It was the best, zingiest, and most fabulous secret Amber had ever had, made all the more bittersweet by the fact that she knew it couldn't last. Before long, Lachlan would inevitably grow bored and move on. But until that happened, she was going to revel in every perfect minute.

And here he was now, but this time, it was 5:30 in the afternoon, and they both had to keep their clothes on, for now at least. Teddy had called and asked them to drop by because he had something he wanted to tell them.

"What if she's pregnant?" said Lachlan as they made their way up the hill to Wood Lane.

Amber was polishing a smudge from her sunglasses. "It won't be that. When I called in a couple of days ago, they were drinking cocktails out in the garden, and I saw how much vodka went into their drinks."

"Well, that's something, I suppose." Lachlan pulled a comical face; he still hadn't been able to get over Teddy's newfound love of porn star martinis.

"Anyway," Amber went on, "I spotted a Cunard brochure while I was over there, so they're probably going to tell us they've booked another cruise."

But it wasn't that either. When they reached the house, Teddy was alone.

"Where's Olga?" said Amber.

"Out shopping. I just wanted to let the two of you know about something I've decided to do." Teddy paused, eyeing each of them in turn. "You both know how I feel about Olga. Well, I'm going to ask her to marry me."

Silence. Then, "Wow." Lachlan shook his head. "Why?"

Hastily, Amber exclaimed, "Teddy, that's *great*," because it was so clearly what he—what anyone—would want to hear.

"Thanks." He turned to Lachlan. "Why would I want to marry Olga? Because I love her, I love being with her, and the thought of not having her in my life fills me with fear. She's a beautiful person, inside and out. She makes me happy every day, happier than I thought I'd ever feel again. And I thank God I was lucky enough to find her."

Amber heard Lachlan take a steadying breath as he battled to conceal his emotions, because he was desperate to protect Teddy from potentially being hurt. He said, "And does Olga genuinely feel the same way about you?"

"I hope so." Teddy was calm.

"You shouldn't hope so. You should be completely sure. Look," said Lachlan gently, "isn't this a bit sudden? I mean, how long have you known her? Really, it's no time at all."

"Two months," said Teddy.

"Two months isn't long though, is it?"

"I met May forty years ago and knew straightaway she was the one for me."

"That was May." There was concern in Lachlan's voice. "This is different."

"It doesn't feel different." Teddy was standing his ground; after all those years of fostering, he'd had plenty of practice at skillfully counteracting arguments. "Olga makes me feel alive again. I never thought I'd meet someone else at my age, but I have. And I'd very much like it if you could be happy for me, but it won't change anything if you can't, because I've made up my mind, and I'm going to be doing it anyway."

Amber hugged him. "Olga's brilliant. I'm so happy for you."

"Thanks, love."

"And I want you to be happy too." It was Lachlan's turn to embrace him. "I hope you will be. When are you thinking of doing it?"

"Asking her? Tonight."

"Well, good luck." Lachlan's voice softened. "And it's not as if there's any need to rush into anything, is there? You can spend plenty of time making plans for the wedding."

"Oh, but I want to rush into it," said Teddy. "Why wait?"

chapter 37

"Morning! I've had a fantastic idea," Olga announced, appearing in the kitchen doorway in a purple jumpsuit as Lachlan was slicing potatoes at the speed of light on a mandoline. "I'm going to show you what I can do!"

Lachlan's grip slipped on the last inch of potato, and the razor-sharp edge of the mandoline sliced into his thumb, spurting blood everywhere.

"Whoops, you need to be more careful—and don't try and make out that was my fault! You should always keep the guard on a mandoline." Dumping the bags she was carrying onto the stainless-steel worktop, Olga opened the first aid tin and took out a blue bandage.

Lachlan ran his thumb under the cold tap, then dried the cut so she could quickly apply the bandage. Had Teddy asked her to marry him last night? Had he also told her about Lachlan's less-than-effusive reaction to the news? Was she perhaps hiding a Taser in one of those bags? He said warily, "What's the fantastic idea?"

Because that was the thing about Olga: you never knew what she might do next.

"OK, I saw my friend Sally yesterday. She's married to Nigel, who plays golf with Teddy, and they have a table for six booked here for tonight. The Hendersons, do you know them?"

Lachlan said, "Don't think so."

"Well, you should. They're very nice. Anyway, their daughter's flying home today from Uganda with her fiancé so they can meet him for the first time. Kate and Alexander got together over there while they were doing voluntary work in an orphanage in Kampala, Sally told me, so it's going to be a very special evening."

"Right." Lachlan was still wondering what was in the bags.

"And guess what? Alexander is Russian! From St. Petersburg, like me, but he hasn't been home for the last three years. So I thought, why don't I make a cake to celebrate them coming here? A traditional Russian honey cake called medovik, decorated with burnt honey icing. It will remind Alexander of home, and he'll love it!"

"You can make him a cake if you want to." Lachlan's thumb was throbbing, and he still wasn't up to speed. "I'm not sure why you're asking me though."

"Oh, sorry, so that you can carry it out to their table at the end of the meal!"

What? "But I don't think—"

"Look, I've brought all the ingredients and those things like big candles that shoot fireworks out of the top! And it'll be a huge cake, so you can give a slice to everyone in the restaurant. Won't that be fun?" As she spoke, Olga was rolling up the sleeves of her jumpsuit and enthusiastically washing her hands. "It's nice to do nice things for people, isn't it?"

Lachlan said, "How do I know it's going to be good enough to serve to my customers?"

Olga's eyebrows arched in disbelief. "Excuse me? Because I'm the one who'll be making it. Medovik is my specialty!"

"But—"

"Oh my God, you're a nightmare, Lachlan! OK, if you don't like it, I promise you can feed it to the gulls!"

To his surprise, she turned out to be a tidy, methodical cook. It took a while to create the first batch of thin, cookie-like sponge layers, then spread each one with a topping of whipped soured and double cream, dulce de leche, runny honey, and sea salt. As she worked, Olga chattered on about the history of the traditional cinnamon-scented cake. "I was seven years old when I tasted it for the first time. I'd been knocking on doors, looking for work, and an old lady with white hair said I could clear the snow from the path at the front of her house. It was a very long path, and I was only small, so it took me hours, and I was so hungry I thought I would pass out! But at last I finished, and the old lady paid me enough kopeks to buy bread. When she opened the front door to give me the money, there was the most amazing smell of baking, and she saw me breathing it in. She went back to her kitchen and came out with a slice of cake wrapped in paper. It tasted of heaven and made me cry. I didn't know what it was, of course, but then she told me. It was medovik. And I know it sounds stupid now, but that was the happiest moment of my life, because until then, I hadn't known anything *could* taste so perfect."

She stopped speaking and turned away.

After a moment, Lachlan said, "Are you crying?"

"Of course not."

He moved around and saw that her eyes were swimming with tears. "Yes, you are."

Olga said fiercely, "Don't you dare laugh at me."

"I'm not laughing."

"It isn't a sad memory. It's a happy one. That was the day I discovered there could be wonderful things in the world. The memory of that first taste of medovik always brings it back." She tipped her head back and blinked rapidly, composing herself. "But you had a hard time too, when you were a boy. You must have a memory of a kind of food that was special to you."

Lachlan put down the lemon he'd been zesting and thought for a moment. "May's cottage pie. It was the first thing she properly taught me how to make. And the weird thing was, mine was good, but it never tasted exactly like hers, no matter how closely I copied everything she did. Even when we made them together, you could always tell which was hers and which was mine."

Olga was smiling now. "That's the magic. But it wasn't the first thing she taught you to make. That was the cake you baked for Ginny's birthday when she was five."

"How do you know that?" Lachlan was taken aback.

"Teddy, of course. He loves telling me about all of you, and I love to listen to his stories. He's proud of every member of his foster family, obviously, but you three are the ones he talks about most." Her eyes danced. "I know everything there is to know about you."

The conversation broke off while Lachlan took delivery of a crate of langoustines. When he returned from packing them into the fridge, Olga was taking the second batch of sponge layers out of the oven and tipping them onto wire racks to cool.

After working together in companionable silence for a few minutes, she said, "I can't believe you haven't mentioned it yet."

"Mentioned what?"

"Teddy asking me to marry him last night."

Lachlan carried on finely chopping basil with his double-handled mezzaluna. "I didn't know for sure he was going to do it."

"You know, sometimes you're a good liar. Other times, not so good." Another wry smile.

"So he did ask you then. Congratulations."

Olga looked sideways at him. "I said no."

That wasn't what he'd been expecting to hear. Lachlan put down the mezzaluna. "Why?"

"Are you ecstatic?"

"I'm surprised. And the reason is…?"

"I knew you and Amber had been around, because I saw the bag of bread rolls for the birds. When Teddy asked me to marry him, I guessed he'd spoken with you about what he was planning to do. So I asked him how you two felt about it."

"And he told you?"

"Hey, this is Teddy. Of course he didn't tell me, because he wouldn't want to hurt my feelings. But I watched him hesitate while he tried to work out what to say." Her expression softened. "Unlike you, Teddy is never good at telling figs."

"Fibs." Her English was so good that the occasional slipup made him smile.

"Yes, sorry. Funny word. So then I said, if I'd left my phone in the room, recording your reaction, would I want to play it back and hear it for myself? And that's when I saw the look in his eyes and knew for sure." Olga paused, then shrugged. "What could I do except say no?"

Had he actually said anything that bad? Not really, not compared with some of the comments he'd made in previous weeks. "You could have said yes."

"And risk hurting Teddy? Causing upset to him and the family he loves? That would be cruel. I already know what you think of me." Olga expertly tested the springiness of the sponges cooling on their racks. "I can't prove to you that I'm not the kind of person you think I am. And I'm not a troublemaker either. So it's easier to turn down Teddy's offer of marriage. Better all around, don't you agree?"

Lachlan hesitated. It was frustrating that she was being so reasonable and honorable about it, almost as if she were on his side.

"And now you're wondering if I'm playing a bluff with you." Olga appeared to be reading his mind. Mischievously she added, "Ooh, or is it maybe a double bluff? Who can tell?"

"You only met Teddy two months ago."

"I know. I told him that. He said none of us knows how long we have left here on this earth. Anyway, I just thought you'd like to be reassured. You won't need to get your best suit out. Well, not for a while yet."

Lachlan nodded, relieved. "That's sensible."

"Or maybe I'm being extra clever." Olga's emerald eyes sparkled. "After all, a talented gold digger might choose to wait in case there's more gold out there somewhere waiting to be dug up!"

This was the kind of comment she liked to drop into conversations, almost as if for the sheer fun of it. Lachlan smiled briefly and started chopping again. "I think you're saying that to get a reaction."

"Maybe. Actually, I like that you're looking out for Teddy because you love him so much. It's a good thing, to be wary. And I know you still don't trust me. Because I look the way I do, is that the reason?" She gestured toward her face, her hair, her slinky body beneath the apron she was wearing over the purple jumpsuit. "Maybe I should make myself more ugly, stop wearing makeup, cut off all my hair with a big knife… Would that help?" She pulled a comical old-crone face, then reverted to normal and shrugged. "But Teddy likes me the way I am. And I do love him, just so you know. More than you'll ever understand."

If she were any more convincing, he might end up believing her.

Lachlan swept the mound of finely chopped herbs into a bowl. "I hope you do."

....

The restaurant was full and noisy, but despite being rushed off his feet, Lachlan hadn't been able to resist keeping an eye on table two, where Sally and Nigel Henderson were meeting their daughter's Russian fiancé for the first time and getting to know him. The first twenty minutes had been a bit stiff, with both sides desperate to make a good impression. Now, an hour and a half and two bottles of wine later, all four had relaxed visibly and seemed to be getting along well together.

"They've just asked to see the dessert menu." Jo came into the kitchen with an armful of plates.

"OK, let's get the cake out." It was all ready, waiting to be carried to the table, a huge creation topped with silver fountain candles. Olga had made another much smaller cake so that Lachlan had been able to taste it earlier and give it his approval.

"Well?" She'd watched him swallow. "Do the gulls get it?"

He'd said, "Sadly for them, no."

Now, crossing to the music system, Lachlan turned down the track currently playing and replaced it with the one Olga had downloaded, an old but rousing version by a male-voice choir of the famous Russian folk song "Kalinka." He'd had his doubts when she'd come up with the idea, but Olga had been insistent.

"He'll love it. Everyone in the restaurant will love it. It's OK." She had laughed at his distinct lack of enthusiasm. "You don't have to perform the dance, I promise."

Slowly now, Lachlan increased the volume and saw, out in the restaurant, the occupants of table two take notice.

"Right." He lit the three fountain candles and stepped back. "You can take it over to them."

"It's your restaurant," said Jo. "I think you should do it."

OK, there was no time to waste; the firework candles would burn out in under a minute. Seizing the cake, Lachlan said, "Open the door then," and carried it out into the restaurant.

The music was gathering pace—"Ka-linka, kalinka, kalinka moya"—and the customers had already begun to clap in time with it. The look on Alexander's face as he realized that both the song and the cake were for him was a sight to behold. Now everyone was whooping and applauding as Lachlan reached table two.

"I can't believe you've done all this for me." Overcome with emotion, Alexander glanced at Kate's parents.

"We didn't," Sally exclaimed. "It wasn't us. We had no idea this was going to happen."

"It's a medovik cake." Alexander pressed his hand to his chest. "The best cake in the world. This is amazing."

"It's huge." Kate clapped her hands in delight. "We can't eat all that!"

"Well, if it's the best cake in the world and you can't manage it all yourselves," said a man at the next table, "we'll volunteer to help you out."

....

"The whole restaurant was buzzing for the rest of the evening." Lachlan had arrived back at Amber's cottage at midnight, later than usual. "Every single customer wanted a slice of that cake. Plus everyone was congratulating the happy couple. It got quite emotional—Sally Henderson was so happy she burst into tears. Look." He showed her one of the photos a customer had already posted on Twitter. "It was great. You should have been there to see it."

"You mean Olga did a nice thing out of the goodness of her heart, and it all worked out really well?"

"I know, I know. Don't look at me like that."

"Olga should have been there to see it."

"I know that too. I did tell the Hendersons it was her idea, and they called her to see if she wanted to come down and join them, but she said it was their night. They've made plans to get together tomorrow instead. Olga and Teddy are going to meet up with them for lunch."

"She's a kind person," Amber said simply. "I really like her. Everyone likes her except you."

"Hey, she's growing on me. I'm on Teddy's side, that's all. Being cautious, making sure he's OK."

"Maybe Olga's on Teddy's side too."

"Come here. We aren't going to argue about this." Lachlan kissed her; it was crazy, but being at work and away from Amber even for a few hours felt like too long. He loved her. He knew that, but she mustn't know it. As far as she was concerned, they were friends with benefits, nothing more. It was torture in a way, but a sweet kind of torture. Keeping his true feelings hidden might be hard, but giving up sleeping with her now they'd crossed that line was unthinkable.

"Anyway," she murmured against his mouth, "did you bring back any of this amazing medovik?"

By way of reply, Lachlan guided her hand around to the pocket of his thin black cotton jacket. "Maybe I didn't, maybe I did."

"Oh my." A slow smile spread across Amber's face as she located the well-wrapped package between them. "Is that a parcel of Russian honey cake, or are you just extremely pleased to see me?"

chapter 38

BENJIE WAS COMING BACK AFTER DELIVERING A PAINTING TO ITS new owners, an elderly couple from Harrogate who were renting one of the holiday cottages overlooking the quieter, craggier end of Lanrock's East Beach. As he made his way along the scenic cliff path, he was actually feeling quite cheerful until his heart gave a jolt of recognition and he realized the figure approaching from the other direction and still some distance away was Jo.

Oh God, not again.

He veered off the narrow path, up onto the flat expanse of grass at the top of the cliff, and instinctively pulled out his phone to give himself something to be engrossed in. Jo had Moose with her, but he was on his lead this time, which was a relief.

But when he casually glanced up from his phone a minute later, he saw that Jo had also left the path in order to reach the flat area of grass on the clifftop. She'd unfastened Moose's lead and was now throwing his favorite yellow ball into the air, away from the edge of the cliff and in the direction of the clump of trees that blocked the view of the parking lot. Hopefully the dog would concentrate on chasing and retrieving the ball this time rather than lolloping over to greet him.

The next moment, from over the ridge to the right came the sound of laughter, then Teddy Penhaligon and his glamorous Russian girlfriend came into view. If you could still call someone a girlfriend when they were in their forties. The locals had been agog when Olga had first arrived in Lanrock; her appearance had given them plenty to gossip about, particularly when she'd started doing yoga on the beach in her striking bikinis, but Benjie liked her a lot. She'd been into the gallery on several occasions, admiring the various pieces of art and chatting vivaciously in a way that had at first left him a bit tongue-tied. After the third or fourth visit, however, he'd found himself relaxing under the sheer force of her friendliness. As far as he was concerned, she was great.

Recognizing him now, Olga waved at him. Today she was wearing a glittery white sleeveless top and tight-fitting lime-green trousers with white sandals. Benjie waved back at them both, then watched as Olga held up her phone and moved away from Teddy in order to take a photo of him with the sea behind him. Backing up further still, she called out, "Turn your head to the left…and a little more, that's it… Oh, you look so handsome, like a Hollywood film star!"

"*Noooo*, come here, Moose. STOP IT."

All heads turned at the sound of Jo's voice, in time to see Moose shoot out of the thicket of trees with a large snarling dog in hot pursuit. They circled the grass, barking furiously, then paused to confront each other before setting off again. There was no playfulness, no tail wagging involved. Racing up to them, Jo attempted to get the lead back on Moose, but the bigger dog growled menacingly, causing Moose to leap away and set off again.

"Moose, *here*," Jo yelled, but another volley of barks was followed by the bigger dog baring its teeth and launching itself at Moose, who skidded into reverse, then shot off to the left, perilously close to the cliff edge.

"It's all right. I'll get him." Teddy, who was closest, moved toward Moose and held out his hand, murmuring, "Here, boy. It's OK…"

Moose promptly slid through a gap in the iron railings and, with a high-pitched yelp, disappeared from view.

"Oh *God*." In a panic, Teddy grabbed the railing, clambered over it, and lost his footing, stumbling on the loose stones and crashing to the ground on the other side. As he let out a shout of alarm, Moose reappeared, paws scrabbling madly as he managed to climb back to safety. At that moment, as the rest of them watched in horror, the edge of the cliff began to crumble, rocks and stones loosening and breaking away, taking Teddy with them as they fell.

In the space of a couple of seconds, an unremarkable afternoon had turned into a nightmare. Olga let out an unearthly shriek of anguish as Teddy vanished. The rest of them raced over to the railings, fearing the worst. Down on the beach, people were screaming, looking up.

A narrow ledge a few meters below the clifftop had broken Teddy's fall, for now at least. He was lying half on his side, holding his arm and gasping with pain. Another walker ran across the grass to the railings, shouting that he was calling the emergency services. Jo, trembling, grabbed a chastened Moose by the collar and refastened his lead. The larger dog had disappeared.

Benjie looked at Olga in horror. "What are you d-doing?" But it was too late to stop her; she had already vaulted over the railing and thrown herself flat on the remaining narrow strip of ground in order to see Teddy properly.

"Teddy?" she shouted. "Oh, Teddy, are you hurt?"

Teddy shifted slightly, then let out a sudden loud groan as the pain caught him in its grip. Olga, her face contorted with terror, yelled, "It's OK! Don't move. I'm coming down!"

"You can't!" Benjie reached through the railings to try and stop her, but Olga slithered out of reach, grabbing hold of a flimsy handful of branches and easing her legs over the edge.

"Fuck, she's mad," shouted the man who'd just called the emergency number. "She's going to die…"

"Teddy, hold on. I'm on my way!" Olga found her footing and a rock to grab hold of a split second before the roots of the branches were ripped out of the shallow sandy soil.

"Ow…ow…ow." Teddy's face creased as he clutched his arm. Looking up and seeing Olga descending toward him, he shouted, "It's too dangerous. Go back."

"No! I love you!" Then, her left foot slipped, and for a moment, she was dangling by her fingertips, prompting those above her to shriek with fright. But she managed to gain another foothold before half sliding down the remaining distance and launching herself sideways to land on the ledge where Teddy was stuck.

"Oh thank God." Benjie felt sick, watching as she crawled alongside Teddy and wrapped her arms around him.

"Are you hurt? It's OK, my darling. I'm here." Stroking his face, Olga murmured endearments, unaware that above them, the man who'd called the emergency services was now climbing through the railings himself.

"What are you *doing*?" Benjie shouted at him; there definitely wasn't room for three people on the narrow ledge below.

"I'm not going down there, just trying to get a better angle. This is going on my YouTube channel." But as the man leaned over with his phone, he dislodged another shower of small stones. Grabbing hold of the railing, he yelped, "Oh shit!" before hastily scuttling back to safety.

"No!" Covering Teddy's head with her hands, Olga threw herself on top of him to shield his body from further injury. But the ground had been weakened, and a bigger stone the size of a grapefruit went plummeting down and landed on the back of her left hand.

"What was that?" Teddy gasped, his scalp protected by the hand that had just borne the brunt of the impact.

"It's nothing," Olga reassured him. "It's all fine, sweetheart. Don't worry. You're OK."

The man next to Benjie was still videoing them. He said with relish, "If that ledge gives way, they'll both be killed when they land on those rocks."

"Oh God," Benjie heard Jo say faintly on the other side of him. "I can't bear it. This is all my fault."

....

Lachlan had been making tarragon sauce in the kitchen when he heard his phone ring and ignored it. A couple of minutes later, playing the voice message Jo had left for him, he heard her tell him in a shaky voice what had happened and where she was.

When he reached the clifftop, the coast guard and ambulance had arrived ahead of him. Lachlan's heart felt as if it was about to explode in his chest as he approached the cordon the coast guard had set up.

White-faced, Jo came toward him with Moose on a lead. "They're bringing him up now. I'm so sorry."

At that moment, they saw the team of coast guards winch Teddy up in a harness. He was lifted into the back of the waiting ambulance. Explaining to the paramedics that he was Teddy's next of kin, Lachlan was allowed into the ambulance while he was being checked out.

"I'm fine, I'm fine," Teddy was protesting as they gave him the once-over.

Lachlan said, "How can you be fine? You fell down a cliff!"

"I'm not hurt though." Teddy shrugged.

"But Jo called and told me you were injured. I could hear you on the phone in the background, shouting out in pain."

"Oh, that was when I tried to turn over." Propped up on the gurney while a paramedic took his blood pressure, Teddy held up his arm to show Lachlan. "That's what made me yell. Hurt like nobody's business."

Lachlan stared in disbelief at Teddy's outstretched forearm, bearing a tattoo that hadn't been there before.

"Whoa, that's brand new," said the cheerful paramedic. "No wonder it hurt! And you've got some dirt in it too… I'll clean that up for you in a minute."

"We had them done this morning," Teddy said proudly. "Matching ones, at that new tattoo parlor on Tresilian Road, next to the Sailor's Rest."

The sizeable tattoo, on the inside of his forearm, was of his and Olga's initials entwined within a heart, with the words *Love you forever* inscribed in curly italics around it.

All the adrenaline that had been surging through Lachlan's body since receiving Jo's phone call had nowhere to go. With rising exasperation, he blurted out, "So if Olga's that much in love with you, where is she now? Busy doing yoga, I suppose, in a gold bikini on the beach."

As they surveyed each other, a ragged cheer went up outside the confines of the ambulance. With characteristic patience, Teddy said, "Why don't you go and see what's happening out there? Pop outside and take a look."

The moment Lachlan saw, he felt the overwhelming sense of shame he'd habitually experienced after first arriving in Lanrock. Each time he'd behaved badly, he'd expected his new foster parents to betray their anger and disappointment and react accordingly. But Teddy and May never had. With that rare skill of theirs, they'd allowed him to see for himself why it would have been better if he hadn't reacted in the way he had.

And now here he was, all these years later, experiencing that exact same feeling all over again.

Leaving the ambulance, he went over to rejoin Jo and Moose, and together they watched from behind the cordon as Olga was checked over, then released from the harness that had winched her up to the top of the cliff.

"You didn't tell me she fell down too," said Lachlan.

"I thought Teddy was the one you'd be worried about. And she didn't fall," Jo explained. "She threw herself down there to be with him. Is Teddy OK?"

"He is, thank God." Even from twenty meters away, Lachlan could see that Olga had come off worse; there was blood on her face and hands and splattered over her glittery white shirt. Spotting him in turn, she peered around the paramedic who was examining an injury to her neck and shouted, "Lachlan, have you seen Teddy? Tell me the truth. Is he really OK?"

Suddenly there was a lump in Lachlan's throat. He nodded and called back, "He's good."

Then Olga was taken into the ambulance to be checked over too, leaving most of the gawping tourists to lose interest and wander off. Moose, also bored, wagged his tail and dropped his ball at Jo's feet, indicating that the time had come to do some more throwing and chasing.

"Are you all right?" Lachlan asked, because Jo was twisting the lead around her fingers, looking pale and distracted.

She started, then nodded. "Yes."

"So how did it happen?"

"Teddy slipped and lost his balance. Olga was distraught. She was *so* brave. Sorry, I have to go." Glancing over her shoulder, she gave the dog's lead a little tug. "Come on, Moose. We're off."

When Jo had scurried away, Lachlan turned and saw that the person coming up behind him was Peggy's son.

"Hi," he said to Benjie. "Did you see it all? Jo was about to tell me what happened, but she had to leave in a hurry. She seemed a bit shell-shocked."

Benjie took a breath. "It was Moose. He was b-being chased by another dog and nearly went over the edge. Teddy tried to grab him and missed, then lost his b-balance."

"Wow, he was lucky." Lachlan surveyed the cliff edge, the perilous drop, the rocks below. "Jo said Olga was pretty brave."

This time, Benjie nodded. "She could have been killed. We tried to stop her, but she was in a complete p-panic, worried about Teddy. She had to be with him. Then the rocks started to fall, and she threw herself on top of him to stop him getting hurt. One rock landed on her face, that's where all the b-blood came from, and another came down on her hand, but she kept hold of him and wouldn't m-move or cover her own head." He looked steadily at Lachlan. "I know you don't trust her. My mum told me. But she was like a superhero today. If you'd been here to see it, you'd change your mind about her."

chapter 39

IT WAS AS HE WAS MAKING HIS WAY HOME THAT BENJIE SPOTTED the two figures in the distance, down on West Beach. Altering course for the second time today, he headed toward Jo and Moose, sitting together on the sand.

When she looked up and saw him approaching her, she visibly flinched.

"Are you OK?" said Benjie.

Jo stared at the crumpled tissue in her left hand. "You mean am I OK considering I nearly killed someone this afternoon? Oh yes, never better."

"You didn't kill him." They hadn't spoken since their showdown. She was looking terrible, drawn and devastated, with pink-rimmed eyes. Despite everything, Benjie's heart went out to her.

"It was all my fault that it happened."

"You could say it was the other dog's fault for chasing Moose. Or it was Moose's fault for running away, not looking where he was g-going."

A fresh tear rolled down Jo's pale freckled cheek. "You can't blame the dogs."

Moose glanced up at Benjie, suitably sorrowful. For once, he wasn't bouncing around like an overeager groupie.

"Or you could say it was Teddy Penhaligon's fault for climbing over the railings," Benjie went on.

Another tear dripped off her chin. "He was trying to rescue Moose. Oh God, and I should have told Lachlan when he asked me what happened, but I just couldn't. I was too ashamed."

"Do you want a handkerchief?"

"Now you're being nice, after what I did to you…and I c-can't b-bear it." Jo's chest juddered.

"Hey, I'm the one with the stammer around here, not you." It was her look of utter despair that did it; Benjie sat down next to her and put his arm around her shoulders, prompting an outburst of sobbing that tore at his heart. He sat quietly, rubbing his hand in comforting circles over her back and letting her tears soak into the shoulder of his gray-and-white-striped shirt, the one she'd once declared her favorite.

When she finally showed signs of slowing down, he said, "You don't have to worry about telling Lachlan, anyway. I already did."

Jo lifted her head. "You said it was my fault?"

"No, but I told him Moose almost ran over the edge. Which obviously means he was off his lead. He knows that m-much. Are you worried he's going to sack you? Don't worry. I really don't think he will."

Her auburn curls were all over her face. She made a half-sobbing, half-trumpeting sound, startling two small boys building a sandcastle nearby.

"I mean it," said Benjie.

Jo looked up at him. "That's not what I'm worried about. It isn't why I'm in this state." Wiping her eyes, she steadied her breathing, then went on, "I'm crying because you're being kind to me. And I know I don't deserve it…but it's just the best feeling in the world. I'm so sorry about what happened… I want to pay back all the money. Will you at least let me do that, *please*?"

"No need." Despite his best efforts, he'd been unable to dismiss Danny's comments from his mind. Because Danny had been right: anyone in need of money would have to be a saint to turn down the offer of a job that was both easy and legal. Yes, it had been completely humiliating to find himself on the receiving end, but he was able to accept now that he'd been unfair.

"I never meant to hurt you." Her mouth wobbled. "I've never felt so awful in my life. And I've missed you so much. You have no idea."

"I probably do," said Benjie. "I've m-missed you too."

"Can we be friends again?" Jo searched his face.

"Yes please."

"Oh thank God!" She hugged him so hard they both almost toppled over on the sand. "Thank you! And does that mean we can go out to places and have more adventures?"

Benjie nodded. Not that they had long before she'd be heading off on her travels; September would be here soon enough, but at least they could make the most of the few weeks they had left.

"It'll be great." Already Jo was sounding like her old self. "I love doing things with you."

"Same." Her eyes were shining and her face was close enough for him to tilt forward and kiss. In theory, anyway. Benjie checked himself; it wasn't the first time this thought had sprung fully formed into his mind. Thank goodness he'd never acted on impulse and attempted to cross *that* line before. And he mustn't do it now either. That she wanted them to be friends again was enough. More than enough.

"What are you thinking?" said Jo.

"I'm wondering what we're g-going to do next. Maybe paragliding. Or wing-walking." In a small corner of his mind, Benjie was aware that he'd said all this and only stammered once. Somehow, the muscles in his mouth felt more relaxed, as if they were celebrating the release of tension in his chest.

"Or skydiving. Or swimming with sharks."

He laughed, and even his laugh felt more natural. "Do they have many sharks around here?"

"Maybe not. Well, we could swim with sardines instead." Dreamily, Jo said, "We can do absolutely anything we want to do. Isn't that great? Oh, I haven't even asked you. How are things going with Dani? All good?"

Moose had long ago lost interest in the conversation and was dozing beside them. To their left, a group of teenage girls were playing music and singing along to Ariana Grande, and over to their right, the two small boys were now energetically digging a hole big enough to bury their father up to his neck in sand. As the sun beat down and the gulls wheeled overhead, Benjie told Jo everything that had happened and showed her photos on his phone of himself with the real Danny, the one she'd seen him with ten days ago, here on the beach.

"Wow," she marveled, "that's amazing. You must have been devastated though, when you first found out."

"You'd think so, wouldn't you? But I wasn't. It was weird. I just couldn't be angry. He hadn't done it in a m-mean way. He was just lonely and wanted someone to talk to online, and once we started chatting, it was too late to admit what he'd done, because he didn't want it to stop."

"So you're still in touch?"

"All the time. Danny's great."

"That's so cool. Do you think he was secretly hoping you might turn out to be gay too?"

"Maybe, but he always knew I wasn't. We're just friends. Really good friends though." Benjie flicked away a wasp that had settled on Moose's tail. "Actually, it was Danny who told me I shouldn't blame you for what happened."

Jo's mouth opened. "He said that?"

"He asked me what I'd do if I was hungry and someone offered to pay me to eat a plate of steak and fries."

"Oh!" She blinked.

"He also said only a saint would turn down an offer like the one my mother made you."

"I'm not a saint. I'm just…human."

Benjie nodded. "I know. Me too."

"Well, I might not have met your friend Danny, but I like him already."

"You'll like him even more when you do meet him."

"I still can't get over how well you've taken it, finding out he wasn't who you thought he was. You were crazy about her."

Benjie nodded. "And I liked having someone to pretend to be crazy about. But it was only ever an online relationship. I always knew it wasn't real." He couldn't admit to Jo that he'd been more attracted to her than to the fictional girl in his life. Nor could he confess that it was the fact that he'd developed real feelings for her that had made the discovery about the money aspect so hard to bear.

Then he saw the way Jo was looking at him and self-consciously rubbed a hand over his nose. "What is it? What's wrong? Do I have something on my f-face?"

She smiled. "Nothing's wrong. I'm glad you aren't crazy about someone else… *Oh.*" She turned pink. "I didn't mean it like that."

"Didn't you?" Wow, she really was a champion blusher. Feeling suddenly very brave indeed, Benjie said, "That's a shame."

And now Jo was gazing into his eyes, as if checking he really meant it. Slowly, and with a pulse jumping in her jaw, she whispered, "Maybe I meant it a little bit like that."

"Only a l-little bit?" Oh my God, listen to him! Had he really just said that? He couldn't quite believe this was happening; it felt like he was acting in a film of his own life!

"Maybe…quite a lot of a bit." Jo was moving closer.

And closer.

And closer still…

And then they were kissing, right there on the beach in front of dozens of strangers, and it was even better than all those times he'd imagined how it would feel to kiss her.

Better still, it *was* actually happening.

When they finally moved apart, Benjie and Jo gazed at each other in mutual wonder. Then they heard a high-pitched whine and saw Moose with his eyes closed and his paws twitching madly as he dreamed of chasing gulls he was destined never to catch.

"Typical," said Jo. "I just had the best kiss of my life, and my crazy dog managed to sleep through it."

The best kiss of her life? Had she really just said that?

"Hey, Moose." As soon as Benjie uttered his name, the dog's eyes opened, his tail thumping hopefully on the sand.

"Right, let's do that again." Taking Jo back into his arms, Benjie gave Moose a stern look. "And this time, try to stay awake."

Amber had spent the afternoon in Salcombe with a drug-addled ex-rock star who'd stayed at Dom's hotel in Notting Hill last week and fallen in love with the giant octopus chandelier. It had taken her a good two hours to convince him that an even more enormous tarantula suspended over the swimming pool in his ten-acre garden probably wasn't the most practical idea.

"Hey." The rock star was accustomed to having his every wish granted. "Who gives a toss about practical? It'd look cool, babe."

She'd eventually persuaded him to commission a smaller tarantula for the hallway of his house instead, which hopefully wouldn't get blasted with the BB gun that was his latest new toy.

"There was me thinking I had a good story to tell you," she marveled now. "And then I come back to this."

"I didn't call you because there was nothing you could do," Lachlan explained. "I didn't want you rushing off in the middle of your meeting."

"He probably wouldn't have noticed. He got through half a bottle of tequila while I was measuring up the hallway. Anyway, at least Teddy and Olga are OK. Thank God." She shuddered at the thought of how it could have ended. Teddy had called Lachlan from the hospital to let him know they'd be home in an hour or so. "Come on then. Show me the video."

The holidaymaker, who'd come down from Doncaster for a week with his wife, had already been videoing the view from the clifftop when Teddy had stumbled and fallen almost directly in front of him. The man had carried on filming, capturing everything on his phone, then uploading it to his YouTube channel. It had promptly been picked up by the local TV station he'd tagged, who had aired it with the headline "Russian Beauty Risks Life to Save Husband in Lanrock."

"Oh my God…" Even though she knew it ended well, Amber's heart was in her mouth as she watched the video. She flinched as the loose rocks showered down, landing on Olga. You could hear her reassuring Teddy, telling him it was OK, he was safe, and the coast guard were on their way. Even as the blood from her injuries dripped down her face and soaked into her sparkly white shirt, she was holding onto Teddy and telling him she loved him.

When the video finally ended, Amber gave Lachlan a long look.

"All right, all right," said Lachlan. "You don't have to say it. I know."

They'd reached the house. Lachlan took a deep breath and rang the doorbell.

"Hello, my darlings. Come in, come in. Now, no need to make a fuss. I'm fine. Just not a pretty sight!" Olga beamed as she welcomed them inside.

She'd changed out of her bloodstained clothes into a scarlet kaftan and black leggings. The stitched-together gash across her temple was swollen and bruised, she was sporting a spectacular black eye, and the two broken fingers on her left hand had been splinted.

"The TV people just called," Teddy announced. "They wanted to come here tomorrow and do an interview with us. But Olga said no."

"Of course I said no! Why would I want to be on TV looking ugly? You know how vain I am!"

"You could never look ugly. You're a star." Amber gave her a gentle hug, then spotted Olga's right forearm. "And Lachlan told me about this—I can't believe you got matching tattoos! When we were teenagers, Teddy always talked us out of having them…and now you've talked him into it!"

"Ah, but I didn't," said Olga. "It was Teddy's idea—he insisted!"

Stunned, Lachlan swung around. "Seriously?"

Teddy shrugged. "I asked her to marry me, and she turned me down. She said she loved me, but she couldn't do it. And I said in that case, how could I be sure she loved me?"

Lachlan experienced a fresh twist of guilt, because that had all been down to him.

"And I said how about if I got his name tattooed across my chest?" Olga continued. "But it was just a joke—I didn't mean it!"

"I thought it was a great idea. A bit of fun," said Teddy. "So I said we should both do it. Only maybe not across our chests." He held out his arm so Amber could admire the artwork. "Come on. Let's go through to the sitting room. We've got a bottle of champagne on ice to celebrate us both still being alive."

When their glasses were full, Lachlan braced himself and cleared his throat. The time had come. "OK, you all know how much I hate it when

I'm wrong and everyone else is right." He turned to Olga and raised his glass to her. "If I'm honest, it's been creeping up on me for a while. But today has finally proved to me just how wrong I was. Maybe it was a bit of a drastic way of going about it," he went on with a smile, "but all's well that ends well, and it's time to admit the truth. Olga, you're amazing, and Teddy's lucky to have you. We're all lucky to have you in our lives."

"Oh, Lachlan…" Olga's green eyes filled. "Don't you dare make me cry."

"Hey, let me finish." He raked his fingers through his hair, giving himself a moment to find the words. "I'm a work in progress. I told you before, it takes me a while to learn to trust people. That's just the way I am. But I get there eventually. And I'm so sorry I gave you a hard time. You make Teddy happy, and I definitely think you should marry him."

When Olga had stopped hugging him, she said, "So I didn't need to get this tattoo after all!"

And much later that evening, while Teddy and Amber were chatting on Zoom with Raffaele and Vee in London, Olga murmured into Lachlan's ear, "I do know, by the way, how you feel about Amber."

He froze. "You do?"

"Oh yes. You're crazy about her."

"How do you know?"

Olga's tone was playful. "Maybe I'm a witch. I can sense the magic. Other people might not be able to see it, but I can." Her eyes sparkled. "It's very nice."

"Right." Lachlan hesitated; he knew that too but was still struggling to trust himself.

"And I think you're worrying too much." Olga's voice was low and encouraging. "You and Amber would be perfect together. I think maybe, deep down, she's completely crazy about you too."

It was good to hear but also kind of funny to think that Mystic Olga had picked up on half of it but not the rest. Amused, he said, "You think I should make a play for her then?"

"Oh, sweetheart, I'm not talking about sex. It's obvious the two of you are already sleeping together." Olga gave him a glittering yet compassionate smile and briefly patted the left side of his chest. "I'm talking about the next level after that."

....

"Hello, love! Surprise!"

Olga blinked, because it *was* a surprise. For a moment, when the name Bernard had flashed up on her phone, she'd been none the wiser. But now, hearing those bluff tones, it all came back to her. Bernard from the cruise, who'd bought himself the beautiful Breitling watch.

"Bernard, how very lovely to hear your voice! How *are* you?"

"I'm well, thanks. Calling from Geirangerfjord. Just climbed to the top of a giant waterfall. And you sound as if you're only down the road, clear as a bell. Isn't technology marvelous?"

"You're on another cruise? Oh my word!" She remembered him saying he liked to take several each year.

"Well, what else am I going to spend my money on? Can't take it with me when I pop my clogs, can I? Anyway, had to give you a call—just picked up an English newspaper and saw what happened to you and Teddy the other day! I've told all my friends on the ship that I know you!"

Olga understood why the story had attracted more press interest than it might otherwise have done; people had loved to emphasize the apparent unlikeliness of their pairing as a couple. She found the sly comments faintly insulting but really not worth bothering about. Who cared what a bunch of ignorant trolls thought?

She said, "Well, that's nice. I'm fine, Bernard. A few cuts and bruises and a couple of broken fingers, that's all."

"Listen, we must meet up! Once this cruise is over, why don't I drive down to see you? It's so easy to lose touch, and we mustn't let that happen. I'm so happy you and Teddy are still together," he added cheerfully. "Gives me hope for the future!"

Poor Bernard, he had a kind heart and more money than he knew what to do with. Olga suspected he'd had a bit of a crush on her, but he wasn't her type at all—even if she hadn't already fallen head over heels in love with her darling Teddy. On impulse, she said, "Of course we mustn't lose touch! Listen, we're having a party here a few weeks from now, once my face is all healed up. You must come along. It would be so wonderful to see you again, Bernard."

chapter 40

IT HAD BEEN AN EVENTFUL SUMMER. AND NOW, ON THE SECOND Sunday in September, it was coming to an end. The party had been Teddy's idea, and Amber had arrived early to help him and Olga with the preparations. When May had still been alive, happy gatherings at their house on Wood Lane had been a regular occurrence, but following her death, Teddy hadn't had the heart to plan them. Now, though, the time had come for the tradition to be revived, and Olga had needed no persuading to bake another of her many-layered Russian honey cakes for the day.

She'd actually prepared this one on Friday evening, before any of them had known how doubly significant the making of the first medovik would turn out to have been.

Amber paused to watch Lachlan working away at top speed as usual in the family kitchen where he'd first learned to cook, whisking trays in and out of the oven while preparing yet more food for the party. Sensing her gaze on him, he looked up, and Amber's heart flipped, her grin matching his, because she knew he was still replaying the words of the review on a loop in his head.

The restaurant critic of the UK's best-regarded Sunday broadsheet was entirely anonymous; working under the name Carina O'Keeffe, she'd kept her identity a secret for over a decade. Her food knowledge was legendary, and she was admired worldwide for her forthright opinions. She had the power to make or break a business, and it could happen at any time.

At midnight last night, the Sunday edition of the paper had appeared online. Within minutes, Lachlan's phone had begun to buzz with texts and messages from friends in the business who'd just seen the critic's review of a restaurant she'd visited weeks earlier.

"I don't believe it. Fuck, this is… Oh my God, I can't take this in."

Next to him in bed, seeing the color drain from his face as he skimmed the review, Amber had instantly feared the worst. Then she'd read it herself and had barely been able to make out the last lines through a sheen of tears, because the critic had been blown away by the quality of Lachlan's cooking, describing each course in detail. She'd also written:

> What made the evening extra special, however, was the willingness of this restaurant to go the extra mile, surprising a table with the carrying in of a perfect medovik in order to welcome a Russian visitor to Lanrock. Seated behind the table in question, I know for a fact that these diners had neither requested nor expected such a surprise. It was both a heart-warming gesture and a spectacularly good cake, as I discovered when it was divided up and shared around the rest of the diners, much to their delight. I have to say, in all my years in this job, I've never known an atmosphere as warm and inclusive in a restaurant full of strangers. What an utterly magical experience my time at McCarthy's was. Food, 10/10. Value for money, 10/10. Handsomeness of chef, 12/10 (not that I would allow such a frivolous detail to affect my judgment in any way. Ahem).

Amber dried her eyes on the edge of the duvet. "I always did like reading her columns. But this one's my favorite." A review like this would be a game changer.

"She said the smoked almond pesto was the best she'd ever tasted."

"It might be the only smoked almond pesto she's ever tasted," Amber teased. It wouldn't do to let him get too big-headed.

"Twelve out of ten for handsomeness of chef." Lachlan shook his head. "Not thirteen?"

"You're getting old. Losing your looks. Won't be long before I have to trade you in for a younger model." Their friends-with-benefits relationship was still going strong; she was growing ever more skillful at keeping her true feelings hidden, and no one else had so much as an inkling about it. Their secret was as watertight as ever.

"What are you thinking?" Amber saw that he was now staring into space, frowning slightly.

"I've just realized something." The frown faded, and Lachlan broke into a grin. "If Carina O'Keeffe was sitting at the table behind the Hendersons, she's definitely a bloke."

That had been last night. And now a middle-aged man Amber didn't recognize was making his way up to the house, clutching a fancily wrapped bouquet of pink peonies.

"Someone's early," she announced.

Olga peered out the open window and clapped her hands. "Oh, it's Bernard!" Having greeted him, she brought him into the house. "Such gorgeous flowers! Amber, this is lovely Bernard from the cruise, and he's already been on another one, to the fjords. Teddy and I can't wait to go there—everyone says it's so beautiful."

"Oh, it's outstanding. I couldn't stop taking photos." Eagerly, Bernard reached for his phone. "You must let me show them to you."

Olga said brightly, "We'll do that later, shall we? Let me put these flowers in water and get you a drink. Oh, Teddy, there you are. Look who's here…"

An hour later, the house had filled up, and the party was in full swing. By sheer bad luck, Amber had paused to offer Bernard a mini lobster hors d'oeuvre from the tray she'd been passing around and had somehow ended up trapped in a corner of the sitting room, smiling politely while he talked her through hundreds of photos of glassily smooth fjords, craggy mountains, red-roofed Scandinavian houses, and dressed-to-the-nines strangers sitting around a huge oval table in an ornately decorated dining room.

"Now this was Jonathan, he was a nice chap, a consultant neurologist, you know! Not much he doesn't know about the brain, I can tell you. And next to him, there on the left, that's Marjorie, she's a traffic warden. Doesn't look like one, does she? She had some funny stories to tell us about—"

"Ooh, sorry, I can see someone who's going to need a bit of help," Amber said hastily, peering past him out the window. It was a fib, but she was desperate, and Peggy *was* making her way up the drive lugging a canvas almost as big as herself, which was a whole new problem in its own right but thankfully not hers to deal with. With an apologetic look at Bernard, she hurried out into the hall to open the front door.

"Peggy, let me give you a hand."

"Thank you, darling." Sweeping past her in a swirl of rainbow kaftan and silver necklaces, Peggy said, "And where are Olga and Teddy? Ah, there they are!" She carried the wrapped canvas through to the sitting room and greeted each of them with a big kiss. "Now, I have a little something for you…well, quite a big something actually. You're going to love it." Turning, she gestured toward the fireplace. "And I already have the perfect place for it, d'you see? Just take that mirror down, and you can hang this there instead."

The rest of the conversation in the room had died down; everyone who knew Peggy was waiting in various stages of apprehension for the piece of art to be ceremoniously unveiled.

Enjoying the moment, Peggy gazed around and grandly announced, "The title is *Love in Peril*, and this is my gift to you!"

Across the room, Amber caught Lachlan's eye and saw that he was on the alert, ready to glare at anyone who might be tempted to snigger when the painting was revealed.

With a flourish, Peggy tore off the brown wrapping paper and stepped to one side so everyone could admire her latest creation. It was dark brown and rocky, with hints of angry gray sea below and splashes of crimson surrounding two pale elongated blobs, each in turn containing two smaller heart-shaped blobs.

"Well. I am…overcome with emotion," Olga exclaimed, her hands clasped to her chest. "I don't know what to say!"

Teddy hugged Peggy. "You're too generous, Peg. Thank you so much."

The next moment, Amber realized that Bernard had left his chair over by the window and was now standing beside her, shaking his head in amazement.

"I don't believe this. I've spent the last year searching for an artist, and…" He looked at Olga, then pointed toward the canvas. "May I take a closer look?"

Olga deftly stepped aside. "Of course. Take as many looks as you like!"

Bernard moved forward and studied the painting in closer detail. He bent his knees and peered at the signature, then said, "I knew it. I recognized the style straightaway... Still can't make out the name though. Well, how extraordinary. You're not going to believe this." Sliding into raconteur mode, he turned to face the gathered guests. "Just over a year ago, I was driving through Southampton when I passed a junk shop and spotted a painting in the window that stopped me in my tracks. I parked up, went inside, and bought it on the spot, because it was the most amazing work of art I'd ever seen. It just...*spoke* to me, you know? And it's been hanging in pride of place in my living room ever since."

"That's—" began Peggy before Bernard raised a hand to prevent interruption.

"But I was never able to find out who the artist was, despite searching online and taking it along to a couple of galleries to ask the experts who worked there. Who turned out not to be experts after all," he went on dismissively, "because they didn't have a clue. So I was stuck, because the signature just wasn't clear enough. It starts with a P or a D, but after that, it's just a squiggle. Which was incredibly frustrating, because I was desperate to find out everything I could about the artist and buy more of his work... Oh my God, hang on..." He turned to gaze again at the painting, then at Peggy. "I've just realized, this is a depiction of what happened on the cliff, isn't it? Which means you actually commissioned the artist to paint it...which means you can tell me who he is!"

Along with most of the other assembled guests, Amber did her best to hide a smile, because Peggy's face was by this time an absolute picture. Reaching for Bernard's hand, she shook it and said proudly, "Pleased to meet you. Peggy Smart."

"I do apologize. How rude of me." Still vigorously shaking her hand, Bernard said, "And I'm Bernard Lewis. Well, this is turning into a momentous day. Does the artist live near here by any chance?"

Peggy nodded. "Just a mile and a half away."

"How *extraordinary*. And does he exhibit in a gallery? Because if he does, I need to get there before it shuts. Oh my goodness, you don't know what this means to me."

"Same." Beaming up at him, Peggy drew him back to the canvas and pointed to the bottom right-hand corner. "See the P? That stands for Peggy. And the first squiggle is an S, then the rest of it spells Smart."

"Oh my word, you're not serious." Bernard's reaction was gratifyingly cartoonish as the penny dropped at last. "It's you? Are you sure? I mean, of course you're sure… I'm in a right dither here! I know I said I'd been trying to track you down for the last year, but it feels like I've been searching for this kind of art my whole life. Sorry if that sounds completely crazy—"

"It doesn't," Peggy blurted out. "It sounds wonderful. You can't imagine how much it means to me to hear someone say they love my work. Most people don't understand what I'm aiming to achieve. They can't appreciate the effort that goes into creating my art."

"Ignore them." Bernard's tone was forceful; he was shaking his head like a bear. "They're just ignorant."

"I know." Peggy nodded in agreement. "I tell myself they're the same kind of people who laughed at Vincent van Gogh."

"They're the ones missing out. They don't understand genius." Bernard dismissed the naysayers with a swipe of his hand. "I still feel as if I'm dreaming."

"I can't believe you found my painting in a junk shop. That's *so* insulting. Which canvas was it?"

Bernard took out his phone and showed her. He nodded proudly. "It's my screen saver on all my devices."

"Oh, I don't believe it—that's *Drowning in Mud*, one of my favorites!" Peggy sounded outraged. "I donated it to a charity auction. Whoever won it must have chucked it away. How *rude*."

"Their loss. My gain." Bernard reached for her hand and clasped it between both of his. "Peggy, I'm not exaggerating when I say this could be the happiest day of my life."

chapter 41

BENJIE AND JO WERE WATCHING THE EXCHANGE UNFOLD BEFORE them, both agog.

"Who *is* he?" whispered Jo.

Benjie shrugged. "No idea. I hope someone didn't pay him to turn up and pretend to be her b-biggest fan."

Behind them, Olga tapped him on the shoulder. "Trust me, it's all real. We met Bernard on our cruise. He's the sweetest man, single and ready to jingle."

"Mingle," Benjie gently corrected her, but only because he knew Olga wanted to be corrected.

"Mingle. Thank you, darling. Funny word! And look at them. They're gazing at each other like teenagers. Give it another hour and they'll be outside, canoodling in the hot tub."

Alarmed, Benjie said, "I hope not."

"Oh, I'm sorry. She's your mum. You don't want to hear about old people kissing! Never mind," Olga went on playfully. "By this time tomorrow, you two will be gone, and Peggy'll be free to get up to all sorts with whoever she likes!"

"Eurgh," said Benjie.

Jo laughed at the look on his face. "Oh, now he's traumatized."

Unperturbed, Olga said, "Me and my big mouth! Anyway, how's everything going? Are you all packed and ready to leave?"

Jo nodded, and Benjie managed to remove troublesome mental images of hot tub frolicking from his mind. The day after the clifftop rescue, he'd come along here with Jo so she could apologize to Teddy and Olga for having inadvertently caused the accident. Olga had promptly informed her that she wasn't remotely to blame; it had been Teddy's fault entirely for climbing over the safety railings, thinking he was Spider-Man, when he knew perfectly well it was an idiotic thing to do.

Then she had insisted they stay for a drink in the garden and had asked loads of questions, hearing all about Jo's plans to head off in September on her belated gap year.

"Oh my goodness, but won't you miss her terribly when she's gone?" Olga had gazed in dismay at Benjie.

"Well, I suppose so, b-but it's what she's always wanted to do." He'd felt his pulse quicken, because Olga was voicing thoughts he hadn't felt able to say himself. "And we'll be able to keep in touch… It'll b-be OK."

"Why don't you both go?" Olga raised her eyebrows.

"Um…er…I've got my job at the g-gallery."

Her shrug was dismissive. "It's Peggy's gallery. I think you don't much enjoy working there anyway. Why don't you tell your mother you'd rather go traveling?"

Benjie's mind was in a whirl. "B-but then she'd have to find someone to take over from me."

"Pfft! It's a nice job! In fact, my friend Sally is looking for work, something sociable that involves talking to people—she'd be great in the gallery! And I think Peggy would be very happy to see you heading off. Anyway, just a thought!"

Benjie had blushed then, awash with memories of being back at school and seeing fellow pupils grimace when the teacher announced, "You can pair up with Benjie." Because it had been Jo's plan to travel the world, and she might want to do it on her own. Having someone else tagging along could be her worst nightmare.

But when they'd left Teddy and Olga's house and begun to make their way back down the hill, Jo had said, "Look, I know it's probably not your idea of fun, but if you did think you might want to give it a go, that'd be fine with me."

Up until twenty minutes previously, the prospect of traveling, backpacking, and exploring different countries in a nonholiday way had simply never occurred to him. But Benjie was beginning to wonder why not.

"Let me have a think about it," he'd said to Jo. "If you're sure you wouldn't mind." They were still a bit shy with each other after yesterday's conversation on the beach…followed by yesterday's kissing on the beach…

"Hey." Jo had stopped walking and turned to face him. "I wouldn't ask if I didn't mean it. I think Olga knew what she was doing when she brought it up." Reaching up on tiptoe, she gave him another kiss, then said, "We could have brilliant adventures together. How about that? I'd love it."

And now here he was, several weeks on from that afternoon, back at Teddy and Olga's house with an entirely different year ahead of him than the one he'd expected. Which just went to show, you never knew when a sliding-doors moment might be about to come along and change the course of your life. If he hadn't volunteered to deliver the framed print to the holidaying couple in the rented cottage, he wouldn't have witnessed the cliff incident. If he hadn't approached Jo afterward on the beach, would they ever have healed their rift? If he hadn't kissed her, would they still just be friends who secretly fancied each other?

And he'd still be facing a future stuck in his mother's art gallery, having to tolerate tourists making rude comments about her art.

It had taken a day before he'd plucked up the courage to tell Peggy the new plan, which also went to show that you never knew how people might react to unexpected news. He'd expected his overprotective mother to be dismayed, maybe even distraught. Instead she'd been over the moon.

An hour later, Sally Henderson had been equally delighted, leaping at the chance to take over his job. The next morning, she'd come into the gallery to learn the ropes and had proven herself entirely suited to the role. Chatty, no-nonsense Sally was enthusiastic and welcoming to everyone who ventured over the threshold but took no prisoners if they showed any inclination to step out of line. When a middle-aged Bristolian couple had begun nudging each other and smirking at Peggy's canvases, Benjie had felt the familiar rising spiral of anxiety, because this was what he most dreaded happening, and it invariably made his stammer worse.

Whereas Sally Henderson, up until that moment cheerful and

friendly, had said to the couple, "Oh my word, did no one ever teach you basic manners when you were growing up? How rude, and how ashamed of yourselves you should be. If you don't understand art, I don't think you belong in here, do you?"

After the chastened couple had hurried out, Benjie had felt the panic slowly subside. "That was b-brilliant. I don't know how you can be so… you know…"

"Confident? Benjie, I used to be a captain in the British Army. A couple of pig-ignorant tourists don't scare me. People like that can take a hike."

Her smile was serene; she was going to be perfect. But also, he had to know the truth. Lowering his voice—even though the gallery was empty—he ventured cautiously, "Do you th-think my mum's paintings are…good?"

Sally straightened the one nearest to them, a violently purple abstract titled *Creatures of the Deep*, featuring mustard and midnight-blue shapes strewn across the canvas. "Beauty is in the eye of the beholder, darling. They're not my cup of tea."

"They're not many people's cup of t-tea," said Benjie.

"But there's a pot for every lid, isn't there? That's the great thing about art—some people might not be too keen, but others will love her work. We just have to make sure we encourage the second lot into the shop so they can buy it." Sally exuded confidence. "And boot out the dross!"

Now, back at the party, Benjie's attention was caught by Sally on the other side of the room. Indicating Peggy and Bernard, gazing into each other's eyes and lost in a world of their own, she winked at him and mouthed, *A pot for every lid*.

Benjie nodded and felt himself relax, because he'd been concerned about leaving his mother here on her own. Then again, maybe he wasn't quite as indispensable as he'd thought.

....

"I'm moving back to London," Raffaele told Amber, and she threw her arms around him. It wasn't a surprise; he and Vee were well and truly back together now. Having lived together in their old basement flat throughout her recuperation from the surgery, their feelings for each other had regrown.

Like kintsugi, the Japanese art of repairing broken pottery with gold, they'd overcome their difficulties and were now whole again, their love for each other stronger than ever. Vee was her old self once more, and there was no question of them being apart.

"We'll miss you," Amber told them both. "But we all knew it was going to happen."

"And you'll still come up and see us," Vee reminded her. "As often as you can get away. You and Lachlan can both stay—we've got a new sofa bed, so he can sleep on that while you have the spare room." She spread her hands. "Sorted."

"Perfect!" Amber nodded brightly. Vee and Raffaele still had no idea at all about her and Lachlan's clandestine relationship; neither of them wanted to find themselves on the receiving end of a lecture from Raffaele. Instead they were waiting for the novelty to wear off—Lachlan because he had no idea how she really felt about him, and herself because…well, this was Lachlan they were talking about, and for him, the novelty would obviously wear off soon enough.

She was dreading it happening, though she knew it must be imminent. A million times, she'd tried to prepare herself by imagining Lachlan telling her it had been fun while it lasted but the time had come to put it behind them and move on. The thought destroyed her, but all she could do was pray she'd have the courage and the Streep-level acting ability to agree with him and not make an almighty fool of herself.

Waiting for it to happen was like watching grains of sand fall through an hourglass. The longer it went on, the more agonizing the end was going to be. It was her own fault; she'd thought she could handle it and keep her emotions under control.

But now she knew she couldn't. She'd gotten herself in way too deep. Which made it more vital than ever that their arrangement remained a secret. On top of all the heartbreak and misery, she just couldn't cope with Raffaele—or anyone else for that matter—shaking his head and saying *I told you so.*

That would be unbearable.

In the meantime, all she could do was wait and pray that Lachlan would do or say something so completely unforgivable that she would go off him of her own accord.

"Hey." Vee waved a hand in front of her face. "You're miles away."

Amber dragged herself back to the present. "Only because you and Raff are going to be miles away."

"We'll be coming down to visit as often as we can," Vee reminded her. "You won't be stuck here with Lachlan the whole time."

Give it another month at the outside and she wouldn't be stuck here with Lachlan at all; by then, he'd be off with someone else. OK, time to put *those* mental images out of her mind. Amber turned to Raffaele. "So what's going to happen to the salon down here? Will you sell it?"

"I'll keep it running. I've spoken to Anna and Kim, and they're both keen to step up their hours. We'll rent out the other two chairs. And I have someone else interested in getting involved too." He raised a playful eyebrow. "Someone you know, actually."

Amber was pretty sure she didn't know any other hairdressers. "Who?"

Vee turned and beckoned Olga over. "Amber was just wondering who's going to be joining the salon down here."

"Oh, someone *marvelous*." Olga did excited jazz hands. "It's me!"

Amber blinked. "But you're not a hairdresser."

"Not a qualified one, I admit. But how hard can it be? Snip, snip, snip with the scissors, easy as pie!"

Was Raffaele serious? Bewildered, Amber said, "But it isn't easy. You need to be qualified!"

Olga laughed. "It's too easy to tease you today. Your mind is like spaghetti! Don't worry. I'm a beautician, remember? That's what I'm going to be doing…threading, facials, nail treatments… I need to get back to work and be busy. I want to be the best beautician in Lanrock and make Teddy proud."

"He's already proud." Lachlan had joined them.

"I hope so." Olga patted his arm. "And thank you so much for doing the food today. It's fantastic."

"My pleasure," said Lachlan. "Listen, though, you might want to rescue Teddy. Looks like he's gotten himself trapped over there."

They glanced across at Teddy, who'd stopped to chat with Bernard and Peggy and been inveigled into looking at something on Bernard's phone. He'd been there for several minutes now, Amber realized, and was indeed looking trapped.

"Oh, poor darling," Olga exclaimed. "It's all my fault for inviting Bernard. I'd better help him to escape."

....

Olga made her way over.

"There you are. Come and join us!" Bernard patted the seat to the right of him at the table in the corner. "I've just been showing Ted and Peggy some of the photos from my last cruise… Here you go, look at this one. That's the theater. The shows they put on in there are first class. Peggy's never been on a cruise, did you know that? I've just been telling her how wonderful they are for making new friends."

He'd made her sit down; now she was trapped too. Still, she couldn't be rude and rush off. "Absolutely," said Olga.

"And this is the chandelier in the ballroom, how about that? Sixty thousand crystals, it said in the brochure!"

For some reason, Peggy didn't seem to mind the endless photos; she was asking loads of questions and listening avidly to the answers. As Bernard continued, Olga zoned out slightly and watched Teddy instead as he made a valiant attempt to seem interested. Oh, she'd been so lucky to meet him. He was such a genuine, warm-hearted man, so thoughtful and kind…

"And here we are, dressed up for dinner on the formal night."

Peggy said, "Oh, look at you. All smart in your tuxedo!"

Bernard looked pleased. "I scrub up quite well, don't I? On the other side of the table you've got Derek and Shauna…and that's Marco, he's an archaeologist. And next to me is Dorinda—hang on, let me find a better one of her… Oh, here we are together." Proudly, he held up the phone.

"Glamorous," said Peggy.

"Very. Drank a lot. Jolly good company though."

Olga felt Teddy nudge her foot under the table and realized she was being shown the photo. She focused on the bright-green ostrich-feather boa around tanned shoulders, then the shimmering blue and green rose-patterned silk of the woman's low-cut dress before—

"I don't believe this." Her mouth fell open. "It's *her*."

"Who, Dorinda?" Bernard looked delighted. "Do you know her?"

"She was on our cruise! She accused me of stealing her diamond bangle!" Jerking upright on her chair, Olga reached for the phone and expanded the photo. "Yes, that's definitely her!"

She showed it to Teddy, who pointed at the screen. "And…is that the bangle?"

"*What?*" Taking another look, Olga let out a shriek of outrage. "Oh my God, it is!" How had this woman described it when she'd been searching on her sun lounger? A wide platinum band studded with diamonds and sapphires. And there she was in the photo, wearing an identical one. *That evil witch*.

"She shouted at me, accused me of stealing her bangle. In front of everyone else on the top deck." Olga's heart was racing. "I was never so angry in my life."

"You didn't mention it at dinner." Bernard looked surprised. "I'd have remembered."

"Of course I didn't mention it, because I was so humiliated! To be accused of stealing is the most horrible thing. I thought you might all think I was a thief." Pressing her hand to her cleavage, Olga looked at Teddy. "I was so scared you might wonder if I'd taken her stupid bangle. I mean, I knew I hadn't, but what if a tiny corner of your mind was thinking I might be a thief."

"I didn't think that for one second," said Teddy.

"But now the bangle is back on her arm." Olga's breathing was rapid. "So it was never stolen."

"Unless she claimed on the insurance and bought another one just like it," said Peggy.

Olga shook her head. "Well, now I need to know."

"In that case," said Bernard, "why don't I give her a call?"

He evidently made a habit of exchanging numbers with the people he met on his travels. Olga gave him back his phone and watched as he dialed.

"Put her on speaker," she said just before Dorinda came on the line, and they all listened while Bernard explained the situation.

"Oh, I remember that." Dorinda trilled with laughter. "I woke up on my sun lounger and the bangle was gone, so I thought there was only one person who could have taken it. We had a bit of a ding-dong about it, then I left. And it was hilarious. When I got back to my cabin, I found a hole in the lining of my bag…and there was my bangle. It had slipped right through! Can you believe that? *So* funny!"

She was now cackling like a hyena. Teddy, reaching across the table, gave Olga's hand a reassuring squeeze. And Olga realized just how much of a calming influence he'd been on her over the last months, because not long ago, she would have grabbed the phone and told Dorinda exactly what she thought of her and called her all manner of choice names too.

But what good would that do, really? And this was one of the many, *many* lessons Teddy had taught her during their time together. For so many years, he and May had welcomed children into their home; with love and boundaries, humor and patience, they'd helped them in countless ways toward adulthood. Olga's heart swelled now as she gazed at him; just thinking of the lives they'd improved made her realize how wonderful he was and how lucky she was to have met this perfect, gentle man.

"Do you want to yell at her?" Teddy asked. "Will it make you feel better?"

Would it? Actually, no. She broke into a smile and shook her head at Bernard. "It's OK. I'm not going to yell. You can hang up now."

"And she didn't even bother to say sorry?" Peggy was incandescent on her behalf. "Wow, I'd have told that woman exactly what I thought of her."

"I don't need to tell her," Olga said cheerfully. "I'll just think it a lot inside my head."

....

When Lachlan had arrived at her cottage after work, Amber had felt the crackle of paper in the back pocket of his jeans.

Now, coming into the kitchen, she caught him standing with his back to her, reading something that looked like a letter, and simultaneously noted that the outline of the envelope in his back pocket was missing.

"What's that?" It had been an entirely innocent question until she saw his reaction.

Lachlan said, "Nothing," and quickly refolded the sheet of paper, pushing it back into his pocket.

It was classic guilty behavior, and her heart did a swallow dive inside her chest, because hadn't she known it was only a matter of time?

She didn't press him; no one likes a jealous girlfriend. Plus the last thing she was was his girlfriend. But an hour later, the note was no longer in his pocket. And when she opened the lid of the kitchen garbage while Lachlan was in the bathroom, there it was, crumpled up and thrown away.

Oh God, but it was better to know. Mentally braced for the worst, she fished it out, uncrumpled it, and scanned the handwritten lines:

Hello love,

This is just to say, you'll never know the difference your parcels make. I look forward to them every week—you're so kind and I'm very grateful. I know you said not to tell anyone, but I did tell Jo when she called from Phuket last night, and she said you're nicer than you pretend to be! Sounds like her and Benjie are having a wonderful time. I miss her so much—the house is so quiet now—but at least I still have Moose to keep me company.
Anyway, thank you again.

Love,
Barbara (and Moose) xxx

A tidal wave of relief washed over Amber, followed by a jolt of panic as she heard a theatrical cough behind her. Oh *no*, now it was her turn to have been caught red-handed.

"Rummaging in bins?" Lachlan grinned. "Classy."

She did her best to brazen it out. "I was curious, that's all. Thought it might be another parking fine."

"Nice try." He wrapped his arms around her. "You thought it was a love letter from some other woman."

"Of course I did, because now we're back in the eighteenth century where everyone writes love letters on actual paper."

Lachlan studied her face. "Are you jealous?"

Oh God, he was looking serious. If he thought she was, this could be the end of their arrangement. It was the reason he invariably ended them, calmly explaining that the time had come to call a halt to proceedings before anyone got hurt. Then again, maybe she should be the one to say it, because endlessly waiting for the guillotine to fall was doing her no good at all. Basically, she was a wreck.

OK, I will. Just not quite yet. Not tonight.

"You didn't mention this." She reverted to well-honed flippant mode and waved the letter at him. "What's in the parcels? Class A drugs?"

"Just a couple of meals, nothing major." He shrugged. "Jo brought her to the restaurant for her eightieth birthday last year—she loves good food but isn't much of a cook. Then I happened to bump into her the day after Jo and Benjie left, and she was feeling a bit low, suffering from empty nest syndrome. So I just drop a parcel over to her every Friday afternoon. That's all."

Be flippant, be flippant, and definitely don't cry.

"My God." Amber feigned shock. "Who knew? You *are* nicer than you pretend to be."

"Occasionally," said Lachlan.

But how much longer could she keep going while simultaneously never wanting it to stop? For weeks now, she'd been actively searching for reasons to go off Lachlan, simply because it felt like the most painless way to do it. Like a leopard waiting to pounce, she watched and listened for anything that could conceivably be chalked up against him. Over the years, she'd gone off men because they drank gulpily, chewed noisily, sniffed too often, interrupted other people's conversations, thought they were being hilarious when they weren't, and took too long combing their hair.

But Lachlan was still failing to come up with any annoying habits. Even when he did his infamous impression of Tom Jones singing "Delilah" in a Geordie accent, she found it funny rather than ridiculous.

For goodness' sake, couldn't he do anything wrong?

Then a few nights later, it happened. Amber was in the shower washing her hair when she heard a female voice in the flat. Baffled and without stopping to rinse off the shampoo, she stepped out and wrapped a towel around herself, because someone was definitely out there. The next moment, she opened the bathroom door and her blood ran cold, because now she recognized the voice; it belonged to Cass, the new waitress at the restaurant. Slim and pretty, she'd taken over after Jo had left…but what was she doing here at this time of night? It made no sense…

Silently, she pushed open the bedroom door—and found out what Cass was doing here. She and Lachlan were in bed together, naked. Frozen in the doorway, Amber croaked, "What…what's going on?" even though it was obvious. And here it came, the world of pain and anguish she'd been expecting for months now, because sooner or later, it had always been bound to happen. "*Noooo…*"

Eyeing her calmly from the bed, Cass said, "Look, sorry to have to be the one to tell you this, but that wasn't shampoo you were using. It was hair removal cream."

And when Amber clapped her hands to her head, she discovered she was bald.

The next moment, even though Lachlan was over there on the bed with Cass, somehow his voice was simultaneously in her ear.

"Amber, shh. It's OK. You're fine."

Amber's eyes snapped open. She gazed around wildly, her brain attempting to catch up. "Where is she?"

Because if she's still here in this bed with us, that's just gross.

"Where's who?"

"Cass." The moment the name was out, Amber was awake enough to wish she hadn't said it. She took a shaky breath. "It was a dream, wasn't it?" *Oh, thank God for that.*

"I don't know what Cass was doing in it. But yes, you were dreaming." Lachlan held her while she regained control of her breathing.

Amber tilted her head so she could just make out his profile in the shadows. "What's happened to your face?"

"Oh, is it a mess? That's where you hit me."

"I *what*?"

"Not on purpose. You were swinging your arms and caught me on the nose."

"God, I'm sorry." She sat up and switched on the bedside lamp, then gave a yelp, because there was blood on his face, and it was dripping onto his chest. "*Waah!*"

"Don't panic. I'm fine," Lachlan assured her.

"You look like something out of *Nightmare on Elm Street*."

"Doesn't matter. It was an accident."

"Is it broken?"

"Maybe." He touched the sides of his nose, then smiled. "Anything Raff can do, I can do better. Always wanted a nose like his."

"You could have me arrested for assault," said Amber.

He slid out of bed and surveyed himself in the wardrobe mirror. Blood continued to drip from his chin, and he caught it in his hand. Smiling at her mortified reflection, he said, "I'll let you off. I'm going to clean myself up in the shower."

"Don't use the sham—" Amber skidded to a halt.

"Don't use the shampoo? Why not?"

She fell back against the pillows. "I dreamed it was hair removal cream."

Laughing, Lachlan disappeared into the bathroom. The moment he'd switched on the shower, Amber burst into tears. It was no good. There was no way out. She couldn't do it. She just couldn't do this anymore.

The sound of the gushing water meant she could make as much

noise as she needed to make. Which was…a lot. She wasn't a crier as a rule; not for herself at any rate. But the emotions had been building up for what felt like forever, and now they were exploding out of her like a volcano.

She sobbed. She wept. She howled and hiccupped her way through handfuls of tissues, hoping it would prove to be cathartic. But as the tears continued to pour out and the skin on her face grew increasingly sore and tight, the misery showed no sign of lessening. She'd made her bed, and now she was being punished for it, as any sensible friend could have warned her would happen. Which was why she hadn't confided in any friends at all, sensible or otherwise.

She jumped as the water pipes went *clunk*, letting her know that the shower had been turned off. Lachlan would be out any second now, and she couldn't bear for him to see her like this. She pulled on a pair of shorts and a blue top, ready to rush out of the cottage, but her face was scary, she looked a fright, and her bladder was perilously full.

Plus the bathroom door was opening. Letting out a bat-squeak of panic, Amber threw on a hoodie and tugged the hood over her head, pulling the cords tight so most of her face was hidden. As Lachlan emerged naked, dripping wet and carrying a towel, she kept her head down and scooted past him into the bathroom, locking the door behind her.

Surprised, he said, "You OK?"

"Fine." But it was no good. The next wave of grief was on its unstoppable way.

Ten minutes later, he tapped on the door. "Hey, what's going on?"

I can't stop blubbing like a pathetic baby. Is that a good enough answer? Amber gazed in abject despair at her reflection in the mirror over the sink. She'd brushed her teeth and had a shower herself, but the tears continued to leak out.

Lachlan said, "Are you still in there, or have you escaped through the window?"

"I'm still in here." It came out as a bunged-up croak.

"Are you *crying*?" He sounded shocked.

"No." She sighed. "Maybe."

"Because you broke my nose? Listen, you sound worse than I do. I don't think it's broken anyway."

"Good." Amber winced at the sight of her swollen eyelids and reddened eyes. "But that's not why I'm crying."

"Open the door."

She hiccupped and wiped her face with the sleeve of her hoodie. "I can't."

"You have to. You can't stay in there forever. And I'm not going anywhere."

It came out as a whisper. "Still can't."

After a long silence, Lachlan said, "Are you pregnant? Are we having a baby? Because—"

"No! I'm not pregnant!"

"Are you ill?"

"Not ill either." She screwed her eyes shut. "Lachlan, I just can't do this anymore."

"Do what?"

"This. Us. You and me." The words were out; she'd said them at last. It was easier with a door between them.

After a second, he said, "Why?"

"It's just…not working."

"In what way isn't it working?"

This was like amputating one's own arm. "Every way."

"Amber, I need to know what's going on here. If you don't come out and say it to my face, I'm going to…"

"Going to what?"

"Kick the door down."

It was an old, stone-built cottage with a sturdy, solid oak bathroom door.

"You'd break your foot."

"OK, I'll go to the garden center and buy a chainsaw. Look, this is crazy. You have to tell me what the problem is."

He had a point. It wasn't practical to hide in here forever. She took a deep breath. "OK, that thing we said would never happen? Well, it did."

Silence. Oh God, the horror, the shame. How could she live it down? How could they ever get past this and go back to being just friends again, both of them knowing how she felt about him? Because she knew she was going to feel this way until the day she died; it wasn't a love that would ever disappear. She'd just managed to condemn herself to a lifetime of awkwardness and pity.

"What did?" said Lachlan.

"I got emotionally involved, OK?"

He paused, then said, "Really? Me too."

"No, you don't understand. I got the feelings we told each other we wouldn't get."

"Same."

"Don't patronize me." Unable to bear it, Amber unlocked the door and faced him, breathing fast. "It's far worse than that. And it's all your fault for not having any faults. I've tried so hard to make it stop, but you keep *doing* things."

"What kind of things?"

She gestured wildly. "Being nice to people! Taking meals to Jo's gran to cheer her up! Looking after the stupid seagull with the broken leg that taps on the window for food because otherwise it won't get any. I mean, for God's sake, who looks after a lame *seagull*?"

"Any more things you can think of? Being fantastic in bed maybe?" Lachlan suggested.

"That too!" There, she'd said it all now. Well, nearly all.

Lachlan reached for her hands and pulled her to him, and her heart plummeted, because here came the bit where he said all the nice things and tried to let her down gently.

"I love you." He gazed into her eyes, and Amber flinched, practically able to hear every word in advance, as if he were reading from a script she'd already learned off by heart... *You're a great girl, and I hope we'll always be friends, but maybe it's best if we—*

"More than you'll ever know," Lachlan continued. "And if you think you have feelings for me...well, you have no idea how far ahead of you I am. I don't want anyone else. It's you or no one at all, and I mean it.

These last couple of months have been the happiest of my life, and having to pretend it was just a bit of fun has killed me, because all I wanted was more." He paused to take a couple of deep breaths, and Amber realized he was trembling, which was a very un-Lachlan thing to do. "All I *do* want is more. I love you, and not in a friends-with-benefits way. In a full-on, forever-and-ever, just-you-and-me way. Because it's you. You're the one. You've always been the only one for me."

Amber's mouth was dry and her legs were like jelly. This was the kind of scenario she'd never even allowed herself to fantasize about. The fingertips of his left hand were lightly circling the birthmark on her right thigh, the one he loved to trace because he said it looked like South America. She reached up and touched the side of his face, then ran a finger along the ridge of his beautiful, slightly swollen but hopefully not broken nose. "Are you serious?"

"Completely. What were you dreaming about earlier?" He raised an eyebrow. "You said Cass's name. And you thought she was here."

Poor sweet Cass, how was she ever going to be able to look her in the eye again? "It wasn't a dream. It was a nightmare."

"You thought I was sleeping with her?"

She nodded. "Yes."

"I've had those dreams too. And that's never happened to me before. Because I've never cared enough about anyone to worry about it, I guess." Lachlan's smile was wry. "But in the last few weeks, I've dreamed about losing you to Dom. I was terrified it would happen."

"Dom's not my type. It's never going to happen."

"It could though. He's a charming guy, good company, got loads of hotels."

"Maybe, but my type is pretty specific." Breaking into a huge smile and thanking her lucky stars they didn't have to rush off to work just yet, Amber wrapped her arms around his neck and kissed him so they didn't have to waste any more time talking about Dom or Cass or their fears of committing themselves to a relationship they'd both been too scared to acknowledge.

When they came up for air, Lachlan said, "What's your type, then? And how specific are we talking?"

Amber's heart ached, but this time with happiness. Lacing her fingers between his, she kissed him again. "Well, I've spent a lot of time narrowing it down," she murmured, millimeters from his mouth. "And believe it or not, it turns out it's you."

chapter 42

Three years later

AMBER LAY BACK IN THE RECLINING CHAIR WITH HER EYES covered. Had it really been three years since that particular Sunday morning in October? She marveled at how perfectly every last detail had been preserved in her brain.

It was the day her life had changed for the oh-so-very-much-better, the day they'd realized that sometimes you had to stop fighting it, take the risk, and go with your heart.

She also remembered the two of them video-calling Raff and Vee in London to break it to them that they were a couple and Raff and Vee's reaction to the news.

"So you're finally admitting it? About time too." They'd cracked up laughing at the indignant expression on Lachlan's face.

"What are you talking about? It's only just happened."

Raff said, "No, it hasn't. You've been sleeping together for weeks."

"What?" Lachlan did a double take. "How do you *know* that?"

"Olga told us," Vee said cheerfully.

"And how did Olga know?" He turned to Amber. "Did you tell her?"

"No!" It had been Amber's turn to be indignant.

"She didn't need to," Raffaele explained. "Olga just knew. And as soon as she told us, we could see it too."

"That woman." Lachlan sighed. "I swear she's a witch."

Now, a voice above Amber's head announced, "Time's up! Let's have a look at you, shall we?"

Thank goodness. Amber blinked as the clammy face mask was lifted off and the cold compress removed from her eyes. Beauty treatments really weren't her thing, but Olga had insisted on treating her to a pamper session, so how could she refuse?

"Oh, you look amazing." Olga clapped her hands with delight. "All glowy and gorgeous!"

Amber sat up and peered into the mirror; to her relief, the compresses had done their work, and the skin beneath her just-threaded eyebrows was no longer bright pink. And her skin did feel silky soft…

"See? You didn't want it done, but now you're glad you did." Olga's smile was triumphant. "You forgot that I'm always right. Now, makeup…"

"There's no point," Amber protested. "All I'm doing is going to the beach."

"Just a touch." Olga was already wheeling over the trolley bursting with makeup and brushes. "Two minutes, that's all. I promise."

It ended up taking eight minutes, but that was good going for Olga, who loved nothing more than giving someone the full RuPaul. Finally allowed to escape, Amber gave her a hug. "You're brilliant. Thanks so much."

"I'll walk down with you," said Olga. "I fancy an ice cream before heading back." She quickly texted Teddy to let him know, then they locked up the salon and made their way down to the beach.

"Look at you, smiling," Olga observed as they drew near.

Amber knew it sounded daft, but she couldn't help it. "Because I know what I'm about to see." The sense of happy anticipation never faded. They rounded the corner, and there was the bay ahead of them. She paused on the sidewalk, searching among the end-of-season tourists on East Beach. Then her heart did that familiar joyful flip as she spotted them on the sand, unaware that she was watching them but waiting for her nonetheless. The next moment, Lachlan turned and saw her and waved. As Amber waved back, he said something to one-year-old May on his hip, who'd been making him play the nose-booping game she loved so much and never tired of. When May heard what he was saying to her and followed the direction of his pointing finger, she kicked her legs and let out a shriek of delight.

Amber's eyes filled. Since giving birth to May, she'd experienced a whole new set of heightened emotions.

My family.

My everything.

She still missed her own mother, of course she did, but the genes that had caused May to inherit her grandmother's smile and partner it with Lachlan's eyes to miraculous effect meant the memories would never be forgotten. And what they might lack in blood-related family, they more than made up for in the found kind. Thanks to Teddy and May, she and Lachlan had found each other and created a new life of their own.

Belatedly, Amber noticed all the blankets spread out on the sand, the seating, the many large wicker hampers, and the eclectic collection of silver wine coolers with bottles sticking out of them. She turned to Olga. "He said it was just going to be a few bits to eat for the three of us. This is crazy. Look how much stuff he's brought with him."

"It does seem like a bit much." Olga lifted her turquoise-rimmed sunglasses in order to take a better look. "If you twist my arm, I could come down and help you get through some of it, if you like."

They made their way across the sun-warmed sand, and Olga swooped on May, lifting her out of Lachlan's arms and covering her with noisy kisses.

In return, May spluttered with laughter, booped the tip of Olga's nose with her forefinger, and cried, "*No,*" which was her way of saying nose.

"What's going on?" Baffled, Amber wondered why Lachlan was looking so pleased with himself. "You've got enough food here to feed a hundred people."

His dark eyes were sparkling. "Have I? Turn around."

She turned, looked along the beach. "What? I can't see anything."

Lachlan held her by the elbows and swiveled her ninety degrees to the left. "See the road you just came down? Look who was behind you."

The sun was blazing down, right into her eyes. It wasn't until she shielded them with her hand and the people moved closer that she was able to make them out. She gasped as realization dawned, because there was Teddy, not waiting at home for Olga to return after all, and with him were Vee and Raffaele, who'd told her they were spending the weekend in Dublin.

And there was Jo, who now worked for Amber, taking care of the studio while she was at home with May. And next to Jo was Benjie, who'd returned from their gap year a changed man. His romance with Jo might not have worked out—after a few months, they'd both realized it had run its course—but the two of them had remained close friends, and Jo had been instrumental in helping Benjie to set up the ice cream shop on the seafront that had won countless awards and put countless inches on the waists of its many fans.

And there too, behind them, were Lachlan's sous chef, Paolo, and his smiling boyfriend, Daniel, who worked alongside Benjie in the ice cream shop.

Next came Eamonn and his wife, Mandy, who'd bought one of the trailers at the trailer park and often came down to stay when Vee and Raffaele were visiting Lanrock.

There was Jo's grandmother, arm in arm with Mervyn the traffic warden, who was evidently taking a few hours off from being the scourge of all visitors hoping to park in Lanrock. From the looks of it, Mervyn was going to have his work cut out keeping an overexcited Moose out of the hampers of food.

And now here was Dom, for whom Amber had just finished creating her eleventh stained-glass chandelier, one for each of his hotels to date. As he'd so confidently predicted three years ago, visitors and guests loved to be photographed beneath what had swiftly become the signature feature of the Burton Hotel Group.

And holding Dom's hand was his latest stunning girlfriend, who worked for the TV production company that made *Cooking for the Enemy* and had been trying without success to persuade Lachlan to appear on the show alongside Gerry Walsh. So far, each time Lachlan had turned her down, the company had come back with the offer of an increased fee.

Amber said, "*Oh*," and clapped her hand over her mouth, because still they were coming, a whole procession of friends making their way down to join them on the beach: the brilliant women she'd gotten to know during her prenatal classes, now carrying their own babies and clutching balloons, and the girls who worked in the restaurant, and there was Peggy, resplendent in a psychedelic green kaftan, almost tripping over a sunbathing tourist and being rescued in the nick of time by Bernard, who'd moved in with her last year but had yet to persuade her to go on a cruise.

And look, there were Sally and Nigel Henderson, who'd just returned from visiting their daughter and Russian son-in-law in Norfolk following the birth of their twins…

So many people, so many wonderful friends. Her heart full, Amber leaned against Lachlan. "No one's ever thrown me a surprise picnic on the beach before. I can't believe you arranged all this."

....

Lachlan couldn't believe it either. He'd never been the type of person who'd gone out of his way to do extravagantly nice things for other people in the past. But being with Amber—*properly* being with her— had changed him. He no longer had the restless urge to meet and flirt with attractive women; that aspect of his character was behind him now. If they weren't Amber, he simply wasn't interested. Thanks to her, he had everything he'd ever wanted, a more perfect life than he could have dreamed of.

Should he have told her earlier how he felt about her? It was a question he still wondered about, even now, because the idea that they might have missed out on more years of being together was something that still haunted him. But Amber was certain he'd been right not to, just as she had done the right thing by simultaneously keeping her own feelings for him to herself. They'd both needed that time to grow and mature, to live their own lives, in order to be able to know for sure that their emotions were genuine. If either of them had told the other too soon, they might not be together now. It had eventually happened, she was convinced, at exactly the right moment for both of them. Sometimes you just needed to wait for that perfect time to come along.

And thank God it had. She'd made him a better person, and for that, every day he loved her more. Amber and May were his whole world. Sliding an arm around her waist, he said, "At least it isn't raining, because we definitely wouldn't have been able to squeeze this many people into the restaurant."

Amber was still gazing in wonder at the crowd assembling on the beach. "It isn't even my birthday though."

Lachlan reached over to retrieve May. "It's better than that. It's the third anniversary of the best day of my life." As May grabbed a handful of his hair, he planted a quick kiss on his daughter's petal-soft cheek, then a longer one on Amber's mouth. "The day you very nearly broke my nose."

about the author

With over thirteen million copies sold, *New York Times* and *USA Today* bestselling author Jill Mansell writes irresistible, funny, poignant, and romantic tales for women in the tradition of Marian Keyes, Sophie Kinsella, and Jojo Moyes. She lives with her partner and their children in Bristol, England.

IT STARTED WITH A SECRET

Their happy-ever-after is within reach...but only
if they're willing to tell the truth.

Lainey and Kit arrive at their new jobs in blissful, summery Cornwall only to find themselves in the midst of a lovable but chaotic family—where every member is having an identity crisis at the same time. Widowed mom Majella has done her best for years, but can't quite grasp why things are falling apart. It's what she doesn't know that's causing the chaos, because everyone is keeping secrets.

In classic Jill Mansell style, our heroine and her friends are drawn through a hilarious multi-generational soap opera in which, by the end, happily-ever-afters are available to anyone willing to tell the truth about their heart's desire.

**"A little blast of sunshine—uplifting, heartwarming,
and supremely feel-good."**

—Sophie Kinsella, #1 *New York Times* bestselling author

CPSIA information can be obtained
at www.ICGtesting.com
Printed in the USA
LVHW100206110622
721009LV00002B/5